BOOK ONE
THE DEVIL'S CHILDREN

BOOK TWO
HEARTSEASE

BOOK THREE
THE WEATHERMONGER

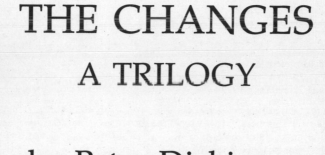

# THE CHANGES

## A TRILOGY

by Peter Dickinson

A Dell Trade Paperback

A DELL TRADE PAPERBACK
Published by
Dell Publishing
a division of
Bantam Doubleday Dell Publishing Group, Inc.
666 Fifth Avenue
New York, New York 10103

ISBN: 0-440-50413-9

Reprinted by arrangement with Delacorte Press

Printed in the United States of America

Published simultaneously in Canada

December 1991

10 9 8 7 6 5 4 3 2 1

BVG

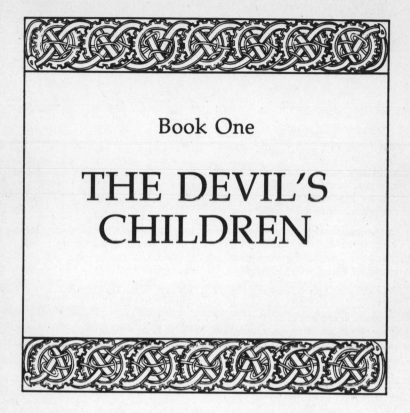

Book One

# THE DEVIL'S CHILDREN

for Rani Gagan Deep Singh

# The Beginning

*The tunnel is dark and clammy, raw earth crudely propped. Bent double under its low roof an elderly man jabs with his crowbar at the work face, levers loose earth away, rests panting for several heartbeats and then jabs again. This time the crowbar strikes a hard surface just below the earth. He mutters and tries again, jabbing in different places, only to find each time the same smooth hardness blocking his path, sloping upward away from him. Wearily he fetches a camper's gas lamp and peers at the obstacle, picking loose earth away from it with shaking fingers, and muttering to himself all the time. Suddenly he bends closer, pursing his lips, and runs a torn thumbnail down a crack in the smooth surface. The crack goes straight as a ruler, and meets the edge of the slab at an exact right angle. It is not natural rock, but stone measured and cut by masons.*

*His heart, which a moment before had been thudding with exhaustion, is now thudding with excitement. But he is a tidy-minded man and works methodically to clear a whole slab, and then to find leverage under it for his crowbar. Several hours pass, but at last he settles the steel into a crevice and leans his weight on it. The stone groans as it lifts. The man has a pebble ready to wedge the slit open. As he steps back to rest from that first effort he knocks his lamp over. In the new dark he sees that the slit is glowing, with a pale faint light, like a watch dial. So The Changes begin.*

*On a fine June night the Cardiff express drummed below the dark hills. The moon had set and the stars were soft but strong. In the fourteen coaches passengers slumped half* asleep, frowsting and prickly. In the cab the driver stared ahead as the green lights called him on from section to section; the rails glistened ahead like faint antennae probing into the soft wall of night. How could he know at what moment the nightmare began, when the details of the nightmare were exactly the same as those of the journey he'd made so often before? Only inside him the horror swelled and burst into a scream as he leaped from his seat. His hand came off the Dead Man's Handle, so the brakes cut in as the drive cut out. The deceleration slung him against the dialed control board, stunning him. He lay still on the cab floor while his train, untouched by the nightmare because it had no brain to infect, brought itself to a stop with its useless engine still drumming in the dark.

The shudders of braking startled the passengers awake. They stared around them. A man yelled and beat at the windows with bare fists. Before the train stopped they were running up and down the coaches, looking for a way of escape. By accident a man scrabbled a window open (the door latch was now a mystery) and they all fought each other to get through it, to drop into the dark, scramble up the embankment and run at random into the still fields.

On roads and motorways drivers forgot their skill and sat helpless while their cars or lorries hurtled off the tarmac. In factories the night shifts rioted and smashed. At Port Talbot a freak storm gathered and raged above the steel works until the lightning made the whole huge complex a destroying furnace. In ordinary houses, as dawn came on, the alarm clocks rang and sleepers woke to stare at the horrible thing clanging beside them. Some hands, out of sheer muscular habit, reached out for the lightswitch, only to snatch themselves back as though the touch of plastic stung like acid.

Day after day followed of panic and rumor. Cities began to burn, amid looting and riot. Then the main flights started, hundreds of thousands of people streaming away from their homes to look for food, safety, peace. It was no wonder that many families became split up; no wonder that in London, for instance, one particular girl decided that the best thing to do was to go back to her deserted house and wait for her mother and father to come and look for her.

# Chapter 1

# BECOMING A CANARY

"Nicola Gore," said Nicky. "I am Nicola Gore."

She turned on her right heel, kicking herself around and around with her left foot, until the leather of the heel began to drill a neat, satisfying hole among the roots of the six-inch grass.

"Nicola Gore," she said as she spun. "Nicola Gore. Nicola Gore. Nicola Gore."

She was talking to herself, of course, because there was no one else to talk to. The last living person she'd seen had been the one-legged old man who sat on his doorstep in the sun, waiting to die and talking about his boyhood in Hammersmith more than sixty years ago, when the noise of London traffic had been the rattle and grate of iron wheels on cobbles.

Now the only noise was birdsong, and Nicky saying her own name to herself, aloud in the enormous loneliness.

The old man had gone from his doorstep twelve days ago.

She had promised not to try and look for him, because he had said his going would be the sign.

And it was nineteen days before that since she'd last talked to anyone she really knew, anyone who loved her. She turned and turned. It was taking longer to get dizzy now than it had when she'd first discovered the trick.

They weren't going to come and find her now, were they? She'd done what she'd always been told to, if ever she was lost—waited where she'd last seen Mummy and Daddy, waited for a day and a night and another day, watching the dull-eyed ranks of refugees straggle toward Dover. Then she had set her chin and walked the other way, back to the drained city, looking at all the faces of the people who were leaving but not answering any questions, no matter how kindly. If she went *home*, someone would come and look for her, surely.

But they hadn't.

Just in time, before the tears came, the long wave of dizziness began to wash over her. Nicky had discovered this trick quite early. If you could get yourself dizzy enough, you stopped being Nicola Gore, alone and frightened and miserable in great empty London, and you became a sort of daze without a name, a blurred bit of a blurred world. She went on turning as long as she could still stand. Then she fell.

When the blurs began to settle into shapes again they were the tops of trees. She lay on her back in the spider-peopled grass and looked at the blue, unmottled sky. It had been like that every day, except for the hideous thunderstorm on the road to Dover. Would it last forever? No, it was July now, but one day it would be winter. She'd have to go before then. She ought to go now, before she caught the sickness down the road, or another sickness from living on lemon soda and pretzels and nuts looted out of empty pubs. She must set her chin again, become hard and uncaring, endure a world of strangers.

She knew that when it came to leaving she would need something to *make* her do it, but the impulse to action levered her out of the grass. Listlessly she looked around the place which five weeks ago had been called Shepherd's Bush Green, London, W.14. A four-acre triangle of turf, crisscrossed with paths and dotted with trees; around it ran a wide road; blank shops lined the northern side, and unfinished towers of flats and offices rose to the south. Nasty engines squatted in the road, silent and useless; they were all dead, since the people who had once made them work and move had left, but even so Nicky preferred not to go near them. Luckily there were gaps between them, where Nicky could tiptoe through, then scamper along the pavement of Shepherd's Bush Road, around the corner and home.

That's where she ought to be now, waiting in case they came after all, but it was better here among the trees. This was where you could get furthest from the dead machines and the black unnatural roads that stank strangely under the downright sun. And she *had* pinned her notice to the door, saying where she was, just as she'd done for the last twenty-eight days. Still, perhaps she'd better go and see.

She turned listlessly on her heel again, knowing it was useless to go back home and that she would have to make the effort not to cry when she got there and found the notice untouched. Dully she kept turning, like a slow top, and felt her heel beginning to bite yet another neat round hole into the earth below the squashed grass.

About the ninth time she went around she saw a movement up at the east end of the Green.

At first she thought that it was just the dizziness, coming sooner than usual and making the world tilt about, but next time around she stopped being a top and stood swaying and peering. The movement was people.

For no reason she slid toward the nearest tree trunk and hid.

There were quite a lot of them, and the colors were wrong. It was like a procession in fancy dress. All the men had beards, and they wore mauve and pink and purple hats. No, not hats. There was a word for them . . . and there was a word for the women's bright, slim dresses, which reached right down to their ankles . . . and another word for these people with their strange clothes and beards and brown skins . . . or was it all something she had once dreamed she knew about? There were blank bits in her mind nowadays. Perhaps it was the loneliness.

Four of the men came in front, carrying heavy sticks; behind them marched a big group pushing carts and prams or carrying bright-colored bundles; several children walked among the prams; one cart was covered with cushions, on which an old lady was propped up; at the back came another four men, also armed with heavy sticks. They moved very slowly, like a funeral, along the north side of the Green. They were quite silent, apart from the iron wheels of the handcarts grating on the tarmac, until they were nearly opposite where Nicky was hiding. Then a high voice shrieked an incomprehensible sentence from amid the group of prams and the whole procession halted. They all began talking together as they spread themselves out on the grass, sat down and started to eat the food which the women passed among them.

The dizziness had gone from Nicky's body but her mind still seemed fuzzy with it. These people . . . she'd seen men and women like them before, strolling along these very pavements, doing their weekend shopping . . . but that was in the part of her memories which nowadays she seemed to find it hard to think about, like dreams you know you've had but somehow can't bring back when you're awake. Now, staring at these dark-skinned, bright-dressed people, she only felt their difference and their strangeness.

But they were people, and they were going somewhere.

Her mind made itself up without being asked. She slipped away along the tree trunks, across the road at the gap between the bad machines, along the pavement to where the old traffic lights stood blind as stone, left down Shepherd's Bush Road—walking now, and panting with the heat, and her neck sore from where the collar of her filthy shirt stuck to the sweaty skin—and along her home street.

Not home anymore. The street was dead, and buzzing with flies in the stinking, tarry heat.

Yes, her note was pinned to the pink door, untouched; but this time she didn't feel her throat narrowing and her eyes peppery with useless tears. She pushed the door open and ran up the stairs to her own room. Even this, with its brown carpet and the pictures of ships on the walls, didn't feel like home now. She took her satchel from the shelf, wiped the dust off it with her sleeve, undid the straps and tilted the meaningless books out onto the floor. Into the bottom of the satchel she stuffed a jersey, a spare skirt, her party blouse, the socks she'd managed to wash in soda water, and her gym shoes.

Anything else which she needed or wanted? Not Teddy, comfort though he'd been. None of the school uniforms. Nothing to make her remember home or Mummy or Daddy. That was all over now—it had happened to somebody else, a girl with parents to love her and look after her. But Nicola Gore was going to look after herself, and not let anybody love her again, ever. It wasn't worth the loss.

Out of her desk drawer she took the blunt hunting knife which she'd bought with her own money at the fair when she was staying with Granny at Hertford; and from the blue jar on the mantelpiece she took the coral and gold necklace which one of her godmothers had given her at her christening, but she could never remember which.

Then she ran down to the kitchen, picking her way to the larder between the horrible smashed machines. Two bottles of lemon soda and one of soda water from her last pub raid; the packets of nuts and the salty biscuits. Her satchel was full now, and heavy too. She slung its strap over her shoulder, picked up her pencil from the hall table, and pushed the door wide open until she could lean against it to write on her notice without its moving away.

She crossed out her last message, about being up at the Green, and wrote beneath it "I'm going away now. I waited for twenty-eight days."

She was pulling the door shut when she thought that that sounded as though she was blaming them, so she pushed it open again and wrote underneath "I'm sure you would have come if you could. Love, Nicky."

When she pulled the door shut for the last time she felt that there ought to be some way of fastening it, but she couldn't remember how the lock worked. So she just made certain that the drawing pins were firmly fastened into her note, turned away and walked down the street without once looking back. She started to be afraid that she would be too late, but it was awkward to run with her satchel so heavy. It didn't matter; they were still there when she reached the Green again; the strange, dark children were playing a game of "touch" under the trees.

Beyond them the adults lolled or squatted on the grass. The whole group chattered like roosting starlings. The noise of their talk bounced off the shop fronts, and all of a sudden made the Green feel as though people were living there once again. Yes, thought Nicky, these foreign-looking folk would do. She could go with them, and yet stay strangers always. It was a good thing they were so different. She sidled like a hunter toward the scampering children.

She was waiting by a tree trunk, beyond the fringe of the game, when one of the smaller boys scuttered from an exploding group which the "he" had raided. He came straight toward her squealing with laughter until he was hardly six feet away; and then he saw her. At once he stopped dead, called with a shrill new note, and pointed at her. Then he stood staring. His eyes were very dark; his hair was black and gathered into a little topknot behind his head. His skin looked smooth as silk and was a curious, pale brown—not the yellow-brown of suntan, but a grayer color, as if it was always like that. His mouth pouted.

The game stopped at his call, not quite at once, but in spasms of scuttering which stilled into the same dark stare. Now the adults' heads were turning too; the thick beards wagging around; the worried, triangular faces of the women turning toward Nicky. One of the women called; two children ran to her side and stared from there. The other children melted back toward the adults, looking over their shoulders once or twice. Several of the men were on their feet, grasping their heavy staves and peering not at her but up and down the Green. Now the whole group was standing, except for the little old woman who had ridden on the cart; she still sat on the ground and gazed with piercing fierceness at Nicky from among the legs of the men. Then she cried out suddenly, only three or four words, like the call of a bird. The words were not English.

A big man bent and scooped her off the grass, like a

mother picking up her baby; he carried her to the cushioned cart, which was brightly painted with swirling patterns—it was the sort of handcart that street-market stall holders had used for pushing their goods about. The old woman settled herself on the cushions, stared at Nicky again, and called another few words. At once the whole group trooped off the grass and took up their positions for the march.

Nicky ran forward from under the trees. They were all watching her still, as though she might be the bait in some unimaginable trap.

"Please," she called. "May I come with you?"

A rustle ran through the group like the rustle of dead leaves stirring under a finger of wind. One of the worried women said something, and three of the men answered her. Nicky could tell from their voices that they were disagreeing with her. The old woman spoke a single syllable, and the nearest man shook his head at Nicky. He was short and fat and his beard was flecked with gray; his hat was pink, only it wasn't a hat, of course—it was a long piece of cloth wound in and out of itself in clever folds to cover his head and hair.

"Please," she said again. "I'm all alone and I don't know where to go."

"Go away, little girl," said the fat man. "We can't help you. You are not one of us. We owe you nothing."

"Please," began Nicky, but the old woman called again and at once the whole group began to move.

They walked off quite slowly, not because they wanted to move like a funeral, but because they couldn't go faster than the slowest child. Nicky stood and watched them, all shriveled with despair at the thought of facing the huge loneliness of London once again.

She stepped into the road to watch the strange people turn the corner north. (If they'd wanted to go south they would have started down the other side of the Green.) But instead they went straight ahead, up the Uxbridge Road, toward the doorstep where the one-legged man had sat in the sun.

Nicky began to run.

Her satchel dragged her sideways and thudded unsteadily into her hip. A rat tail of dirty fair hair twisted into her mouth and she spat it out. Her soles slapped on the hot pavement and the echo slapped back at her off the empty shops. When she crossed the big road at the end of the Green the strange people were only a hundred yards down it, so slow was their march. She ran on, gasping.

They must have heard her coming, because one of the four men who walked in the rear came striding back toward her, his stave grasped in both hands like a weapon.

"Go away, little girl," he said sharply. "We don't want you. We can't help you."

Nicky stopped. He was taller and younger than the fat man who had spoken to her before, and frowned at her very fiercely.

"No! Don't go that way!" she said between gasps. "There's a bad sickness that way. An old man told me. He said he was going to catch the sickness and die. He made me promise not to go down there. He said he'd seen people staggering about and then falling down dead in the street."

The dark man moved his stave, so that it stopped being a weapon and became a stick to lean on.

"This is true?" he asked.

"Yes, of course."

He looked at her for several seconds, just as fiercely as before. Then, without another word to her, he turned and called after the procession in the strange language. Beyond him Nicky could see two or three faces turn. A cry came back, the man answered and another cry came. By this time the whole group had stopped.

"Come with me," said the man without looking around, and strode off up the street. Nicky followed.

Men, women and children stood staring and unsmiling, still as a grove of trees, while she walked between them. When they reached the cushioned cart where the old woman lay, the man stopped and spoke for some time. The old woman creaked a few words back at him. Her face was all shriveled into wrinkles and folds as though it had been soaked too long in water, but her thin hooky nose stood out of the wrinkles like the beak of a hawk, and her dark brown eyes shone with angry life. She looked like a queen witch.

"Tell your story again, please, miss," said the man.

Nicky had stopped panting, so she could fit her words

together into proper sentences; but she was so afraid of the old woman that she found she could hardly speak above a whisper. She felt the other people drawing closer, so as to be able to hear.

"I used to bring food for an old man who sat on a door-step," she said. "He only had one leg, which is why he hadn't gone away. He told me that quite a lot of people further down this road had stayed too, and now they'd got very sick and if you went near them you might catch their sickness. It was the sort of sickness you die of, he said. He said that they crawled out into the street, like rats coming into the open when they've eaten poison, but some of them danced and staggered about before they fell down. He made me promise not to go this way if he wasn't on his doorstep, because that would be the sign that the sickness had come up the street as far as where he lived. He wasn't here when I came to look for him twelve days ago, and he hasn't come back. That's where he used to sit, down there, opposite the church."

The group was still no longer, but wavering and rustling. Suddenly the starling clamor of voices broke out, all of them seeming to speak at the same time. The women drew their children close to them, and the men's hands began to gesture in several directions. A younger man with a very glossy beard spoke directly to Nicky, in English.

"Cholera, perhaps," he said. "Or plague."

He sounded interested, as though he'd have liked to explore further up the road and see which guess was right.

The big man who pushed the old woman's cart had pulled a red book from under the cushions and was peering at it amid the clamor; two of the other men, still arguing at the tops of their voices, craned over his shoulders. The old woman held up her arms suddenly and screeched like a wild animal, and the shouting stopped. She asked a short question, and was answered by a mild-faced young woman in a blue dress. The old woman nodded, pointed south, and spoke again. The crowd murmured agreement. The big man ran his finger down a page of the book, flipped over some more pages, and ran his finger on—he must be tracing a road on a map. Then the whole group picked up all they had been carrying; the pram pushers and cart pushers circled around; the old woman screeched and they all started back toward the Green. They filed around Nicky as though she were a rock in the road.

She stood, running her thumb back and forward under her satchel strap, and let them trail past. Nobody said a word, and only one or two of the smallest children stared. When the last four, the stave carriers, had gone she followed behind. One of them glanced over his shoulder and spoke to the man who had led her into the group. He glanced back too, said something, shrugged and walked on. Nicky trudged behind.

They turned right at the Green, south. Their pace was a dreary dawdle as they went down Shepherd's Bush Road, which Nicky had so often scampered along. Carefully she didn't look up the side street to where her note was pinned to the pink door, but studied instead a gang of scrawny cats which watched from a garden wall on the other side of the road; already they were as wild as squirrels.

Yes, she thought, I am right to go now. If I stay any longer I will become like those cats. She remembered how neat the strange children had seemed, even while they were playing their game of "touch," and wondered how she herself looked. You can't wash much in soda water.

At Hammersmith Broadway there had been either an accident or a battle, for two buses lay on their sides and a vegetable lorry had charged into the ruin, scattering crates of lettuce about. The wreckage stank and the procession edged well clear of it. A minute or two later they were on Hammersmith Bridge.

Here the whole group stopped and the adults broke into their cackle of many-voiced argument while the children crowded to the railings and gazed at the still and shining water. Small brown arms pointed at floating gulls or bits of waterlogged driftwood, ignoring the wrangle that raged behind them. Nicky wondered how they ever could decide anything if they were all allowed to speak at the same time. The big man found a sheet of paper under the cushions, a real map with many folds, and this was pored over until, once more, the harsh creak of the old woman decided the question. Mothers called their children to them; burdens were hefted; the march dawdled on.

They went so slowly that Nicky decided she could afford a few minutes more on the bridge; she would be able to catch them without hurrying. The river was beautiful, full from bank to bank as high tide began to ebb unhurriedly toward the sea. A sailing dinghy fidgeted around at its moorings as the water changed direction. Something about the river's calm and shining orderliness washed away all Nicky's resolution—the river ran to the sea, and over the sea lay France, and that's where Mummy and Daddy were, and a little boat like that couldn't be hard to sail. She could swim out to it and row it ashore, and then stock it up with pretzels and lemon soda and sail down the river, around the coast and over the Channel. And then it would be only a matter of finding them, among all the millions of strangers. They *must* have left a message, somewhere. Sailing would be nice —alone, but going to meet the people who were waiting for you, who would kiss you and not ask questions and show you the room they had kept ready for you. . . .

Nicky's whole skeleton was shaken by a tearing shudder, like the jerk of nerves that sometimes shocks the body wide awake just as it is melting into sleep, only this shudder went on and on. Nicky knew it well. It had shaken her all that first nightmare morning, and once or twice since. It was a sign that somewhere a hellish machine was working.

She looked wildly about for a few seconds, not feeling how her mouth and lips were pulling themselves into a hard snarl like a dog's, nor how her legs were running down the street called Castelnau faster than they'd ever run when she'd asked them, nor how her hand was groping in her satchel for the hunting knife.

A bus towered in the road; the strange people crowded around it, chattering again. Nicky jostled between them and hurled herself at the young man who stood smiling beside the vile engine which churned its sick stink and noise into the air. Her knife was held for killing. The young man was the only person looking in her direction. He shouted before she was quite through the crowd, and started to back away around the bus. A hard thing rammed into her ear and

cheekbone, jarring her head so that for an instant she could
not see. In fact she could not remember falling, but now she
was on her hands and knees groping dazedly for the
dropped knife, not finding it, then crawling toward the
drumming engine and feeling again in her satchel for a bottle to hit with.

The world seemed to be shouting. Tough hands gripped
her arms and hoisted her up. She struggled toward the bus,
but the hands held her, hard as rope. The young man was
climbing again through the door of the bus. She lunged at
the hands with her teeth, but the men who held her did so in
such a way that she couldn't reach.

All at once the foul drumming stopped, and only the stink
of it hung between the houses. A voice croaked an order.
They all moved on, up Castelnau.

Slowly, like the panic of nightmare dying as you lie in the
half-dark and work out that you really are in your own bed
between safe walls, the lust of hatred ebbed. She felt her
neck muscles unlock. Her hands and knees, where she had
fallen, stung with sudden pain. She was so tired that she
would have dropped but for the hands that gripped her. She
let her head droop.

It might have been a signal for the others to stop, and for
the clatter of arguing voices to break out again. Most of the
voices were men's, but sometimes a woman joined in. At
last something was settled.

"Are you all right now, miss?" said a man.

Nicky nodded.

"Why did you do that?" said the man.

"Do what?"

"Try to kill Kewal?"

"He made the thing go," she said. "He mustn't. I had to
stop him."

"Who told you to?"

"I don't know."

"Do you want to kill him now?"

Nicky looked around the dark, silent faces. The young
man she'd charged at stood directly before her, smiling, his
small teeth brilliant amid the gorgeous beard. Only one of

his eyes looked directly at her. The other one squinted crazily over her right shoulder. "No," she said.

"But if he tried to make the bus go again?" asked the man. "Yes," she said.

The hands let go of her and she swayed. An arm curled round her shoulders to stop her falling—a woman's arm this time.

"You will come with us," said the man. It wasn't a question. Now, at last, she looked up and saw that the speaker was the big man who had been pushing the old woman on the cart. A woman in a blue dress, the one who'd answered the question about the sickness, knelt down in the road and started to sponge Nicky's bleeding knees.

"Yes," said the young man, Kewal, smiling and squinting. "You will be our canary."

"Kaya?" said one of the women.

"When the miners go into the coal mines," explained the young man importantly, "they take a canary with them; if there is firedamp about—that is carbon monoxide, you know—the bird feels it before the miners. Just so this girl . . . what is your name, miss?"

"Nicola Gore."

"Just so Miss Gore will be able to warn us of dangers which we cannot perceive."

"You are willing?" asked the big man.

"Most people call me Nicky," she explained.

"Good," he said, as if she had answered "Yes." She had in a way.

"Our names are easy too," said Kewal. "All the men are called Singh and all the women are called Kaur."

Several of the group laughed in a fashion that told Nicky that it was an old joke. A high, imperious voice croaked from the handcart.

"My grandmother does not speak English," explained Kewal as the big man turned and began a conversation in the strange language. The woman who had been dabbing at her knees rose and took her hand and started to clean the grazes.

"How is your head?" said a voice at her side. "I regret that I had to hit you so forcibly."

She turned and saw the fat man who had first spoken to her. He was smiling nervously. His eyes had the look of a dog's which thinks it may have done something bad but doesn't want you to think so.

"My uncle is very quick and strong," said Kewal. "Although he does not look it."

There was another little laugh among the group. Nicky felt her cheek.

"It's all right," she said. "It's still a bit sore but it's all right. It doesn't matter, Mr.—er—Singh?"

Her voice turned the last two words into a question. She knew that Kewal had been joking, but she didn't know what the joke was. However, the fat man smiled and nodded. The old voice creaked another order. You could hear it quite plainly through the chatter of the rest of the group.

"Come," said Kewal. "My grandmother wishes to speak to you."

The old woman was still just as terrifying as before. She lay on her elbow on the cushions and stared. She wore about five necklaces, and every finger of her left hand had at least two rings on it. Nicky wanted to propitiate her, to make her less fierce and strange, so without taking her eyes from the many-wrinkled face she began to grope in her satchel. The old woman spoke two sentences and the big man laughed.

"My mother is pleased with you," he said. "She says you fight well, like a Sikh. But now you must fight for us, and not against."

Nicky's fingers found what she wanted. She walked right up to the cart.

"Would you like this?" she said, giving a little half-curtsey: the old woman might be a witch, but she was a queen too. Nicky put the gold and coral necklace down on a blue satin cushion. The ringed claw picked it up and the bright eyes examined it, stone by stone. The old woman clucked, spoke again and put it down on the cushion.

"My mother is grateful," said the big man. "She says it is good gold and well-carved beads, but you must keep the necklace. You are to help us and we are to help you, so there is no need for an exchange of gifts. We will protect you, and share our food and drink with you. In return you will warn us if we seem to you to be embarking on anything which is dangerous or wrong. Things like Kewal starting the engine of that bus. Do you understand?"

Nicky tore her eyes at last from the old woman's.

"Yes, Mr. Singh," she said, more confidently this time.

The big man's lips moved into a smile under his dark-gray beard.

"You will have to learn our other names too, you know," he said. "Now we must march on. You will walk with my sister's family. Neena!"

Nicky picked the necklace off the blue cushion. She was glad she hadn't had to give it away.

# Chapter 2

# FIRST NIGHT

Neena, the big man's sister, was a dark little woman, only two or three inches taller than Nicky.

"You can put your satchel into my pram," she said. "I expect you're pretty tired."

She spoke so softly that Nicky could hardly hear her. She looked tired and worried herself. A sulky baby sat in the pram, almost hidden by a hill of bundles.

"Thank you," said Nicky, and propped the satchel on the handles of the pram, leaning it against the bundles. Then she found she was still holding the soda bottle which she'd taken out to fight with, so she unscrewed the top and started to drink. The lemon soda was nastily sweet and warm, and very fizzy with the shaking it had had, so that the froth bubbled back into her nose and made her sneeze; through her snortings she heard the boy in the pram begin a slow wail.

"Oh dear," said Nicky, "is that my fault?"

"He's thirsty," said Neena, "and we cannot spare much water because we have to boil it all."

She leaned her light weight against the handles to get the pram going as the rest of the group moved off. Nicky, walking beside her, felt in the satchel for another bottle and handed it to Neena. The baby was watching; its wail softened to a snivel.

"No," said Neena, "it's yours. You will need it."

"I can easily break into another pub," said Nicky. "That's how I got these."

Neena looked at her doubtfully for a moment.

"Thank you, Nicky," she said. "Push the pram please, Gopal."

A boy about Nicky's size took the handles and started to shove while Neena rummaged in her bundles for a mug; she filled it from the lemon soda bottle and tilted it carefully to the baby's lips. The baby put up a hand to steady it, but did not help much; still, Neena managed very cleverly despite having to glide beside the pram.

"My brother is nicer than this, really," said Gopal, "but he knows that something is wrong and that my mother is worried."

"Are you really all called Singh?" said Nicky in a half-whisper.

"Yes. It was an order of the guru three hundred years ago that all Sikhs are called Singh. It means 'lion,' and we are a soldier people."

He spoke very proudly and seriously.

"What are Sikhs?" said Nicky.

"We are Sikhs. My people are Indians—Indian Indians, of course, not American Indians—but many of us came to England, especially after the Hitler war. We have a different religion from you and from other Indians, and we carry five signs that we are different. Other Indians wear the turban, for instance, but we do not cut our hair or beards at all, ever; we carry a sword, to show we are soldiers; we wear a steel bracelet; we . . ."

"I can't see any swords," said Nicky, who had been puzzled by the explanation. She felt that she ought to know about the Hitler war, and about Indians, just as she ought to have known about turbans, but she'd forgotten. She was irritated by being forced to recognize another of those mo-

ments when she saw or heard something which felt as
though she'd dreamed it before, but had forgotten the
dream.

Gopal laughed and felt in the back of his turban. From it
he produced a square wooden comb to which was fastened
a toy scimitar two inches long.

"You can't wear a sword if you are working in a bank," he
said, "or driving a train in the underground. Not a real killing sword. So we wear our swords like this, but they are still
a sign of our faith and a sign that we are a soldier people.
We are a very proud race, you know. When a man joins the
Sikh religion he becomes taller and stronger and braver. It
has often happened. I've read it in my history books."

"How old are you?" said Nicky.

"Thirteen."

"I'm twelve. Shall I help you push the pram or are you too
proud?"

He laughed again, as though he was used to being teased
and didn't mind. His face was thin and his skin looked silky
soft; he moved his brown eyes about a lot when he spoke or
listened, in a way that was full of meanings. Nicky decided
that she liked him, but that he was a bit girlish. It was only
later that she found he was a true lion, worthy of his name.

"You can help me up the next hill," he said. "We'll give my
mother a rest."

Neena—Mrs. Singh or Mrs. Kaur, Nicky decided she
ought to call her—turned her weary face to smile at her son,
then started to arrange the bundles on the pram so that the
little boy could sleep.

In fact the next hill was a long time coming.

Castelnau is a flat mile from end to end, between friendly
Victorian mansions; then it bends and becomes Ranelagh
Gardens, quaintly ornate red houses with little unusable
balconies crowding all down one side, and on the other a
six-foot wooden fence screening Barn Elms Park from the
street. Ranelagh Gardens twists to cross the miniature scrub
desert of Barnes Common. Here a bedraggled horse stumbled out of the bushes and followed them, until one of the
rear guard tried to catch it and it shied away.

On the far side of the common the road humps itself up

over a railway. Nicky fulfilled her bargain by toiling beside Gopal to heave the pram up to the ridge of the hummock, but she could only just manage it, so much of her strength had the rage of her fight taken. On the bridge some of the children crowded to the wall and gossiped in English about the odd little station with its lacelike fringes of fretted wood, until angry voices called them back to the line of march. Down the far slope a pram ran away from its pusher and was caught amid excited shouts by the advance guard. It seemed to Nicky that the shouting and the excitement were much more than were needed for an ordinary pram trundling downhill with nobody in it, only bundles and cardboard boxes.

The long climb up Roehampton Lane was another matter. Ropes and straps were produced and tied to every cart and pram, so that two could pull and one could push. The men in the rear guard and advance guard had to do their share as well, but they pulled with one hand while the other held their thick staves ready over their shoulders. Neena returned to the handles of the pram and Nicky and Gopal each took a strap. It didn't seem hard work for the first few steps, but as the wide road curved endlessly upward Nicky began to stagger with weariness. Nobody spoke. The iron rims of the cartwheels crunched on the tarmac, and the eighty feet padded or scraped according to how they were shod. Nicky bent her head and hauled, seeing nothing but the backward-sliding road beneath her, hearing nothing but the thin whistle of her breath in her throat. She stumbled, and stumbled again.

As she was still reeling from the daze of her second stumble she heard the old woman's voice creak, and a man shouted "Ho, Kaka, you fat villain, give Miss Nicky a rest and work off some of your grease by pulling on a rope."

Nicky looked up hopefully. A roly-poly boy about eight years old came and held out his hand for the strap.

"Please," he said shyly.

"This is my cousin Kaka," said Gopal from the other side of the pram. "I have twenty-seven cousins, and Kaka is the worst."

Kaka smiled through his shyness as though Gopal had

been paying him a compliment, and immediately gave such a sturdy tug at the strap that the pram shot sideways across the procession and Neena locked wheels with the pram next door. Even the weary women laughed as they scolded Kaka, and the men halted and leaned on their staves to watch the fun.

The march only stopped for a couple of minutes, but it felt like a proper rest. Nicky walked beside Gopal on the other side of the pram. It was interesting to see how warily the leading men looked into every driveway and side road as they went past, and how often the others glanced from side to side or looked over their shoulders, as though every garden of the whole blind and silent suburb might hide an ambush.

"Is everybody here your relation?" she said.

"No," said Gopal. "Daya Wanti—that's the old lady on the cart—is my grandmother, and she has four sons and two daughters. My mother's the youngest. All my uncles and aunts have married, and they have children. Some of the children are grown up, like my cousin Kewal and my cousin Punam, who washed your knees; and then my father has a sister who is married and has children, and there's a family who are relations of the lady who married my uncle Chacha Rahmta. He's the one who knocked you over."

"But everybody here is your relation or married one of your relations or something like that?"

"No, not quite. We have some friends who had come alone from India and decided to live near us. When the madness happened to all the English people, they gathered to us for safety. You don't mind me talking about the madness? That's what we call it."

"I expect so," said Nicky without thinking about it. "Is your grandmother the chief?"

"Oh no. The women have an equal voice with the men, and of course the voice of the older people is more respected than the voice of the younger people; but we all decide together what to do, and then . . ."

"And then my mother tells us what we are going to do despite that," interrupted a man from Nicky's other side. It was Uncle Chacha Rahmta, pulling steadily on a rope which was tied to a handcart laden with cardboard cartons. As he spoke, the old woman screeched from her cart and the whole party stopped as if she had been a sergeant major calling "Halt!"

"You see what I mean?" said Uncle Chacha Rahmta.

They had reached the ridge of the hill. Ahead the road dipped and curved into the small valley of Roehampton Village, and then rose almost at once toward Putney Heath and Wimbledon Common. But behind and below them were roof tiles, mile upon lifeless mile, spreading right across the Thames Valley and up the far northern hills. Perhaps a few hundred people were still living among those millions of rooms, eating what they could scavenge, like rats in a stable; otherwise it was barren as a desert, just long dunes of brick and cement and slate and asphalt. Far to the east something big was burning, where a huge ragged curve of smoke tilted under the mild wind.

The Sikhs broke into their clattering gossip even before they settled for their rest. The children were too tired now for running-about games, but pointed and badgered their elders about the cluster of high-rise flats which stood close to the road, like the broken pillars of some temple of the giants. The baby in the pram woke, and was lifted out to totter around on the pavement. The adults sat along a low wall, and passed bottles of water from hand to hand, from which each drank a few sips. Nicky felt thirsty again, but didn't dare start her last bottle for fear of making the baby cry. Perhaps if she moved further away . . .

Down in the dip, right in the middle of the village, was a pub. She stood up and trotted down the hill. A voice cried after her, but she waved her hand without looking around, to show that she knew what she was doing. The rosebed in the forecourt of the pub was edged with tilted bricks; she prized one out and used it to hammer at the pane of frosted glass which was the top half of the door; the glass clashed and tinkled as it fell to the floor inside. The first blow was the dangerous one, because the glass might go anywhere; after that, if you were sensible, it was quite easy to knock away the jagged lengths of pane around the central hole, until you were tapping away the last sharp splinters along the wooden rim at the bottom.

That done, Nicky took her spare skirt out of her satchel and laid it along the wood; she put her hands on the skirt, bounced twice on her toes to get the feel of the ground, and flicked herself neatly through the gap. Gym had been her best subject, once.

The saloon bar was the usual mess, with all the glasses smashed and empty bottles of beer and wine and whisky littering the floor. The room reeked of stale drink. But, as usual, the men who had roared and rioted in here a month ago had not been interested in the soft drinks, except as things to throw and fight with; there were several crates of ginger ale and lemon soda and tonic water under the bar counter. She heaved one out and started to drag it to the door. The light changed; there was a crash and a thump behind her; Gopal was sprawling across the floor, gasping and giggling, his feet still scuffling among the smashed splinters.

"Are you all right?" said Nicky. "Don't cut yourself."

"I'm less good at jumping than you are," he said, turning around to look at the door while he brushed his front with his hands. "If we turn your crate on its end we'll be able to unbolt the door. Then we can drag your loot out."

But outside the door stood Uncle Chacha Rahmta, looking serious. Kewal was hurrying up, while Neena watched anxiously from halfway down the slope.

"You are a bad little boy, Gopal," said Uncle Chacha. "You must not wander away like this. Your mother is very worried."

Probably he spoke in English so that Nicky could share in the reproof.

"It's quite safe," she said. "We're only getting some lemon soda for the children."

(She didn't tell him about the pub she'd broken into north of Shepherd's Bush where a dead man had sat, sprawled across a shiny red table, with a knife in his side.)

"It is notorious that Indian parents overprotect their children," said Kewal. "But that is what they do, Miss Nicky Gore, and you must respect their anxieties."

"All right," said Nicky. "Will you help us with this crate? There's plenty for everybody."

"But we cannot take this," said Uncle Chacha slowly. "It is not our property."

"It isn't anybody's," said Nicky. "They've all gone."

"We could put some money in the till," suggested Kewal.

"It's smashed," said Gopal. "I noticed."

Uncle Chacha walked into the pub, very careful and light on his feet, like a wild animal sniffing into a trap. He counted five green pieces of paper into a broken drawer. Kewal waved to the crowd on the hill and they gathered themselves into line of march and trooped down to the pub. Kewal explained what had happened, and half a dozen angry voices answered him, all together. Several faces looked at Nicky. The women joined in the row. Suddenly something was settled and four of the men went into the pub to fetch more crates, and cans of peanuts and cheese biscuits. The whole party settled to an impromptu picnic. The children recovered strength and began a squealing game of chain tag. The towers of empty flats brooded silent in the dusty afternoon air. The men settled into one group, and the women into another. Every half minute a mother would look up from her gossip and call to a child in words that Nicky couldn't understand, but in the tone that all mothers everywhere use when they are warning their children to be careful. Nicky, all of a sudden, felt just as lonely and left out as she had that morning on the Green, before the Sikhs had come.

"Do you not wish to join the game," said Kewal, who had appeared silently beside her. "Are you too old for that sort of thing, perhaps? Look, Gopal is playing."

"I'm too tired and hot," said Nicky, sighing to keep the crossness out of her voice. "What's the name of the language you talk among yourselves?"

"It's Punjabi—that's the normal language Sikhs use in India. Most of us speak English here—in fact I've friends who only know a few words of Punjabi—but in our family my grandmother has always insisted that even the kids have got to speak Punjabi at home. When my grandmother insists on something, it happens. Some of us used to resent it and stick to English when she wasn't around, but now, since the madness happened, we all seem to have become more Sikh. Sometimes I find myself actually thinking in Punjabi. I never used to."

"Why are you all still here? Why did you leave so late? Everybody else went away a long time ago."

"Oh," said Kewal, "at first we couldn't decide what was happening. Some of us used to work for London Transport, but when the early shift went to get the buses out they were attacked by mobs of Englishmen. Even the little children threw stones as soon as an engine started. And they weren't like you—they didn't stop when the engines were turned off. Perhaps it was because there were so many of them; it's difficult, you know, for a whole crowd to stop rioting once they've started. But none of my relations was killed, though my cousin Surbans Singh was badly beaten. So they came home, and the rest of us couldn't go to work because none of the buses and trains were running. I started to bicycle to the university—I'm a student—but I was chased by shouting people so I came home too. We shut ourselves in our houses —we have three houses all together in the same road—and held a council. We decided that all the English people had been infected by a madness against machines, which for some reason did not affect us Sikhs. Oh, now I'll tell you something interesting and significant. The Jamaicans had also gone to get the buses out, but my cousin Surbans said that they were extremely clumsy and giggled all the time when they made a mistake. He thought they'd all been drinking—at four o'clock in the morning, which is not impossible with Jamaicans. So perhaps they too were a little affected by the madness, but not in the same manner as the English. Anyway our council decided that we'd wait until the madness passed. But it didn't pass. One of my uncles owns a store, so there was enough to eat, but water became difficult and sanitary arrangements too. And it was difficult to cook without . . . What's the matter, Miss Gore?"

Nicky had only been able to understand about half of what Kewal said. His explanation seemed full of nasty, fuzzy words and ideas, such as "bicycle." She felt a qualm of the old sick rage bubbling up inside her—the rage she'd felt in Castelnau, or on that first morning when Daddy had gone around the house with his hammer smashing all the nasty gadgets of their lost life. But it was only a qualm this time, not strong enough for killing or smashing. She put her head between her hands and waited for the qualm to seep away. Kewal watched her in silence.

"Please don't talk about things like that," she said at last. "You mustn't."

"Why?"

"I don't know why, but you mustn't."

He smiled.

"You're a good canary," he said. "You will be really useful to us. I must go and tell my uncles what you say."

"No, wait," said Nicky. "I think I can explain a bit more. Gopal was talking to me before, and he said things which worried me in a different kind of way. The things you were talking about made me feel very angry, very mad really. I don't mind your calling it madness, because it's just like that. But Gopal was talking about India, and the war and things which I'm sure I knew about once. But now it's . . . it's as if they'd become so . . . so *boring*, I suppose, that my brain goes to sleep before I can think about them. I couldn't remember the word for your hats until he told me it was 'turbans.' Do you understand?"

"Aha!" said Kewal, his terrible squint sparkling with pleasure at his own cleverness, "I begin to see. Shall I explain my theorem to you?"

"No, please," said Nicky, who had only just managed to struggle through the discomfort of trying to think about the shut places of her own mind. "Go and tell your uncles."

That caused further delay while the two groups of grownups joined to discuss Nicky; at one point a quarrel broke out and excitable fists were flung skyward, but it was all over as suddenly as a child's tantrums. Then at last they were on the march again, hauling prams and carts up the steep slope to the common, then turning right to trundle down toward Kingston. The children who had darted so eagerly through their game became tired almost at once, oppressed by the dreariness of the slow walk. By the time they came to Robin Hood Roundabout, where the road divides, one of the smallest ones was sniveling and several mothers had found space for an extra burden on their prams. Nicky helped fat Kaka up onto the old lady's cart.

"I shall not be able to push a great weight like yours except downhill," said the big man severely. Kaka grinned between fat cheeks and reached for his grandmother's hand. Or perhaps she was his great-grandmother, Nicky thought. All the grown-ups seemed to show a special kindness toward the small children, despite their strange, fierce looks.

At the roundabout a further conference was held. Nicky lounged amid the incomprehensible babble and looked north, through Robin Hood Gate, to where the green reaches of Richmond Park lay quiet in the westering sun.

"Miss Gore," a voice called. It was the big uncle.

"Yes."

"We are discussing whether we should go through Kingston or along the bypass. It is shorter to go through, although there is a big hill. Would it, shall I say, *affect* you if we went one way or the other?"

"I don't know," said Nicky. "Couldn't we go in there?"

She pointed to the inviting greenness of the park. Some of the mothers made approving noises. The discussion in Punjabi clattered out again. Really, Nicky couldn't understand how any of them could be *listening* with so many of them talking all together. This time the women seemed to have more to say than the men, but at last the noise quietened and in the lull Gopal's grandmother said something decisive. The march wheeled into the park.

"We've decided that the children have gone far enough," said Neena, "so we shall camp here for the night. The women wanted to sleep in a house, but the men said there was more danger of sickness. My mother said that we shall have to camp often, and this would be a warm fine night, with no enemies about, for practice."

"Oh, this is much nicer than houses," said Nicky.

The grass stood tall, shivering in faint slow waves under a breeze so slight that it seemed to be the sunlight itself that moved the stems. The copses looked cool and dark. A cackle of interest burst from several lips together; following the pointing arms Nicky saw a troop of deer move out of shade into sunlight. The big uncle studied his map and then led the march right to where a swift brook flowed in a banked channel.

Here, while a dozen mothers scolded children in Punjabi about the dangers of falling in, they began to set up camp, slowly, arguing about every detail, four people fussing over some easy matter while a fifth struggled alone with an unmanageable load. The fifth might shout angrily for help, but his voice went unnoticed amid the clamor.

Then, quite suddenly, everything was sorted out to everyone's satisfaction and the women started to fill pots from the stream while the men and the older boys straggled off toward the nearest copse.

"You come too, Nicky," called Gopal.

Halfway to the trees they came to a neat stack of fencing posts which the men picked up and carried back for firewood while the boys and Nicky went on.

As they reached the edge of the wood they heard a scuffling and snorting, and about twenty deer flounced away uphill, then turned to watch them from beyond throwing range.

"If only I had a gun!" said one of the older boys with a laugh. "Pow! Wump! Kerzoingg!"

"No!" cried Nicky.

"A bow and arrow, perhaps," said Gopal in a teasing voice.

"Yes, that would be all right," said Nicky, seriously.

It took them some time to gather dry twigs and branches and pile them together for dragging down to the camp. By then the men had fetched the whole pile of fencing posts and were sawing them into short logs. Soon four neat fires were sending invisible flames into the strong, slant sun. Pots boiled. Some of the men were cutting bracken up the hill, others were rigging a mysterious screen. A child fell into the stream, but luckily Kewal was sitting on the bank, brooding at the passing water, and he snatched it out. The child was scolded for falling in and Kewal for not doing his share of the work. Nicky half dozed, and wondered whether it was all a dream.

"Come and wash, Nicky," said Neena, "if you want to."

There was nothing she wanted more. The women were queueing to wash behind the screen, using barely more than a mugful of hot water each in a collapsible canvas baby bath. Nicky, ashamed at her month's grime, used more than her share of water, but nobody complained. Cousin Punam inspected her scratches and dabbed some nasty-smelling stuff along the sore place where her collar had been rubbing. Neena borrowed clean clothes for her from another mother. Then she joined the chattering laundry party.

A frowning woman, darker than the others and with flecks of gray in her hair, hung out her own clothes beside Nicky and looked at her several times without speaking.

"We Sikhs are a very clean people," she said at last, in an accusing voice. "We are cleaner than Europeans."

"I like being clean too," said Nicky.

"Good," said the woman without smiling.

Then Nicky was called over to where the men, who had also been washing and laundering, were holding a council. Gopal had told them about the gun and the bow, and now they settled down to ask her random questions about what they could or could not do with safety. It was difficult because some of the questions made her sick and unhappy again; besides, the way they all asked different questions at the same time, or started discussions in Punjabi among themselves, or became involved in flaring arguments about things that didn't seem to matter at all—all this muddled her attempts at sensible answers. If she hadn't been so tired she would have laughed at them several times, but soon she realized that it wouldn't have been a good idea. They were too proud and prickly to take kindly to being laughed at by an outsider. She thought they wouldn't actually hurt her, not now; but looking at the rich beards and the strong teeth and the dark eyes, fiery and secret, she was sure that they could be very cruel to their enemies.

And Nicky wasn't an enemy—but she was determined not to be a friend either. As the big uncle had said, she was to help them and they were to help her, but one day that would end, and it must end without hurting her. She realized that her raid on the pub had been partly a way of saying that she didn't belong, that the Sikhs had no other claims on her than the single contract of alliance. She was their canary, but she was neither friend nor enemy.

While one of the longest arguments straggled on, Nicky noticed a movement just beyond the group. Four or five deer, long accustomed to the idea that people mean picnickers, and picnickers mean scraps of food, had come nosing up. Uncle Chacha, who hadn't spoken as much as the others so far, now broke into the argument in Punjabi, shifting a couple of feet back out of the circle as he did so. The deer shied away at his movement, then drifted slowly in again.

"Do not look at them, Miss Gore," said one of the uncles. "A wild animal is made more nervous by the gaze of the hunter."

"I do wish everyone would call me Nicky," she said. "Miss Gore sounds like somebody's aunt."

Smiles glowed amid the beards.

"Okay," said several voices; but they said it quietly, and when the discussion rambled on it did so without any sudden bursts of shouting which might disturb a wild animal.

She never saw Uncle Chacha strike because she was carefully not looking straight at the deer. But in the corner of her eye there was a flash of movement, a silent explosion followed by one sharp thud. Then the deer were bounding away and all the Sikhs were on their feet, crowding around and cheering. Nicky jostled through to see what had happened and found Uncle Chacha standing, stave in hand, by what looked like a pale brown sack. He hung his head with exactly Kaka's shyness—he must be the fat boy's father. Then Nicky saw that the sack had a spindly leg, and a round eye big as a halfpenny, dull and unwinking.

"He broke its neck with his lathi," said Kewal proudly. "One blow, bim, like that. We'll have roast venison for supper."

The council was over. Nicky raced twigs on the stream with Gopal and his friends for a bit, then joined in a game of blindman's buff. Then all the children sat in a circle around the cart to hear the old lady tell them a story. Nicky went off to play with a tiny brown baby, Neena's niece, who kicked and gurgled on a pink towel. After that she curled up and slept amid the tickling grasses.

It was almost dark when they woke her, and the dewy dusk smelled beautifully of roasted meat. They all sat on the trampled grass in a ragged circle around the fires; even the smallest babies were awake again, staring from their mothers' laps at the wavering flames. The Sikhs looked stranger still as the night deepened; the men's beards became huge shadows—shadows with no shape to cast them—and in these shadows a row of teeth would gleam for a moment when a mouth opened to talk or smile or chew; the eyes too shone weird in the weird light. They looked like a ring of pirates, murderous invaders.

The venison was charred at the edges and tough to chew, but full of delicious juices even if you did have to spit out the pithy gobbets of fiber that were left unswallowable at the end of each mouthful. The Sikhs had made a curry sauce to dip the meat into, and passed it around in pots, but it was too hot for Nicky. The grown-ups ate a flattish scone-like bread called chapati, which they'd brought with them, but the children preferred to finish off the cheese biscuits from the pub. The drinking water was still tepid from its boiling, but delicious after a month of lemon soda.

When they'd finished eating, the big man stood up by the old lady's cart and read in a solemn voice from a book. Sometimes the Sikhs answered him, all together.

"Prayers," whispered Gopal in Nicky's ear.

Some of the babies were asleep again before he'd finished, and now they were settled into their prams. An awning had been built over the old lady's cart, and the cut bracken piled into mounds under that and the other carts for the smaller children to sleep on. The older children and the grown-ups slept in the open, women and girls in one group, men and boys in the other. Somebody had a spare blanket to lend to Nicky. The bracken was surprisingly comfortable.

"You see?" said Neena as they were sorting themselves out. "It takes a long time to make a camp. It's a lot of work. We cannot hope to march more than ten miles a day, with the children to think about and the carts and prams to push."

"Where are you going to?" said Nicky.

"We do not know. We'll just go until we can find a place where we can live. Perhaps it is across the sea, but I hope not."

# Chapter 3

# GOOD LAND, CLEAN WATER

A place where they could live.

They came to it eight days later, but did not recognize it at first. They thought it was just a sensible place to stop for a few days so that Rani, Neena's sister-in-law, could have her baby. On the left of the lane stood a raw, ugly square brick farmhouse with metal-frame windows; then, a little further up the hill, was a brick shed; then a tiny brand-new bungalow; and then, for them to camp in, an old brick farmyard built like a fort with a single gateway, an old barn down one side, and on the others single-story cattle sheds and grain stores. A hundred yards on, right on the ridge of the hill, loomed two vast new concrete barns and a cluster of grain towers. On the other side of the lane there was only a single house, opposite the farmyard. Once it had been two old cottages for farm laborers, but someone had run them together and smartened them up for an artist to live in.

He'd gone, and so had all the other people. Every house was empty. No cattle lowed for milking, no cat miaowed on any doorstep. Hundreds of birds clattered in the hedges around the artist's cottage, but the farmer had hauled out every other hedge on his land to make it easier to cultivate the flowing steppes of hay and wheat and barley that now stood rippling in the upland wind across six hundred acres.

A mile and a half down the hill you could see the tower of Felpham Church, warm brick, rising amid lindens, seeming to move nearer when the afternoon sun shone full on it, and then to drift away when a cloud shadow hit the sun. You could see only a few roofs of Felpham, although it was quite a big village. Beyond that was distance.

And the distance really was distance, although the farm stood barely a hundred and fifty feet above the plain which stretched to the northeast. For twenty miles there was nothing else as high. There were no real landmarks, except the now useless electric pylons. A double row of these swooped across the slope between the farm and the village, but Nicky tried not to see them. Instead she gazed out beyond them to the mottled leagues, blue and gray and green, that reached toward London. Though they had been settled here for weeks she felt that she still could count every footstep of the road they had come.

It was the people she remembered most. First the old tramp who had come, snuffling like a hedgehog, up to their camp on Esher Common and asked for food. The Sikhs had simply made room for him, dirty as he was, and fed him all he wanted. He must have been half crazy, for he seemed to notice no difference between them and other people, nor between these times and other times, but just mumbled and chewed, and at last lurched away into the dark without a word of thanks.

But the first real people they'd met—ordinary English people, wearing English clothes—had been at Ripley. And they'd been enemies. A dozen men and women had run out of a pub at the sound of the iron wheels on the road. For a while they'd simply stared as the march of Sikhs moved slowly past, but then one of the women had said something mocking to the men, then a man had shouted and all the men were throwing stones and bottles at the Sikhs while the women cursed and jeered. Kaka had been hit by a stone, but

had managed not to cry. Nicky had rushed from the line,
shouting to the men to stop it; their attitude changed, and
for a moment she'd thought they'd heard her and understood, until the rear guard of the Sikhs rushed past her,
staves whirling. The Englishmen had broken and run, while
their women cowered against the wall. As the procession
moved out of Ripley there were catcalls from behind walls,
and clods of earth lobbed into the line, but no one had followed them. And the people working the fields paid no attention as they marched by, grim and silent.

They'd camped that night in a field north of Guildford, on
the banks of the river Wey, and had held another council.
The discussion sounded earnest and subdued, and after it a
party of men had gone night-raiding into Guildford, though
there'd still seemed to be plenty of food left in the cardboard boxes on the carts. (Seeing a can opened made Nicky
uneasy, but the meat inside tasted all right.)

They'd decided to head for the coast, but to avoid towns
and villages even if it meant going the long way around.
However, the houses in the Home Counties are so close
sown that they were bound to pass some of them, and at the
very next hamlet two or three faces had leaned out of windows and called cheerily for news, just as though columns
of bearded foreigners passed that way so often that there
was nothing strange about it. So for a while they'd felt more
optimistic, but as they steadily trudged the days away they'd
learned that every village was different, and that the frowning ones were commoner than the smiling ones. And people
seemed to have little idea of what was happening more than
a mile or two from their own doors.

No more stones were thrown at them, but they had
thrown some themselves. This was in their second battle, on
the outskirts of Aldershot, a much nastier business than the
skirmish at Ripley. The enemy had been a wandering gang
of robbers, though at first they'd looked like another procession, trundling down the sunk road toward the Sikhs; but
almost at once a dozen young men armed with pick helves
had charged shouting and yelling, forcing the Sikhs' advance guard back against the group of women and children.
Uncle Chacha had brought the rear guard up in a counterat-

tack. While the grunts and bellows rose Nicky stared wildly around for something she could do. Gopal grabbed her elbow and pointed to the flinty chalk at the top of the embankment, and the next moment they were scrambling desperately up. There'd been seven of the children up there, screaming and hurling flints, by the time the robbers broke and ran back to where four or five dirty women had been watching the fun from among their own prams and barrows. The angry Sikhs had driven the lot of them on down the road, hitting as hard as they could. Nicky had stopped to look at the robbers' baggage, which had turned out to be a hoard of cheap looted jewelry, a lot of boxes of sweets and some moldy loaves. The Sikhs left it all where it was.

Mr. Gurchuran Singh had hurt his leg in the battle, so they'd decided to rest for a couple of days where they next found water. They had posted extra sentries that night, and after supper the big uncle, whose name was Mr. Jagindar Singh, had spoken very earnestly to Nicky.

"We think you should leave us," he said, "as soon as we next meet friendly people. You will be safer with them than with us. We propose to try to reach the sea and go away to France. We listened to the Paris radio in London, and they are free from this madness there."

"But what will you do for a canary?" Nicky had said.

"Oh, we shall be careful. You have taught us much."

"I'd rather come with you for a bit longer, Mr. Singh."

"We do not consider it wise."

"What does your mother say?"

"Ha, you have bewitched her, Nicky. She says that it is no business of ours, and that you are to make up your own mind."

Nicky had looked toward the cushioned cart and seen the bird-bright eyes watching her through the gloom.

"Please, then," she'd said. "I'd much rather stay. I don't want to have to learn to know a *new* lot of people. Have you still got the . . . the thing you listened to France with?"

"Kaka knocked it off the table and none of us knew how to mend it."

"Good."

She'd meant what she'd said about the new people. They

would be English, like her, and the kindlier they were the
worse it would be, day after day probing to pierce through
the clumsy armor she'd built around her heart. They would
try to be mothers, and fathers, and perhaps even the sisters
and brothers she had never had. And only she would know,
all the time, in waking nightmares as well as the deeps of
dream, how such a home can be smashed in a single morning. She couldn't live through that again.

Besides, against all her reason, she had made a new
friend. Kaka's elder sister Ajeet was a very quiet girl whom
Nicky had at first thought was seven or eight; in fact the two
of them had been born only a week apart. They had fallen
into that instant, easy friendship which feels as though it
had begun before any of your memories and will last until
you are so old that the humped veins on the back of your
hands show dark blue-purple through your wax-white skin.
Ajeet's mother—Uncle Chacha's wife—was the fat frowning
woman, and she seemed anxious to know about every
breath her children drew, but they all seemed happy enough
when you got to know them. At least she didn't try to be a
mother to Nicky.

They had to move before Mr. Gurchuran Singh's leg was
properly healed, because a passing horseman had shouted
to them that there was plague in Aldershot. That had meant
a long journey around the northern edge of that ugly, shambling town, so in the end they had come to Felpham from
the north, taking eight days to get there from London.
Felpham was a frowning village, but not a stone-throwing
one, so they had trudged silently through and begun the
long push up Strake Lane, never guessing that they were
nearly home. In fact Nicky almost refused to pass the
double line of pylons, because they seemed so much worse
than the single ones which she'd crossed with a slight shudder before, but Gopal cajoled her under.

It had rained twice that day, and there were looming
clouds about, so they were glad of the farmyard roofs and
the dry hay beneath them. Four of the men pushed a cart
laden with pots to Strake, two miles further along the road.
There was a pond marked on the map at Strake.

It was Nicky who found the old well, which had enabled

the farm to be built there in the first place. The close eye
which the Sikh parents kept on their children irked her,
though she didn't like to say so; but she tended to drift off
and explore as soon as she had done what she could to help
set up camp; it was her way of saying that she wasn't going
to let herself be watched and pampered like that. Once or
twice Gopal had slipped away and come with her, only to be
scolded when they got back, but this time she was alone.

The artist's cottage was locked. Nose against windows,
Nicky could see a low-ceilinged kitchen and another big
room which had been made by knocking down several
walls. Light streamed into it through a big skylight in the far
roof. She didn't feel like visiting the huge barns because
they'd be full of engines, and everywhere else was nothing
but rippling wheat; so she sat on a low circular flint wall,
topped with a line of brick, and thought about nothing
much. The shouting and chatter of the encampment washed
over her unheeded. The center of the flint wall was covered
with a four-foot round of wood; she thought vaguely that it
must be some sort of garden table, uncomfortable because
you couldn't get your knees under it. She slapped the timber
with her palm.

A slow boom answered, as though the whole hill were
speaking, the million-year-old chalk answering her knock in
tones almost too deep to hear. Each slap or rap produced
the same bass reply. She got her fingers under the edge of
the wood and it came up like a lid.

The hole in the center of the circle was black. It was a
tunnel of night defying the gay sun. The palms of her hands
went chilly as she clutched the brick rim and peered in. At
first she could see nothing, but then there was a faint light, a
circle of sky with a head and shoulders in the middle. The
rough chalk walls dwindled down, becoming invisible in
darkness before they reached the water. She dropped a
stone but it fell crooked, clacking several times from wall to
wall before the splash. She went to fetch Kewal.

He dropped three or four stones, with his other hand feeling his pulse. Even when the stones fell straight it seemed
ages before the splash answered.

"About fifty feet to the water," he said. "If we can get it up, and if the water is good, it means we can stay here for a while. The women say that Rani's baby will be born in two or three days."

They found a rope and bucket in the sheds, but it took a lot of trial and error and a lot of many-voiced arguments before the men rigged up a method of getting a bucket down all that distance and making it lie sideways when it reached the water, so that it filled, and then tilted upright when it was full. Hauling a full bucket up from fifty feet was tiring, too, but it was better than walking to Strake. And the water when it came was so sweet and clean that Cousin Punam decided it was safe to drink without boiling.

It was Gopal who found the corn. While Rani was in labor, three days later, the older children were shushed away. Nicky didn't follow them up to the big barns because she felt uncomfortable there. She was looking, with little luck, for late wild strawberries in the matted grass on the banks of the lane when Gopal came hurrying past, his hands cupped close together as if he was trying to carry water. Nicky thought he'd caught a bird and ran to look.

"Nicky, you're thick," he said. "This is *food*. I climbed an iron ladder up one of those round towers and opened a lid at the top and it's full of corn. There's enough to feed us for a year. Look, it's dry and good."

He ran on to show his treasure to the menfolk, while Nicky returned to combing through the weeds for strawberries. She found no more of the little red globules of sweetness, but caught a grasshopper instead, let it tickle her prisoning palms for a moment, then held it free and watched it tense itself for its leap, and vanish.

The baby was born in a cow stall. It was a boy. That night the Sikhs held full council. It was just as noisy and muddled with cross talk as any of the ones they'd held on the road, but Nicky got the feeling that even in the middle of rowdy arguments they were being more serious, paying more attention to what the others said. From time to time they would ask her a question.

"We can't use any of the tractors, can we, Nicky?"

She shook her head.

"But we can reap and plow and dig and plant by hand?"

"Oh yes."

"And there's nothing wrong with this wheat?"

"Wrong?" She looked through the gateway to where the beautiful tall blades waved, gray as fungus under the big moon, but already tinged with yellow by daylight as the year edged toward harvest.

"Oh yes," said Mr. Surbans Singh, "this is a modern cross-bred variety of wheat, and another of barley. The madness does not apply to them, you think?"

"Oh no!"

Another long fusillade of Punjabi followed. Then . . .

"Nicky, would the madness make the villagers come and destroy us if we were to set up a blacksmith's shop?"

"What would you do?"

"Make and mend spades and sickles and plows and other tools."

"I mean, how would you do it? What would you use?"

"We'd have to make charcoal first, which is done by burning wood very slowly under a mound of earth. Then we'd have to contrive a furnace, with bellows to keep the charcoal burning fiercely. And when the iron was red-hot we'd hammer it, and bend it with vises and pincers, and then temper it in water or oil."

"Water," said Nicky. "Where would you get the iron from?"

"There is plenty lying around the farm."

"I *think* that would be all right. You could try, and I could always tell you if I thought it wasn't. Why do you want to know?"

"First, because if we are to stay here we shall need hand tools. This farm is highly mechanized, which is no doubt why the farmer left; he felt he couldn't work it without his tractors. But secondly, we shall need more to eat than wheat. We shall have to barter for meat and vegetables until we can produce our own. Some of us have seen smithwork done in India, in very primitive conditions; Mr. Jagindar Singh was a skilled metalworker in London, and two more of us have done similar work in factories and garages; so we think we can set up an efficient smithy. But perhaps the villagers will not have our advantages, so we shall be able to

barter metalwork with them in exchange for the things we
need."

"That's a good idea," said Nicky, astonished again by the
amount of sense that seemed to come out of all the clamor
and repetition. "But do you think the villagers will actually
trade with you? They didn't look very friendly when we
came through, and they haven't come up here at all."

"If we make something they need, they will trade with
us," said Uncle Jagindar somberly. "It does not matter how
much they dislike us. We have found this in other times."

The whole council muttered agreement. Kewal gave a
sharp, snorting laugh which Nicky hadn't heard before.

"We must be careful," he said. "If we become too rich they
will want to take our wealth away from us."

"I expect there are quite a lot of robbers in England now,"
said Nicky. "Like those ones we fought on the other side of
Aldershot—men who've got no way of getting food except
by robbing the ones who have."

This set off another round of argument and discussion in
Punjabi. The men seemed to become very excited; voices
rose, eyes flashed, an insignificant uncle even beat his chest.
Nicky edged back out of the circle to ask Gopal what they
were talking about. He was allowed at the council, but he
was thought too young to speak (Nicky wouldn't have been
listened to either if she hadn't been the Sikhs' canary).

Gopal laughed scornfully, but he looked as excited as the
rest.

"They are going to make weapons," he said. "Swords and
spears and steel-tipped arrows. A Sikh should carry a real
sword when times are dangerous. But I'll tell you a joke—
we Sikhs won most of our battles with guns; we used to run
forward, fire a volley and then run back until we had time
to reload. It doesn't sound very brave, but all India feared us
then. What's the matter, Nicky? Oh, I'm sorry, I forgot. But
they won't make guns now; instead they'll turn this farmyard into a fort which we can defend against the robbers."

After that the council became less serious, dwindling into
boastings and warlike imaginings. Gopal translated the
louder bits.

"My Uncle Gurchuran says we must capture horses and

turn ourselves into cavalry, and then we can protect the whole countryside for a fee. A protection racket. We often lived like that in the old days. . . . Mr. Parnad Singh says his father was Risaldar at an archery club in Simla, and he will teach us all to shoot. A risaldar is a sort of sergeant. . . . My Uncle Chacha is teasing him and Mr. Parnad Singh is angry. . . . My Uncle Jagindar is trying to smooth him down; he says it will be useful to have a good shot with a bow for hunting, and that Uncle Chacha must be careful what he says, because he is so fat that he'll make an easy target. That's unfair because Uncle Chacha is the quickest of them all, and the best fighter. You saw how he fought against those robbers. Now he's pretending to be angry with Uncle Jagindar, but *that* doesn't matter because it's inside the family. . . . My grandmother is speaking. She says we must all be careful how we talk to one another, because we are in a dangerous world and we can't afford to have feuds with one another. My goodness, she says, we Sikhs are a quick tempered people. She's beginning to tell a story. She tells pretty good stories, for children and adults too."

The council had fallen silent at the creak of the old woman's voice. There had been a brief guffaw of laughter at her second sentence, but that was all. One of the men turned to glare at Gopal because his translation was spoiling the silence. He too stopped talking.

The story was not long, but the old woman told it with careful and elaborate gestures of the hands, as though she were the storyteller at some great court and had been sent for after supper to entertain the princes. Nicky could hear, even in the unknown language, that it was the story of a fierce quarrel between two proud men. She looked along the outer circle of children and saw Ajeet sitting entranced, mouth slightly parted and head craning forward as she listened and stared at the elaborate ceremony of the fluttering hands. Ajeet's lips were moving with the words, and her hands made faint unconscious efforts to flutter themselves.

All the Sikhs laughed when the story ended, then broke into smaller chattering groups. Nicky crossed to where Ajeet still sat staring at the orange firelight.

"What was the story about, Ajeet?" she said.

"Oh, I don't know," said Ajeet in her usual near whisper, shy and confused.

"Please tell me. I like to know anything your grandmother says. She is so . . . so special."

"Oh, it was a tale of two Sikh brothers, farmers, whom my grandmother knew in India, and how they quarreled over a dead pigeon, and in the end lost their farm and their wives and everything. Listen. It was like this."

Her voice changed and strengthened. She drew her head back and sat very upright, freeing her hands for gestures. The history of that forgotten feud rolled out in vivid, exact words, each phrase underlined with just the same gesture of finger or wrist that her grandmother had used. Once or twice she hesitated over a word, and Nicky realized that she was turning familiar Punjabi into English which didn't quite fit. When she finished Nicky found herself laughing at the ridiculous disaster, just as the men had laughed, and heard more voices laughing behind her. Kewal and three of the other men had been standing around in silence to hear the same story all over again.

"Very excellent," said Kewal, only half mocking.

One of the men called in Punjabi over his shoulder, and was answered by a pleased cackle from the open stall where the old woman lay on her cushions; she had been watching the show too. Ajeet accepted the compliments gravely, without any of her usual shyness, then took Nicky off to say good night to the old lady.

This had become a sort of ritual for Nicky, a good-luck thing, wherever they were. They couldn't say much to each other, even with Ajeet to translate, because their lives had been so different, but somehow it ended the day on a comfortable note.

As they crossed the yard back to the shed where the women slept, Nicky looked around the firelit walls and the black-shadowed crannies. So this was home, now.

Provided nobody came to drive them out.

They settled in slowly. The bungalow had been left unlocked, and the first thing the Sikhs did was to redecorate the bedroom with rich hangings. They took their shoes off

when they went into the room. Uncle Jagindar carried the
old lady in when it was finished, and she clucked her satisfaction, though she wanted several details changed. Nicky
watched fascinated from the doorway.

"It is a place to keep our holy book," explained Kewal.
"My family are very orthodox Sikhs. Before these troubles
some of us younger ones didn't treat our religion as earnestly as the elders, but now it seems more important. It
will help to keep us together."

"We'll have to use the other houses to sleep in when the
winter comes," said Nicky. "It'll be too cold to sleep out in
the sheds."

"You are very practical-minded. That was how the English
ruled India. They would go and admire the Taj Mahal, but
all the time they were thinking about drains. Anyway, my
uncles don't feel it proper to break into other people's
houses, even if the people have gone away."

"They'll have to in the end," said Nicky. "I don't mind
doing the burgling, and then once the doors are open you
could all come and use the houses like you are doing this
one."

Kewal laughed and pulled his glossy beard.

"That would be an acceptable compromise," he said. "But
I think we won't tell my uncles until you've done it. I will
attend and supervise, because in my opinion your tech-
niques of burglary are a little crude."

But you have to be crude with metal-framed windows.
They fit too tight for you to be able to slide a knife or wire
through to loose the catch. Nicky broke two panes, opened
two windows, climbed into two musty and silent houses,
and tiptoed through the dank air to unbolt two doors. The
artist's cottage was full of lovely bric-a-brac—a deer head,
and straw ornaments that were made for the finials of
hayricks, and Trinidadian steel drums. Kewal delightedly
began to tonk out a pop tune, but Nicky (frightened now of
what she'd done) dragged him away.

And the uncles *were* cross when she told them. (She left
Kewal out of her story.) But when the women found that
there was an open hearth in the cottage and a big closed
stove in the farmhouse, in both of which you could burn

logs, they told the uncles to stop being so high-minded. Here was somewhere to bathe and attend to small babies in the warm. And though the electric cookers were useless, a little bricklaying would turn the artist's drawing-room fireplace into a primitive but practical oven and stove for a communal kitchen.

Even so, Uncle Jagindar spoke very seriously to Nicky.

"It is difficult for us," he said. "If you were my child, or one of my nieces, I would punish you for this. Perhaps you are right and we will have to use these houses in winter, but you are wrong to take decisions on your own account against the wishes of us older people. If you continue to do this, then perhaps our own children will start to copy you, and then we will have to send you away. We will be sad, but we will do it."

"I'm sorry," said Nicky. "My own family weren't so . . . so . . ."

"If your own family were more like us," said Uncle Jagindar, "you would not have become separated from them as you did, even though a mad priest caused a panic."

Nicky was surprised. Ajeet was the only person she'd told about that wild Dervish who'd pranced red-eyed beside the retreating Londoners yelling about fire and brimstone; and the thunderstorm; and the hideous mass panic; and the long, sick misery of loss. Ajeet must have told her frowning mother, who must have passed the story on. But Uncle Jagindar was being unfair—anybody could have got lost in that screaming mob.

"All right," she said. "I'll try not to be a bad influence." That was her own joke—Miss Calthrop at school used to talk about girls who were bad influences, but had spoiled her case by always picking on the girls who were most fun to be with. Uncle Jagindar nodded, and Nicky went up across the fields to the wood to see how the charcoal burners were getting on.

They had made an eight-foot pyramid of logs, covered them with wet bracken, and then sealed the pile with ashes and burned earth. Then the pile was lit by the tedious process of dropping embers down the central funnel and carefully blocking them in with straight sticks. A pockmarked man was in charge, because he had done the job in India. Nicky hardly knew him, as he was one of the Sikhs who was not related to the main families and spoke little English; but now he leaned on his spade by the water hole he had dug and gave orders to the two men who were building a second pyramid of logs.

Gopal came into the clearing with his father, shoving a handcart laden with more logs for the pile.

"Wouldn't it be better sense to burn the charcoal near the log stack?" said Nicky. "Or to cut your wood from these trees here?"

"Wrong both times," said Gopal. "Nought out of ten. You must have seasoned wood, and we were lucky to find that big stack up by the road. And you must have water to quench the charcoal with when you take the pile to bits. If Mr. Harbans Singh hadn't found that spring, we might have had to carry the wood all the way down to the well."

"How long before you get any charcoal?"

"Three days, Mr. Harbans says, but the first lot may not be very good. Have you finished your bow, Risaldar?"

They all called Mr. Parnad Singh Risaldar now. It was a joke in a way, but he seemed to like it. Perhaps it reminded him of the glories of his father's Simla club. He was an older man than the others, his beard a splendid gray waterfall. He looked up from where he was whittling at a long stave.

"In a year's time, perhaps," he said, "unless I can find some seasoned ash or yew before then. With something like this, I'd be lucky to kill a rabbit at twenty paces. But tell me, Nicky—if I used tempered steel from the farmyard—the right piece, I mean—would it be safe to use that?"

"I think so," said Nicky uncertainly.

"Let's try," said Gopal. "There's all sorts of metal littered about the barn."

Halfway down the huge field two bright-colored figures were working, a man in a crimson turban and a woman in an orange sari. When the children came nearer they saw that it was Mr. Surbans Singh and his wife Mohindar, he scything, she raking. Mr. Surbans Singh had appointed himself head farmer.

"What are you doing?" called Gopal.

Mr. Surbans Singh straightened up, but his wife (whom Nicky thought the prettiest of all the Sikhs) went on tedding the grass he'd cut into a loose line.

"I found this scythe in a shed," he said. "It is very bad, and the hay is grown too coarse to be good feed, but poor hay will be better than none if we are to keep sheep through the winter."

"Sheep?" said Nicky, surprised.

"I hope so," said Mr. Surbans Singh. "I would not like to eat nothing but chapati all the year round. Eh, my dear?"

Mrs. Mohindar stopped raking and smiled at him.

"I have married a greedy man," she said.

Mr. Surbans Singh looked at the tiny patch he had cut, and then at the vast sweep of the hayfield.

"We have a long way to go," he said ruefully, and bent to his scything.

From the gray-white hulk of the barns came an erratic clinking of metal. Nicky noticed Gopal looking at her out of the corner of his eye as they walked down the slope.

"What are they up to?" she said nervously.

"Come and see."

She wouldn't actually go in under the big roof, but the barn was open at both ends and she could see the whole scene. All down one side a rank of bright-colored engines, gawky with insectlike joints and limbs, stood silent. Other machines and parts of machines littered the floor of the barn, leaving only just enough passageway for the tractors to haul the attachments they needed in and out.

"This farmer liked gadgets," said Gopal. "Three combines, two hay balers, six different tractors, all the latest devices."

"What are the men doing?" said Nicky, quivering.

Uncle Jagindar was walking about among the engines with a hammer. From time to time he would tap at one, which produced the clinking, and call a man over to him, point and explain.

"Iron and steel are funny stuff," said Gopal. "There are lots of different kinds. Some you can work with, and some you can't—it is too hard, or its softening point is too high, or it comes from the forge too brittle. My Uncle Jagindar wants ordinary mild steel, and he's looking for bits he can use; the others are trying to take them off the tractors and attachments."

"And the things won't go when they're taken to bits?" said Nicky.

"That would suit you?"

"Yes, but it's not as good as smashing them."

She was quite serious, but Gopal laughed and Uncle Jagindar heard the noise and came out into the sunlight. He was interested in the idea about the bow, but said he didn't think they'd find steel whippy enough, and he didn't think he could temper a rod to that state either. Besides, it would be very dangerous to the bowman if it snapped under tension. Then he shouted to one of the men, who brought out an old sickle without a handle which they'd unearthed. Uncle Jagindar sharpened it with a stone and bound sacking tightly around the tang until it was comfortable to hold. Gopal, much to his disgust, was sent up to help Mr. Surbans Singh in the hayfield, and Nicky went with him to turn the hay.

It was surprising how much got cut, provided you didn't stop every few minutes to look and see how you were getting on.

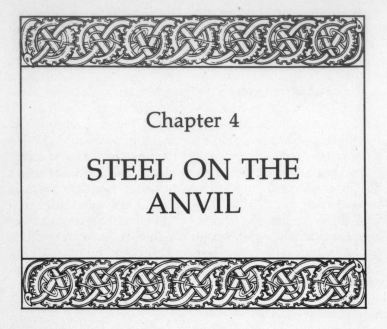

# Chapter 4

# STEEL ON THE ANVIL

Eight days later Nicky went down to the village. She bent her head and ran with a shudder of disgust under the double set of power lines that swooped from pylon to pylon across the lane.

"You are afraid that they will fall on you?" asked Uncle Chacha, rolling cat-footed beside her.

"No, it isn't that. But they feel like a . . . like a curse."

"Probably that is why the village people have not come up to disturb us, then."

"I expect so."

In fact she could see a whole party of villagers in a field up to their right, almost half a mile away. They were loading a wagon with hay; the wagon was pulled by eight ponies. She pointed.

"They've quite enough fields to work on near the village," she said, "without coming up our way."

"It is curious that they are all working together," said Uncle Chacha. "I would have expected them to be cultivating separate patches—that is more the English style. Perhaps somebody has organized them."

He walked on the verge, keeping close in under the ragged hedge. He was wearing his dull green turban, for extra camouflage. They stopped about fifty yards from the first house, and he tucked himself in behind a bulge of hawthorn.

"If you are in trouble, run this way," he said. "But I will not come to help you unless you scream or call."

"All right," said Nicky. "But I'm sure you needn't worry."

She walked on. It had taken a lot of argument at the council before the Sikhs had agreed that the best way to make contact with the village was for her to go down alone and try to find somebody to talk to. Most of the women had thought it was dangerous, and the men had also felt that it was dishonorable to let a girl take the risk. But the old grandmother had been her ally in the argument, and together they'd won.

The first few houses were larger than cottages and looked empty. In front of one of them was a small paddock littered with striped pony jumps. The next houses were smaller and looked lived in, but there was no sign of life. She rounded the corner into the wider bit of road which is called the Borough, and there, under the inn sign of the Five Bells, three men sat on a bench with pewter mugs in their hands.

They looked up as soon as they heard her footfall.

"Good morning," said Nicky.

The nearest man pushed a battered brown felt hat back over his short-cropped gray hair. His face was brown with sun, and his small gray eyes sharp and suspicious. But he spoke friendly enough.

"And good morning to you, miss," he said. "Where're you from, then?"

"I'm staying on the farm up the hill," said Nicky.

The group tensed. A lean-faced young man with a half-grown beard said, "Booker's Farm, that'd be?"

"I don't know its name," said Nicky. "We just came there and stayed because one of my friends was going to have a baby."

"How many o' you?" said the hat wearer.

"About forty."

They looked at each other.

"That's them," said a little old man in shirtsleeves. He spoke with an odd, crowing note.

The others nodded.

"I know what," said the beard grower. "They kep' her prisoner and now she's run away and come to us."

"No," said Nicky. "They helped me get out of London, and so I stayed with them."

"Bad place, London," said the man in the hat.

"You aren't one on 'em, though?" crowed the man in shirtsleeves.

"No," said Nicky. "They're called Sikhs."

"Know what we call 'em?" said the man in the hat. "We call 'em the Devil's Children."

"But they aren't like that at all," said Nicky.

"Leastways they aren't like other folk," said the man in the hat. "Not like good Christian folk. You grant me that."

"They've been very good to me," said Nicky.

"That's as may be," said the man in shirtsleeves. "We don't want nothing to do with 'em. That's what the Master tells us, and he's right again, too."

"Is there a smith in the village?" said Nicky.

"Neither there isn't," said the man in the hat. "And if there was, he wouldn't care to work for the Devil's Children, would he now?"

The men seemed to become more hostile and suspicious every word they spoke.

"Oh, *we* don't need a smith," she said. "But we thought *you* might. For making plows and mending spades and things like that. The Sikhs are very good smiths."

She hoped that was true. The first furnace hadn't blown hot enough, and had had to be rebuilt. But the big double bellows had been fashioned from wood and canvas and proved to spout a steady blast of air; and though the first mound of charcoal opened had been poor stuff, and the second not much better, they were all delighted with the product of the new one which had been built on the site of the first.

The three villagers looked at each other, and the one in shirtsleeves rose to his feet.

"Perhaps I'd best go and fetch him, then," he said.

"Right you are, Maxie," said the man in the hat. Maxie scuttled away around the corner.

"And you'd best be up the hayfield, Dunc," said the man in the hat, "afore he finds you sitting here swilling of a morning."

The beard grower stood up too, but didn't leave.

"Funny thing," he said. "I remember my granny telling me stories about the Queer Folk, and as often as not they was smiths and ironworkers. Under the hills they used to live then, she said."

"That's a fact," said the man in the hat. "I remember that too. Not as I actually thought on it for years and years, but maybe there's something in it. Maybe they went up to London after."

"They'll bring you luck, if only you don't cross 'em," said the beard grower eagerly.

"Best have nothing to do with them," said the man in the hat.

"But good iron they made," said the beard grower. "Never wore out, my granny told me."

Yes, thought Nicky, it would be easy to believe the Sikhs were some sort of hobgoblins, if living with them day by day didn't keep reminding you that they were ordinary people—bones and veins and muscles and fat. Even she could only recall in shifting glimpses that other world, before all these changes happened, where you actually *knew* about Sikhs and foreigners without (perhaps) ever having met any. But these fancies were going to make barter difficult. On the other hand it meant that the villagers were less likely to come raiding up to the farm. . . .

She was still hesitating what to say next when the little man, Maxie, came back.

Beside him strode a giant. A man seven feet tall, red-faced and blue-eyed. He had no waist at all, but a broad leather belt held shirt and trousers together at the equator of his prodigious torso. Another strap hung across his shoulder and from it dangled a naked cutlass. His cheeks were so fat

that separate pads of brick-red flesh bobbled below his eye
sockets. Nicky noticed that the man in the hat had stood up
when he appeared. The other man, the beard grower, was
already standing, and it was at him that the giant stared.

" 'Morning, Arthur," said the man in the hat.

"What you doing down here, Dunc?" said the giant. "The
rest of 'em's up at the hayfield. Them as don't work this
summer won't eat this winter."

"Right you are, Arthur," said the beard grower. "My foot's
been playing me up, but it's better now."

He slipped away, and the blue gaze turned itself on Nicky.

"Who's this, then?" said the giant. His voice was a slow
purr, like a well-fed tabby's.

"She says as she lives with the Devil's Children," explained
the man in the hat. "And she says as they've blacksmiths up
there, willing to make and mend for us."

"So Maxie told me," said the giant. "You think we got
nothing to do but break good tools, miss?"

"Oh no," said Nicky. "But however careful you are, things
do get broken, and it isn't going to be so easy to mend them
now, or to buy new ones. And I expect there are things you
haven't got, like plows which you can pull by hand or behind a horse. All the plows up at the farm are made for
pulling behind those . . . you know . . . tractors."

As she got the nasty word out the giant took a quick pace
forward. She saw a pink thing wheeling toward her but before she had time to duck, his open palm, large as a dish,
smacked into the side of her head and sent her sprawling.
She hadn't even stopped her scraping slide across the dusty
tarmac when her shoulders were seized and she was lifted
into the air.

She opened her eyes and through the dizziness and tears
she saw that the giant was holding her at arm's length, three
feet above the ground, so that his face was directly opposite
hers. He began to shake her to and fro. As he shook he
spoke, in just the same purring voice.

"I'll have no talk *(shake)* like that *(shake)* in my village
*(shake)*. Not one word of it *(shake)*. D'you hear *(shake)*? I'll
have no talk *(shake)* like that *(shake)* in my village."

"Easy, Arthur, easy!" The little man was hanging on to the

giant's left elbow. His weight seemed to make no difference at all to the shaking.

"She's only a kid," crowed the little man, as though he were speaking to the deaf.

The giant stopped shaking and put Nicky down.

"I'd treat my own kids a sight rougher if I heard 'em talking that kind of filth," he purred.

"But what d'you make of what she was saying before?" said the man in the hat. "I got a spud-fork needs a good weld. And we'll be crying for hand plows come seed time."

"Fetch her your fork then," said the giant. "Let's see what sort of a job they do. And then maybe they can show us a plowshare. You, girl, they'll be wanting something out of us in exchange, won't they, or my name's not Arthur Barnard."

The vast forefinger pointed suddenly at Nicky as though she'd been trying to cheat him.

"Milk and vegetables and vegetable seed for next year and meat," she gabbled. "Not beef. They aren't allowed to eat beef in their religion."

"Heathen," purred the giant. "I'm not having them come among *my* streets, not with fifty plows. Fetch her your fork, Tom, and let's see what kind of a job they make of it."

He turned on his heel and strolled away with four-foot paces. The man and the girl watched him until he was out of earshot.

"Sorry he hit you like that, miss, but it was your fault for talking nastiness."

"Yes. Shall I call you Mr. Tom?"

"That'll do. Tom Pritchard's me full name."

"But who is *he*?"

"Arthur Barnard. The Master we call him now. Time was Felpham was full of a different crowd of folk—men went up to London most days, children went away to school, women didn't have enough to do. So *they* ran the village. Then they left, all of a sudden, and only us kind of folk remained. Soon after that a band of ruffians come along, more than twenty of 'em, came here to break and steal and to gobble what food we had. They were that fierce and that rough that most of us were scared to stand up to 'em, but Arthur Barnard—cowman he used to be, up at Ironside's—he drove 'em out. Took that sword he wears out of the old admiral's cottage and drove 'em out. Pretty nigh on single-handed he did it. Since then what he says goes, like as you've seen. You come with me, miss, and we'll find that fork."

He limped away to his council house up beyond the church. The fork had been broken just above where the handle joined the tines. One long strip of iron still ran up the front of the wood, but the wood itself was snapped and the strip of iron behind had rusted right through.

Uncle Chacha turned the tool over discontentedly in the shelter of the hedge and listened to Nicky's story.

"I don't know," he said. "Perhaps Jagindar can mend it, but it doesn't look easy. This is not my trade; I am a checker in a warehouse, not a blacksmith. Does your head hurt where the man hit you?"

"I'm getting used to being hit," said Nicky, fingering the bruised bone. "He wasn't quite so quick as you are, but his hand was much heavier."

Uncle Chacha nodded, put the fork over his shoulder and started on the trudge up the lane. After a while he said, "This man sounds interesting. A smaller fighter can sometimes defeat a bigger one because he is quicker, but a man who is very big and quite quick will usually win."

"If you were a checker in a warehouse," said Nicky, "how do you know so much about fighting, and why are you so good at it?"

"I am very quick," said Uncle Chacha, "because all my life I have played squash. I am quite good—I have played in the national championships, though I didn't get very far. I have also learned some judo, because I was not very popular at the warehouse when I first went there. The other men were racially intolerant, and I wished to be able to defend myself. A Sikh should know how to fight."

"But swords and things," said Nicky.

"Oh, we will have to see."

They got the forge going properly two days later. Nicky stood in the doorway of the shed, where the stolid sun beat brilliant against the brick, and watched a pair of uncles pumping rhythmically at the bellows bar in the dusky interior. The pulses of air roared with a deep, hungry note as they drove through the glowing charcoal, turning it from dull red to orange and from orange to searing yellow. Uncle Jagindar stood in the orange cone of light from the furnace door, shading his eyes as he gazed against the glare. He was stripped to the waist and the weird light cast blue shadows between the ridges of his muscles. At last he grunted and nodded, and Mr. Gurchuran Singh picked up a pair of pincers and lifted a short bar of white-hot metal from the furnace. When it was firm on the anvil Uncle Jagindar smote steadily at it with a four-pound hammer. The brightness died out of it as though the blows were killing the light; the crash of each blow rang so sharp, and the next crash followed it so quickly, that Nicky's head began to ring with the racket and she put her hands to her ears. Kewal took her by the elbow and led her away.

"Is it all right?" he said. His anxiety seemed to make his squint worse than ever.

"Oh yes," said Nicky. "Only it's so *noisy*. What are they making?"

"Just a practice piece, a small sword for one of the children. It may not be very good because Jagindar isn't sure of the quality of the steel he is using. Steel is a mixture of iron and carbon in exact quantities, and the hot charcoal adds more carbon to the iron, so you achieve steel of a different temper. In primitive conditions like this it is all a matter of judgment, so the first few things he makes will probably be flawed or brittle."

Nicky looked down the slope to where two extraordinary figures were prancing on the unmown lawn behind the farmhouse. Their padded necks and shoulders made them look heavy and gawky, but they skipped around each other like hares in March, taking vicious swipes at the padding with short, curved staves. Few of the swipes reached their target because the figures ducked and backed so agilely, or took the blow cunningly on the little round leather shields which Uncle Chacha had cut from old trunks in the farmhouse attic. Suddenly Nicky realized that the six-yard folds of fine linen from which the Sikhs contrived their turbans would be almost as useful in battle as a steel helmet. The fencing practice stopped, and Uncle Chacha and Mr.

Harbans Singh leaned on their staves and discussed what
they had learned.

"Yes," said Nicky, "I suppose a brittle sword wouldn't last
long with that amount of bashing. But I thought proper
fencers prodded at each other with the points of their
swords, instead of swiping like that."

"It's a different type of sword," said Kewal. "We Sikhs
have always used the tulwar, which you call a saber. The
curve of the blade helps the cutting edge to slice through
whatever you strike at. You Europeans invented the dueling
sword, using the point to pierce your enemy before he could
reach you, but even European cavalry has always used the
saber, because the horse carries a man to close quarters
where the cutting edge is handier than the point."

"I hope he doesn't make Mr. Tom's fork brittle," said
Nicky. "Let's go and help in the hayfield."

Kewal made a face, but walked up the path beside her.
Nicky was learning all sorts of surprising differences between the Sikhs, who had at first seemed so like each other.
Kewal, for instance, was quick and clever, but lazy and
vain; most days he seemed to have some reason to wear his
smartest clothes, and the clothes then became a reason for
not doing any hard or dirty work—though he was usually
on the fringe of any working party, criticizing and giving
advice. If Nicky had suggested going up to the wood to help
in the endless job of carting charcoal down to the forge, he'd
have found a reason for doing something else. The black
and brittle treasure from the opened mounds filled all the
air around with a fine and filthy dust. That was work too
dirty for Kewal.

Suddenly Nicky laughed aloud. *She* was going up to the
hayfield as an excuse for not taking her turn at the flour
milling, which she thought the dreariest job on the whole
farm: you pounded and rubbed and sieved for an hour, and
finished with two cupfuls. Kewal looked to see if she would
share the joke, but she shook her head.

The toy sword was given to Kaka, and he swaggered
about with it stuck into his straining belt, looking just like a
miniature version of the giant down in the village. Uncle
Jagindar was pleased with it, because it didn't snap when

you bent it or banged the anvil with it, and the edge came up killing sharp. He practiced all next day at the forge and on the third day he mended Mr. Tom's fork, welding a new length of steel up the back. The risaldar shaped a new handle, and the finished job looked almost as good as a fork from a shop. Nicky was ready to take it down at once, but Gopal said, "No, listen!"

The bells were going in the church tower, tumbling sweetly through their changes. It must be Sunday. The Sikhs didn't keep Sunday or any other day as special; instead they had long prayers and readings from their holy book morning and evening. Yes, it would be a mistake to go down on a Sunday, another sign of how different the two communities were.

She found Mr. Tom at his house on Monday morning. He fingered the weld and the new handle with hands so harsh that you could hear his skin scrape across the surface.

"Clean and sturdy, I'd say," he said. "We'll show the Master. He's in court, Mondays."

They found the giant in what had been a classroom in the school. Mr. Tom led Nicky quietly in and pointed to a bench where she could sit. Twenty other villagers were there, cramped behind child-sized desks; the giant sat up on the dais, also cramped, though his desk had been made for a grown man. Maxie sat at a table below the dais, scribbling in a ledger. A dark, angry-looking woman stood in front of the desk complaining about something. When she stopped she sat down. The giant looked at the room in silence for a full minute.

Then he nodded to Maxie, who had stopped writing. Maxie leaped to his feet and crowed like a cock.

"Now hear this!" were the words he crowed. The giant purred into the silence.

"Mrs. Sallow," he said, "has brought a complaint against her neighbor Mr. Goddard, saying that his dog spoils her flower beds by burying bones in 'em. There are three points to this case. Firstly, it is the nature of a dog to bury its bones where it feels like, and you can't change that. Secondly, flower beds aren't of no account in Felpham no more—it's vegetables we'll be needing, beans and such, to see us through the coming winter. Thirdly, which falls into two parts, a man must have a good dog, and if that dog goes digging up the neighbor's flower beds the neighbor has to put up with it, though it would be different, like I said, if it was vegetables. And moreover it is the use and custom of Felpham that a woman is subservient to a man, and when it comes to a complaint, other things being equal, the man shall have the best of it. Case dismissed."

"Case dismissed," crowed Maxie, and began to scribble again in his ledger.

The dark woman, looking angrier than ever, bustled out of the classroom.

"That's the last case, eh, Maxie?" said the giant.

"Yessir."

Mr. Tom stood up.

"The girl's brought my spud fork back from the Devil's Children," he said. "Seems like a good mend to me."

"Let's have a squint at it," said the giant.

Tom took the fork up to the dais and the giant rose from his desk. First he waggled the tool to and fro in his huge hands, then he peered at the actual join, then he took the tines in one hand and the handle in the other, put his knee to the join and heaved.

"Oi!" cried Mr. Tom. "Don't you go busting of it, Arthur!"

The giant stopped heaving and gazed at Mr. Tom from under reddish eyebrows. Mr. Tom looked away, and the giant resumed heaving. Nicky could see the squares of his checked shirt change shape where they crossed his shoulders as the oxlike muscles bulged with the effort. The classroom was silent as a funeral. Suddenly there came a crack and a twang, and the fork changed shape.

The giant straightened and held it up. He had snapped the wooden handle clean in two, and one of the steel supports had broken with it, but the other had held. It was the piece Uncle Jagindar had mended which had stayed unbroken.

"Now hear this," purred the giant, panting slightly with the aftermath of that great spasm of strength.

"Now hear this!" crowed Maxie.

"We'll be needing a fair whack of honest tools," said the giant. "Some will want mending, and some we haven't got.

You all know how the Devil's Children have settled in up at Booker's, and how near we came to raiding up there and driving 'em out, bad wires or no bad wires. Now it turns out that they've blacksmiths among them, as will make and mend ironwork for us, and do an honest job at it. So I say this: if a man wants a piece of iron mended, or made, he'll come to me and tell me what he wants, and I'll fix a fair price for him with this girl here as lives with the Devil's Children. If you want a job done, you must pay a fair price. But I won't fix a price which the village or the man can't spare, I promise you that. It'll be a bag of carrots, maybe, for a mended spade, and a lamb or two for a new plow. And I hereby appoint Tom Pritchard my deputy to handle this trade, seeing as I broke your fork, Tom, though I'll oversee it myself till we've got it running smoothly. But if I find one of you, or any other man or woman in Felpham, dealing with the Devil's Children direct, other than through me or Tom Pritchard and this girl here, I'll skin 'em alive, I promise you that. We have to trade with 'em, but they're heathen, outlandish heathen, and apart from trade we don't want to see nor hide nor hair of 'em. I've heard some of you talking fancy about them, saying as they're the Queer Folk and suchlike rubbish. I don't want to hear no more of that. They're mortal flesh, like you and me. But they're heathen foreigners besides, and it is the use and custom of Felpham to have nothing to do with 'em. Now, such of you as've got metal to make and mend, you're to bring it to the Borough, or drawings of what you want. Maxie, you can cry the news through the village. Court adjourned."

"Court adjourned," crowed Maxie, and whisked out of the room like a blown leaf. Tom went ruefully up to the dais to collect his ruined fork; Nicky saw that he was too afraid of the giant to complain. She sat where she was while the room cleared; all the time the giant stared at the wall above the door, as though he could see through it.

When the last of the villagers had gone he yawned, scratched the back of his head, stood up, settled his cutlass strap over his shoulder, covered it with an orange cloak which he pinned in place with a big brooch, clapped a broad hat with a plume in it onto his head and strode toward the door. Nicky saw that he was wearing boots now, and that the cloak had once been a curtain. The room boomed at every footfall. He stopped suddenly, as though he'd only just noticed her.

"What are you waiting for, girl?" he said.

"I wanted to ask you how we're going to fix a proper price for the work if you won't meet any of the Sikhs."

"The Devil's Children," he said.

"They aren't like that at all," said Nicky. "They're proud, and they wear funny clothes, and they talk a lot, but when you get to know them they're really like anybody else. Just ordinary."

"None of my folk's going to get to know the Devil's Children," said the giant without looking at her. "But I give you my honor I'll strike a fair price. Think, girl, it's in my interest till we can find a smith of our own; there's a heap of metalwork to be done before winter if we're to come through it short of starving. I don't want your people trading over to Aston, nor Fadlingfield, because they think we've cheated 'em here. Now you run along. This afternoon I'll send a barrow of stuff up as far as the bad wires; you can fetch it back, mended, this day week. We're vicious short on scythes, too, so you can get your friends to forge us half a dozen new 'uns—we'll shape the handles."

"All right," said Nicky, and turned to go.

"Come back, girl," said the giant. "I've more to say. You heard what I told my people about having nothing to do with the Devil's Children. You tell your friends the same. If I see one of those brown skins down this side of the bad wires I'll tear him apart, man, woman or child. Joint by joint I'll tear him."

There was no point in arguing, so Nicky walked out into the midmorning glare and ran down the street, left through the Borough and up the lane to where Kewal was waiting for her in the shadow of the hedge. (Now that the job was known to be safe he had volunteered for it because it was also known to be easy.) He was almost as interested by the description of the court as Uncle Chacha had been by the first meeting with the giant.

"Yes," he said. "He is becoming a feudal baron, and he is

setting about it the right way. It would be curious to know whether he has thought it out or whether his behavior is instinctive. The first step is to make all the villagers obey him, and this he must do partly by frequent demonstrations of his physical strength—that was why he broke the fork— and partly by laying down strict rules which they *can* obey. And at the same time he must channel all the business of the village through his own hands. Now a man who wants a fork mended or a scythe made must come to him, and if that man is out of favor with him then the work will not be done. So our forge is another source of power for him."

"He protects them too, don't forget," said Nicky. "And I thought they seemed to like being bullied like that, in a funny way."

"Oh yes, of course. Most people prefer to have their thinking done for them. Democracy is not a natural growth, it is a weary responsibility. You have to be sterling fellows, such as we Sikhs are, to make it work."

That afternoon two barrow loads of broken implements waited where the power lines crossed the lane. Uncle Jagindar and his assistants toiled in the roaring and clanging smithy as long as there was light. By Friday the work was done.

The giant scrutinized tool after tool in the Borough before handing them back to their owners, but as far as Nicky could tell from the blue, unwinking eyes and the blubbery cheeks he was satisfied. She explained about the pieces which Uncle Jagindar had said were past mending, and he nodded. Half an hour later she was herding two fat lambs up the lane, while a disgruntled Kewal toiled behind her shoving a barrow piled high with vegetables.

# Chapter 5

# LOST BOY

The sheep meant more work—hurdles to be woven from thin-sliced strips of chestnut wood, posts to be rammed into the ground to hold the hurdles steady in sheep-proof fences around an area where the hay had been cut. Then the fences had to be moved every two days to allow the flock to get at fresh grass. And men had to sleep out at the sheepfold all night to scare away wild dogs and foxes. The flock grew to about thirty animals by the end of August, so steadily did the smithy work; in fact Nicky and Kewal decided that the giant must be extending his empire by trading in metalwork with villages on the far side of Felpham, so many broken tools did he seem to find, so many orders for scythes and plowshares and horse harness were left each week with the barrows.

Nicky asked the giant one day if he could pay for the next big load with a horse, but he stared at her angrily and shook his head.

"I hear as they're carrying swords now," he purred suspiciously; the huge hand crept to the pommel of his cutlass.

"Yes," said Nicky. "It's part of their religion. They were soldiers ages ago, and they've always carried swords. My friends used to wear a little toy sword before . . . before . . . you know; now they've made themselves proper ones again, in case they have to fight somebody."

"And now they're wanting horses too," said the giant. Suddenly Nicky saw what was worrying him.

"But they don't want horses for fighting on," she said. "They don't want to fight anybody. They'd like horses for plowing and pulling carts and so on."

"That's as may be," said the giant. "But I'm not sparing any horses. I've given you a fair price for the work so far, haven't I?"

"Oh yes," said Nicky, and looked at a crate of baffled hens which was balanced across one of the barrows. "The Sikhs are very pleased."

"And so they ought to be," said the giant. "Well, if they're making swords for themselves, they can make 'em for me too."

"I'll ask," said Nicky doubtfully.

"You do that," said the giant, and sauntered down the hill. He moved nowadays with a slow and lordly gait which seemed to imply that all the wide landscape belonged to him, and every creature in it.

But Uncle Jagindar refused to make weapons for anybody except his own people, and the Sikh council (though they argued the question around for twenty minutes) all agreed with him. When he heard the news the giant became surlier than ever with Nicky, and the villagers copied him. Partly, Nicky decided, this was because they just did whatever *he* did out of sheer awe for him; but it was also partly because of the way they had built up a whole network of myths and imaginings around the Sikhs. One or two things that Maxie said, or that Mr. Tom said when he was talking over smithwork to be done, showed that their heads were full of crazy notions. They stopped looking her in the face when they spoke to her, as though they were afraid of some power that might rest in her eye. Also, if there were children in the

Borough when she came past, mothers' voices would yell a warning and little legs would scuttle for doorways. Once Nicky even saw a soapy arm reach through a window and grab a baby by the leg from where it was sleeping in a sort of wooden pram.

The giant still looked her straight in the eye, and raged in his purring voice if he heard anyone suggest or hint that the Devil's Children were other than human flesh, but the scary whisperings went on behind his back. Nicky first realized how strong these dotty beliefs had become when she found the lost boy.

August had been a furiously busy month. The smithy furnace still roared all day, eating charcoal by the sackful. Ajeet and Nicky were officially in charge of the chickens, but that didn't excuse them from any other work that needed doing—looking after babies, or chasing escaped sheep, or dreary milling, or binding and stooking the untidy sheaves as the first wheat was reaped, and there were six scythes now to do the reaping. And then, a few days later, the dried sheaves were carried down to the lane and spread about for threshing; and that was woman's work, though after twenty minutes' drubbing at the gold mass with the clumsy threshing flail your neck and shoulders ached with sharp pain and your hands were all blisters.

But even threshing was better than plowing, which Mr. Surbans Singh insisted on making an experimental start on as soon as the sheaves were off the stubble.

"We're learning new sums," whispered Ajeet. "Four children equal one horse."

Nicky only grunted. She was trudging with six-inch steps through the shin-scratching stalks, leaning her weight right forward against the rope that led over the pad on her shoulder and back to the plow frame. Ajeet trudged beside her with another rope, and Gopal and his cousin Harpit just ahead; behind her Mr. Surbans Singh wrestled with the bucking plow handles as the blade surged in jolts and rushes through roots and flinty earth. It was very slow, very tiring, and turned only a wiggling, shallow furrow. When at last Mr. Surbans Singh called a halt, all four children sank groaning to the bristly stubble and watched while Mr.

Surbans Singh and Uncle Jagindar and Mr. Wazir Singh (who had once been a farmer) scuffed at the turned earth with their feet, bent to trickle it through their fingers, and discussed the tilt and angle of the blade.

"Not bad," said Mr. Surbans Singh at last. "We cannot plow all these acres. The next thing is to take sharp poles and search for the best patches of earth."

"You can run away and play now, children," said Mr. Wazir Singh, who was one of those people who always manage to talk to children as though they are small and stupid and anything they do, even when they've been helping for all they're worth, is of no interest or importance.

"Thank you, Nicky," said Mr. Surbans Singh with his brilliant smile. She could see where broad streams of sweat had runneled through the dust on his face, and realized that he must have been toiling twice as hard as any of them.

"Thank you, Ajeet and Gopal and Harpit," he went on. "Ask your Aunt Mohindar to give you each an apple."

The apples in the artist's cottage garden weren't ready for eating yet, but the village had paid for some of the last lot of work with a sack of James Grieves. The children sat on the wall around the well and bit into the white flesh, so juicy that there was no way of stopping the sweet liquid flowing down the outside of their chins in wasteful dribbles. Nicky looked over the wide gold landscape, where the swifts hurtled and wheeled above wheat that would never be harvested, and felt the wanderlust on her. Suddenly the close community, busy with its ceaseless effort for survival, seemed stifling.

Usually she would have gone for rest and calm to sit by the old lady's cart under the wych elm and watch the babies playing. Even when Ajeet came to translate, she and the old lady did not speak much, though sometimes the old lady would tell her of extraordinary things she had seen and done in that other life before she came to England—not really as though she was trying to entertain Nicky, more to teach her, to instruct, to pass on precious knowledge. And when they didn't speak, it still was soothing to be near her, in a way that Nicky couldn't explain; she guessed that the old lady felt the same, but there was no way of asking.

But today the old lady had one of her little illnesses and had stayed in bed, not wanting to see anybody except her daughters, and then only to complain to them about something. So now Nicky longed to be out of earshot of the clang of the forge and the thud of the flails, away from the pricking and clotting dust which all this hard work stirred into the air, somewhere else.

"I'm going for a walk," she said as she threw her core away.

Harpit groaned. Gopal sighed.

"So I shall have to come with you," he said, "to slaughter your enemies."

He patted the three-quarter-size sword that swung against his hip. He was very proud of it because Uncle Jagindar said it was the best blade he'd made. One corner of the forge held a pile of snapped blades which hadn't stood up to the cruel testing the smiths gave them. ("What use is a sword," Uncle Chacha had asked, "if you strike with it once and then there is nothing left in your hand but the hilt?") Gopal joined the adults for fencing practice these days.

Now he patted his sword like a warrior and stood up.

"I'm afraid I haven't got any enemies for you," said Nicky as she stood too.

"Not even the bad baron?" said Harpit. That was what the children called the giant down in the village. It was funny to think that Nicky was the only one who'd ever seen him.

"No, he's not my enemy," said Nicky. "He's all right—in fact he's a hero, sort of."

"I must tell my mother where we're going," whispered Ajeet.

"I'll tell her," said Harpit, "and that means I needn't come on this idiot expedition. Where are you going, Nicky?"

"Up to the common."

Despite Gopal's sword, Nicky was the one who led the way down the curving line of elms and oaks that had been allowed to stay on the boundary between one farm and the next; the ripe barley brushed against their left shoulders; they dipped into the place where the line of trees became a farm track, whose slope took them down to join a magical and haunted lane, untarred, running nearly fifteen feet below the level of the surrounding fields. The hedge trees at the top of the banks on either side met far above their heads, so that the children walked in a cool green silence and looked up into the caverns where the earth had been washed away from between blanched tree roots. In that convenient dark the animals of the night laired. It was a street of foxes.

Then, too soon, they were out into the broad evening sun and turning left up the grassy track to the common. Swayne's farm, deserted now, stood silent on the corner— mainly a long wall of windowless brick, with gates opening into yards where cattle had once mooched and scuffled. Gopal, driven by some impulse to assert himself against the brooding stillness, drew the gray curved blade from his belt and lunged at imaginary foes; with each lunge he gave a grunting cry. The echo bounced off the brick wall on the far side of the farmyard, and died into stillness.

"Please stop it," said Ajeet. Gopal sheathed his sword, grinning.

The echo continued. It said "Help!"

Nicky climbed the gate into the farmyard. The dry litter rustled under her feet.

"Where are you?" she called.

"Here," said the faint voice. "Help! I'm stuck!"

They found him in the loft over a hay barn. A ladder lay on the floor of the barn, and in the square black hole in the ceiling a wan face floated. Nicky and Gopal lifted the fallen ladder back into place.

"I can't climb down," said the face. "I've hurt my foot." It began to sob.

"I'll come up and help you," said Gopal. "Don't worry. It's all right."

"Not you!" wailed the face. "I've got a brick. I'll hit you!"

Gopal took his hand off the rung and shrugged.

Nicky climbed slowly up the ladder. The face shifted in the square, and in the dimness behind she saw an arm move upward. She stopped climbing.

"It's quite all right," she said. "I won't hurt you. My name's Nicky Gore. What's yours?"

"Shan't tell you."

The arm with the brick wavered uncertainly. Nicky flinched.

"Look," she said, "if I'd got magic, your brick wouldn't hurt me, but if I haven't got magic, then you'd be hurting somebody just like yourself, somebody who's trying to help you."

"What about him?" said the boy, still panting with sobs.

"He wants to help you too. His name's Gopal. He's my friend. And the other one's Ajeet—she tells wonderful stories."

"Tell 'em to go away."

Nicky looked over her shoulder. Ajeet was already floating out like a shadow. Gopal shrugged again, tested the bottom of the ladder, and went to the door.

"Be careful," he said. "I *think* it's steady, but not if you start fighting on it."

Nicky managed a sort of laugh as she climbed into the darkness.

"How long have you been here?" she said.

"I been here all day. I was looking for treasure. There's a heap of treasure buried up on the common, folk say, but when I come to the farm I thought the farm folk might have found some, so I started looking here, and then I knocked the ladder down, and then I trod on a bit o' glass and it come clean through my foot. . . ."

He was about eight, very dirty, the dirt on his face all streaked with blubbering.

"Wriggle it around over the hole," said Nicky, "and I'll have a look."

He did so, with slow care; his groans sounded like acting, but the foot really did look horrid; the worn sneaker was covered with dried blood and the foot seemed to bulge unnaturally inside the canvas. The laces were taut and too knotted to undo, so Nicky drew her hunting knife (which Uncle Chacha had honed for her to a desperate sharpness) and sliced them delicately through. The boy cried aloud as the pressure altered, then sat sobbing. Nicky realized that she'd probably done the wrong thing. They must get him to an adult as soon as possible.

"Look," she said, "if I go down the ladder the wrong way

around, then you can get yourself further over the hole, and I'll come back up until you're sitting on my shoulders. Then I can give you a piggyback down."

The boy nodded dully. Nicky stepped onto the ladder and went down until her head was below floor level. There she turned so that her heels were on the rungs.

"Now," she said, "see if you can wriggle your bottom along until your good leg is right over this side. A bit further. Now I'm coming up a rung. I'll hold your bad leg so that it doesn't bang anything."

"It hurts frightful when I drop it," groaned the boy.

"All right, I'll hold it up. Now you take hold of the ladder, lean forward against my head, and see if you can lift your bottom across so that you're sitting on the rung. Well done! Now let yourself slide down onto my shoulders; hold on to my forehead. Higher, you're covering my eyes. Hold tight. Down we go!"

The ladder creaked beneath the double weight. Nicky moved one heel carefully to the next rung, bending her knee out steadily so as to lower the two of them without a jolt. The wounded foot came through the opening with an inch to spare. Each rung seemed to take ages, as the thigh muscles above her bending knee were stretched to aching iron. She'd done five and was resting for the next when the grip on her forehead suddenly gave way.

"Hold tight!" she cried, and flung up her hand from the ladder to catch the slipping arm.

"Are you all right?" she said.

There was no answer. The boy's weight was now quite limp. Fresh blood was seeping, bright scarlet, through the crackled dark rind of the blood which had dried on his shoe before. Gopal, who must have been watching through the doorway, ran in and held the bottom of the ladder. She came down the last few rungs in one rush, trying to hold the boy from falling by forcing the back of her head into his stomach to slide him down the rungs. The top of the ladder bounced and rattled in the trapdoor, but stayed put.

"I've got his shoulders," said Gopal. "We've found something to carry him on outside. Can you manage?"

Nicky staggered out into the sunlight and saw Ajeet spreading hay onto a hurdle.

"This end," said Gopal. "Turn your back to it. Now get down as low as you can and I'll lift him off."

Nicky crouched, then sat; she twisted to ease the wounded leg onto the hay, and at last stood, shuddering with the long effort and feeling such sudden lightness that a breeze could have blown her away.

"Well done, Nicky," said Gopal. "Lift his leg, Ajeet, while I put more hay under it. If we get it higher than the body it might bleed a bit less. And then we'll need to lash it into place, so that it doesn't flop about while we are carrying him. A rope or a strap."

"No," said Ajeet, "something softer. What about your puggri?"

"It's such a bind to do up again," said Gopal, but he began to unwind the long folds of his turban. His black hair fell over his shoulders, like a girl's, but he twisted it up with a few practiced flicks and pinned it into place with the square wooden comb. The cloth was long enough to go three times around the hurdle, lashing the leg comfortably firm. The child muttered and stirred, but did not wake. His face looked a nasty yellowy gray beneath the tear-streaked dirt.

"Where shall we take him?" said Nicky.

"Up to the farm," said Gopal.

"He won't like that," said Nicky. "Nor will the villagers. They'll think we've stolen his soul away, or something."

"Never mind," said Gopal. "First, we don't know which house he belongs at, or even which village. Second, he must have proper medical attention, and he won't get *that* in the village."

"All right," said Nicky.

Gopal took the front of the hurdle, Nicky and Ajeet the two back corners. The first stretch along the deep lane was manageable, but after that it became harder even than plowing, and they had to rest every fifty yards. They were battling up through the barley field when a voice hissed at them from the trees. They all stopped and looked into the shadow, too tired to be frightened.

It was the risaldar, statuesque with his long bow, waiting

for a rabbit or a pheasant. Obviously he was cross that they had spoilt his hunting, but after a question or two in Punjabi, answered by Gopal, he stepped out from his cover, handed the bow to Nicky, and took the girls' end of the hurdle. For the rest of the journey the children worked shift and shift on the front corners.

The communal supper was being carried out of the artist's cottage when they at last settled the hurdle wearily across the wellhead. The usual cackle of argument rose as the women gathered around the wounded boy, while the steam from the big bowls of curry rose pungent through the evening air. But Cousin Punam shushed the cooks away and had the hurdle carried into one of the sheds beside the farmyard.

"We will take the sock and shoe off while he's still fainted," she said, snipping busily with a pair of nail scissors. "Then he will never know how much it hurts, eh? I did not think, when I was doing my training, that so soon I would have to be a qualified doctor. A little boiled water, a little disinfectant, cotton wool . . . Ai, but that's a nasty cut! Pull very gently at this bit of sock, Nicky, while I cut here. Ah, how dirty! That's it, good—throw it straight on the fire. And don't come back for five minutes, Nicky, because now I must do something you will not like."

It was still more than an hour till nightfall. The last gold of sunset lay slant across the fields and in it the swifts still wheeled, hundreds of feet up, too high for her to hear their bloodless screaming. It was going to be another blazing day tomorrow, just right for the dreary toil of reaping and threshing. She leaned against the cottage wall and looked down at the square brick tower of the church, warm in that warm light. What next? The boy would be in trouble in the village if they learned he had crossed the bad wires; if the Sikhs simply put him on the hurdle and carried him down to the Borough, they could expect more suspicion than gratitude—and Cousin Punam *had* been going to do something "wrong" to him. . . . Nicky would have to remind her to tie the wound up with a clean rag, and not anything out of her bag. . . .

Cousin Punam had finished, but was talking to someone.

Nicky heard the words ". . . tetanus injection . . ." before
she called out to ask whether she could come in. Neena was
sponging the grime off the sleeping face.

"When will he wake up?" said Nicky.

"Quite soon, perhaps," said Cousin Punam.

"It sounds awful," said Nicky, "but he'll be terrified if he
sees you. Let me wait, and I'll find out where he lives. Then
we can take him back."

Cousin Punam sighed and shrugged, just as Gopal had
done down at Swayne's.

"Have you had your supper, Nicky?" said Neena.

"Not yet."

"I'll send you some."

"Thank you," said Nicky. "And thank you, Punam, for
. . . for everything."

She stumbled over the words, half conscious that she was
speaking for the boy and his mother and the whole village
words that they would never learn to say. The women left.
Ajeet came back with a chapati—the heavy, sconelike bread
which the Sikhs made—and mutton curry. Nicky was just
learning to like the taste now that the Sikhs were beginning
to run out of curry powder.

Perhaps it was the smell of food which woke the boy,
because he tried to sit up when Ajeet was hardly out of the
stall. Nicky rose from the floor, her mouth crammed with
bread and curry.

"Don't try to move," she mumbled. "How does your leg
feel?"

He looked at it as though he'd forgotten how it hurt, then
at her, then, wide-eyed, around the dim unfamiliar stall.

"Where's the rest of them?" he whispered.

"Having their supper. You're all right. We'll look after
you."

"I'm not telling you my name," he whispered fiercely. "My
mum says don't you tell 'em your name if they catch you,
and they've got no power on you, 'cause they don't know
what to call you in their spells."

"If you'll tell me where you live, we'll carry you home as
soon as it's dark."

"Oh," he said with a note of surprise.

"I thought we could say you'd been looking for birds' nests in that hedge below the bad wires, and one of us heard you calling and found you'd hurt your foot and brought you up here. Then nobody'd know you'd crossed the wires."

"Much too late for birds' nests," he said. "Where you come from, if you don't know that?"

"London," said Nicky. "Well, you think of something you might have been looking for at this time of year."

"Too early for crab apples or nuts," said the boy. "Tell you what: I could have been looking for a rabbit run to put a snare in."

"That'll do," said Nicky, thinking that she ought to tell the risaldar about rabbit snares. "Do you live in the village, or outside it?"

"Right agin the edge," he said. "You can cut across to our back garden through Mr. Banstead's paddock."

"Good," said Nicky. "We won't go till it's nearly dark. I'm afraid your mother will be worrying for you."

"That she will," said the boy.

"Are you hungry?"

Suspicion tightened the lines of his face again.

"I'm not eating the Queer Folk's food," he muttered.

"I could bring you water from the well," Nicky suggested. "That was here before us. And there's a bag of apples which came up from the village only yesterday morning."

He thought for a few seconds, hunger and terror fighting.

"All right," he said at last.

After supper they lifted him gently back onto his hurdle and four of the uncles carried him down the lane. He stared at his bearers in mute fear until, between step and step, he fell deep asleep. Nicky had to shake him awake at the edge of the village so that he could tell them their way through the dusk.

It was the last cottage in the lane to Halling Down. The uncles lowered the hurdle onto the dewy grass and stole off into the darkness by the paddock hedge. A dog yelped in the cottage next door as Nicky pushed the sagging gate open. A man's voice shouted at the dog. The door at the end of the path opened, sending faint gold across a cabbage patch. A woman stood in the rectangle of light. Nicky walked up the path.

"That you, Mike?" called the woman.

The boy cried faintly to her from his hurdle.

"I found him hurt," said Nicky, "so we bandaged him up and brought him home."

The woman picked up her long skirt and rushed down the path. It was the same Mrs. Sallow who'd been complaining in court about her neighbor's dog. When Nicky got back to the paddock she was kneeling by the stretcher with her arm under the boy's shoulders.

"His foot's very bad," said Nicky. "I think I could manage one end if you do the other."

Mrs. Sallow stood up and looked despairingly around. Obviously her feud with the dog owner meant she could expect no help from there, and she had no neighbor on the other side.

"All right," she said. "But mind you, I owe you nothing."

"Of course not," said Nicky.

The boy and the hurdle weighed like death. The boy groaned as they tilted through the gateway. The woman said nothing. Nicky lowered her end on the path outside the door.

"I'll cope from here," said the woman. She knelt by the hurdle and pulled the boy to her. Then with a painful effort she staggered to her feet. Nicky held the door open for her.

"You keep out," said the woman.

"I never told 'em my name, Mum," said the boy.

"Good lad," said the woman.

"But, Mum . . ." said the boy.

"Tell me later," she said, and kicked the door shut with her heel.

Nicky had dragged the hurdle down the path and joined the uncles by the hedge when the cottage door opened again. Mrs. Sallow stood in the doorway, hands on her hips, head thrown back.

"You people," she called. "I give you my thanks for what you have done for my boy."

The door shut as the neighbor's dog exploded into an ecstasy of yelping.

"What was the significance of that?" said Mr. Surbans Singh.

"It's unlucky to take help from fairies," explained Nicky, "if you don't thank them. All the stories say so. Goodness I'm tired."

"In that case," said Mr. Surbans Singh, "it is most fortunate that we happen to have a magic hurdle here, with four demons to carry it."

So Nicky rode home through the dark while the uncles made low-voiced jokes about their supernatural powers. It was almost a month before she saw Mike Sallow again.

# Chapter 6

# THIEVES' HARVEST

They had been plowing all day, with four plows going and every man and woman, as well as all the older children, taking turns at the heavy chore. Between turns they worked at the two strips which were wanted for autumn sowing, breaking down the clods with hoes and dragging the harrow to and fro to produce a fine tilth. The thin strips of turned earth looked pitiful amid the rolling steppes of stubble and unmown wheat. The strips were scattered apparently at random over the farm, wherever prodding with sticks had shown the soil to be deepest or least flinty, or where there seemed some promise of shelter from the winds. There'd been no rain for a week, so the soil was light and workable, which was why the whole community was slaving at it today. On other days logging parties had been up in the woods, getting in fuel for the winter. And twice a raiding party had set off at dusk, trekked the twenty miles to Reading through the safe night, stayed in the empty city all day, and trekked back laden with stores and blocks of the most precious stuff in all England, salt.

But today had been stolid plowing. Resting between her turns, Nicky had been vaguely conscious that something was happening down in the village. The bells rang for a minute, not their proper changes, and then stopped. Shouts drifted up against the breeze, but so faint and far that she didn't piece them together into a coherent sequence, or even realize that they were more and louder than they might have been.

About six it was time to go and get the hens in by scattering corn in their coops. If you left it later than that they tried to roost out in the shrubs of the farmhouse garden. She was helping Ajeet search the tattered lavender bushes for hidden nests when she saw, down the lane and out of the corner of her eye, a furtive movement—somebody ducking into the crook of the bank to avoid being seen. Kewal, she thought, out checking the rabbit snares to escape his share of plowing. But Kewal had been up in the field, lugging at the ropes as steadily as anyone (it was really only that he didn't like *starting* jobs) and besides, hadn't the shape in the lane had fair hair? And wasn't there something awkward about the way it had moved?

Inquisitive, she slid down the bank and stole along the lane. They all went barefooted as often as possible now, because shoes were wearing out and making new ones was a job for winter evenings. No council workmen had been along the lanes of England that summer, keeping the verges trim, so you could bury yourself deep in the rank grasses. Mike, peering between the stems, must have seen her coming; but he stayed where he was. He had been crying, but now his mouth was working down and sideways as though something sticky had lodged in the corner of his jaw; his lungs pumped in dry, jerking spasms.

"What's the matter, Mike?" said Nicky, forgetting that she wasn't supposed to know his name. But he'd forgotten too.

"The robbers have come!" he gasped. "The robbers have come!"

Nicky stared at him, not taking it in.

"They was herding all the children together," said Mike,

"and taking 'em off somewheres. I was abed still, with my foot, but my mum shoved me out of the back gate and says to come to you. I been crawling across the fields, but I dursn't come no further, though you done me good once. My mum says you done my foot good."

"But what about Mr. Barnard—the Master? Didn't he stop them?"

"They killed him! They killed him!"

Mike began to wail, and Nicky's whole being was flooded by a chill of shock at the thought of that huge life murdered. She put her arm around Mike's shoulders and waited for the sobbing to stop.

"Come with me," she said. "My friends will know what to do. Shall I give you a piggyback again?"

"I'll do," sniffled the boy. "There's not nowhere else to go, is there?"

"That's right," said Nicky, and helped him, half hobbling and half hopping, up the lane. His foot was still clearly very sore, and she could see from his scrattled knees that he really must have crawled most of the way.

Ajeet was standing in the lane with the basket of eggs. The boy flinched when he saw her, but came on.

"Come and help me talk to your grandmother," said Nicky. "Robbers have come to the village and killed the big man. They're taking all the children somewhere, Mike says —as hostages, I suppose. That means they're going to stay."

Ajeet never looked as though anything had surprised her. Now she just nodded her small head and walked up to the wych elm where the old lady held court on fine days. The big tree stood right against the lane above the farmyard and here in a flattened and dusty area of what had been barley field the small children scuffled and dug, while the old lady lay on her cushions in the shade and gave orders to everything that came in sight, or gathered her grandchildren and great-grandchildren into a ring and told them long, marvelous fairy tales. One of the mothers was always there to do the donkey work of the nursery, but the old lady was its genius.

By the time Nicky had brought Mike hobbling up and settled him in comfort in the dust, Ajeet had told the news.

Nicky turned toward the tree, put her palms together under her chin and bowed. The old lady did the same on her cushions, just as if Nicky were an important person come from many miles away to visit her. The old lady rattled a sharp sentence at the children who'd gathered to listen, and they scattered.

Ajeet said, "My grandmother wants the boy to tell his story again."

Mike was staring at the old lady with quivering lips. Nicky remembered how terrified *she'd* been when she first faced those brilliant eyes.

"He told me that robbers had come to the village," she said. "They'd started herding the children together and taking them somewhere. He was in bed with his bad foot, and his mother smuggled him out of the back door and told him to come to us. He said the robbers had killed the big man. Do you know any more, Mike?"

"My mum said they was on horses, in armor," he whispered.

Ajeet translated. Mike couldn't remember any more. He'd seen nothing himself, though he'd heard the cries from his bed, and the church bell ringing its alarm and then stopping.

The old lady spoke to Tara Deep, the mother who'd been looking after the nursery. She nodded and began to walk up to the plowmen, quick and graceful in her blue sari. The old lady spoke directly to Nicky.

"My grandmother wants to know what *you* think we should do," said Ajeet.

"First we've got to make ourselves as safe as we can," said Nicky, "and then we've got to find out more, how many of them there are, and what they're going to do next. We can't decide anything until we get more news. The only thing is, the robbers won't mind crossing the bad wires—they must have passed things just as bad to get to the village at all."

"I just shuts my eyes and ducks under," said Mike.

"The farmyard's almost a fort already," said Nicky. "We could get food and water in, and the sheep, and strengthen it. And as soon as it's dark I'll go down across the fields and try and find somebody I know. Mr. Tom's house has its back to the school playground, and then there's a path and then fields, so I might be able to get to him without going through the village at all. After all, we aren't really sure that Mike's got his story right—his mother must have been very hurried and worried."

Ajeet had been translating as Nicky went along. The old lady raised a ringed hand, palm toward Nicky in a sort of salute, and answered. Ajeet laughed.

"My grandmother says you'll make a very good wife for a soldier someday," she said.

Nicky nodded, unsmiling. She was frightened, of course, by what she had suggested, but another part of her felt a strange, grim satisfaction in the risks and dangers. They would force her to rebuild the armor around her heart, which during the last few weeks she had allowed to become so full of chinks and weaknesses. She bowed her head and stared at the scuffled dust; at the thought of the coming action her heart began to hammer—as though there were a small smithy in there, retempering the rusted steel.

By now the men were trooping down from the field, talking excitedly and looking northeast across the swooping acres to where the church tower stood peaceful among its lindens. The women called their own children to them as they came, and cajoled them into stillness and silence. A big orderly circle gathered under the wych elm, the men stopped chattering and the old woman spoke. Nicky heard her own name jut out from the fuzz of Punjabi; heads turned toward her. Then, as usual, twenty voices broke into argument together; the old lady screeched, and Uncle Jagindar was talking alone. Voices grunted agreement. He turned to Nicky.

"This sounds dangerous," he said, "but we can send a guard with you."

"I don't think it's *very* dangerous," said Nicky. "If they catch me, they'll think I'm one of the village children and put me with the others as a hostage. But I don't see why they should—they can't watch the whole village, all the way around. If you do send a guard, you won't have so many men for the defense up here, supposing they decided to attack tonight, which would be the sensible thing for them.

It'd be a waste of our men. You'll need sentries all night, too."

She could see heads nodding.

"Perhaps Gopal could come with me," she said. "Not to fight or anything, but to bring back news if I do get caught. The thing is, I'm sure I'm the only person Mr. Tom or any of them would talk to, so it's no use any of you going. They're a bit scared of me, but not half so much as they are of you. That's right, isn't it, Mike?"

"Yes, that's right," he whispered, staring around at the dark and bearded faces.

"And we've got to *know*, haven't we?" she said. "We can't decide anything till then."

Uncle Jagindar wheeled to the ring of Sikhs.

"That is agreed, my friends?" he asked.

"Agreed," boomed the council.

He started to allot tasks in Punjabi. Gopal came, serious-faced, to Nicky.

"Our job is to eat and rest," he said. "Mike looks as if he needs a rest too."

The boy nodded, but they had to help him to his feet and support him, swaying, down to the farmyard. Already the water carriers were bringing bucket after bucket clanking from the well, while the carts creaked up from the farmhouse with larderfuls of dry stores and cans. Sacks of charcoal were carried in from the smithy, for cooking, and mounds of hay down from the big barn for the sheep. Soon the sheep themselves flooded, baaing with amazement, into the bustling square. The cooped hens were trundled up the lane; barrows of blankets and bedding came from the houses, sacks of new corn from the storage towers. The old lady was ensconced in an open stall, and the holy book carried reverently in from the bungalow.

As dusk fell the courtyard was still a shouting and baaing and cackling confusion. The communal supper was going to be very late, cooked on the faint-flamed and smokeless charcoal instead of the roaring logs they'd used when they first spent a night there. But Nicky had already eaten; her fair hair was covered with a dark scarf; she wore a navy blue jersey and a pair of dark gray trousers belonging to Gopal;

she would have liked to blacken her face, but could imagine the effect on an already terrified Mr. Tom if a dark face hissed at him out of the night. His was obviously the first house to try.

After the clamor and reek and dust of the courtyard, the dewy air of nightfall would have seemed bliss to breathe if her heart hadn't been beating so fiercely. Gopal eased his sword in its scabbard, then frowned at the slight click. They stole down the familiar lane side by side. Mr. Kirpal Singh, crouched by a lone bush on the bank, whispered them good luck. (Five sentries watching for two hours each: everyone was going to be very tired tomorrow.)

There was a copse on the right of the lane below the bad wires. They headed south beside it, and on up the slope under the cover of a hedge which had not been hauled out because it marked the boundary between two farms. After two hundred yards they turned east again, leaving the hedge to slip like hunting stoats along the edge of a stand of barley. There was no hurry. The night was still dark gray, and Nicky didn't want to reach the playing field until it was fully black. So where the barley stopped, because that was as far as the reapers had mown, they lay on their stomachs, trying to suck the last inch of seeing out of the shortening distances, peering and listening for dangers. A lone pheasant clacked in a copse to their right.

"They can't post sentries all around a village as big as this," whispered Gopal. "Not unless there are hundreds of men. In any case they don't need to defend the whole village now they have hostages. They'll guard the place where they've set up camp, and then perhaps they'll send out patrols. That's what we must watch out for."

Beyond the reaped stubble was a pasture field where cows stumbled and snorted, invisible from twenty yards. Knowing what inquisitive brutes cows can be the children steered to the right, where an extra loom in the dark promised the shelter of another hedge. But when it came it was double, and a lane ran down the middle. Nicky shook her head—such a path was a likely route for a patrol. They scouted left, and the lane bent at right angles; flitting through a gap in the hedges, they found themselves once more at a place

where unreaped wheat ran beside stubble, and ran in what
Nicky, even after that bout of dodging, still thought was the
right direction. Then another lane to cross, and empty pasture beyond. It was too dark to see more than ten yards
now.

After a whispered talk, Gopal dropped behind and Nicky
tucked a white rag into her belt for him to follow her by,
like the scut of a rabbit. (If they were chased, she'd have to
remember to snatch it out.) Darkness made the middle of
fields seem safer than hedges; but coming in darkness to the
village, by this unfamiliar way, she might easily have
missed her direction. The wind had been steady from the
southwest all day, surely. Just as she decided to stop and
reconsider, the church clock began to clang sweetly to her
left. Eight. More to her front, but further away, urgent
voices yelled. In the fresh silence the tussocky grass of the
pasture seemed to swish horribly loudly, however carefully
she moved her feet; anyone waiting in the coming hedge
would be bound to hear her—though she couldn't hear
Gopal ten paces behind her. Encouraged, she stole forward.

This hedge was double too, but the path down the middle
was only a yard across. So she knew where she was, at least;
this was the footpath that ran south between the church and
the school. The nearer hedge was strengthened with the
thorny wire she hated so much. As she squatted and wondered whether there'd be a gap further along, Gopal edged
quietly up beside her.

"Barbed wire?" he whispered. "Wait a moment."

He crouched by the fence, holding some sort of tool in his
hand. Two clicks, and he dragged a strand of wire away.

"My own idea," he whispered. "Wire cutters. You can
crawl through now. Is it far from here?"

"Only across the playing field."

"Then tie your rag to the other hedge so that we can find
the place coming back."

Most of the householders in the council estate kept a dog,
but Mr. Tom preferred his scarred old tabby; so if they came
up straight behind the right house there oughtn't to be any
barking. Nicky lay in the dewy grass and tried to make out

the roof lines; Mrs. Bower's chimney, next door, had a big hunched cowl. So . . .

Only firelight showed through Mr. Tom's parlor window. Nicky edged an eye above the sill, hoping that he hadn't gone to bed yet. No. He was curled in a chair by the dying fire, his head in his hands but held so low that it was almost on his knees; he looked very old and beaten. Nicky tapped cautiously on the pane. At the third tap he looked over his shoulder like a haunted man, and then put his head back between his hands. She kept on tapping, in a steady double rhythm which couldn't have been caused by anything accidental, such as a flying beetle. At last he staggered from the chair, crossed the room and opened the window half an inch.

"Who's there?" he whispered.

"Me. The girl from Booker's Farm. I want to talk to you."

"I'll have nothing to do with you," he hissed, and tried to shut the window. But Nicky was ready for him and jammed the hilt of her knife into the crack.

"We want to help you," she whispered. "But we can't until we know what's happening."

"How many o' you's out there, then?"

"Only me and a boy. He'll rap on the window if he hears anyone coming."

"Okay," said Mr. Tom after a pause. "I'll let you in."

"I'll climb through the window," said Nicky. He opened it wide and she flicked herself through. The moment she was in he fastened it tight, while Nicky tucked herself into a corner where she couldn't be seen from outside.

"Sit like you were sitting before," she suggested. "Talk as though you were talking to yourself. Mike Sallow came up to the farm and told us that robbers had come to the village and killed Mr. Barnard and taken all the children somewhere."

"True enough," groaned Mr. Tom. "They killed the Master. I was there, waiting for the fun of seeing him drive 'em off, but there was three of them on horses, wearing armor. They charged him down and skewered him through and through, so's he never got not one blow in with that sword of his. And then they cut his head off and stuck it on the pole of the Five

Bells, for the wide world to see what manner of men they
are. And herded all the children together, all as they could
find, and took 'em down to a barn behind White House; and
they put 'em in a loft with a pile of hay and timber down
below, and they made old Maxie cry through the streets that
they'll set fire to the whole shoot if they have a mite more
trouble out of us during their stay."

"How long will that be?" said Nicky.

"As long as there's a morsel left to eat, that's my guess.
And the Master was that set on us coming through the win-
ter short of starving that we've barnfuls of stores waiting.
You mark my words, we'll have 'em for months yet."

"How many of them are there?"

"Thirty. Maybe thirty-five."

"But there must be more than a hundred men in the village!"

"I know what you're thinking, girl, but they fell on us that
sudden, and we had't nothing to fight 'em with, save a few
cudgels. The Master, he'd been set on getting us swords, so
he could have his own little army, but your folk wouldn't
make 'em for us, remember? And these robbers come with
spears, and horsemen in armor, and now they've got the
children—though I've none of my own, thank God—and
we're bound hand and foot, hand and foot."

"Do you think they'd actually burn the children if there
was trouble?"

"I don't know, a course; but I do know they'd do *something*, and something pretty cruel, too. There was one of
'em, one of the ones on horseback, and while the footmen
were hacking off the Master's head I saw him throw back
his helmet to wipe his face. Curly hair, he had, and a broken
nose, though he was scarce more than a boy. And when he
saw Arthur's head dripping up there on the pole, he laughed
like a lover. Like a lover in spring. I slunk away and come
back here, and the rest I know from Maxie's crying."

He had been half out of his chair, glaring around the
room as he tried to tell her the horror of his story, but a
faint rap on the window made him shrink and curl like a
snail. Nicky made a dart for the window, heard the footsteps, knew it was too late and slid herself under an old Put-

U-Up bed where she lay, barely breathing, against the wall.
A hard fist thundered at the front door. She could see Mr.
Tom's feet rise from the floor, as though he were trying to
curl himself even further into his chair.

"Go and answer him," whispered Nicky. "It'll be worse if
you don't."

The feet doddered back to the floor. The legs stumbled
past the dying fire. Then a bolt was drawn, slap. Then
voices.

"What's your name, gaffer?"

"T-t-tom Pritchard."

"Tom Pritchard, eh? Fetch us each a mug of ale, Tom
Pritchard."

More than one of them, then.

Shufflings, another door moving, palsied clinking of glass,
more shufflings. Silence. Then the smash and tinkle of deliberately dropped tumblers.

"We hear you were a crony of the big man's, Tom Pritchard."

"N-n-no, not me. He broke my fork a-purpose."

"What d'you know about the lot they call the Devil's Children, Tom Pritchard? We hear as you had dealings with
'em."

"N-n-not much. They live up at Booker's, 'tother side of
the bad wires. Three months back they came there. I had a
bit of dealings with the girl as lives with them. She's an
ordinary girl, to look at. The Master wouldn't have none of
'em but her in the village, and then only to do dealings in
smithwork. They make and mend iron for us, they do, and
sometimes I helped with the dealings. I never seen none of
the others, saving the girl."

"Ah."

A low discussion.

"What are you doing still dressed this time o' night, Tom
Pritchard? Thinking of going out, eh?"

"I . . . I couldn't sleep. I was sitting by the fire. I hadn't a
light showing. I heard the orders."

"At least you ain't deaf, then, Tom Pritchard. Well, it's
time good little gaffers were in bed, even them that can't
sleep. I want to see you going up them stairs, Tom Pritch-

ard. You can sleep now, gaffer. The Devil's Children needn't fright your dreams no more, not now we're here to look after you. We'll nip up there and sort 'em out for you, soon as we're settled. Up you go now, like a good gaffer."

A grunt, and the stumble and thud of Mr. Tom being shoved so hard along the hallway that he fell. Slow steps on the stairs. More talk at the porch, then footsteps coming, but turning off through the other door. A curse as something fell from a larder shelf. Voices in the hallway.

"Nice drop of ale they brew, leastways."

"Yeah. Cozy old spot to winter out. Scour around for more hosses, get them Devil's Children to run us up armor for the lot of us . . ."

"How'll you manage that, then?"

"Same as here. Devil's Children got children of their own, ain't they?"

Laughter.

"Be getting along then. Hey, Maxie, who's next?"

The crow of the clerk's voice from the street, shrill with terror.

"Sim Jenkins, sir."

Heels crunching through the broken tumblers on the doorstep. Going.

Nicky lay in the stillness and counted two thousand. She had an instinct that the robbers were the sort of people who would do the thing properly, when they wanted to scare a village into obedient terror. They wouldn't leave Mr. Tom quivering in the shameful dark without letting him know that they were still keeping an eye on him. And sure enough, when she was in the sixteen hundreds, another light tap came from the window. Thirty seconds later the front door slammed open, feet drummed on the stairs, more doors crashed and banged upstairs, and the hard voice shouted "Just come to tuck you up, gaffer. See that you *are* in bed, eh? Sweet dreams."

Feet on the stairs again, and the door walloping shut, and the crunched glass. Then the dreary business of starting once more at one, two, three . . .

She was so stiff when she edged the window open that she had to clamber through like an old woman. Halfway up the garden Gopal floated beside her from behind the runner beans; he touched her cheek with his hand in gentle welcome, then led the way back across the school playground to where the faint whiteness of their rag in the hedge marked the cut wires.

They took the journey home as carefully as they'd come, but nothing stopped or even scared them until their own sentry hissed at them out of his hiding and made their tired hearts bounce. Though it was well past midnight, every adult Sikh was awake and waiting in the dark farmyard. Nicky told her story in English, breaking it into short lengths so that Uncle Jagindar could turn it into Punjabi for the old lady. The pauses while he spoke enabled her to think, so that she left nothing out. When she had finished, five of the men crept out to relieve the sentries; for them she told the whole story all over again. Now every Sikh knew, and Nicky could sleep.

They held a council as soon as breakfast and the morning prayers were over. Daylight meant that Gopal and Harpit and the other children could stand sentry; from the upstairs windows of the farmhouse, from the hayrick in the big barn, from the upper branches of the wych elm, every scrap of country could be seen. The sheep were driven out to a new pen, close to the farmyard, but the hens were left to cluck and scrattle while the council talked. Nicky was there, with Ajeet to tell her what was said. Otherwise there was nobody younger than Kewal.

"Uncle Jagindar is asking if there is anyone who thinks we must move from here . . . they all say no . . . Mr. Kirpal Singh says we can either wait and defend ourselves if they attack us, or attack them before they are ready . . . Aunt Neena says they may not attack us . . . several people say they will . . . my grandmother is calling for quiet. . . ."

"Nicky," said Uncle Jagindar, "you heard the men say they would not leave us alone, I think."

"Yes," said Nicky. "They told Mr. Tom that they were going to come and, er, 'sort you out' as soon as they were settled in the village. And they want you to make more armor for them. They were going to take the children as hostages."

The murmur of voices broke into fresh clamor. Ajeet sorted out what mattered.

"Mr. Wazir Singh says we could defend ourselves here forever. My father says no, not against thirty-five men with the only water on the other side of the road. My grandmother says the place would be a trap—a week, safe; a month, death. Mr. Wazir Singh says how can fifteen men attack thirty-five. And they have hostages, my mother says. Take them at dawn before they are ready, says Uncle Jagindar. Take the barn where the children are first, says the risaldar. Kill as many as we can in their beds, says my grandmother. My father says first we must watch them, to find out where the sentries are and what they do, especially at night. Scouts must go and watch, says Uncle Jagindar, but they must be careful not to be seen lest they put the robbers on their guard. Watch for two nights, strike on the third, says my grandmother. Mr. Surbans Singh says that meanwhile we must seem to be farming exactly as usual, but keep a secret watch out everywhere around the farm. They will send scouts up soon. Aunt Neena says that the children must stay near the farmyard. My grandmother tells me to tell you that the order includes you, Nicky. . . ."

Nicky nodded, to show she had understood.

". . . now the risaldar says we must pretend to be felling wood for the winter, and cut the nearest trees in the row beyond the cottage so that they cannot creep up on us that way. And set fire to the barley, says my grandmother. . . ."

"Nicky," said Uncle Jagindar, "is there anything more? You know the village and we do not."

"I think White House must be that very big one out on the far side, but I haven't seen it since we first came through. The other thing is the hostages. We've got to think of a plan to keep them safe. It's not just because they're children. If we attack the robbers and the robbers kill the children in revenge, then the village will come and massacre all of us. There's over a hundred men in Felpham, and once they really get angry . . ."

"You are right," said Uncle Chacha. "We must be quick

and careful when the time comes. And we must be ready to run away if we fail."

The council shambled on, going over the same points several times, but slowly reaching the practical business of sentry duty and scout duty. At last they all dispersed to the tense charade of pretending to be innocent farmers while watching every hedge and hollow in case it should hide an ambush, and at the same time planning a murderous onslaught on an army more than twice their size. There was one false alarm that day: the enemy spy, sneaking up the line of trees in the dusk, turned out to be Mrs. Sallow, bedraggled and terrified but determined to know whether her son was safe. She sat in silence by Mike's straw, but after supper Nicky wheedled out of her some useful news of the robbers' arrangements.

Next day tempers were short with lack of sleep. The men took turns to rest, but some had to be on show for the benefit of the robber spies who lurked along the hillside; they thought they spotted three of these, but had to act as if they hadn't.

In the dark hour after the third midnight a whisper went around the farmyard. The women turned out with swords and spears to stand sentry, while the raiding party stole up the hill; fifteen grown men, and four lads. And Nicky. If the first phase of the attack succeeded, somebody would have to keep the rescued children from squealing panic, or the sleeping robbers would be woken and the second phase ruined. And that would have to be Nicky.

She thought she was the youngest of the long line creeping through the dark, until a hand took hers. It was Ajeet. None of the men noticed the extra child.

The wide loop around the village, taken at a stalker's pace, with many pauses, lasted hours, but they were still too early.

In that first faint grayness when the birds begin to whistle in the copses, they struck.

# Chapter 7

# BLOOD ON THE SWORDS

Nicky lay on her stomach on the chill bank of a ditch; or perhaps it was the beginnings of a stream, for her legs were wet to the knee, despite the dry spell they'd been having. To left and right of her, like troops waiting to attack from a trench, was the tiny Sikh army. The blackness of night seemed no less than it had been, but now she could be sure of the hulk of the barn; the big house, over to her right, was still an undistinguishable mass of roof and treetops and out-buildings. She was rubbery cold, and thankful that the Sikhs (full of the sensible instincts of campaigning) had made her wear twice the clothes she'd thought she'd need.

In the dark ahead of her Uncle Chacha was stalking the sentry. Two of the robbers slept in the barn, taking turn and turn to watch outside while the other slept by a brazier. An oil-soaked torch was ready there, which the inside man could thrust into the brazier and bring to crackling life. Dry straw, dry hay, dry brushwood were heaped along the tarred timber of the walls; and there were two wicked cars there, whose tanks would explode if the fire blazed hot enough. The whole room was a bomb, and above it slept the children. (Mrs. Sallow had told them these details, because the robbers had shown the mothers of Felpham their precautions on the very first morning.) The Sikh scouts had studied the movements of the sentries; and the first thing was to catch the outside one just before the time for the last changeover. About now, in this dimness . . .

Only the nervy ears of the watchers in the ditch could have caught that faint thud. There was no cry. Shadows shifted to her left—Uncle Jagindar and the risaldar stealing forward. Three short raps and a long pause and two more short raps was the signal the sentries used. It had to be given two or three times, so that the man inside had time to know where he was—sleeping in a straw-filled barn by a brazier, with forty terrified children in the loft above.

The raps came loud as doom through the still, chill air. The watchers waited. Then the signal again. And . . . but it was interrupted the third time by creaking hinges.

Now there was a cry, but faint—more of a gargling snort than any noise a man makes when he means something. But a meaning was there and Nicky shuddered in the ditch: there is only one sure way of keeping an enemy silent, the Sikhs had insisted, and that is to kill him. The hulk of the barn altered its shape: a big door swinging open, but no orange glow from fire beginning to gnaw into hay and timber. The army rose from its trench and crept toward the barn, Kewal and Gopal carrying plastic buckets filled from the ditch. In the doorway they met Uncle Jagindar and the risaldar carrying the brazier out on poles, while Uncle Chacha walked beside them holding a piece of tarpaulin to screen the light of it from any possible watcher in the house. Kewal and Gopal threw the water in their buckets across the piled hay and went back for more. The robbers had also kept buckets of water ready by the brazier (though they hadn't shown the Felpham women this precaution) and one of the uncles scattered their contents about.

Nicky felt her way up the steep stair and slid back the bolt of the door. The door rasped horribly as she edged it inward, and she looked down to see whether the noise had worried the Sikhs; but only Gopal and Ajeet stood in the grayness that came through the barn door. The others must already be stealing off across the unmown lawn toward the big house.

Inside the loft a child, children, began to wail. Nicky stood on the top step, gulping with rage at her own stupidity —she should never have climbed to the loft until a child stirred. But it was too late now. She pushed the door wide and stepped in.

The loft stank. Five windows gave real light. Dawn was coming fast. Sleeping children littered the moldy hay, in attitudes horribly like those of the two dead robbers on the grass outside the barn. But three were already woken to the nightmare day, and wailing. Nicky put her finger to her lips. The wailing stopped, but the wailers shrank from her as though she'd been a poisonous spider. More of them were stirring now—older ones.

"It's quite all right," said Nicky. "We've come to help you."

The words came out all strange and awkward. Nicky wasn't used to being hated and feared.

"Go away!" said a redheaded girl, about her own age.

More children were moving. A six-year-old boy sat suddenly bolt up, as though someone had pinched him; he stared at Nicky for five full seconds and began to screech. Some of them were standing now, but still cowering away from her. A babble like a playground rose—this was wrong, awful, dangerous. Everything depended on keeping the children quiet until the attack on the house had started.

"Shut up!" shouted Nicky, and stamped her foot. There was a moment's silence, then the noise began to bubble up again, then it hushed. Ajeet walked past Nicky as though she wasn't there, right to the end of the stinking loft, turned, settled cross-legged onto a bale and held the whole room still with her dark, beautiful eyes. Just as the silence was beginning to crumble, she spoke.

"Be quiet, please," she said in a clear voice. "I am going to tell you a story. Will you all sit down please?"

Every child settled.

"There was a tiger once which had no soul," said Ajeet. "All day and all night it raged through the forest, seeking a soul which it could make its own. Now, in those forests there lived a woodman, and he had two sons . . ."

Her hands were moving already. The jungle grew at her fingertips, and through it the tiger stalked and roared, and the woodman's sons adventured. Nicky saw a child which had slept through the din wake slowly, sit up and start listening, as though this were how every morning of its life began. Terrified of breaking the spell, Nicky tiptoed to a window.

She could see the house clearly now; white and square, very big, with a low slate roof ending in a brim like a Chinese peasant's hat. Here a cheerful stockbroker had lived six months before; along these paths his children had larked or mooned as the mood took them; an old gardener had mown the big lawns smooth enough for croquet. And now they were all gone, and the lawns were lank, and murder crept across them. Any minute now . . .

A crash of glass, and a cry, and then a wild yelling. A naked white man was running across the lawn with a Sikh after him. The naked man ran faster and disappeared among trees, and the Sikh stopped and trotted back to the house. A cracked bell began a raucous clank—the alarm signal—but stopped before it had rung a dozen times. One, two, three, four men jumped from an upstairs window and ran to the largest of the outbuildings. From another window a figure flew, tumbling as he fell; when he hit the grass he lay still, and a second later Nicky heard the crash of the big pane through which he had been thrown. In the twanging silence that followed, Nicky studied the geography of the buildings and tried to plan for disaster. Suppose a sortie of robbers rushed from the house, would there be time to get the children down the stairs? The robbers had chosen the barn for their hostages because it was set nearly a hundred yards from the other buildings, and they could fire it without endangering themselves. Supposing the four men now cowering in the large outbuilding—just as far away across the paddock-like turf, but more to the left—plucked up their courage for revenge. . . . A hoarse yell wavered across the grass, rising to a sharp scream, cut short.

Nicky looked over her shoulder to see how the children

were taking these desperate noises. Should they leave now, and risk meeting a party of escaping robbers, or a returning patrol? No. Ajeet still held them enthralled: the woodman's second son was exchanging riddles with the tiger that had no soul. The tiger had already possessed the soul of the elder son, but needed a second man's soul to make up a whole tiger's soul. Nicky crossed the room and looked down the steep stair. Gopal had finished soaking the straw and was standing, watchful but relaxed, behind one doorpost. He had closed one leaf of the door. Nicky was on the point of going down to ask what he thought about moving the children when his stance tensed. She darted back to her window.

A man had led a huge horse from the outbuilding door. A strange figure moved beyond the animal and two other men came behind. The horse stopped. The two men went to the strange figure, bent out of sight and heaved.

The knight erupted into his saddle. He still looked strange, because his armor was so clumsy, but now he looked terrifying too—a giant toy which someone has put together from leftover bits of puppets and dolls, and then brought to gawky life. He put out his hand and a man passed him up his spear; a little crimson flag fluttered below the point. Now the man passed him a big timber ax and the knight hooked it into his belt, then turned and said something to the men. Two of them went back into the stables, but the third put a trumpet to his lips and blew a long, shivering note. The knight kicked his heels against the horse's ribs and the big animal started a slow trot over the lawn, toward the barn. Nicky heard the second leaf of the door creak shut, and the bar fall into place. The third man had followed the other two into the stables.

Beyond the knight a dark figure appeared from a downstairs window and stood for a moment, round as a bubble, against the whitewashed wall. Then Uncle Chacha was trotting across the grass, unhurriedly, as though he were slightly late for an appointment. Nicky could see the knight's face now, for the gawky helmet hung back over his shoulders and clanked dully as he bounced in his saddle. His hair was tight gold curls, his cheeks smooth; his nose

was a ruin—broken in some old fight and mended all lopsided; below it his handsome mouth grinned cheerfully. As
he came he fitted the lance into a holder, so that it stood up
like a mast behind his thigh. Now he could wield his ax,
two-handed.

Nicky looked around the room for something to throw,
though none of the windows was near enough over the
door; she might unsettle the horse for a minute, perhaps.
But there seemed to be nothing in the loft except hay and
children. She craned back out of the stench into the murderous sweet air.

The knight had ranged his horse alongside the door and
already the big ax was swung up over his shoulder for a
blow. His armor had gaps between the separate pieces, to
allow his limbs to move freely; really it was only pieces of
boiler and drainpipe held together with straps.

He looked up to Nicky's window; his green mad eyes
caught and held hers; then he laughed, as Mr. Tom had said,
like a lover, and swung the ax. The blade crunched through
the half-rotted planking and he wrenched it free and hefted
it for another blow. Nicky didn't dare look to where Uncle
Chacha came trotting over the sward; his best hope—his
only hope—was to catch the knight unawares and thrust
through one of the joints of his armor. Instead she looked
toward the stable.

The three men were out of the door again, two of them
carrying another brazier and the third an armful of weapons. The carriers put the brazier down and one of them
pointed at Uncle Chacha. The third man dropped the weapons, lifted the trumpet and blew, just as the ax crashed in
again. One fierce note floated across the green.

The knight heard it, looked over his shoulder, saw the
pointing arm, saw his attacker, and kicked the big horse
around. As it turned he hooked the ax back onto his belt and
lifted the lance out of its holder on the return movement.
The pennon dipped. The brazier party stood still to watch
the fun. The knight's boots drubbed mercilessly at the
horse's ribs, so that horse and man rushed on Uncle Chacha
like a landslide. Uncle Chacha glanced once over his shoulder to see whether danger threatened from behind, then

waited for the charge, his curved gray blade held low in his right hand. Nicky tried to look away again, but the dread of the sight held her transfixed.

Uncle Chacha just stood and waited for the lance point. He was a round, easy, still target. Only when the bitter tip was a second away did he begin to move, to his left, out from the path of the horse.

Nicky gulped. He had dodged too soon. The point had followed him around.

But with a single flowing twist, long after he had seemed committed to his leftward dodge, he was rolling and falling to the right, in toward the battering hooves, the way the knight could not expect him to go; and then, as the spear point spiked uselessly past, he was still falling but rolling out, with his sword whistling up behind his back in a long, wristy slash.

The stroke did not seem to have hit anything, but by the time the knight was turning his horse for a fresh charge Uncle Chacha was on his feet and picking up something from the grass—a stick with a red rag near the end. Three foot of severed spear. He felt the point, turned for a moment to wave a cheerful hand to Nicky, threw his small round shield to one side and waited for the knight in the same pose as before—except that now the pennoned point hung parallel to the sword, his left hand grasping the cut shaft.

The three men by the stables had put the brazier down and were sharing out the weapons. One of them shouted to the knight and he called back, then came again more cautiously.

His boots drubbed and the horse bore in. The knight seemed to have an incredible advantage, fighting down at the small round man from that moving tower of muscle, and protected too by all his armor. And his ax—though he had to hold it one-handed, rather far up the shaft, as he needed his other hand for the reins—was so heavy that even held like that any blow from it would surely cleave turban and skull. The knight seemed to think so, for he was grinning as he came.

Uncle Chacha balanced to meet the charge. Nicky thought

she knew what he would do. He would wait again until his enemy was almost on him, feint one way to commit the ax to a blow that side, then dodge around the other side of the horse and either pull the knight from his saddle, or wound or kill the horse so that he could fight the knight level. He would have to be quick, though: the other three men would soon be dangerously near.

But this time he didn't wait. When the horse was six feet away from him he made a long skip to his right, so that the knight had to turn the horse in to him, one-handed. As the big animal came awkwardly around, Uncle Chacha moved again, leaping forward with a shrill, gargling shout. The knight's ax came up, ready for him, but the fat man leaped direct for the charging horse, sweeping the pennoned spear sideways and up in front of its nose at the very moment that the wolf-cry of his shout cut short in a snapping bark. The terrified horse, bred and trained to pull brewers' drays through orderly streets, shied sideways from the onslaught, and half reared in a swirling spasm that gave the knight far too much to do to allow him to smite at his attacker. Uncle Chacha struck with his sword and the knight had to drop the reins and raise his iron arm to parry the whistling blade; even before the steel clanged into the drainpipe, the knight's own spear point was lancing up into the armpit which the raised arm had exposed.

He was still grinning as he toppled.

Uncle Chacha, bouncy as a playful cat, flicked around the plunging animal and his blade flashed through the air again. Nicky heard the thudding jar of the iron doll hitting the turf, but no cry at all. Then the horse was careering off toward the woods and she could see how the knight lay, his feet toward her, his gold curls hidden by the bulk of his armored shoulders, and the half spear still sticking into him, straight up, as though it had been planted there to mark the place where he fell.

The men from the stables were only ten yards further off. Nicky yelled "Look out!" and pointed. Without pausing to study the danger Uncle Chacha lugged the spear from the carcass and ran for the barn. To fight more than one enemy you must have your back against a wall. Nicky left the window and rushed down the stairs, barely noticing as she crossed the loft that Ajeet now had the woodman's son locked in a death wrestle with a six-armed ogre. The children sat as still as if there'd been nothing outside the window but birdsong.

Gopal had been watching the duel through the long slit where the knight's two blows had knocked a whole plank out. Now he was lifting the bar of the door.

"Shut it behind me!" he hissed. "He cannot fight three men!"

"Wait!" whispered Nicky. "Then you might catch one of them from behind."

A thud told that Uncle Chacha had his back to the planking. Peering through the slit, Nicky saw the rush of his pursuers falter as he faced them—they had seen what had happened to the knight. They were all three terribly young, just murderous loutish boys, eighteen at the oldest. Now they quailed before the hard old warrior standing at bay, glanced uncertainly at each other and crept forward with their swords held stiff and low. They must have plundered some museum for them.

Gopal crouched where the doors joined, like a runner settling into his blocks at the start of a race. The robber at the near end passed out of Nicky's line of sight, his back toward her.

"Now!" she whispered, and threw her weight against the big leaf. Gopal stayed in his crouch until the gap was wide enough; just at the moment when steel tinkled on steel outside, he exploded through. Nicky forgot her duty and rushed after him.

The nearest man had heard, or felt, the movement of the door and had half turned, so that the point of Gopal's sword drove into the soft part of his side below the rib cage. His face contorted; with a bubbling yell he buckled and collapsed. But the small blade had gone in so deep that his fall wrenched the hilt out of Gopal's hand, and the boy now stood weaponless.

The middle man, who had just skipped back out of reach of a lunge from Uncle Chacha's lance, wheeled at the cry, then rushed toward this easier victim. Gopal waited his

coming hopelessly, but knowing that you have more chance
if you can see your enemy than if you have your back to
him. Nicky, who had checked her outward rush as the first
man keeled over, scooped up some turf from the stack by
the barn door and hurled it, two-handed, over Gopal's
shoulder into the attacker's face. The brilliant summer had
dried the turf into fine dust, barely held together by the
dying roots of grass. The man staggered in his charge,
blinded, and the next instant Uncle Chacha's lance had
caught him full in the neck.

The third man dropped his sword and ran around the
corner of the barn. No one chased him.

Without a word Nicky and Gopal walked panting to the
other side of the doors, where there were no corpses, and
leaned against the wall. Uncle Chacha picked up his shield
and joined them.

"Three more killed," he said, "and one run away. Not
bad."

"What happened at the house?" said Gopal.

"They are good soldiers. Many of them slept with weapons by their beds. Wazir is dead, and Manhoor, and young
Harpit. We have killed perhaps half of them, but a group are
defending themselves in the big bedrooms on the far side.
We are hunting through the other rooms before we attack
them. Perhaps we will have to burn the house around them.
Look."

A man, an Englishman, was running along the top of an
eight-foot wall. He must have climbed from an upstairs window. Another figure, turbaned, dashed out of a door,
planted its legs wide apart and raised its arms in an age-old
pose. The arc of the risaldar's bow deepened; then it was
straight. The man on the wall threw his arms wide between
pace and pace and tumbled with a crash through a greenhouse roof.

"I must go back," said Uncle Chacha.

"I expect the other horses are in that stable," said Nicky,
"and the rest of the armor. If you turned the horses out you
could set fire to the stable and burn the saddles and things
as well, and then you wouldn't have to fight any more
knights on horseback."

"You are right," said Uncle Chacha, and trotted off across the grass, still as light on his feet as if he hadn't spent the morning fighting for his life against grisly odds.

"You go too," said Nicky. "He'll need a hand with the brazier. I'm going to take the children home."

"That was a good throw, Nicky," said Gopal. "Thank you."

He gave her a gay salute with his bloody sword, made two practice slashes with it, and ran off after his uncle. Nicky climbed to the loft with legs like lead.

Ajeet's tiger was dead, with its skin nailed to the temple door. In the temple the woodman's sons were marrying queens.

Nicky nodded to Ajeet, who put her palms together under her chin.

"And so ends the tale of the tiger who had no soul," she said.

The children watched her in silence.

"Thank you, miss," said the redheaded girl.

"I'm going to take you all to your homes now," said Nicky.

A squealing like a piggery racked the loft.

"Quiet!" she yelled, and the squealing died.

"Now listen to me," said Nicky. "My friends have killed half the robbers. Ajeet's father beat the worst of the men on horses and killed him too. The rest of the robbers are shut up in the house, but a few have run away. Some of them may be hiding in the woods, but it's all right—they can't hurt us if you do what I say. There's a pile of flints by the ditch over there, and I want you each to pick up two of them, or three if you've got a pocket to put the third one in. Choose stones which are the heaviest ones you can throw properly and straight. Carry one in each hand, and if you see anybody who looks like a robber, lift up your arm and be ready to throw, but don't throw till I shout. Do you understand? Just think—thirty big stones, all held ready for throwing. One man won't attack an army like that. You're an army now. Soldiers. And you're going home."

She led them down the ladder. Ajeet came last. By the flint pile she marshaled them into a crocodile, with the smallest children in the middle clutching their useless but heartening pebbles. But the big boys and girls, back and front, were armed with flints that really would make an enemy hesitate. She looked for the last time toward the house. A flurry of shouts and a scream rose from the far side. A wisp of smoke came from the stable, and Gopal was leading a huge horse over the grass toward her.

"The other one bolted," he said, smiling. "But this one is too darn friendly. Can you take him with you?"

Nicky dithered, frightened by the animal's size.

"I'm used to horses, miss," said the redheaded girl. "I'll mind him."

She took the halter and Gopal started back toward the battlefield, in a careful copy of Uncle Chacha's energy-preserving trot.

"Now," said Nicky, "I don't want to go past the house and along the road because that might make things difficult for my friends. Who knows the best way across the fields?"

Several voices answered and all the hands pointed the same way. She chose a dark, sensible-looking boy as her guide and set off. They crossed the big lawn, skirted a little wood, used a tarred footbridge to cross a dry ditch among bamboos, and came to a gate at the end of the garden. They wound slowly up the wheatfield beyond, tramping their path through stalks which had already dropped their seed and were now so brittle that the first gale of winter would push them over to lie and rot. A sudden rustling, as of a large animal disturbed, shook the stems to their left.

"Ready!" shouted Nicky. Thirty fists came up with rocks poised—though the pudgy arms at the center scarcely rose above the wheat stalks. Out of the wheat a naked man bounded like a startled deer. He gazed wild-eyed at the children for a moment; then, amid whoops and jeers, he was scampering up the hill. Nicky called her army into line of march again. That must have been the man she first saw escaping across the lawn in the gray, chill air before sunrise. She looked to her left and was astounded to see that the sun had still not crossed the low hilltop, though the air was gold with its coming. Less than an hour ago, then, the attack had begun.

Her guide led them slantwise up to a second gate, beyond which was a pasture full of cows who stared at them in stolid boredom as they trooped across. The cries from the house were faint and few now, but a strange mutter seemed to be growing in the village. The next gate led into a lane, all arched over with hazels, which her guide wanted to turn along; but Nicky thought they were still dangerously close to the big house and insisted on pushing through the fields behind the straggle of cottages that ran down the main road to the Borough.

More pasture here, and they had to skirt around a marshy piece where the stream that flowed through the White House gardens rose. The mutter from the village was like the roar of surf, and above it floated indistinguishable human shouts. Looking to her right as they slanted down toward the uproar, Nicky saw a slow column of smoke billowing up into the blissful morning. She realized what had happened.

"Run!" she cried. "Run, but keep together!"

If they didn't reach the road in time, a hundred maddened villagers would be roaring down to the big house to slaughter every living thing there, Sikh or robber. It was no use reaching the road alone—she had to come with all the children, safe. The villagers had seen the smoke from the stables and decided that the robbers had fired the barn where their hostages lay. And it would be the Sikhs' fault.

The line moved down hill, slowed to the pace of exhausted and ill-fed six-year-olds stumbling through the tussocks.

"You three," gasped Nicky to the older ones nearest her, "run to the road. Try to stop the village from attacking my friends. Tell them all the children are safe."

The messengers went down the slope in a happy freewheeling gallop, as if it had been a game for a summer evening. Nicky grabbed the wrists of the two smallest children and half helped, half hauled them over the hummocky turf. Other children dropped their flints and copied her. And here was a path, a narrow channel between the wall of a chapel and the fence of a pub garden, and now they were in the road, gasping, while the three messengers shrank from the roaring tide of the enraged village as it poured down the road toward them, led by little old Maxie waving a carpenter's hammer. The men were yelling, but the women were silent, and they were more terrible still: marching in their snowy aprons, faces drawn into gray lines with rage and weeping, fingers clenched around the handles of carving knives and cleavers.

Terrified by the sight, Nicky's army melted to the walls of the road. She stood helpless in the middle, still gripping the fat wrists of the two small children.

The tide of vengeance tried to halt, but the villagers at the back, who could not see what had happened, jostled into the ones who could. The news spread like flame through dry hay. The roaring anger changed and became a great hoarse splendor of cheering and relief. Mother after mother dropped her weapon and ran forward, arms outstretched. They came in a white whirl, like doves homing to the dovecote, and knelt in the road to hug their children.

Nicky ran to Maxie.

"Can you get the men to come and help my friends?" she cried. "They've killed half the robbers, but they're still fighting."

Maxie looked around at the bellowing crowd and nodded.

"Lift me up, Dave," he crowed to the stout man beside him.

Dave and another man swung him up to their shoulders as if he'd been a child held high to watch a king come past. He raised his arms like Moses on the mount and waited for the cheering to die.

"Men o' Felpham," he crowed. "You know as the Devil's Children have rescued our childer out of the hands of the robbers. Now they're fighting them to the death down at White House. Do we go help them?"

A mutter of doubt ran through the crowd.

"We've taken the horses," cried Nicky. "Look, I've brought one. And we've burned the place where the armor was, and we've killed half the robbers. We've killed the worst of the horsemen."

The mutter changed its note, and rose.

"Do we go help them?" crowed Maxie again. "Or do we let it be said that the men o' Felpham stood and watched while a handful of strangers did their fighting for them?"

The mutter returned to the note that Nicky had first heard, the noise of surf in a gale.

"Okay, Dave," said Maxie, "you can put me down."

The women pulled their children aside to let the bellowing army pass. Nicky picked up a fallen cleaver and walked beside Maxie.

"Five of my grandchilder there," he said. "You go home now, girl. This is no business for a child."

"I'm coming to make sure you don't hurt my friends," she said.

"Shan't do that. Not now."

"Well, I'm coming anyway."

Maxie looked over his shoulder.

"Hey!" he crowed. "You get off that horse, Dave Gracey, and let the girl ride. She'll be safer up there."

The stout man slid down, grinning, and whisked Nicky up to the broad and cushiony back. She had ridden ponies on holidays, sometimes, but never a creature as tall as this, never bareback and without reins, though Dave Gracey still held the halter. She seemed a mile in the air, and clutched the coarse mane with her left hand.

But after a minute she found that she wasn't afraid of the height, because the back was so broad and the horse's movement, at this pace, so steady, that she might have been riding on a palanquin. She let go of the mane, rested the cruel cleaver across her lap, straightened her back and neck and rode like a queen.

The exultation of victory thrilled through her blood. They had nearly done it now. All through the long night stalk, and the taut waiting, and the short blind blaze of action, she had felt nothing. She had simply thought and acted as the minute demanded. Even fear (and she had been horribly afraid) came from outside, pulsed through her, and was gone. But now she thought, "We have nearly done it." Glory washed over her like sunrise.

Now she knew why the robber knight had laughed like a lover as he clove at the tarred planks. The same glory was in him; but in him it had gone rancid.

It was a good half mile from the Borough to the White House. The village bellowed its coming all the way.

The besieged robbers must have heard them, realized that flight was the only hope now and made a desperate sortie. For as the village turned into the White House drive they met a dozen of their oppressors. Beyond, on the far side of a little bridge, came the weary Sikhs.

The village halted, faced by these armed and pitiless enemies. Another second and their courage might have oozed away as fast as it had risen; but Nicky kicked as hard as she could at the horse's sides, swung her cleaver up and shouted "Come on!"

The great beast trundled forward and the roaring rose behind her once again. A robber lunged at her with a short lance, but she saw the stroke coming and bashed the point aside with the flat of her cleaver. Another man fell as the horse simply breasted him over. The second rank of robbers turned to run back over the bridge. But there on the other side, swords ready, waited the grim Sikhs. The robbers hesitated, and the village churned over them.

Nicky was already among her friends. Gopal was there and Uncle Chacha and Kewal and the risaldar, weary as death but smiling welcome amid their beards. She dropped from the horse and ran to drag Maxie out of a ring of shouting and backslapping friends. He came without question.

"This is Mr. Maxie," she said. "This is Mr. Jagindar Singh."

The two men shook hands. Blood was still seeping from a crooked slash that ran from Uncle Jagindar's wrist to his elbow.

"I reckon we owe you a lot, sir," said Maxie. "More'n we can rightly pay."

"You will pay us well if we can now be friends," said Uncle Jagindar.

# Chapter 8

# FIVE STONES

Kaka and Gurdial and Parsan won the fancy-dress parade at the spring festival. Kaka was the back legs of the elephant, Gurdial was the front legs, and Parsan, aged two, dressed in brilliant silks and jewels, rode in the tiny howdah and was the princess. In fact the Sikh children, with their unfair advantage of looking slightly fancy-dress anyway, might have won every prize in the parade if the vicar hadn't been diplomatic enough to give the second prize to Sarah Pritchard, who came as a flaunting gypsy. She was Mr. Tom's great-niece.

On the other hand the village won the tug-of-war and (to the risaldar's disgust) the archery; and, of course, all the cake-making contests—there was no prize for chapati. But then Mr. Surbans Singh won the plowing match, cleaving a line so straight behind his big dray horse that you'd have thought he had a cord to steer by. Nicky didn't win anything, though she bowled and bowled for the pig. Kewal told her that if there'd been a disobedience prize, the dog which she'd found limping through the January snow on the common would have beaten any dog the village could put up. Kewal was wearing his gold turban and had spent all night with his beard in curlers; every girl in the village made eyes at him, and with his squint he had the advantage of being able to ogle two at a time. He strutted as though he'd won the battle against the robbers single-handed. (He had, in fact, been very brave but not—Uncle Chacha once hinted—very skillful, having neglected his sword practice.)

After the fancy dress parade was over and Kaka and Gurdial and Parsan had been given their prize—a white rabbit—the trumpet sounded for the main event of the festival. The trumpet was the one the robbers had used for their signals; before that it must have blown in a pop group; now it was half the village band.

The bowling for the pig stopped, and the women left off chaffering at the stalls and began to summon their children from their squealing chase among the elders' legs. Everybody trooped away, the young men down to the old cricket pavilion to collect their weapons, and the rest to line the Borough and the short street up to the churchyard. The old lady, Ajeet's grandmother, waited on her cart at the widest part of the Borough and Maxie stood on a crate beside her. Maxie was mayor now; the village hadn't fancied being ruled by another Master, so, soon after the battle, they had elected a mayor and councillors. Uncle Jagindar was a councillor.

Away to the right, from the cricket pavilion, the trumpet blew again. This time it was playing not a call but a tune, "The British Grenadiers," which was the only march the trumpeter could get the whole way through. A clumsy drum rattled in support. The village stood murmuring and craning, waiting for the soldiers to pass.

First marched the two standards. Kewal carried a gold lion embroidered on a black cloth, to symbolize the fact that "Singh" means "lion." The village had chosen, mysteriously, a sheep. (The vicar had liked that, and had preached a sermon on the text "The lion and the lamb shall lie down together.") The sheep was white, on a green cloth, and one of Mrs. Sallow's cousins carried it.

Next came the trumpet and the drum, and behind them the risaldar and the six bowmen from the village. If you knew the risaldar well you could see that beneath his proud bearing he was still sulking about the archery contest. Last of all came the infantry, fifty swords strong. Uncle Jagindar had hammered and tested every sword.

There was no cavalry, because all the village ponies were too busy hauling and plowing to be trained for warfare. The big dray horses which the robbers had brought hauled and plowed too: neither Sikhs nor villagers had thought it right that three men should ride proud while the rest walked.

The soldiers saluted the old lady and Mr. Maxie with their swords as they passed; they all looked as though they knew how to handle their weapons. Mr. Maxie waved an affable hand, as though he were saying good-bye to a visitor from his doorstep, and the old lady put her palms together and bowed with antique grace. The procession wheeled right, up toward the church, and the whole village and all the watching Sikhs crowded behind. Nicky and Ajeet and Kaka and Gurdial trundled the old lady's cart up the slope.

Mr. Tom's brilliant notion had solved the puzzling question of the monument. The three dead Sikhs were of course not Christians, and neither Sikh nor villager thought it proper that their monument should be in the churchyard. But two villagers had also died, one first of all and the other by a bitter fluke meeting a robber's sword in that last rush over the bridge. These two were Christians—at least since May. So five great stones had been found, and a stonemason had been brought over from Bradley to square them up and set them into the churchyard wall ("neither in nor out," as Mr. Tom had claimed). The mason had then cut a single name deep into each stone.

> ARTHUR BARNARD
> WAZIR SINGH
> MANHOOR SINGH
> HARPIT SINGH
> DAVID GRACEY

Thousands of daffodils and a few hellebores and primroses stood in vases and jars along the top of the wall and in a thick mass on the ground below it.

The vicar, very nervous and breathy with emotion, preached a short sermon from the old mounting block beside the monument. Despite his donnish accent he managed to say what everybody felt was right, about how the two communities needed each other, both in peace and war. Uncle Jagindar read a brief prayer in Punjabi and then translated it into English, adding that words like "courage" and "love" meant the same thing in any language. Finally the trumpet played "God Save the Queen," just as if anybody knew what had happened to the Queen since May. Everyone cheered.

"Very English," whispered Kewal in Nicky's ear. She trod on his foot, on purpose.

The army dispersed and the weapons were put away, though many of the villagers now copied the Sikhs and wore their swords wherever they went; the men relaxed and chatted while the women got supper ready and the village children taught the Sikh children how a maypole worked and the bigger boys played football. Nicky noticed an odd group around the old lady's cart, Mr. Maxie and Mr. Tom and Neena and Uncle Jagindar, all talking earnestly. Quite often one of them would glance across to where she sat against the pavilion wall fondling her stray dog's ears.

It was a lucky night, warmer than usual for April, under a dull sky. Stars would have been pretty but would have meant frost, which no one wanted either for sitting out in or for the sake of the vegetable patches which were sown and showing. But even in that comparative mildness they were glad to sit within feel of the huge bonfires which had been built at the bottom of the recreation ground. The spit-roast mutton was very good, and the home-baked bread much nicer than chapati, Nicky decided.

After supper she didn't feel like joining in anything, though there was dancing between the bonfires—whole lines or circles of dancers moving in patterns with a prancing motion which overcame the roughnesses of the turf, while Mr. Tom's lion-headed fiddle sawed out the six-hundred-year-old tunes. Ajeet had attracted a ring of small children around her, a little beyond the circle, and was telling them a story which made some of them tumble about with laughter. Nicky sat and leaned her back against the wheel of the old lady's cart and longed to be less stupid at Punjabi, so that she could talk to her without a translator. They were somehow the same kind of people, Nicky knew, herself and the old lady—hard, practical, wild, loving. But though Ajeet or Gopal gave her a long lesson every day, so that she could now understand quite a bit of the talk, she couldn't speak more than the easiest sentences back. She had never been any good at languages, not French, not German, and now not Punjabi.

So she leaned against the wheel and watched the pattern of dancers in the orange light of the bonfires, and the huge oval of faces, and the sudden fountain of curling sparks that erupted when a log collapsed. Neena came out of the dark and sat beside her.

"Are you happy, Nicky?"

"No, I don't think so. I don't know. I ought to be, but I'm not."

"What do you want?"

"I don't know that either."

"We've been talking about you."

"Yes, I noticed."

"We think it's time we tried to get you back to your own family."

"Please don't talk about it. Please!"

"No, listen, Nicky. Mr. Maxie's cousin is a sailor at Dover. Mr. Maxie sent a message to him and he heard the answer yesterday. Ever since . . . since all these changes happened, boats have been going over to France, ferrying people away. Millions of people have gone. And the French have set up offices all along the coast, where they take everybody's name very carefully. The French are good at that sort of thing. It may take a little while, but in the end they will find your parents for you, and all this will become just like a dream, or a story that Ajeet tells."

"But why should anyone take me to France? What can I do in exchange?"

"We will pay them."

"But no one's got any money, not anymore."

"The smallest of my mother's rings would buy a fishing boat ten times over. And she would give every jewel she owns to make you happy, Nicky. I sometimes think she loves you more than any of her own children or grandchildren. It is strange, is it not, how sometimes a soul will speak to a soul across language, across the generations, across every difference of race and birth and breeding."

Neena spoke some sentences of Punjabi. Nicky knew enough to understand that she was translating what she had just said. Nicky put up her hand and felt the other hand take it, felt the hard, cold knuckles and the harder rings.

"Mr. Maxie's cousin will come and fetch you next week," said Neena. "He will see you safely right out to the middle of the Channel, where the big ships wait and the madness ends. Mrs. Sallow insists that she will go with you as far as the sea, so that you are not among strangers."

"I don't want to go," said Nicky. "I daren't."

"But why? You have dared and adventured much more terrible things. This should not frighten you."

"It's not that kind of fright. It's . . . I don't want to explain."

Neena spoke quietly in Punjabi, and there was a short silence.

"Nick-ke," said the old voice above her head.

"Ai?" said Nicky.

The old lady began to speak, her voice dry and quiet, like the sound of a snake rustling across hot rocks in her own far country. This time it was she who spoke in short sentences, so that Neena could translate.

"Nicky, you are in danger. It is not the sort of danger we have fought through this last year. It is inside you. We have been in bad times. We have all had to be hard and fierce. But you have made yourself harder and fiercer than any of us, even than us Sikhs. In bad times you have to wear armor around your heart, but when times are better you must take it off. Or it becomes a prison for your soul. You grow to the shape of it, as a tortoise grows to the shape of its shell.

Nicky, you must go to a place where you can take your armor off. That place is your parents' hearth."

Nicky felt a chill in her bones which was not the chill of the night air. The small smithy under her ribs started its hammering, and in her mind's eye she saw the iron doll topple, grinning and jointless from his huge horse.

"How did you know about the armor?" she whispered.

Neena translated, and the old lady's cackling laugh surprised the night. Then the snake-rustling sentences began again.

"I was married when I was twelve. To a man I had never seen. It was the custom of our people. I loved my parents and my brothers and sisters and our happy house, and then I was taken away from them. I too put armor around my heart. But I was luckier than you, Nicky, for my husband— oh, how old he seemed—was kind and patient and clever. He made a place, a world, in which I wanted to take my armor off."

"Perhaps they're dead," said Nicky.

"Perhaps they are not. Perhaps you will not find them. Who can say? But until you have tried to find them you will make yourself stay hard and fierce. That is the danger of which I spoke. It is in your nature to become like that forever."

And that was true. Nicky knew that her kinship with the robber knight went deeper than the armor, deeper than the glorious wash of victory she had felt on the morning of the battle. Yes, she must go. But still she felt reluctant.

"Must I go so soon?" she said. "Next week is . . ."

"You must go now," said Neena decisively. "We have not talked to the village about this, but we think that all this island is closing in on itself. Soon they will have forgotten about how to get people away; they will have forgotten about France. We must expect difficult times."

"Then I ought to stay and help you," said Nicky obstinately.

"No. We have learned to be careful. We will survive and prosper. If you ever come back, you will probably find that Jagindar is an earl. Nicky, you don't have to go. We all love you here, and we should like you to stay, out of our own selfishness. But we think you should try to go to your family."

Nicky made up her mind, as usual, in one irrevocable rush.

"Yes," she said. "Yes, I will go. But perhaps one of you could come with me as far as the sea. Kewal or Uncle Chacha or Mr. Surbans Singh."

Neena sighed in the dark, and Nicky could hear the rustle of her sari as her shoulders made the familiar shrug.

"It would be nice, Nicky, but it would not be safe. Outside these few fields we are still the Devil's Children."

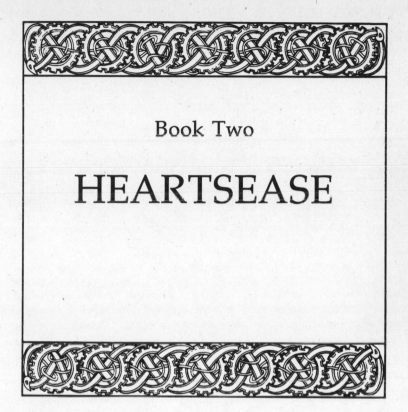

Book Two

# HEARTSEASE

for Philippa and Polly

# While Four Years Pass

*Nicky was lucky. She bought a passage on an almost empty fishing boat. In mid-Channel they hove to beside a large steamer and she climbed aboard, only finding it strange that she did not find it strange. At Calais the refugee agencies searched their files and sent her to a camp where she found her parents waiting in the long queue, as they'd done every day for many months. Despite the drabness of the huts, finding them was like coming out of an icy, drizzling street into a warm house full of friendship.*

*Nicky's ship was one of the last few to leave. Britain, as Neena had foreseen, closed in on itself, like an anemone in a rock pool closing at a touch. When other nations tried to probe into the island, the island seemed to grow a mysterious wall around it. It was very difficult to get even a single spy through.*

*But behind the wall we began to change. The Changes were mostly inside us, in our minds, but a few were outside. In a bare hill valley a great oakwood grew, overnight, with a tower in the middle of it. In Surrey that wild Dervish who had caused the panic when Nicky lost her parents discovered that the thunderstorm had been no accident. He had willed it into being, and now he could will any weather he chose. He didn't know how, nor did the others (a boy in Weymouth, a schoolmaster in Norwich, for instance) who found they had the same gift. In a year or two it was just a commonplace that there would be sun for harvest and snow in December, accepted by everyone in much the same way that they accepted that a chestnut tree would grow its five-fingered leaves every spring.*

But not everyone was aware of the weathermongers at work, because not every district had its own weathermonger, and just as the island closed in on itself, so the cells inside it also closed. Men lived by rumor. Events in the next county became strange and far away. One winter, for instance, it was said in Yorkshire that dragons had begun to stir in the Pennine hills; quite sensible farmers took to sleeping with buckets of water beside their beds, ready to quench the fiery breath.

Most of the customs that grew up were concerned with witchcraft (as the use of machines was called). These also varied from shire to shire. Hereford, for instance, was very little troubled by witches and the reason for this (men believed) was the great Hereford Flower Dance, which lasted for fourteen days in May and was a time of singing and happiness, a celebration of the power of Nature against the horror of engines.

By contrast there were the great witch-findings in Durham Cathedral, with three thousand people massed under the frowning Norman arches, pale-cheeked and sweating, groaning all together as name after name was called, neighbors and wives and sons and cronies, to stand the unappealable tests.

In an island like this, so secretive, so unpredictable, how could a spy from the outside world survive? As he set up his little transmitter in a Cotswold copse, working with difficulty because the controls and connections seemed suddenly unfamiliar and awkward, how could he know that he would be smelt out, ambushed, seized and stunned, and then wake to find his legs shackled by oak stocks, his back against a wall, and himself facing a baying crowd of villagers? And then the brief, jeering trial and the hail of stones.

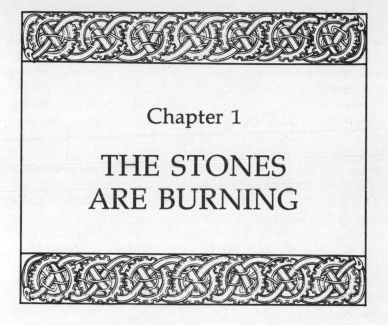

# Chapter 1

# THE STONES ARE BURNING

It was the last of the soft days of autumn. As dusk fell, you could feel the frosts coming, a smell of steel in the air.

If it hadn't been so nearly dark Margaret would have gone the long way around; but she was tired and Scrub was even tireder, his head drooping, his mane clotted with sweat, his hooves not making their proper clipclop, but muddling the sound with a scrapy noise because he wasn't lifting them up properly. Even so she began to lead him the long way, without thinking about it. It was only the clank of a milking bucket from Fatchet's cowshed reminded her that Uncle Peter would be finished milking soon; if she came back after he'd sat down in his rocking chair in the farm kitchen and begun to drink his evening's cider from the big blue-and-white mug, he'd beat her with his belt until she was sore for days.

She turned back and led the pony down Tibbins Lane, toward the stocks where the dead witch lay under the new heap of stones.

She started to sing a carol, "The Holly and the Ivy," but found her voice wouldn't rise above a mumble, and even that noise dried in her mouth before she was halfway down the lane. She tried again and managed a whole verse at a bare whisper, and then the muscles in her throat turned the words into no sound at all. She would have run if she'd been alone, but Scrub was past anything except his dragging walk. Clip, scrape, clop went his hooves on the old tarmac, clip, scrape, clop. She could see the heap of stones now, lying against the Rectory wall as though they'd just been tipped from a cart—not brought in baskets and barrows by a hundred villagers for throwing.

All at once she thought of Jonathan; just like him to be helping Aunt Anne with the baking that morning, so that he hadn't been made to go and watch the stoning. He'd laugh at her, his sharp snorting laugh, if she told him she'd ridden so far to get away from this heap of stones that now she had to come back right past it. Jonathan always thought things out before he did them. Come on, Margaret, it's only a heap of stones and what's left of a foreign witch. Come on.

As she passed the neat pile the stones groaned.

Margaret dropped the reins and ran. Forty yards on, where the walls narrowed into an alleyway between two cottages, she waited, panting, for Scrub. He clopped down in the near-dark and nuzzled against her shoulder, but nothing else moved in the dusk behind him.

Uncle Peter was still whistling shrilly at his milking stool when she led the pony past the cowshed toward the little paddock which he shared with poor neglected Caesar. Jonathan was waiting for her, leaning against the pillar of the log-store, his little pointed face just like a gnome's under his shaggy black hair.

"What's wrong, Marge?" he said.

"Nothing."

"Is it to do with the witch? You didn't watch, did you?"

"No, of course not."

"But it is, isn't it?"

"Oh, Jo, it was . . . I had to come back down Tibbins Lane because I was so late, and when I passed him he groaned. I thought witches died, just like anybody else."

Jonathan tilted his head over the other way, still watching her with his bright, strange eyes—like a bird deciding whether to come for the crumbs you are holding in the palm of your hand.

"You're not making this up, are you, Marge?"

"No, of course not!"

"All right. Now listen. I'll take Scrub out and put his harness away. You—"

"But why?"

"Listen! You go and offer to carry one of Father's buckets in—he won't let you, but it'll tell him you're home. Go and say hello to Mother, then go upstairs noisily and quietly into my room. Climb out along the shed roof and jump down into the old hay. I'll meet you there."

"But why, Jo?"

"Because he's still alive, of course. We've got to get him out. Tim'll help us, but we'll need you too."

"Jo, you'll—"

"Yes, I'll take care of your precious Scrub. Go slowly, Marge. Talk slowly. Try and sound just tired, and nothing else."

She gave him the reins, started to walk toward the cowshed door, turned back to shout to him to see that there was enough water in the trough, realized that it would be dangerous to shout (dangerous now, in a house which was safe this morning) and walked on.

Uncle Peter was milking Florence, so he must be almost finished. There were two full buckets by the door, so he'd be middling pleased—last week he hadn't managed to fill even two most days.

"Can I carry one of these in for you, Uncle Peter?"

He grunted but didn't look up. "You leave 'em be," he said. "Too heavy for a slip like you, Marge. Where you been all day, then?"

"Riding."

"Long ride. Didn't you fancy what we did to that foreigner this morning?"

Margaret said nothing.

"Ach, don't you be feared to tell *me*. You're a good lass, Marge, and I wouldn't have you hard-hearted, but you must understand that it's necessary. Thou shalt not suffer a witch to live, the Book says. Look now, I took nigh on half a bucket out of Maisie, who was dry as an old carrot till this very day, when she should by all rights have been flowing with milk like the land of Canaan—what was that but witch-craft?"

"I suppose you're right, Uncle Peter."

"Course I am, girl. You go in now. You'll have forgot all about it by tomorrow."

Aunt Anne was in the kitchen, which had been the living room before the Changes came. She was rocking her chair an inch to and fro in front of the bread-oven, staring at nothing, her face drawn down into deep lines as though she wanted to cry but couldn't. Margaret said hello but she didn't answer, so it seemed best to go thumpingly up the stairs, tiptoe into Jonathan's room, wriggle out through his window and crawl down the edge of the shed where the tiles were less likely to break.

The hay was last year's, gray with mustiness, but thick enough to break a clumsy jump. She picked herself up and moved into the shadow of a stack of bean poles which Uncle Peter had leaned against the shed wall. It really was night now, with a half-moon coming and going behind slow-moving clouds, and the air chill for waiting in; but before she began to feel cold inside herself she heard a low bubbling sound which meant that Tim was coming up the path from his hut in the orchard. The moon edged out as he reached the shed, and she saw that he was carrying a sheep hurdle under one arm and a full sack on his other shoulder. Jonathan was with him.

"You there, Marge?" he whispered. "Good. Hold this. I won't be long."

He handed her a saw and scampered off down the path. Tim at once began to make his bubbling noise more loudly, because Jonathan was the only person he knew and trusted, apart from his own sister, Lucy. Other people teased him and threw things at him, or were frightened of him and kept away; but inside his poor muddled brain he knew that Jonathan really thought of him as a person, and not as an animal who happened to be shaped like a man.

"It's all right, Tim," whispered Margaret, speaking as she might have done to Scrub, "he's coming back. Be brave." The whisper seemed to make Tim feel he was with someone who wouldn't hurt him, so he settled down to wait and the bubbling quietened in his throat. Jonathan was away several minutes, and when he came back he walked slowly, bent sideways by the weight of the heavy thing he was carrying.

"What's that?" said Margaret.

"Petrol, I think. It burns. I found a few tins hidden under the straw in the old barn where the machines are."

"But you aren't allowed to go there!" whispered Margaret.

"Tim can carry it," said Jonathan. "And the sack. There won't be anyone in the road now it's really dark. I'll manage the hurdle and you take the saw, Marge. Keep in the shadows. If someone does come, stand still until you're sure they've seen you. If you have to run away, don't drop the saw or they'll know where it came from. Climb up the ivy on the other side of this wall and you can get back onto the roof. Off we go."

Tim followed him like a dog at its master's heels. The alley between the cottages was a black canyon, but beyond it the moon shone clear against the Rectory wall. Tim moved more quietly than the children because he didn't have proper shoes, not even clogs; his feet were wrapped in straw which he tied into place with strips of old rag. The stocks had been set opposite the gate into Squire's house, where the road was wider, so that there would be plenty of room for the villagers to gather round and throw things at whoever was in them—soft fruit and rotten eggs and clods of turf at ordinary bad people, stones at witches.

The pile was silent now, but Jonathan didn't stop to listen to it. He started lifting the stones away, not dropping them but putting them down carefully so as not to make any noise. Tim watched, bubbling quietly, and then began to help. When Margaret lifted her first stone the witch groaned again.

There weren't as many stones as there seemed. The pile looked big because Mr. Gordon, the fierce old sexton, had made the men pick the loose ones up when the stoning was

over and heap them into a neat cairn. Before long Margaret
tried to pull a bigger stone out but found it was soft and
warm—a legging with a leg inside it. In a few minutes more
they had cleared the legs up as far as the stocks.

"You two carry on with the top half," said Jonathan,
"while I cut through here."

"But Jo," whispered Margaret, "won't they start hunting
for him when they see it's sawn through? They'll know
someone's got him out."

"That's what the petrol's for."

He was already sawing, slowly but firmly, making as little
noise as possible. Margaret and Tim labored on, lift, stoop,
lift, stoop, lift, stoop. No single stone seemed to make the
cairn any smaller, but soon they had cleared the body up to
the waist. Tim had stopped his bubbling and was working
with increasing urgency now that he could see enough of
the witch's body to know what it was; he cooed once or
twice, a noise which Margaret hadn't heard him make before. The witch had sheltered his head behind crooked
arms, but these were now stuck to the mess of clotted blood
and clothing and hair around his face; when Margaret tried
to move an arm to get at a stone which had lodged in the
bend of the elbow he groaned with a new, sharp note.

"He ought to be dead," whispered Jonathan. "Perhaps he's
wearing some kind of armor under his clothes."

Tim knelt down beside the bloodied head and with slow
tenderness, cooing like a distant pigeon in June, lifted the
wincing tangle and cradled it against his dirty chest while
Margaret picked out the last stone and eased the arms down
into the man's lap. Jonathan sawed with even strokes, as
though he was in no hurry at all.

"Oak," he whispered. "About three minutes more. Watch
out up the lane, Marge, just in case."

The last tough sliver gave beneath the sawteeth and he
lifted the imprisoning timber from the man's ankles. Then
he fetched the hurdle and laid it beside the body. Tim, without being told, eased the wounded man on.

"We'll each take a corner in front, Marge. Tim can carry
the back."

The weight was heavy but manageable. As soon as they

were well clear of the rubble Jonathan lowered his corner to the ground so that Margaret and Tim had to do so too. Then he tipped the contents of the sack out and arranged them carefully around the stocks—straw and kindling and a few small pieces of plank. He opened the can and poured its contents over his bonfire and the surrounding stones. An extraordinary smell rose into the night air, and all at once Margaret remembered the seaside, which she'd completely forgotten about for five years—a smooth sea, hot sun, sand crawling with people, and behind it all a road where just such a smell came from, because a lot of machines were waiting there for three ladies in white coats to—she remembered the right words—fill them up. She hadn't thought of petrol, or the sea, or machines as things which took you to places, for ages—not since she was how old? The Changes were five years back, she and Jonathan were fourteen now, so not since she was nine. Now this smell, sharp, rather nasty, filling your nose like chopped onions, brought all the pictures back.

"We'll let it soak while we get him down to the barn," whispered Jonathan. "I'll come back with a lantern to light it. People will run out if they see the flames now."

"Why do you want to burn the stocks?" said Margaret as she picked up her corner of the hurdle.

"Burn the saw marks. Then people might think he got away by witchcraft."

They didn't talk again as they carried the witch through the alley, along the stretch of road at the bottom, down through the farm gate and yard and along the steep path behind the pigsties to the big barn where the wicked machines stood in their rusting rows. Jonathan seemed to know his way about and led them unstumbling through the blackness to a place where there was a little hut inside the barn. He pushed a door open, and another forgotten smell lifted out into the night, more oily than petroly this time.

"I think he'll be safe here," he said. "There's a big engine without wheels in the middle; I don't know what it was for but it drove a big fan and pushed air into those towers outside. Marge, you'll have to climb up the ivy to my room and

get some coverings to keep him warm. Straw, Tim. Straw.
Straw. Good boy."

Tim bubbled his understanding and slouched out. Jonathan was shuffling around in the blackness, making a
sweeping noise. Margaret waited, jobless, to help shift the
witch. Then the faint square of lighter blackness in the
doorway was blocked and she could smell fresh straw—Tim
must have robbed the stack by the pigsties.

"I've cleared a place here," said Jonathan. "Hurry, Marge
—we can move him."

The ivy was harder to climb than Jonathan had implied,
but she managed it on the third go. She whisked the blankets off his bed, threw them out of the window, and went
slowly down the stairs. Aunt Anne was still sitting in tragic
stillness by the ovens, but this time she looked up when
Margaret came in.

"Pete should be back in ten minutes," she said. "He's talking to Mr. Gordon. You must be hungry after all that riding
—there's mutton and bread in the larder if you want something to keep you going."

"Oh, yes, please," said Margaret. "I've just remembered I
didn't check whether the ponies had enough water. I won't
be out long."

She found what she wanted in the larder: two fresh rolls,
apples, slices of mutton, and one of the little bottles of cordial which Aunt Anne had brewed last March. She took the
bottle from the back of the shelf and hoped it wouldn't be
missed. As she was going out through the porch she had
another thought and picked up one of the half-dozen lanterns which were always there. Aunt Anne didn't even move
her eyes when she crossed the kitchen and lit the wick with
a spill from the fire. Jonathan met her just outside the
porch.

"Bit of luck," he whispered. "I thought I'd have to sneak in
to light mine. Put it down—I've got a bit of dry straw. Shield
the light as you go down the path, Marge."

He knelt in the moonlight and flipped the little doors
open; deft and sure he lit his straw and moved the quick
flame into the other lantern in time to light the wick before
the straw was all burned. Margaret carried her lantern

around the corner of the house where the pile of bedding
lay, picked the blankets up and hid its light among them.

The witch was moaning on his straw. His face in the yellow lantern light was an ugly mess of raw flesh, his lips fat
with bruising, his eyes too puffy to open. Margaret tucked
her blankets around him, put the food where he could reach
it, opened the bottle and tried to push its neck between his
lips. With a jerky movement the man's hand came up and
grabbed at the bottle, tilting it up until the yellow stuff was
pouring out of the corners of the hurt mouth. He swallowed
four times and then let his hand fall so that Margaret had to
snatch at the bottle to prevent it from spilling all over him.

"Thanks," he whispered.

She started to sponge the cordial from his jaw with a corner of her skirt, but stopped in a welter of panic—someone
was moving out in the barn. She knelt, quite still, then realized that the lantern was more betraying than any movement—rats scuttle, but they don't send out a steady gold
glow. As she was moving to blow it out she heard the man in
the barn make a different noise, a faint bubbling, Tim.

The big zany shambled through the door, carrying more
straw and an indescribable mixture of old rags. He walked
toward the wounded witch as if he was going to dump his
load on him, then stopped. He stared at the blankets, then at
the lantern, then at Margaret. Then he cooed and added a
quiet little cluck of satisfaction before he took his bundle
over to another corner of the hut and began to spread it
about. Margaret realized that he'd brought his own bedding
to keep the wounded witch warm, and now he intended to
spend the night there to look after him. She decided to leave
the lantern; Lucy was such a lazy slut that she'd never notice
there was one missing when she cleaned and filled them in
the morning.

As she stood up she looked for the first time at the other
thing in the hut, the hulking old engine, bolted down into
the concrete floor, streaked orange and black with dribbles
of rust and the ooze of oil. She fitted her lantern into a nook
where a lot of pipes masked it from three sides, in case
there were cracks in the outside wall where the light could
shine through and betray them. Then she left.

Uncle Peter was in his chair, and Aunt Anne and Lucy were putting supper out on the table, home bread and boiled mutton and turnips. The steamy richness filled the kitchen.

"Where you been, Marge?" he said.

"I'd forgotten to see if there was enough water for the ponies."

"Good lass, but I can't have you traipsing about the farm at all hours of darkness. You must learn to do things while it's still daylight. But never mind this time. Where's that son of mine, though?"

Feet clattered on the stairs and Jonathan rushed into the room, flushed and bright-eyed.

"Sorry I'm late," he said, "but I was looking out of my window and a great big fire started up suddenly in the lane. It doesn't look like an ordinary fire. One minute there wasn't anything, then it was like sunrise. What do you think's happening?"

Uncle Peter jumped to his feet, picked his cloak off the settle and his cudgel from behind the door, and strode growling out. Aunt Anne stood with the ladle in one hand, the other clutching the back of a chair, her face as gray as porridge. Then she sighed, shrugged, and began to spoon meat and gravy and turnips into bowls. Lucy took the big cleaving knife and hacked off clumsy chunks of bread, which she handed around. Aunt Anne mumbled a quick grace and they sat down.

At once Jonathan was talking about a bird he'd seen that afternoon, which he thought might be a harrier. He held a piece of mutton on the point of his knife and waved it over the table to show how the bird had spiraled up out of the valley; then he popped the meat into his neat little mouth (which looked too small to take it) and settled down to chewing. Nobody else said anything. Margaret knew that she ought to be hungry after all that misery and riding and excitement, but the excitement was still buzzing in her, making her blood run too fast through her veins to allow it to settle down to anything so stolid and everyday as eating and digesting. She dipped a morsel of bread into gravy and watched the brown juice soak up through its cells; she ate that slowly, and then picked up the smallest piece of meat on her plate with the point of her knife and managed to swallow that too. Lucy had gobbled, and was already giving herself a second helping. Aunt Anne ate almost nothing.

After twenty minutes Uncle Peter flung through the door, his cheeks crimson above his beard. He tossed his cudgel into the corner.

"Gone!" he cried.

"Gone?" said Aunt Anne, shrilly.

"Gone to his master the Devil!" shouted Uncle Peter. "I tell you, the stones were burning!"

"What does that mean?" said Jonathan in an interested voice.

"They were burning," said Uncle Peter solemnly. "Not much, by the time I came there, but I could see where they'd been blackened with big flames. And they weren't honest Christian flames, neither—the whole lane reeked of the Devil—the stink of wickedness—you know it when you smell it. And the little flames that were left, they were yellow but blue at the edges, not like mortal fire."

"Were the stocks all burned too?" said Margaret. Uncle Peter was too excited to notice how strained her voice came out, but Jonathan glanced sharply toward her.

"Burntest of all," said Uncle Peter. "Roaring and stinking still."

"Oh dear," said Aunt Anne. "I don't know what to think. We've kept your supper warm for you, Pete."

"We'll know tomorrow," said Uncle Peter, "when I've done milking Maisie. I reckon the witch has gone home to his master, and she'll be carrying a full bag."

He sat down and plunged into the business of eating, tearing off great hunks of bread and sloshing them around his platter before stuffing them into the red hole in the middle of his ginger beard, where the yellow teeth chomped and the throat golloped the lumps down. Margaret, who did not like to watch this process, looked away and her eye fell on Lucy. Lucy was a house servant, so she did not speak unless she was spoken to, though she sat at the same table with them all. (Where else was there for her to sit, if she wasn't to share a shed with her poor mad brother?) Now her black

eyes sparkled above her plump red cheeks as she drank the
excitement, looking from face to face; but the moment she
saw Margaret watching her she dropped her glance de-
murely to the table. She was a funny secret person, Margaret thought, just as much a foreigner as the witch, really.
Four years back she'd led Tim into the village—she'd been
twelve then, she said, and Tim must have been about fifteen,
but nobody knew for certain—and asked for shelter. They'd
stayed ever since, but Margaret knew her no better than the
day she came.

The moment Uncle Peter had speared his last chunk of
mutton and thrust it into his mouth, Lucy was on her feet to
take his plate and bring him the big round of cheese. He was
swilling at his mug of rough cider when the door was
racked with knocking. Aunt Anne started nervously to her
feet and Uncle Peter shouted, "Come in!" It was Mr. Gordon,
the sexton, his broad hat pulled down to hide most of his
knobbly face, his shoulders hunched with rheumatism, but
his blackthorn stick held forward in triumph like an emper-
or's staff.

"The Devil has taken his own!" he cried.

"Off to bed with you, children," said Aunt Anne, with a
sudden echo of the brisk command she used to own before
she became so silent. "I'll clear, thank you, Lucy."

Lucy curtsied and said good night in her soft voice and
slipped up the stairs. Margaret kissed her aunt on the cheek,
bobbed to her uncle and went too. Jonathan came last, and
above the noise of his shoes on the bare stairs Margaret
could hear Mr. Gordon and Uncle Peter settling down to
excited talk over the meaning of the magical fire. As she
undressed she saw how extraordinary it was that they
shouldn't even think of petrol—they'd been grown men before the Changes. Then she remembered that she'd only
found the picture of the seaside in a dark cranny at the back
of her mind—a place which she knew she was supposed to
keep shut, without ever having been told so. And Jonathan
was a funny boy, treating the adventure so calmly, knowing
just what to do all the time, thinking things out all the time
behind his ugly little cat-face. He must have remembered
about petrol and machines long ago, if he'd been exploring

in the barn enough to know his way through it in the pitch dark.

She herself remembered about central heating as she rushed the last piece of undressing, wriggled into her flannel nightdress and jumped into bed. Once the house had been warm enough for her to open her presents on Christmas morning, wearing only her pajamas. Why . . .

She sat bolt upright in bed, knowing that if she asked that sort of question aloud Uncle Peter and Mr. Gordon and the others would be stoning *her* for a witch. She shivered, but not with cold this time, and blew out her candle. At once the horrible business of the morning floated up through her mind—the jostling onlookers, and the cheering, and the straining shoulders of the men as they poised their stones for throwing. She tried to shut it out, twice two is four and four is eight and eight is sixteen and sixteen is thirty-two and thirty-two is sixty-four and sixty-four is, is a hundred and twenty-eight and . . . but each time she got stuck the pictures came flooding back. She heard Mr. Gordon cackle exultantly from the door as he left, and Uncle Peter's booming good-nights. Still she lay, afraid to shut her eyes, staring through the diamond-paned window to where Orion was just lifting over the crest of Cranham woods.

Something scratched at the door.

"Who is it?" she croaked.

"Me," whispered Jonathan through the slight creak of the opening door. "I must oil that. Come and listen. Quietly."

She put on her cloak and tiptoed onto the landing. Flickering light came up the stairs as the fire spurted. Jonathan caught her by her elbow in the darkness.

"Stop there," he whispered. "The floor squeaks further on. You can hear from here."

Aunt Anne and Uncle Peter were still in the kitchen, arguing. Uncle Peter's voice was rumbly with cider and not always clear, but Aunt Anne's had a hysterical edge which carried every syllable up to the listeners.

"I tell you I can't stand it any longer," she was saying. "Everything that's happened is wicked, wicked! What harm had that poor man done us this morning, harm that you can prove, prove like you know that if you drop a stone it will

fall? And forcing the children up there to see him die. I kept
Jo back, and I'd do so again, but Marge is like a walking
ghost. Oh, Pete, you must see, it can't be right to do that to
children!"

"Rumble mumble Maisie nigh filled a bucket tonight
when she was dry mumble rumble answer me that woman!"

"Oh, for God's sake, you know as well as I do that you've
only just moved the cows down to the meadow pasture.
They *always* make more milk the first couple of days there."

"Rumble bang shout off you go before I take my cudgel to
you!"

A gulping noise. Aunt Anne was really crying now.

"Wouldn't she help?" whispered Margaret.

"She's too near breaking as it is," whispered Jonathan.
"But Lucy will be useful."

"Lucy! But she's . . ."

"You've never even thought about her, Marge. Just look
what she's managed for Tim. And anyway, Tim's deep in it,
so she'll *have* to help. Thank you for asking about the
stocks. Bed now."

This time Margaret found she could shut her eyes and
there was a different picture in her mind: she'd reined Scrub
up for a breather on the very top of the Beacon and looked
northwest toward Wales. The limestone hill plunged at her
feet toward the Vale; there lay the diminishing copses and
farms, and beyond them the gray smudge which was the
dead city of Gloucester, and beyond that, green so distant
that it was almost the color of smoke—but through those far
fields snaked the gleaming windings of the Severn toward,
in the distant west (often you couldn't be sure whether what
you were seeing was cloud or land or water, but today you
could) the Bristol Channel. The sea.

# Chapter 2

# DOG PACK

The frosts came, and shriveled the last runner beans. Even at midday the air had a tang to it which meant that soon there would be real winter. Any wind made whirlpools of fallen leaves in odd corners.

It was three days before the witch spoke. To either of the children, that is—maybe he talked to Tim, but if so Tim couldn't tell them. And it was dangerous to go down much to the old tractor barn where the wicked machines stood.

"If you've got to go," said Jonathan, "look as if you're making for Tim's shed. Carry something he might need—food or an old rag. Then sneak round the back of the barn. And once you're past Tim's shed walk on a fresh bit of grass each time, or you'll make a path and someone will spot it. You do realize we're stuck with a dangerous job, Marge?"

"Stuck?"

"Well, wouldn't you rather you'd never heard him? Rather someone else had? Then we could have rubbed along as we were."

Margaret didn't know what she'd rather, so she hadn't said anything. Next time she went to the barn she carried a knuckle of mutton with a bit of meat still on it, and actually walked into Tim's shed as if she was going to leave it for him. She looked around at the stinking heaps of straw, with the late-autumn flies hazing about in the dimness, and wondered how she'd never thought about the way Tim lived, any more than she thought about the cows who came squelching through the miry gates to milking. She'd thought far more about Scrub than Tim.

Ashamed, she looked around the dank lean-to to find something she could do now, at once, to make the zany more comfortable. There was nothing, but in her search she saw a triangular hole in the corrugated iron which formed the back of the shed. And on the other side of the hole was the wheel of a wicked machine, a . . . a . . . a *tractor*. Of course, this shed was propped against the back of the barn, and if the hole were larger she could slip through to where the witch lay, and there'd be no danger of leaving a track through the rank grasses below the barn.

She tugged at the ragged edge of metal, and the whole sheet gave and fell out on top of her. It left a hole just like a door. Inside were the derelict machines and the little brick hut in the corner. And inside that were the rusting engine, Tim, and the witch. He looked a little better, but not enough; it was difficult to tell because of the deceiving yellow light from the lantern and because his face was still livid and puffy with bruising. Tim squatted in his corner of the shed, watching her as suspiciously as a bitch watches you when you come to inspect her puppies. Margaret took the bone to him, then knelt beside the witch. She'd brought a corner of fresh bread spread with cream cheese; she broke bits off and popped them into the smashed mouth whenever it opened—it was like feeding a nestling sparrow, except that nestlings are greedy. It took him a long time to chew each piece, and longer still to swallow.

"Looks to me as if he could do with a wash," said a soft voice.

Chill with terror Margaret swung around. Lucy was standing in the doorway, her hands on her hips, her face more foreign than ever—elfish, almost—in the faint light of the lantern. She wasn't looking at Margaret, but down at the wounded witch.

"Yeah," he said with a rasping sigh, "water would be good."

"But how are we going to get it here without anyone . . ." She stopped. In the panicky silence she could hear Tim gnawing a morsel of mutton out from a cranny of bone. She stood up, trying to seem (and feel) like a mistress talking to a servant.

"Lucy," she said hotly, "if you tell anyone . . ."

But Lucy was smiling, and Margaret could think of no threats that would mean anything.

"It's I could be menacing you, Miss Margaret, and not t'other way about. But I'll help you for Tim's sake. I mind him sitting by my bed when I had the measles, afore they took him away, just bubbling, but he made me feel better nor any of the medicines they gave me. He'd have been a doctor, Tim would, supposing he'd been in his right mind."

"Doctor?"

"Leech, then, but a proper un. I'll be fetching hot water. Fruit's what he needs, miss, not that pappy bread."

"What shall I do? Can I help?"

Lucy looked at her again—not her secret, half-mocking glance, but something new, considering, only a little suspicious.

"Aye," she said at last, "mebbe you could. We'll make as if we're mucking out Tim's shed, which I should a done weeks back. The Master's in Low Pasture, and your aunt's too fazed to notice what we do. So I'll go and set the big kettle on the stove, and you could mebbe fork all that straw out of Tim's shed and set light to it. Mind you don't burn his treasures—you'll find 'em under a bit of planking in the back corner."

She slipped out, silent as a stoat. Margaret had to run and scramble over the tow-bars in the dark barn to call after her in a straining whisper, "I'll come and help you with the kettle, Lucy."

Lucy turned, black in the bright rectangular gap where the iron sheet had been, nodded in silence and flitted away.

There was a hayfork by the midden above the orchard. Margaret scrattled the straw in the shed together—it was cleaner than she'd thought, just musty with damp from the bare earth beneath; and really there were no more flies under the low roof than there were in any other shed on the farm. The plank in the corner she left where it was, after inquisitively lifting it to see what Tim's "treasures" were: a broken orange Dinky-toy earth-shifter; a plastic water pistol; the shiny top of a soda siphon; a child's watch which could never tell the time because the knob at the side only made the big and little hands move around the dial together. As she put the plank back Margaret was astonished that she should know what they all were—four days ago they would have been meaningless, except that she'd have known they were wicked.

She picked the driest straw she could see from her heap, twisted it together and took it back into the hut where the witch lay. Tim began to croak with alarm when she opened the lantern to poke it into the flame, so she carried the lantern out into the shed, lit her wisp of straw there and thrust it into the heap. After she'd put the lantern back she stood for several minutes leaning on her fork and watching the yellow stems shrivel into black threads which wriggled as the fire ate into the innards of the pile. Her cheeks were sharp with heat when she began to walk up through the orchard toward the house.

Lucy was in the kitchen, struggling to carry the steaming kettle single-handed. Aunt Anne sat on one side of the stove in an upright chair and Mr. Gordon sat in the rocking chair between the stove and the fire, rocking and clucking. Neither of them looked as though they would pay any more attention to the comings and goings of children than they did to the tortoiseshell butterfly which pattered against the windowpane.

"Can I help you with that, Lucy?" said Margaret.

"If you please, Miss Margaret," said Lucy. "I thought I'd best clean out Tim's shed afore winter sets in."

Margaret picked up a cloth and gripped one handle of the kettle with it. But it wasn't a kettle, she thought. A kettle was a small shiny thing with a cord going in at the back. You didn't put it on the stove, but it got hot from inside because the cord was . . . was electric. This big pan they were edging out through the door, very carefully so that the hot water wouldn't slop over, was a . . . a . . . preserving pan. She looked excitedly at Lucy's down-bent face.

"I say, Lucy, I've just remembered . . ."

"Careful, Miss Margaret, or you'll be spilling it all, and then we'll have our work wasted."

The interruption was soft and easy, but the glance from under the little lace cap was as fierce as a branding iron. Margaret suddenly saw what a comfortable time she'd had of it since the Changes—Scrub to break and ride and care for, a share of housework, only the occasional belting from Uncle Peter to be afraid of. Wary, of course, but never till now Lucy's cowering softness, like the stillness of a mouse when a hawk crosses the sky above it. Not even Jonathan's dangerous adventuring.

Those times were over, since they'd rescued the witch. She would have to cower and adventure with the others. This was what Jonathan had meant about being stuck.

They could never have cleaned the witch without Tim. At first, while Lucy dabbed at the spoiled face, bristly with beard between the scabs, he squatted beside the bedding and watched with the soft glance of a clever spaniel. But as soon as they tried to lift their patient and undress him Tim pushed gently between them and ran his arm under the limp shoulders, lifting the body this way and that while the girls eased the torn and blood-clotted rags off.

"We'd best be burning most of this too," said Lucy. "D'you think you could find some old clothes of the Master's, Miss Margaret—nothing that he'll miss, mind?"

"I'll try," said Margaret. "Jo was right—he is wearing some kind of armor."

"Yeah," said the witch faintly. "Bulletproof, but not rockproof. I figure I got two or three busted ribs, and a busted arm, and I don't seem to move my legs like I used to. You some sort of resistance movement, huh?"

"Resistance?" said Margaret.

"I guessed . . ." said the witch, and paused. "Oh, forget it, you're only kids, anyway. Who knows I'm here?"

"Me and Jonathan and Lucy and Tim," said Margaret. "I heard you groaning under the stones and I told Jonathan and we got Tim to help us bring you down here. Uncle Peter would kill you if he knew, though."

"Us too, mebbe," said Lucy, so softly that Margaret only just caught the words. Then she added in a brisker voice, "Which is your bad arm, mister?"

"Left. Roll me over on my right side and you can unzip my armor."

They had to show Tim what they wanted, and he turned the witch over as gently as a shepherd handling a lamb. The man's legs flopped uncontrolledly, not seeming to move properly with him, like a puppet's. Then the zip puzzled them for a few seconds, but they both remembered in the same instant and reached out to pull the tag down.

"You'd best be looking for them clothes, Miss Margaret," chided Lucy. "If we let him chill off, he'll catch his death, surely."

Margaret walked slowly up through the orchard, coming to terms with this new Lucy, not the slut who didn't fill the lamps or rake out the ashes or scrub the step clean, but a different girl, a stranger, who knew just what needed doing. Rather than risk Mr. Gordon's fierce and knowing glance she climbed the ivy and crawled in through Jonathan's window—much easier by daylight than it had been in the dark. When she tiptoed out onto the landing she saw Jonathan crouched at the top of the stairs; he looked around at her and put his finger to his lips.

"What's happening?" whispered Margaret.

He beckoned, then pointed to the floor; he must be showing her which board creaked, so she stepped over it and crouched by his side. He said nothing, but the steady clack of Mr. Gordon's rocking chair came up the stairs, mixed with his wheezing and clucking.

"He's waiting for her to break," whispered Jonathan at last. "I don't know what to do. He's willing her to it."

"Can you go in and interrupt them?"

"No, I daren't—she's protecting me. She knows, somehow, though I've never told her. And he seems to know she knows."

"Oh." Margaret felt despairing. It was so unlike Jonathan not to have a plan. Well, at least *she* could try.

"Find some of Uncle Peter's old clothes," she whispered, "ones he never uses. Take them down to the witch. Lucy's washing him. I'll do something to stop Mr. Gordon."

"Thank you," said Jonathan, and slipped off down the passage toward Aunt Anne's room. Margaret, her gullet hard with fright, crept back into Jonathan's room, out along the shed roof and down the ivy. It would have to be a lie—a good big one.

When she threw open the kitchen door Mr. Gordon was still rocking and clucking, and now Aunt Anne was leaning forward in her chair like a mouse which has caught the eye of an adder. Neither of them looked around when the door banged against the dresser, though she'd pushed it so hard that the blue cups rattled on their saucers.

"Oh, Aunt Anne, Aunt Anne," she croaked (and her terror was real), "a ginger cat just spoke to me. He said 'Good morning.'"

The rocker stopped its clack. Aunt Anne eased herself back in her chair, gazed at the palm of her left hand, and then turned her head.

"What did you say, darling?" she said dully.

"I went down the lane to see if any of the crab apples had fallen at the back of Mrs. Gryde's, so that we could make some conserve, but before I got there a big ginger cat came out of the hedge from the six-acre and looked at me and said 'Good morning.'"

Mr. Gordon jumped out of the chair, sending his black-thorn stick clattering across the floor. Margaret ran to pick it up for him, but as she knelt his bony hand clawed into her shoulder, so that she dropped the stick again and almost shouted with surprise and hurt. He pulled her close to him; she could see the individual hairs that sprouted from the big wart on the side of his nose. His bloodshot old eyes glittered.

"Mrs. Gryde's cat, that'd be?" he said fiercely.

"No," croaked Margaret. "Hers is quite a little one. This was big, the biggest I've seen, and lame in one leg. It went away up toward the New Wood. Shall I show you?"

Mr. Gordon clucked once or twice, thinking. "Ah," he said at last. "That's where we found the witch. Mebbe he didn't go back to his master after all. Mebbe he turned hisself into a cat—and he'd be lame all right, after the stoning we give him. You bring me along and show me what you seen, lass."

He let go of her shoulder, but gripped it again the instant she'd turned. Aunt Anne had to scrabble for his stick. Then Margaret led him hobbling out into the road, hoping there were no witnesses about; but Mother Fatchet was driving her black pig up the slope toward them. Mr. Gordon stopped her, and the two old people at once began an excited cackling discussion about what might have happened, during which Margaret's invented cat seemed to grow bigger and bigger until she was afraid they wouldn't believe her when she showed them the rabbit run she'd decided on for it to have appeared through—a gravelly place where even the heaviest cat's paw-marks couldn't be expected to show up. But when she showed them the hole they didn't seem to mind that it was small. Mr. Gordon made her tell her lie all over again while he stared hotly up to where the young beeches of New Wood stood russet in the silvery sunlight. Then, at last, he let go of her shoulder and began hobbling up toward the center of the village to roust his cronies out of the pub for another witch-hunt. Mother Fatchet tied her pig to the farm gate and scuttled up the lane so that she should miss none of the blood-soaked fun.

Aunt Anne was at her stove, stirring uselessly at the big gruel pot which simmered there night and day. Margaret slid into the larder, opened one of the little bottles of cordial, poured half of it into a mug and placed that on the stove by Aunt Anne's left hand. Her aunt stopped stirring, picked up the mug and sniffed at it, looked sideways at Margaret, hesitated, then shut her eyes and took three hefty swallows. When she put the mug down she gave a long sigh and reached out to draw Margaret close against her side, as though she was afraid to say thank you out loud, as though even the crannies and shelves of her own kitchen might be full of spies waiting for the betraying word.

It would be dangerous to go back to the barn, Margaret thought—they wouldn't find anything up at the New Wood and then they'd come to look for her to hear her story again. When Aunt Anne let go of her she chose a couple of bruised apples from the larder and ran out to the paddock to talk to Scrub. He was sulking, jealous after three days' neglect, and wouldn't come when she whistled. But Caesar, Jonathan's unloved and melancholy gray, came boredly over and Margaret gave him one of the apples and started to fondle his ears. This was too much for Scrub and he cantered over with a clownish look in his eye as though he'd only just realized she was there. She accepted his pretense and gave him his apple too.

All at once she heard harsh voices shouting on the other side of the road, up in the six-acre; she climbed up onto the second bar of the gate and teetered there trying to crane over the tall hedge. When that wasn't any good she slid across onto Scrub's back and coaxed him along toward the gap further down the field—difficult sitting sideways without saddle or reins, because she had no control at all. But Scrub was in a mood to show how clever he could be, and did what she wanted.

There were eight or nine men standing in a circle just below the New Wood. Three old women in black watched them from twenty yards away. The men all had sticks or cudgels and were taking it in turn to beat something that lay on the grass in the middle of the circle; they shouted at each blow, egging each other on. She could recognize Mr. Gordon by his stoop, and Mr. Syon the smith by his apron, and the two black-bearded brothers from Clapper's Farm. While she was wondering sickly what they'd caught, one of the men struck so hard that he snapped his cudgel; he threw the pieces angrily on the ground and began to walk down across the six-acre toward her. As he came nearer she saw it was one of the stonecutters from the quarry on the Beacon: nearer still, and his cheeks were burning with cider though it was still only the middle of the morning.

"Think your uncle would mind if you lent us a spade, lass?" he shouted.

"I'll get one," Margaret shouted back. She slid off Scrub's back, climbed the fence and ran around to the farmyard. The stonecutter was already staggering in through the gate when she came out of the shed where the garden tools were kept. Aunt Anne had come to the kitchen door to watch.

"What did you find?" asked Margaret as she handed the big man the spade. Her fear and disgust must have sounded just like excitement to him.

"Ah," he answered with gloating pleasure, "he were a clever one, but he weren't so clever as he thought he were. He'd changed hisself into a rook, you see, so's to be able to fly away from where Davey Gordon could smell him out, but he'd forgot as how his arm was broke. The cat you saw was lame, weren't he, missy? So now he was a rook, his wing was broke, and he couldn't fly away after all."

The man gave a bellowing, cider-smelling laugh.

"We smashed him up, that we did," he shouted. "He won't do no more witching now. Thankee, missy—I'll fetch your spade back in half an hour. You done a good morning's work, you have."

He stumped out, too drunk to notice how white Margaret had turned, or how she reeled and hugged the well-pump to keep herself from falling. When the whole hillside and valley had stopped slopping around she found Aunt Anne standing anxious beside her.

"You'd best be away for a few hours, Marge," she said. "If I gave you a pot of damson cheese you could ride over to Cousin Mary's in the Vale. I should have sent it weeks back, but it slipped my mind. I'll pack you up a bit of bread and bacon, too, for your dinner. Mr. Gordon's sure to come round talking to Uncle Peter then, so you'd much best be somewhere else."

"Oh, thank you, Aunt Anne. I'll get Scrub ready."

Twenty minutes later Margaret was clear of the village, riding sidesaddle as she always did. She'd waved to old Mr. Sampson digging his cabbage patch by the almshouses; she'd craned over the Dower House wall to see the yew trees all clipped into shapes of animals; she had sniffed the thymy air as they came out of the woods, and leaned right down over Scrub's mane as the pony took the steep bank up the common grazing ground below the Beacon; it was just like any of a hundred other rides, hill and valley exactly the same as they'd always been, as though nothing had happened to change her world four days ago.

Scrub was skittish and restless with lack of exercise, tossing his head sideways and up as though he wanted to get a better grip of the bit; so she let him canter all the way up the steady slope to the corner of the cemetery, where no one had been buried since the Changes came because people preferred to be buried in the churchyard even if it meant jostling the bones of long-dead generations. As they swept around the corner they hurtled into the middle of a swirling and squawking white riot—they'd gone full tilt into the flock of village geese. Scrub reared and skittered sideways with an awkward bouncy motion, but Margaret had had half a second to see what was going to happen, so she gripped the pommel of her saddle tightly, allowed him a few moments to be stupid (he knew all about geese, really) and then reined him firmly in.

The geese subsided into angry gossip. Mother Fatchet's eldest grandchild was supposed to be herding them but he'd taken time off to swing on a low branch of one of the cemetery pines; now he jumped down, picked up his long stick, put his thumb in his mouth and stood watching her sulkily. Margaret said good morning to him as she rode on, but he didn't answer. For the first time she realized how suspicious everybody was nowadays—suspicious of strangers, suspicious of neighbors. Anyone could betray you. Perhaps other villages were different—friendly and easy—but this village was like a bitch with a hurt foot: move and it snarled.

Of course, people didn't *have* to like each other. Even sweet Aunt Anne had quarreled with jolly Cousin Mary, quarreled twenty years ago about a silver teapot. Now they never visited, never spoke; Cousin Mary sent Aunt Anne a pot of honey in high summer and Aunt Anne sent Cousin Mary a pot of damson cheese in late autumn, and that was all.

But nobody liking or trusting *anybody*—it couldn't have been like that before the Changes.

She made poor Scrub scrabble up the loose-stoned path to the very ridge of the Beacon, though it was just as short and much easier to go around the side. Another curious thing

struck her: the great earth ramparts of the Beacon had been
built thousands of years ago, before the Romans came, but
she only knew that—only knew about the Romans coming,
too—because she'd been told it before the Changes, when
she was less than nine. Nobody told you that sort of thing
nowadays: there wasn't any history. Everyone talked and
behaved as though England had always been the same as it
was now, and always would be; the only thing to mark one
year off from another was a rick catching fire, or a bad
harvest, or a big tree falling, or a witch being caught and
stoned. No one ever mentioned the Changes, if they could
help it.

And that was how she'd thought herself until four days
ago, until Jonathan had spattered the petrol over the stocks
and she'd remembered that seaside filling station.

She reined Scrub in for a breather at the very top of the
Beacon, where the old triangulation point had been (some
fanatic had managed to knock the cement into fragments
with a sledgehammer), and looked at the enormous landscape with new eyes. Always before it had been the dim hills
of Wales which had excited her, and the many-elmed green
leagues between the two escarpments, and the glistening
twists of the Severn. Now it was the gray smudge in the
middle, Gloucester, the dead city.

Always before she had looked away from it, as though it
were something horrible, a stone and slate disease. Now she
wanted to see what it was like since all the people had left it.
You couldn't live in a big city now: there was nothing to live
on, no one to buy from or sell to; besides, the whole place
must smell of the wickedness of machines.

Brookthorpe is the first village in the Vale, just as Edge is
the last village in the hills. Margaret seldom rode down into
the Vale, but she found a way by lanes and footpaths, cutting across fields where no path led in the right direction.
There was much less arable land since tractors were gone,
and cows were mostly herded by children, so many of the
hedges had been allowed to go into gaps.

Cousin Mary had moved. A pretty young woman was living in her cottage and the old apple tree had been cut down.
The new owner said that Cousin Mary had gone to live with

a friend at Hempsted, right down by the river. She told Margaret how to get there.

The Vale has a quite different feel to it from the hills. It's not just that the fields are flatter and most of the houses are brick: the air smells different, and the people have a different look, sly and knowing; the farms are dirtier, too, and the lanes twist for no good reason (up in the hills they twist to take a slope the best way, or so as not to lose height when one is following a contour). Margaret had to ask her way several times, and the answer always came in a strange, soft voice with a sideways look.

She skirted a dead housing development, came to a rotary and rode north along a big road for nearly a mile, looking for a lane to the left. The buildings by the road were rusting old factories and garages, and sometimes a little group of shops with their windows broken and all their goods stolen. Cars and trucks rusted in forecourts, and pale tatters of advertising posters dangled from walls. One place, an open-air used-car mart, had been set on fire, for all the cars were twisted and charred; you'd only have to walk along the lines of them, taking off the filler-caps and poking blazing rags in with a stick—dangerous, but some people were fanatical against machines.

As soon as she'd turned off along the lane to Hempsted, Margaret had a disappointment. A bridge took her over a river, which she at first thought must be the Severn, only it seemed too mean and narrow. She stopped on the bridge and gazed north and south, and saw that the river ran unnaturally straight, and that there were man-made embankments on both sides and a path running all along its bank. So it wasn't a mean and narrow river but a man-made thing, a noble great canal, far wider than the silted thin affair that ran through Stroud. This wasn't dug for narrow barges, but for proper ships; she could see from the color of the water, a flinty gray, that it was deep enough to take seagoing vessels.

Supposing that they could get under the bridge. But no, that wouldn't be necessary, because the whole bridge was made to swivel sideways, out of the way of passing ships. There was even a crankhandle to turn it with.

She was still wondering whether the bridge would really

have swung if she'd had the nerve to turn the handle, when she came into Hempsted. Cousin Mary's new house was a little cottage close in under the churchyard wall. Cousin Mary herself was busy forking dung into the tiny garden, but she stopped her work to receive the precious pot of damson cheese and to ask formally after all her relations up in the hills. She seemed to be not really "living with a friend" as the woman in Brookthorpe had suggested, but to be more of a servant here, like Lucy was on the farm. But she offered to take Margaret into the cottage and show her the place where she'd spilled boiling water on her leg, and it wouldn't heal because Mrs. Barnes down the road had put a spite on her. Margaret said, "No, thank you." There was a great tattered bandage around Cousin Mary's leg, all yellow with new dung and older dirt—no wonder it wouldn't heal. She said good-bye, rode back to the little lane through Hempsted and turned left. She was going to see what Gloucester looked like.

There were houses all along the lane, with fields behind them. Their windows were broken and their tiles were all awry. In a gap between two such houses a man was digging; he stood up and shouted to her as she passed but she couldn't catch what he said—it sounded like something about dogs—so she just waved cheerfully to him. From the slight rise on which Hempsted stands she could see the tower of the cathedral, and the lane led straight toward it. She felt gay, almost heroic, with her adventure, so it took her longer than it usually would have to sense that Scrub was becoming more and more uneasy. Only when he shied across the lane at a big chestnut leaf that floated down in front of his nose did Margaret pay attention to his feelings, and by then they were on the edge of the city itself.

A level crossing over a light railway seemed to mark the real boundary, and there she almost turned back. She was hungry, and Scrub clearly was against going on. But it seemed cowardly, having come so far. What would Jonathan have thought of her? So she dismounted and led Scrub across the rails. The nape of her neck began to prickle; the long, low buildings on either side of the lane were windowless and very silent; by the side of the railway she spotted a bar of rusty iron as thick as a man's thumb and two feet long. She picked it up before she remounted—any weapon was better than none.

The echo of Scrub's hooves tocked back at her off blank walls. In one place the surface of the road had heaved up where frost had reached a pocket of underground water, a burst main, perhaps. On the other side the road became a bridge.

It was a bridge over a canal, the same canal as they'd crossed earlier. On her left was a series of V-shaped gates, two facing inward to hold the water of the canal in, and one outward to control the fast-flowing river which swept round the long curve beyond. On her right were the docks, a wide basin of water surrounded by grim, tall warehouses, and cranes and derricks. Sunken barges lay along the quays, all green with weed. There were two proper ships, with masts and funnels, further down the basin, but one of them was leaning sideways in the water. And against the left-hand quay was a line of three smaller boats, two floating, one waterlogged; the floating ones sat oddly in the water, but looked as though that was how they were meant to be, stern down, bows up, stubby and pugnacious; their funnels were far too big for them. Margaret remembered a jigsaw which she'd been given once when she was ill, a picture of the *Queen Elizabeth* docking. There'd been boats like this in it. They were tugs.

Despite the peeling paint and the rust and the streaks of gulls' droppings they looked undaunted and powerful, an example of the forgotten forces which were on the children's side, if they could be summoned into use again. Margaret began to feel cheerful once more.

But not Scrub. As they rode on, occasionally catching a glimpse of the cathedral tower to guide them, he was tense and quivering. Margaret talked to him to keep his spirits up, but then the sound of her own voice seemed so naked in the empty street that she let it dribble into a whisper, and then into silence. She patted him halfheartedly on the neck and wished she hadn't come.

The street bent left, in the wrong direction, following the curve of the flowing water. This again couldn't be the true

Severn—it was too narrow and controlled—but it must be part of it. Then the street jinked right, away from the water, and crossed a much wider road which led back toward the hills. Margaret turned right.

She almost missed the cathedral because it lay off to the left of this larger road down a narrow alley, but she saw the knobbly pinnacles out of the corner of her eye and wheeled Scrub around into the cathedral grounds. The grass was long and rank, which once had been shaved as close as a mower could be set; it didn't even seem to have been nibbled by rabbits. All the doors were locked fast, so she rode around the gray mass wondering what it was like now inside; she had a dim memory of heavy and shadowed arches, with candles and high, lacy singing; but that might have been some other church. She rode back into the main street and on down to a big crossroads. The sun was halfway down the sky now, and that meant that the proper direction must be . . .

But as she considered the position of the shadows a white mongrel terrier ran out of a lane to her left, threw back its head and howled. The howl was answered by others from all around, and at once the terrier, very lean and dirty but very quick, sprang snarling toward her. Three more dogs wheeled out, baying, further down the left-hand road. Scrub shied, but she kept her seat and shouted and shook the reins. At once he was off up the street in front, the terrier yelping at his heels. Margaret glanced over her shoulder and saw that another dozen dogs poured out of side alleys and were tearing down the road after her. Scrub was already moving at a full gallop, jarring and frightening on the hard uneven road; there was no point in trying to make him go any faster—if he panicked they'd both fall at some pothole. She looked over her shoulder again. Now there were at least thirty dogs in the pack, trailing out all down the street, with the short-legged descendants of corgis and basset hounds far behind while the long-legged Labrador mongrels yelped at Scrub's heels.

A big, wolfish creature with a lot of Alsatian in him made a spurt and leaped, jaws wide, for Scrub's flank. But Margaret happened to be balanced just right to whang him across the forehead with her iron bar. She heard a bone crack and saw him tumble head over heels, and then her eye was caught by an interruption in the level of the road ahead. There had been some sort of explosion—gas perhaps—and fifty yards further on the whole width of the tarmac had been thrown up into a rough barrier which would slow a horse to a walk while the dogs came streaming over it. The streets on either side ran off at right angles, far too sharp to turn a galloping pony into. As they neared the upheaval she saw that right against the left-hand wall, up on the pavement, there was a gap. Scrub had been galloping down the middle of the road, between the blank traffic signals and unreadable police notices, but she coaxed him over toward the wall. He took the curb cleverly, flashed through the gap, pecked as his off forefoot banged into a loose brick, but recovered.

Only a rangy black Labrador was still with them now. Scrub could gallop faster than the dogs could run, but he couldn't keep it up for as long as they could—at least not with a girl and the heavy sidesaddle to carry as well. He would have to ease his pace soon. The black dog bounded along, just out of reach; Margaret lashed at it twice with her bar, but missed; the second time she so nearly unbalanced herself from the saddle that she had to let the weapon drop. Desperately she unbuckled her saddlebag, felt for a slice of bacon, held it out as one holds a chocolate for a begging lapdog, then tossed it in front of the beast's jaws. It slashed at the morsel and missed, but the smell of meat was enough to make it slide to a stop, turn and investigate. The rest of the pack engulfed it while it was still swallowing, then came on. Margaret dug into the saddlebag and flung piece after piece of her picnic behind her, until the street was filled with squabbling hounds. Only the slowest ones came too late to share the feast, and they followed halfheartedly on her trail. Soon she was a hundred yards ahead of the nearest one. Next time she looked around they'd all given up.

Scrub took some slowing, though. The road curved through a section of the city where all the houses had caught fire; it ran under a railway bridge and straightened again before he could be induced to canter, and then to trot.

They were still going a fair lick when they came out into open fields and the road tilted toward the hills.

Two miles further on, among inhabited cottages once more, she dismounted and led him. His coat was rough and bristling, his cheeks and neck rimed with drying foam. Every now and then he tensed and gave a great heaving shudder. When the hill really began to slope steeply, beyond the turning for Upton, she led him onto a wide piece of grassy verge to graze and rest; there were two crusts of bread and a strip of bacon fat left for her lunch, and now it was nearly teatime, but she ate them thankfully, thinking that there are worse things than hunger. Then she looked over his hooves, though it was too soon to see how bruised he'd been by the punishing gallop along the tarmac.

They went home very slowly, Margaret walking most of the way. It was dark before they started down through the long wood that screened the village from the north, and she was already far later than even Aunt Anne's merciful errand would give her an excuse for; so just before she turned the lane where the farm lay she picked up a small stone and rammed it into the groove between Scrub's near front shoe and the tenderer flesh. She led him into the farmyard convincingly lame.

But all the playacting she'd prepared, all the believable lies, all the excuses—they were unnecessary. Uncle Peter was cock-a-hoop at the best milk yield of the year; Aunt Anne wanted to know all about Cousin Mary's new house; Jonathan talked busily about the fox cubs in Low Wood; Lucy was her usual secret self. Any stranger coming in would have thought them a nice, dull, contented family enjoying a plain supper after an ordinary day.

# Chapter 3

# THERE'S WICKEDNESS ABOUT

Margaret was full of sleep—as full as a ripe Victoria plum is of juice—but something was shaking her. Her dream turned it into a bear, and she was too heavy to run away, and she was opening her mouth to cry out for help when she was all at once awake. Not very awake; longing for the warm and private world of sleep again; but awake enough to know that it was Jonathan who was shaking her and the world was too dangerous to cry for help in. She tried to say "Go away" but the noise she made was a guggling grunt, a noise such as a bear might make while shaking a person.

"Oh, wake up, Marge," whispered Jonathan impatiently.

"I'm asleep. Go away."

"Never mind that. He wants to talk to us."

"Who does? The witch?"

"His name's Otto."

"Oh, all right."

She rolled on her back and with a strong spasm of will-power forced herself to sit up while the frosty night sent fingers of gooseflesh down her shoulder blades. Jonathan, thinking ahead as usual, had gathered her clothes onto the table below the window, where she could just see by starlight which way around she was picking them up; but she didn't feel warm even when she was dressed, and stood shivering.

"Shall I go down and get you a coat?" he whispered.

"No," said Margaret, remembering all the betraying creaks in the passage and on the stairs. "I'll be all right. I suppose we're going out through your window. What time is it?"

"Nearly midnight. I took some thistles to bed to keep me awake. Put your cushions under your blankets to make it look as if you're still in bed—Mother might look in—she often goes creeping round the house in the middle of the night. That'll do."

Outside, the frost was deep and hard, the true chill of winter. The stars were thick and steady between the apple branches, the grass crisp under her feet; dead leaves which had been soggy that morning crackled when she trod on them; the air was peppery in her nostrils. It would be hunting weather tomorrow.

As they stepped into the heavy blackness of Tim's shed Jonathan caught her by the arm and stopped her.

"He's ill," he whispered, "and Lucy says she thinks he's getting worse. I've put a splint on his arm and I tried to strap up his ribs, but I don't know if it's any use. He can't move his legs at all. Perhaps he'll die, and all we'll have to do is bury him. But if he's too ill to think and then he doesn't die, we've got to know what we're all going to do. We'd have settled it this morning without you, but Lucy said he was too tired after his washing; he took one of the last of his pills, which are for when something hurts too much, and they make him sleep for twelve hours. So he should be awake now."

She couldn't see at all, but let him guide her through the torn gap in the bare wall, between the bruising tractors and into the engine hut. Here there was a gentle gleam from the shrouded lantern, as faint as the light from the embers of a fire after the lamps are put out.

Lucy was asleep on a pile of straw in the corner, but twitched herself wide awake the moment they came in. Tim was already awake, bubbling quietly, watching them, sitting so close to the lantern that his shadow covered all the far wall. The witch—Otto—was awake too, his eyes quick amid the bruised face. His wounds looked even worse now that the blood and dirt had been washed away, because you could see how much he was really hurt.

"Welcome to Cell One of the British Resistance Movement," he said in his croaking voice. "I'm Otto."

"I'm Margaret."

"Pleased to meet you. I got a fever coming on, and we should get things kind of sorted before. I could have tried earlier, but I figured you were some kind of trap. But Jo tells me I owe you my life, young lady. Such as it is."

"It was Jonathan really," said Margaret. "I wouldn't have known what to do."

"Well, thanks all the same. You reckon they'll stone me all over again if they find me?"

"Yes," said Jonathan.

"And what'll they do to you?" said Otto.

Margaret and Jonathan glanced at each other, and then across at Lucy. She shook her head slightly, meaning that they mustn't tell him, but his eyes were sharp and his mind quick with the coming fever. He understood their glances, plain as speaking.

"Kill you too?" he whispered. "Kids? What kind of folk are they, for God's sake?"

"Not everywhere," said Margaret quickly. "I mean I don't think it's the same all over England. I was wondering about that this morning. This village has gone specially sour, don't you think, Jo?"

"I don't know. I hope so, for the other villages' sake."

"They're so bored," said Margaret. "They haven't anything to do except get drunk and be cruel."

"It's more than that," said Jonathan slowly. "They've done so many awful things that they've *got* to believe they were right. The more they hurt and kill, the more they're proving to themselves they've been doing God's will all along. What do you think, Lucy?"

"That's just about it," said the soft voice from the corner.

"And what started it all?" said Otto.

"The Changes," said Margaret and Jonathan together.

"Huh?"

"We aren't allowed to talk about them," said Margaret. "But everyone woke up feeling different. Everyone started hating machines. A lot of people went away, and the rest of us have gone back and back in time, until . . ."

"But why?" said Otto.

"I don't think anybody knows," said Jonathan.

The girls shook their heads. Tim bubbled. The witch was silent for half a minute.

"Let's try a different tack," he said. "You three don't think machines are wicked. Nor my friend Tim, neither."

"Tim never did," said Lucy.

"I did until four days ago," said Margaret. "But I hadn't thought about them for ages. And I still don't *like* them."

"I do," said Jonathan. "It happened in that very hot week we had during haymaking; I was lugging water out to the ponies and I suddenly felt, Why can't we use the standpipe tap again?"

"Me too," said Lucy, "only it was the stove. I was cleaning it, and I remembered electric cookers didn't need cleaning —not every day, leastways."

"But everyone's afraid to say," said Jonathan.

"It's only worn off some people," said Margaret. "All the men still seem to believe it."

"Course they do," whispered Lucy fiercely. "It means everyone's got to do just what they says."

"It might be something to do with children's minds," said Jonathan in a detached voice. "Not being so set in their ways of thinking."

"Let it go," said the witch restlessly. "You'd best just cart me someplace else and leave me to fend for myself."

The three children were silent, staring at him.

"We can't," said Jonathan at last.

"Why not? You got me here."

"What about Tim?" said Jonathan.

"I don't think he'd let us," said Margaret.

"That he wouldn't," said Lucy.

They all looked to where Tim, scrawny and powerful, crouched amid the tousled straw. There was another long silence.

"Besides," said Jonathan, almost in a whisper, "d'you think you'd ever sleep easy again afterward, Marge?"

She shook her head. There was stretching silence again.

"Where do you come from?" said Jonathan at last.

"America. The States."

They looked at him blankly.

"Davy Crockett," he said. "Cowboys. Injuns. Batman."

Forgotten images stirred.

"Why did you come?" said Margaret. "You must have known it was dangerous."

"They wanted to know what was happening in these parts," said the witch. "I'm a spy. I had a little radio, and I was in the woods up yonder reporting back to my command ship when your folk burst in on me."

"Mr. Gordon smelled your wireless," said Jonathan. "He's like that with machines. You mean that this hasn't happened to the whole world? Only England?"

"England, Scotland, Wales," said the witch. "Not Ireland. Well, then, if Tim won't let you dump me somewhere, how are you going to keep me here?"

"I bring food for Tim," said Lucy. "I can bring enough for you, easy as easy. You won't be eating much, from the look of you."

"I don't like it," he muttered, more to himself than to them.

"We'll work out a story," said Margaret, "something they'll want to believe and that fits in with what they know."

She told them about the cat and the rook.

"And I do have a broken arm," muttered the witch when she'd finished. He was looking much iller now.

"Please, miss," said Lucy, "he's had enough of talking for now."

"All right," said Margaret, "we'll go."

She stood up, but Jonathan stayed where he was.

"What're we going to do if we think it's becoming too risky to keep him here?" he said. "We must have a plan."

"Yes," muttered the witch, "a plan. A man can plan. Can a

man plan? Dan can plan, Anne. Nan can fan a pan, man. Dan . . . Dan . . ."

"He doesn't know what he's saying," said Lucy. "My dad went that way, sometimes, but it was drink did it to him. We shouldn't have kept him talking so long. I'm worried for him, I am."

"We'll have to think of something without him," said Jonathan. "Are you going to stay here all night, Lucy?"

"Aye," she said.

"But will you be all right?" said Margaret fussily. "It doesn't look very comfortable."

Lucy looked at her slyly out of the corner of her eyes.

"I've slept worse," she said. "And it's one less bed to make, isn't it, miss?"

Outside the night air was cold as frozen iron. The moon was up now, putting out half the stars and making the shadows of the orchard trees crisscross the path, so black and hard that you lifted your feet for fear of stumbling over them.

"Jo," said Margaret, "I . . ."

He caught her elbow in an urgent grip; he seemed to know just where she was in spite of the dark. He put his mouth so close to her ear that she could feel the warm droplets condensing in her hair, like a cow's breath.

"Not out here," he whispered. "Sounds are funny at night. Inside."

She went up the ivy first, letting him push her feet into toeholds to save the noise of scrabbling among the hard leaves. She was shivering as she crawled along the wall and in through the window; by the time she was sitting on the edge of his bed, cold was all she could think about. Jonathan came into the room as quietly as a hunting owl, shut the window, opened his big chest (no creak—he must have oiled the hinges) and brought out a couple of thick furs. They wrapped the softness around themselves, hair side inside, and sat together on the rim of the mattress, as close as roosting hens, trying to feel warm by recalling what warmth had once been like.

"What were you going to say, Marge?" he whispered.

"I went right into Gloucester today. A pack of wild dogs

chased me, but that wasn't it. Jo, there are real boats in the town; there's a sort of harbor in the middle of it, with a big canal full of water. If we could get him into one of those and make it go, we might be able to get him away."

"Sailing boats?"

"No, tugs. They sit a funny way in the water as if they were made for pulling things. Do you remember, we used to have a jigsaw puzzle?"

"I had a toy tug. I used to play with it in my bath, but the water always got into the batteries."

"Will these have batteries?"

"Don't be stupid. They'll have proper engines, diesel I should think. If there's a harbor, there should be big tanks with diesel oil in them; perhaps Otto will know how to make it go—he's an engineer, he told us while we were washing him. Lucy's marvelous: she doesn't seem to mind anything."

"One of them's sunk, Jo, but the other two look all right."

"It's been five years, Marge. Engines get rusty, specially sitting down in the water like that. I don't know if you could take a canal boat out to sea—you'd have to be very lucky with the weather."

"But it wasn't that sort of canal, Jo. It was big—twenty yards across, and there were proper ships there, sea ships."

"Oh. Where did the canal lead, then? Out into the Severn?"

"I don't know, but not where I saw, about two miles out of Gloucester. Why do you think it's still full of water? It's much higher than the river."

"They probably built it so that streams keep it filled up. The river wiggles all over the place and goes up and down with the tide and it's full of sandbanks too, I expect. It'd be useful to have a straight canal going out to sea, which you could rely on to have the same amount of water in it always. There'd have to be a lock at the ends, of course."

"What's a lock?"

"Two gates to keep the water from running away when a canal goes downhill or out to sea. You can make the water between them go up and down so that you can get a barge through."

"There were two gates—three gates—at one end, but I don't see how they'd work."

"I've explained it badly. I'll draw you a picture tomorrow. But even if the tugs don't actually go they might be a good place to hide the witch in."

"Provided the dogs don't swim out. They were horrible, Jo."

"Poor Marge. I'll ask him what he thinks tomorrow. Bed now."

But next morning, while Margaret was ladling porridge into the bowls Lucy held for her, the girls' eyes met. Lucy gave a tiny shake of the head, a tiny turndown of the corners of the mouth, before she moved away; so Margaret knew that the witch must be worse. It was a funny feeling, being part of a plot, sharing perilous secrets with somebody you never really thought of as a proper person, only a rather useless and lazy servant. But it was exciting too, especially being able to speak a language they both understood but which Uncle Peter and Aunt Anne didn't even see or hear being spoken.

After breakfast she helped Lucy clear and wash up and then make all the beds, a job she especially hated. Uncle Peter had hired a man to clear the undergrowth in Low Wood and tie all the salable sticks into bundles of bean poles and switches; this meant that he had to go and work alongside the man, partly from pride and partly to be certain he got every last groat of his money's worth out of him. And that meant that poor Jo had to muck out the milking shed after the first milking and take the fourteen cows down to pasture, and then do all the farmyard jobs which Uncle Peter would usually have done. It was midmorning before any of them was free. They couldn't all slink down to the barn, and Margaret was the least likely to be missed.

The witch was very ill, she could see at once; flushed and tossing, his eyes shut and his breath very fast and shallow. The splint on his arm was still tight in its place, but she didn't like to think about his ribs as he fidgeted his shoulders from side to side. Tim knelt at his good elbow, gazing into his face and bubbling very quietly; when the witch's feverish thrashings threw the blankets aside Tim waited for the first faint beginning of a shiver and then drew them back over him as gently as snow falling on pasture. The

moment the gray lips moved, Tim was holding a little
beaker to them and carefully tipping a few drops into the
dry cranny. There was nothing Margaret could do which
Tim couldn't do better, so she sat down with her back
against the engine, taking care to arrange a piece of sack
behind her so that the rusty iron shouldn't leave its betraying orange streaks down her shoulders.

The witch fidgeted and muttered. Tim babied him, eased
water into the tense mouth, bubbled and cooed. When Margaret had been watching for nearly half an hour in the dim
light and was just deciding to leave, the witch sighed suddenly and deeply and the tenseness went out of his body.
His head lay back on the straw, with his mouth open in a
sloping O, like a chicken with the gapes. But this time Tim
didn't pour any water into it; instead he watched for several
minutes, at first with intense concern but gradually re-
laxing. At last he turned to Margaret, bubbled briefly and
shambled out. She was in charge now.

Nothing happened in the first twenty minutes of her
watch. The witch slept unmoving. The harsh lines of action
relaxed into weakness until she could see how young he
really was. Twenty? Twenty-one? She wondered how many
times this had all happened before—the soldier, hunted and
wounded, hopeless, lying feverish on dirty straw in some
secret place while the yellow lamp burned slowly away.
Hundreds of times, after hundreds of battles. But *this*
time . . .

Then the lamp burned blue for a second, recovered,
reeked with black fumes and went out.

Margaret sat in the dark, not knowing what to do. She
could go up to the house and refill the lamp, or just get a
new one; but it would be a funny thing to be seen doing in
midmorning. And it would mean leaving him alone. And if
she stumbled and made a noise in the dark she might wake
him and sleep was better than medicine, Aunt Anne always
said. She stayed where she was; it was quiet and warm and
dark, and after the panics of yesterday and the busyness of
the night she was as tired as a babe at dusk.

Voices woke her. Her legs were numb and creaking with

the pain of long stillness, but she dursn't move because one of the voices was Mr. Gordon's.

"I smell summat," he grumbled.

"Smell, Davey?" said Uncle Peter's voice.

"Arrgh, not smelling with my nose—in my heart I smell it. There's wickedness about, Peter."

"Ah, 'tis nobbut those old engines in the big barn. There's a whole herd of 'em in there, Davey, but they're dead, dead."

"Mebbe you're right," said Mr. Gordon after a pause. "Mebbe you're not. That zany of yourn, Peter, what do you reckon to him?"

"Tim?" said Uncle Peter. Margaret could hear the lilt of surprise in his voice. "He's not in his right wits, but he's as strong as an ox."

"Mebbe, mebbe," said Mr. Gordon. "He'll bear watching, Peter. They're proper cunning, witches are. I wouldn't put it past 'em."

"Making out to be a zany, you mean," said Uncle Peter, still surprised. "But Tim's been with us these four years, and *I've* seen no sign of it. And why, Davey, I told you about the milk, didn't I—how much Maisie gave after we stoned t'other witch up in the stocks? But if Tim was one . . ."

"Your missus don't reckon 'twas more than a change of pasture as made the cattle give so well," said Mr. Gordon sharply.

"Don't you listen to what Anne says," said Uncle Peter with a growl. Mr. Gordon began to cluck. Very slowly, with a rustling like a cow browsing through long grass, they moved away up the orchard. It was minutes before she dared to shift a leg and endure the agonies of pins and needles. Just as the witch was stirring again there came the sound of someone moving quietly through the main barn; the door of the hut rasped as the rusty hinges moved.

"Why are you in the dark?" said Jonathan's voice, very low.

"The lamp went out," whispered Margaret.

"There's another one," he said. "You should have lit it from the old one before it went out. I'll run up to the house and fetch a new light."

"I'm sorry. I didn't know. Be careful, Jo—Mr. Gordon's been nosing round outside."

"Yes, I saw him. They've gone up to the pub, the Seven Stars. I won't be long."

The witch looked no better when the light came, despite his little sleep. Margaret tried to dribble a sip of water between his parted lips as she'd seen Tim doing, but made a mess of the job and spilled half of it down the stubble on his chin. Then she told Jonathan what she'd heard.

"We'll shift Otto as soon as we can, down to those tugs of yours in Gloucester Docks," said Jonathan. "No one goes there, and it's halfway home for him. If only we can last out till the snow comes we can take him down on the logging sledge."

"That'll be at least a month."

"I know. Will you tell Lucy or shall I? About Tim?"

"Tim?"

"What you told me Mr. Gordon said. They like the feel of killing now, that lot—smashing up rooks won't keep them happy for long. They want a real person, human, but somebody who doesn't matter to anyone."

"Except Lucy," said Margaret.

"They wouldn't think she counted. And even if Otto wasn't here, if he was really dead, they'd come and search and find Tim's treasures and stone him for that."

"Jo, oughtn't you to come and see the tugs?"

"Father'll want me on the farm too much."

"Couldn't you sprain an arm or something—something that didn't stop you riding?"

"I suppose so. I ought to have a look at that canal too. I want to know how it gets out into the sea."

"Well, we've got a month," said Margaret. "We'll just have to be careful. I'll go and tell Lucy. Do you think Tim understands about being secret?"

"Sure of it—he's more like a wild animal than a person in some ways. I've noticed he never comes straight down here nowadays."

"How wrong in his mind do you think he really is, Jo?"

"What do you mean?"

"If he were in a country with proper doctors, like there

used to be when we were small, do you think they could
make him all right?"

"I don't know. Perhaps. We'll ask Otto when he gets better."

They sat in the yellow gloom for several minutes. All the
bright outside world seemed more dangerous than this secret cave with the sick man in it; but when Tim came back
they got up wordlessly and left.

Margaret found Lucy putting away a big basket of late-
picked apples on the racks in the apple loft. She did it very
badly, not looking to see whether any of them were bruised,
and sometimes even shoving them so roughly into place
that they were sure to get new bruises. Margaret started to
tell her off, checked herself in mid-nag and said, "I'm sorry.
Let me do it."

Lucy stepped away from the basket with her secret smile
and Margaret's irritation bubbled inside her like milk coming up to boil over. With a wrench of will she stopped herself saying anything and began to stack the apples on the
slats, gentling them into place so that none of them touched
each other but no space was wasted. It was a soothing job;
after she'd done the first row she told Lucy what she'd overheard Mr. Gordon saying about Tim. She finished her story
just when the basket was empty, so she turned it over and
sat on it. Lucy settled opposite, onto an old crate, biting
away at a hangnail.

"Aye," she said at last, "that's just about Mus' Gordon's
way. What did Master Jonathan say?"

"He said I was to tell you."

"He didn't have a plan, then, miss?"

"He thought we should try and move the witch down to
Gloucester—I saw some boats in the harbor where he could
hide—as soon as the first snows come and we can use the
sledge. Perhaps Tim could go with him."

"That'll be a month, maybe."

"Yes, at least."

"But will the old men stay happy till then, without another creature to smash up, miss?"

"I don't know. I think we might be able to invent one or
two things to keep them busy."

"Maybe."

"Lucy . . ."

"Yes, miss."

"I was talking to Jonathan about Tim. If he had proper doctors, like there were before the Changes, do you think they would be able to put him right in his mind?"

"That's why they took him away, miss. They put him in a special school, they called it. They said it was probably too late, but it was worth trying. Then, when the Changes come, my mum and dad took the babies to France—there were two of 'em, a boy and a girl. They wanted to take me, too, but the Changes were a lovely reason for not having to bother with Tim no more, so they was going to leave him behind. It wasn't right, I thought, so I run away and found him and took him away. Sick with worry they teachers was, half of them gone and no electrics no more and no food coming and a herd of idiot boys to care for—they was glad to see the back of one of 'em. So we traveled about a bit and then we come up here."

"I've often wondered," said Margaret. "Thank you for telling me."

"Yes, miss."

"But if we managed to get the witch away to America, you wouldn't mind Tim going with him?"

Lucy started on another nail, one that looked as if it had had as much chewing as it could stand.

"No telling, miss. He's happy here, now. *If* doctors could put him right in his mind, I'd like that. But if they can't, what then? A great big prison of a house, full of other zanies, that's most likely. He's someone here, miss, part of a family, even if he does sleep on straw. And now he's got Otto to fend for . . ."

"Oh dear," said Margaret. "But Mr. Gordon's got his eye on him for his next stoning."

"Aye," said Lucy. "But if it were only that I'd just take him away. We'd find another farm where they can use a maidservant and a strong lad. But it's no use talking of it—I couldn't part him from Otto now. It'd break his heart."

"Poor Tim."

"Don't you go fretting for him, miss. You fret for your auntie."

"I know," said Margaret. "Lucy, if you hear anything . . . anything *dangerous*, you'll let Jonathan or me know quickly, won't you?"

"Yes, miss."

She stood up, carelessly dusting her bottom, and slipped down the ladder. Margaret dropped the empty basket for her to catch and then followed.

The witch lay on his straw, too ill to make plans with, for four whole weeks. Sometimes he could talk sense, but very feebly. Twice they thought he was really better now; four or five times they thought he was dying. It was a hideous age of waiting.

But at least they didn't have to invent diversions for Mr. Gordon and his cronies, because two great excitements came to the village unasked. The first was a visit from the lord of the manor, a great earl who lived far up to the north, beyond Tewkesbury, but who had a habit of rushing around his domains attended by a great crowd of chaplains and clerks and falconers and kennelmen and grooms and leeches and verderers and landless gentlemen who had no job except to hang around, swell their master's retinue, and hope to be of service. Two of these clattered into the village three days after the midnight conference and rummaged around the houses looking for rooms where the small army could sleep. The squire had to move out of his house into the Dower House to make room for the great earl. It was like ripples in a pond all through the village, everyone being jostled into discomfort either to make space for one of the newcomers or for a villager whose bed had been commandeered. So Lucy had to make herself a bed on the floor of her little attic so that Margaret could sleep in *her* bed, so that Margaret's room could be occupied by a gentleman-groom, who slept in Margaret's bed, and a stableboy who slept on the floor. The stableboy normally would have slept in a room above the stables where his precious horses were housed, but the stables at the farm were really the cowshed, and had no room above them. Space had to be cleared to milk the cows in the hay barn.

Lucy slept down in the witch's hut, in fact, but she had to have a bed in the house in case questions were asked.

The gentleman-groom was a shy boy, and the stableboy was a garrulous old man. The gentleman-groom had to be up at the squire's house before dawn and didn't get back till after supper, but the stableboy had little to do except groom and exercise the rangy great horses and tell his endless stories. Margaret found herself spending all day in the stables, leaning against a silky flank and smelling its leathery sweat, while the stableboy talked about horses long dead, about the winners of the Cheltenham Gold Cup thirty years before (all the great earl's retinue rode what once had been steeplechasers or hunters). Sometimes his stories went further back, right into misty legends. He talked about Charles the Second staking the worth of half a county at Newmarket, about Dick Turpin's gallop to York, about Richard the Hunchback yelling for a fresh horse at Bosworth Field.

It didn't have to be racing: anything to do with the noble animals whose service had shaped his life was worth telling. One morning he sat on an upturned bucket and told her about the endurance of horses, about chargers which had fallen dead rather than ease from the gallop their masters had asked of them.

"I'm sure Scrub wouldn't do that," said Margaret.

"Neither he would," said the stableboy, "but he's a pony. Ponies ain't merely small horses—they're a different breed. More sense, they got. If ever you need to cross forty mile in a hurry, missie, you take a horse. But four hundred mile, and you'll be better off with a pony. They'll go an' they'll go, but when they're beat they'll stop."

"But there must be lots with mixed blood," said Margaret.

"Aye," he said, "but there's blood and there's blood. Now I'll tell you summat. In the Armada, fifteen hundred eighty-eight, they Spaniards came to conquer England with a mortal great army, only they had to come in ships seeing the Lord has set us on an island, and Sir Francis Drake he harried 'em and worried 'em until they sheered off and ran right round the north of Scotland and back to Spain thataway. Only the Lord sent fearsome storms that year, and half of 'em sank, and one of the ships as sank had a parcel of Arab horses on her, and one of them horses broke free as the ship went down, and he swam and he swam through the hollerin' waves till he come to a rocky beach where he dragged hisself ashore, and that was Cornwall. And to this day, missie, the wild ponies in Cornwall have a streak of Arab in them plain to see."

"I didn't know horses could swim like that," said Margaret.

The stableboy ran a mottled hand along roan ribs, caressing the faintly shivering hide.

"It's the buoyancy," he said. "They got these mortal great lungs in 'em for galloping, so they float high. Swim with a grown man astride 'em, they will, always provide he leans well forward and don't let hisself slip off over the withers—they keeps their shoulders up and let their hinder end tilt down, y'see. If ever you want to swim with a horse, you hold on to the tail of it, or the saddle."

"But the waves," said Margaret.

"They holds their head that high the waves don't bother 'em," said the stableboy. "Mark you, they gets frighted if they're not used to it, but I'd sooner be a horse nor a man in a rough sea. We haven't the buoyancy, nor the balance neither. Too much in the leg, we got, and only two legs at that. Now another thing, missie . . ."

And he was off again on his endless catalogues of the ways in which the horse excelled all other species, including Man.

Margaret was sorry when he left, swept off in the storm of the great earl's progress. But at least Mr. Gordon and his cronies had been kept active and interested for eight days and would have enough to talk about over their cider mugs for a week besides.

The other excitement didn't happen in the village at all. Just when the witch hunters were tired of gossip over the great earl's visit and were beginning to sniff the wintry air for new sport, a messenger came over from Stonehouse to say that two children had seen a bear in the woods. Nobody had ever been on a bear hunt, but all the men seemed to know exactly what to do. Wicked short spears were improvised and ground to deadly sharpness; Mr. Lyon the smith forged several pounds of extra-heavy arrowheads, to penetrate a tough hide at short range; the best dogs were chosen and starved. Then all the men moved out in a great troop to hunt the bear.

Mr. Gordon insisted on going too, maintaining that the bear must be a witch who had changed his shape but couldn't change back till the new moon, or had simply forgotten the spell. Even his drinking companions privately thought it more likely to be a survivor from the old Bristol zoo, but they didn't care to say so. Instead they built a litter and took turns to carry it; he rode at the head of the mob, hunched in his swaying chair, cackling to his bearers.

The whole of the village changed when they had left. Tensions eased; Aunt Anne smiled sometimes and began to look a little pink; the bursts of gossip you could hear up the street were on a different note—the pitch of women's voices; and it was quieter, so that betweenwhiles the only noise was the knock of the hired man's billhook cutting into an elder stump down in Low Wood.

With Uncle Peter gone, Jonathan was busy all day on the farm, but Margaret stole a satchel of food next evening and asked Lucy to creep up and wake her an hour before dawn. The stars were still sharp in the sky when she set off to explore the canal, and Scrub's breath made crisp little cloudlets in the frosty air. The stars were sharp in the sky again when she got back to find Aunt Anne waiting with a lantern in the porch. Margaret reckoned she'd done over forty miles. After supper Aunt Anne went out to visit a sick neighbor, so the children pulled their chairs up around the red embers of the fire; but in a minute Lucy slid off hers and sat right in under the chimneypiece, her cheeks scarlet with the close heat and every little spurt of flame sending elvish shadows across her face. Jonathan sat out in the gloom, quite silent but twitching like a dreaming hound. Margaret told them what she had found.

"I didn't start from the docks, Jo, because we can ride along that bit when we're taking food down to Lucy—besides, I didn't know how far I'd have to go the other way along the canal. It's miles and miles, and just the same all the way—just the canal and the path beside it. Except that at first it runs between banks and you can't see anything on either side, and later it's up above the rest of the country. *It* doesn't go up and down, of course, only the fields around it do. The towpath is easy to ride on, except for one bad stretch a little way down. There are lots of bridges—I counted them on the way back but I lost count—it's about fifteen, and some of them are open already. . . ."

"Open?" said Jonathan.

"Yes. It's like this: half the bridge is made of stone which juts out into the canal and doesn't move, but the other half's iron, all in one piece, and there's a big handle—you have to unlock the bridge at each end first with a piece of iron which you flip over—and when you turn the handle the whole iron part of the bridge swings around, very slowly though, until it's right out of the way and you can get a boat through. It's a funny feeling—you're moving tons and tons of iron, but it's all so balanced that it moves quite easily. There's a little cottage by each bridge where the people used to live who opened the bridges for the boats, but they're all empty now. Otherwise there aren't a lot of houses by the canal, except for a little village near the end. I got chased by a bull before that."

"Rather you than me," whispered Lucy. Jonathan laughed.

"It wasn't funny," said Margaret, "it was horrid. There's a place where you come out of woods and the canal goes for two miles straight as a plank, but the river's suddenly quite close, across the fields on the right. There's a bridge in the middle of the straight piece—it's called Splatt Bridge, it says; all the bridges have their names on them—and when I got there I thought I'd ride off across the fields and look at the river. I've never seen it close, and I was tired of the canal. The fields were all flat and empty, and I wasn't bothering when I came around a broken piece of hedge quite close to the canal, and it was there, black, bigger than any of the bulls in the village, not making any noise, rushing at us. Scrub saw it before I did, and he got us away, but only just. It was tethered on a long rope through a ring on its nose. It looked mad as Mr. Gordon, Jo, furious, it wanted to kill us, and it came so fast, like a . . . like a . . . ."

"Train," said Jonathan. Margaret shook her head.

"I still can't think like that," she said. "I didn't like opening that bridge, Jo. Not because somebody might catch me,
but just for what it was."

"Poor Marge," said Jonathan cheerfully. "Still, you got
away from the bull. What happened then?"

"Then there's a strange bit, with the river getting nearer
and nearer until there's only a thin strip of land between it
and the canal; and everything's flat and bleak and full of
gulls and the air smells salty and Wales is only just over on
the other side, low red cliffs with trees on them. It's funny
being able to see so far when you're right down in the bottom like that, and the river gets wider and wider all the time
—it's really the sea, I suppose. And then you get to a place
where you're riding between sheds, and there are old railway lines, and huge piles of old timber, some of it in the
open and some of it under roofs, and one enormous tower
without any windows, much bigger than the tower of the
cathedral, and a place like the docks at Gloucester but with
a big ship—a really big one, I couldn't believe it. And then
you come to another lock; at least I think it's a lock but it's
far bigger than the Gloucester one and the gates are made of
steel or iron. And beyond that the water's much lower, inside an enormous pool with sloping sides and places for
tying ships to, and another gate at the far end, and beyond
that there are two enormous wooden arms curving out into
the river, and it's as wild as the end of the world."

"How deep is the canal?" said Jonathan.

"About twelve feet. I measured it with a pole I found,
from two of the bridges. And I couldn't see anywhere where
it looked reedy and silted. There's a place about halfway
along where a stream runs into it, which could help keep it
full. How does a lock work?"

Jonathan took a twig and scratched in the film of gray
ashes which covered the hearthstone.

"It's like this," he said. "The water in the canal is higher
than the water in the pool, so it pushes the top gates shut. If
you want to get a boat out, you push the bottom gates shut,
and then you open special sluices to let the water in the
canal run into the lock. The new water holds the bottom

gates shut, and the water in the lock rises until it's the same level as the water in the canal and you can open the top gates. You sail into the lock and shut them again, and then you shut the top sluices and open the bottom ones and the water runs out of the lock until it's the same level as the water in the pool, and you can open the bottom gates."

Lucy came around and stared at the scrawled lines.

"I don't know how they think of such things," she said at last.

"I see," said Margaret. "At least I sort of see. Oh, Jo, can't we find a big sailing boat and not try to make any beastly engines go?"

"No," said Jonathan. "It would have to be a very big one to go to sea in winter, and all the sailing boats which are big enough will have men on them, using them and looking after them. Besides, we'd never be strong enough to manage the sails, even with Tim's help, and we wouldn't know how, either. But if Otto can show us how to start one of the tugs, then we've got a real chance."

# Chapter 4

# FIRST SNOW

The men came back on the third day, arguing among themselves all the way up the winding hill. Nine villages, it seemed, had gathered for the hunt, and all their eager sportsmen had so hallooed and trampled through the flaming beech groves that the dogs had never had a chance to smell anything except man-sweat. Mr. Lyon had broken an ankle, though; and several small animals had been slaughtered, including five foxes; and Mr. Gordon and his cronies had spent the whole of the second day digging out a badgers' set and killing the snarling inmates as they uncovered them. Mr. Gordon's litter still swayed high above the procession as they tramped wearily up by the churchyard, and in his hand he waved a stick with the gaping head of a badger spiked on its end.

They were busy with boasting for several days after that, and then with critical discussions of the behavior of the people from other villages. So it was thirty-six days (Margaret reckoned them up) after Mr. Gordon had last come nosing around the farm before he came again.

This time he arrived while she was helping Aunt Anne with the heavy irons, lifting them off the stove when you could smell the burning fibers of the cloth you handled them with and carrying them back when they were too cool to press the creases out of the pillowcase. It was a peaceful, repetitive job until the latch lifted and the hunched shape stood outlined against the sharp winter sunlight.

"Mornin'," he grunted, and without waiting for an invitation hobbled across and settled himself in Uncle Peter's chair.

"Good morning, Mr. Gordon," said Aunt Anne, and started to iron a shirt she had just finished with an iron which was already cool. Mr. Gordon clucked.

"Sharpish weather we're having," she said after a while. "There'll be snow before the week's out."

Mr. Gordon clucked again.

When Margaret brought the freshly heated iron she could sense how tense her aunt was. At first she'd hoped to slide away, but now she saw she would have to stay, just in case she could help.

"That Tim," said Mr. Gordon suddenly. "What d'ye reckon to him?"

"Tim?" said Aunt Anne, surprised. "He's just a poor zany."

"Aye," said Mr. Gordon slowly and derisively. "Nobbut a poor zany."

He sat and rocked and clucked while Aunt Anne carefully nosed her iron down the seam of a smock.

"Where'd he come from, then?" he shouted suddenly. "Answer me that!"

Aunt Anne jerked her body upright with shock, and dropped her iron. It made a slamming clatter on the flagged floor.

"I think he came from Bristol," said Margaret.

"Aye, Bristol," muttered Mr. Gordon. "Wicked places, cities."

"That's true," said Aunt Anne.

Mr. Gordon clucked and rocked.

"Why do you want to know?" said Aunt Anne in a shivering voice.

"There's wickedness about," said Mr. Gordon. "I can smell un. It draws me here, same as a ewe draws her lamb home to her."

There was no answer to that, so Aunt Anne went on with her ironing and Margaret with her fetching and carrying of the heavy irons. Mr. Gordon watched them with fierce little eyes amid the wrinkled face, as though every movement was a clue to the wickedness which lay hidden about the farm. The kitchen seemed to get darker. Margaret found she couldn't keep her mind off the witch, tossing feverish on dirty straw. She tried to think about Scrub, or Jonathan, or even Caesar, but all the time the picture inside her skull remained one of dim yellow lantern light, the rusty engine, Tim squatting patient in the shadows, and the sick man whose presence drew Mr. Gordon down to this peaceful farm.

Twice Aunt Anne started to say something, and twice she stopped herself. When Margaret took a new iron to her their eyes met: Aunt Anne's said "Help!" as plain as screaming.

Next time Margaret fetched a hot iron she went over toward the open hearth as if to chivvy the logs, tripped over the corner of the rug, and sprawling across the floor brought the rim of metal hard against the old man's shin. He cried out with a strange, high bellow, leaped to his feet, and before she could crawl out of reach started to belabor her over the shoulders. She cringed under two stinging blows before she glimpsed Aunt Anne's shoes rush past her face; then there was a brief gasping struggle. When she came trembling to her feet Mr. Gordon was slumped back in the chair, panting, and Aunt Anne was standing beside him, very flushed, holding his stick in her hand. They all stayed where they were for a long while, until the rage and panic had faded from their faces. At last Mr. Gordon put out his hand for his stick.

Aunt Anne gave it to him without a word and held the rocking chair steady while he worked himself upright. He took one step, gasped, felt for the arm of the chair and sat down.

"Ye've broken my leg, between ye," he said harshly. "Fetch your man, missus. I'll need carrying."

Aunt Anne walked quietly out into the farmyard, leaving Margaret and the old man together. She wasn't afraid of him for the moment; the fire seemed to have dimmed in his eyes. She began to be sorry she'd hit him so hard until he looked sideways at her from under his scurfy eyebrows and muttered, "No child was ever the worse for a bit o' beating."

Margaret slipped away to the foot of the stairs, where she waited until Uncle Peter came. As soon as he heard the heavy footsteps Mr. Gordon started moaning and groaning to himself. Margaret gritted her teeth and waited for another beating, but Uncle Peter paid no attention to her. Instead he stood in front of Mr. Gordon's chair with his hands on his hips and gazed down at the crumpled figure.

"What the devil d'ye think you're up to, Davey?" he said. "Laying into my kin without my leave?"

Mr. Gordon stopped groaning, gave a pitiful snivel and looked up at the big, angry man.

"I'm hurt, Pete," he said. "Hurt bad. Get me home, so as I can lay up for a couple of days."

"Let's have a look at ye," said Uncle Peter curtly. He knelt down and, pulling out his knife, ripped open the coarse leggings. There seemed to be no end of sackcloth before the blue and blotchy shank came into view. Margaret tiptoed forward and saw where there was a small red weal on the skin that stretched over the shinbone. Now she wished she'd hit him harder.

"I'll fetch the barrow," grunted Uncle Peter, "and I'll wheel you up to the Stars. Two jars of cider and ye'll be skipping about, Davey. But don't you take it into your head to wallop my kin again, not without my say-so."

He lashed the leggings untidily back into position and went out. There came the rumble of an iron-shod wheel on the flagstones outside; then he strode into the kitchen, lifted Mr. Gordon clean out of the chair and carried him to the door. As he turned himself sideways to ease his burden through the gap Mr. Gordon gave a wild cackle.

"Ah," he cried, "what I couldn't do if I was as strong as yourself, Peter lad."

The words sounded forgiving, but the voice rang with mad threats. Uncle Peter didn't say anything, but carried him out and dumped him in the barrow and wheeled him up into the lane.

That afternoon, when she went out to tend to Scrub's needs and poor old Caesar's, she found the stonecutter from the quarry leaning on a low place in the hedge. She called a greeting to him, but he didn't say anything, only watched every move as she walked to and fro. She went back into the house when she'd finished and looked out of an upstairs window; he'd moved up onto the little knoll in the six-acre from which it was possible to see almost every movement on the whole of the farm. He stayed there until it was too dark to see.

Darkness, in fact, came early, under low heavy clouds; but in the last moments of daylight she saw a few big snow-flakes floating past the window. There was an inch of chill whiteness in the yard when she went out to the cowshed to tell Uncle Peter it was time for supper. He was milking the last cow, Daisy, his favorite, by the light of a lantern set on the floor by his stool; the beams were full of looming shadows, and she couldn't see his face when he looked up.

"What the devil happened in the kitchen this morning, Marge?" he said. "Davey will have it you banged his leg a-purpose."

She hesitated, taken by surprise, until it was too late to lie.

"He was worrying Aunt Anne," she said. "I didn't think she could stand it anymore, and I thought I had to try and do something. It was the best thing I could do. Do you think I was wrong, Uncle Peter?"

"No," he said slowly. "No. But Davey's not so crazed as he acts. Just promise me one thing, Marge. You haven't been mucking around with wicked machines, have you, Marge?"

"No, really, I haven't. I promise." She was surprised and frightened. If they didn't get the witch away soon, they'd all be found out.

Uncle Peter turned slowly back to his milking, leaning his cheek against Daisy's haunch as though he were listening for secrets inside her.

"All right," he said at last. "I believe you. But I won't spare nor hide nor hair of you if I find you've deceived me. That's a promise."

"Yes, Uncle Peter. But can't we do something to help Aunt Anne? He doesn't seem to let her alone."

"I don't know, Marge. Honest I don't. Davey's a weird one, but he wouldn't come worriting down here if he didn't feel something was wrong. I don't know what it is. Mebbe he's right about Tim."

"Oh, no!" cried Margaret. "Tim's only a poor zany. He wouldn't hurt anyone."

"You never know," said her uncle darkly. As he stood up and lifted the heavy bucket from under Daisy's bag he said it again, almost to himself, as though he were talking about something else: "You never know."

A glance and a warning jerk of the head were enough, so tense were the children, to call a council after they had all gone yawning up to bed. They sat in the dark in Lucy's room, furthest away from where the adults slept, and talked in whispers. It was very dark outside, with snow still floating down steadily from the low cloud-base. Margaret told them everything that Mr. Gordon had said and done, and then what Uncle Peter had said in the milking shed. When she'd finished she heard Jonathan stirring, then saw his head and shoulders black against the faint grayness of the window.

"If we went now," he said, "the snow would blot out the marks of the runners."

"Now?" said both the girls together.

"Yes. And if we leave it for another night the snow will be so thick that everyone will be able to see the tracks going down to the barn, and we'd never be able to get the sledge across the valley anyway."

"Oh dear," whispered Margaret. Her shoulders began to ache for a mattress and her neck for a pillow.

"Tim must come too," said Jonathan. "And you, Lucy— you'd go with him if he ran away, wouldn't you? They'll just think you overheard something that was being said and decided to take him away. You could stay if you really want to, Marge, but Scrub will pull much better if you're there. Besides, you know the way."

"I could tell you," said Margaret sulkily. "You go up Edge Lane and then . . . then . . . no, it's much too difficult. I'll have to come."

"Good," said Jonathan. "I don't think I could do it alone, honestly. Lucy, there's a pair of Father's boots drying in the pantry. We'll take them for Tim."

Lucy sighed in the dark. "I've never been a thief before," she said.

"You aren't now," said Jonathan. "I'm giving them to you."

Scrub didn't seem at all surprised to be harnessed and led through the orchard to where Jonathan had dragged the log sledge. While Lucy and Jonathan cajoled Tim into his new boots, and then, talking very slowly, persuaded him to carry the witch outside into the dangerous night, Margaret picked up Scrub's hooves one by one and smeared them with lard from a little bowl which she had taken from the larder. That meant the snow wouldn't ball inside his shoes.

All the time the soft, feathery flakes of snow floated down. When they brushed her cheek they felt like the down from the inside of a split pillow, but when they rested for more than a second on bare flesh and began to melt they turned themselves into nasty little patches of killing cold. Tim came cooing out into the darkness. The witch groaned sharply as he was laid on the sledge, made comfortable, and then wrapped by Jonathan in an old tractor tarpaulin.

"Tim," whispered Lucy, "we're going. Going away. We're going."

Tim's bubbling changed, deepened, wavered and then restored itself to its usual note. He lurched into the darkness and they heard him scrabbling in the straw of his shed; then he came back and knelt by the sledge; the tarpaulin rasped twice as he readjusted it. Margaret realized he was taking his treasures with him.

It is steep all the way up to the ridge of Edge Lane. Margaret led the pony between the dark walls of silent houses, only able to see where the road was because of the faint glimmer from fallen snow. The runners of the sledge whimpered gently as they crushed the fluffy crystals to sliding ice. Tim's boots crunched and his throat bubbled. Once or twice Scrub's shoes chinked as they struck through the soft layer of whiteness to a stone underneath. Otherwise they all moved so quietly that Margaret could hear the tiny pattering and rustling of individual flakes falling into the dry leaves of Mrs. Godber's beech hedge.

Scrub took the slope well enough, but Margaret was beginning to worry how he'd manage the real steeps down into the valley and out again, where sometimes the lane tilts almost as sharply as the pitch of a roof. But at least she could see better now. As they came to the short piece of flat at the crest she understood why: the sky ahead really was lighter. Soon they would come out from under the snow cloud into starlight.

"I'll take the brake," said Jonathan. Margaret had been so rapt in her world of stealth and silence that she was startled to hear him speak aloud. She reached up to pat Scrub's neck and steady him for the descent, then heard the iron spike on the end of the brake bar beginning to bite through the snow into the pitted tarmac. Scrub plodded on, unamazed; but when a hundred yards down the hill and just as they were getting to the steepest place, the moon came out and he saw the treacherous white surface falling away at his feet, he snorted and tossed his head and tried to stop. The brake grated sharply as Jonathan hauled at it, but even so the sledge had enough momentum to push the pony forward onto the frightening decline. She felt the wild tide of panic beginning to rush through his blood, and put her hand right up inside the cheekstrap, so that she could at least hold his head still.

"Easy," she said. "Easy. Easy. You'll do it easy."

For a second she thought he wasn't going to believe her. Then he steadied and walked carefully down.

"That's the worst bit," said Jonathan.

The stream in the bottom was a black snake between the white pastures; it hissed like a snake too, and moonlight glistened off its wavelets as it might off polished scales. The old mill, which somebody had rebuilt just before the Changes, was a ruin again now; nobody cared to live so far from the village. They halted for a minute to allow Tim to move the witch around so that his feet would be below his head during the climb.

"We aren't going fast enough," said Jonathan. "It'll be morning before we get back."

"It's not so bad after Edge," said Margaret, "and it'll be much easier with the moon out."

She looked around at the black trees, the ruined mill, the white meadows with the black stream hissing between them; everything in the steep and secret valley looked magical under the chill moon. She'd never have dreamed that a world so dangerous could be so beautiful.

There are two very steep stretches on the far side. Jonathan showed Lucy how to work the brake, then cajoled Tim into hauling on one of the traces on one side of the sledge while he took the other. Scrub stumbled on the second slope, but was on his feet and pulling almost at once, which was lucky because Lucy was thinking about something else and hadn't even begun to use the brake. The pony's knees seemed unhurt, thanks to the cushioning snow, and he toiled bravely on.

Edge, on the last rim of the Cotswolds, was fast asleep, and the road to Gloucester curved through it and into the darkness of beechwoods.

"Do you think you could ride him down here, and get him to trot for a bit?" said Jonathan as soon as they were past the last inhabited house. "There's room for the rest of us on the sledge."

It meant rearranging the sick man again, but they crowded onto the rough slats, with Jonathan at the back to work the brake and Tim clutching the sack of food Jonathan had stolen from the farm. Scrub was uneasy about the changed arrangement, and suspicious of the surface beneath his feet, but Margaret coaxed him into a trot. He faltered, changed pace to a walk and tossed his head.

"Oh, don't be silly," said Margaret. "It's quite safe, and you'll enjoy it. Come on."

She felt his mouth with the reins and nudged his ribs and he tried again, and this time he kept it up. The slope was just right for the sledge: left to itself it would have stopped, with that weight on it, but it needed very little pulling to keep it going and in a minute Scrub had completely changed his mind about the whole affair and was tugging at the bit and trying to stretch into a canter. Margaret looked over her shoulder to her passengers as they passed through a patch of moonlight where no trees masked the sky. Tim was crouched over his sack, staring out sideways at the blinks of light between the trunks. Lucy was smiling her elf smile, looking as wild as the wind that slipped icily past her. Jonathan perched on a nook of sledge between the witch's head and the brake bar, looking intently forward, ready for the next disaster. They could never have got this far without him: he knew what to do because he had thought about it before it happened—and he could think in secret because nobody could tell what was going on behind that funny crumpled face.

"Scrub wants to go faster," she shouted.

"Provided you don't miss your turn," he shouted back. "Throw your hand up when you see it coming."

The next few minutes were heroic adventure—real as the touch of timber but quite different, as different as dreams, from the everyday bothersomeness of roofs and clothing. The icy night air burned past her, long slopes of moonlit snow opened and closed on her left as the trees massed and thinned, Scrub covered the dangerous surface with a muscled and rhythmic confidence while she moved with his movement as a curlew moves with the northwest wind, and the road curved down the long hillside with the generous swoops imposed by the contours—and all the time a lower level of her mind kept telling her that what she was doing was dangerous. And right. Dangerous and right. Right and deadly.

Something nicked the corner of her awareness, the corner of her eye as they raced past—the cottage before the turn. She threw up her arm for a second (you could trust Jo to rely on the briefest signal) and busied herself with the problem of coaxing Scrub to a walk without letting him fall. The brake grated harshly just as she let him feel the pull of the bit.

"Too good to last, boy," she said.

He understood at once, slowing as fast as was safe on that surface and with the danger of the sledge banging into his hind legs. (No horse is really happy about pulling something which hasn't got shafts down a slope—he can't hold it back.)

The ten yards into the lane after the turn is very steep, as steep as Edge Lane, but they took it slowly. After that it levels out and they were able to trot several times, but the exhilaration of the ride down the main road was lost. The night was wheeling on; the high, untended hedges closed them in; they began to feel the secrecy and strangeness of the Vale; the empty city now seemed very near.

"Cheer up, Marge," said Jonathan while they were all rearranging themselves to allow Scrub to cope with a slight rise. "We've just about caught up with the time now. You tired?"

"Not if I don't think about it."

"Is there any way round Hempsted? Someone's bound to hear us with everything so quiet."

"I don't know. Anyway, I probably couldn't find it. This is much the best way in, because the houses are only just on both sides of the road, and not spread out in a great mass. If we try some other way we might meet the dogs."

"All right."

If anyone heard them in Hempsted they gave no sign. It was impossible to tell when they were out of the little inhabited village and into the derelict suburbs. Scrub was tiring now, difficult to coax out of his stolid walk. Margaret dismounted and walked beside him. Tim came and strode on the other side of him, as though he felt some mysterious sympathy with the weary limbs. The moon blanked out, and then there was a swirling flurry of snow, much more wind-driven in this open flatness than it had been up in the hills. Margaret bent her head and plodded on, looking only at the faint whiteness of the road a few feet in front of her. The level crossing told her that they were nearly there—otherwise she might have trudged on forever.

The snow shower stopped again just as they reached the docks, but the moon didn't come out for several minutes, during which she edged forward onto the quay in a panic lest someone would fall into the bitter water. Her memory was mistaken, too; there seemed to be far more obstructions and kinks in the quayside than she'd remembered in the quick glance from the bridge. Then suddenly the light shone down between the blind warehouses and they could all see the whole basin.

"Those were the ones I meant, Jo," she said.

"Yes, the middle one's no good. It must be half full of water. I'll nip ahead and nose around. You come on slowly."

He flitted off between the shadows and was lost. Margaret heard a faint clunking. Scrub was worried and restless, and she herself was too tense to calm him. The water in the basin looked as black as polished slate. Jonathan came back.

"I've found one which will do for the time being," he said. "There's enough room for all three of them, and we needn't try and get Otto down a ladder—I forced the door of the wheelhouse. We can cast off one hawser and slack off the other one and just shove her out into the middle of the basin. Then there shouldn't be any trouble from dogs. But I'm worried about water."

"Water?"

"For them to drink. The stuff in the basin doesn't smell too good."

"Couldn't we melt some snow?"

"Good idea. You scout around and see if you can find something big enough to hold it. Tie Scrub up. Lucy, bring Tim along and I'll show you what I want."

Margaret explored all along the side of the quay, groping into shadows and waiting until the faint light reflected from the snow allowed her to distinguish the blacker shapes of solid objects amid the general blackness. She had in her mind's eye some sort of galvanized iron washtub, and didn't pause to wonder whether any such object was likely to be found in a commercial dockyard, so she came back to the tugs empty-handed after twenty minutes' search. The witch had vanished from the sledge and Tim was gone too. Jonathan and Lucy were performing a curious dance round a chimney-shaped thing, hopping, bending and half straightening before they hopped again. As Margaret came up Jonathan dragged the chimney thing a couple of yards further on.

"No luck, Marge?" he said. "Never mind. Lucy found an

old oil drum with the lid off. I think it'll be all right—it holds water because we tried it in the dock, and it's not too dirty. Give us a hand."

So Margaret joined in the bending and hopping ritual, scooping up the light snow and throwing it into the drum.

"That'll do," said Jonathan at last. "We won't be able to carry it if it gets any heavier. Hang on, Lucy, while I make a lashing; we'll have to get it down into the hold or it won't melt. Fetch that bit of rope you found while I try and get my fingers warm enough to make knots."

Margaret suddenly felt the bitter numbness in her own fingers and put her hands under her armpits and jigged up and down in the puddled snow to get her blood moving. Jonathan swung his arms against his ribs with a dull slapping noise while Lucy slid off into the dark. When she returned there was a long period of just watching and feeling useless while Jonathan fiddled and fussed with the rope. Then Lucy fetched Tim and persuaded him to lift the drum onto the tug and lower it down a hatch.

"That's fine," said Jonathan. "There should be enough melted by morning to drink. Don't drink the water in the basin. Now we'll put you out to sea. All aboard. Got that pole, Lucy?"

"Yes, master," said the quiet voice.

"Show Tim how to push against the quay. I'll shove with my leg. Marge, hang on to my hand so that I can let myself go a bit further, otherwise I'll fall in. Off we go. All together now."

Margaret held his hand and prepared to lean backward against the weight of his stretch out over the water. Lucy found a good hold for the tip of her piece of timber; Jonathan began to shove; Lucy made Tim hold the pole where she'd been holding it and said, "Push. Push. That's right." Nothing happened for what seemed a long time, so that Margaret was sure that the basin must be silted up and the tug stuck. Then, suddenly, she saw a gleam of light between Jonathan's feet, and the oily blackness of the water around the ripple of reflected moonlight.

"Hang on, Marge," said Jonathan. "Don't let him fall over,

Lucy. That's enough. We don't want to shove it right round the other way."

He hauled himself back onto the solid stone, and together they watched the tug drift, inch by inch, out over the water.

"That's fine," said Jonathan at last. "Lucy, you'll have to keep an eye open. If you find yourself drifting too near the quay again Tim can pole you off. And if you want to get ashore just haul on the hawser. You've got enough food for three days, I should think. Marge or I will be down again with more before Friday. All right?"

"Yes, master, and my thanks to you. And to you too, Miss Margaret." Her silky whisper drifted over the water. Far off in the city a dog bayed. Then the moon went out.

"We must be off," said Jonathan. "Do you think Scrub can stand it?"

"Yes. He's been eating snow, which is just as good as drinking, and I think he's found some grass in that corner. He's had a good rest, haven't you, boy?"

She knew he had heard the baying of the dog, and could feel the slight shivering of fright through his hide as she patted him in the pitch dark. He moved eagerly as she untied his reins from the stanchion, and she had a job walking as fast as he wanted to go along the treacherous cobbles, all littered with frozen hawser and rusting chains beneath the snow. Out on the road she climbed into the saddle and heard Jonathan settling at the back of the sledge. Scrub chose a quickish trot and bounced along the winding flat. They both got off to walk up the slight slope into Hempsted, but rode again down to the bridge over the canal.

"Marge," called Jonathan as they crossed the black water, "couldn't we have come along the towpath? It must be quicker."

"I expect so. I didn't think of it. Anyway, it was too dark to be safe."

"Let's try next time we come down."

"Yes."

Then there was the easy straight along the big road that leads to Bristol and another fair stretch along the winding lane toward hills which seemed darker and taller with every pace. In one brief patch of moonlight she saw that it hadn't

snowed here since they came down, for the lines of the
sledge's runners slashed clear through the soft whiteness
and between them were the scuffled ovals of Scrub's hoof-
prints. Her legs were very tired when she dismounted to
begin on the long climb up to Edge, and felt tireder still
when the snow started again before they were halfway up to
the main road. So there was nearly an hour's slow plodding
(head bent, shoulders hunched, little runnels of melting
coldness beginning to find their way into the cringing skin)
before they could once again start down the hill to the valley. Margaret was too tired to think about risks; she let
Scrub take it at a dangerous, wallowing canter through the
dizzying flakes. Jonathan had to shout to warn her at the
two very steep places, but she didn't even dismount then,
only slowing the pony to a slithering walk while the brake
scraped behind them. She had to walk up the far edge of the
valley, and it took years of darkness (though she knew from
daytime blackberrying that it was really only ten minutes'
stroll). Then they were in the village again, coming down
between houses with the snow falling as thick as flour from
the runnel of a millstone. She could see neither sky nor star
nor horizon through the swirling murk, but the habit of
living without clocks told her there were two hours till
dawn. She led Scrub into his paddock, heartlessly leaving
him to lick snow and rummage for grass, while Jonathan
dragged the sledge back into the timber store.

When she came reeling back to the tack room with the
harness and the heavy saddle he was waiting for her.

"Marge!" he hissed, as though he had something vital to
tell her. "She's called *Heartsease.*"

"Who is?" said Margaret.

"The tug. I spelled it out by moonlight. It's the name of
Mother's favorite flower—I thought it might be lucky."

"Luck's what we need," said Margaret crossly. She hung
her gear in the darkest corner, shifted a dry saddle and
reins to the place where she usually kept hers, and then, wet
and miserable as a storm-wrecked bird, climbed the freezing ivy, crept along the passage, hid her wet clothes under
the bed, snuggled between sheets and allowed herself to
drown in sleep.

Chapter 5

# WE NEED A BOMB

But even in sleep there was no safety. She dreamed about the bull which had chased her at Splatt Bridge, and woke from the nightmare in a wringing sweat, to lie in the faint grayness of first light and remember how huge and murderous he had seemed, how slowly Scrub had answered the rein and then had vanished, so that she was standing in the sopping grass while the bull hurtled down toward her, foaming, mad, untethered. . . . It was a long time before she slept again.

The proper morning began with bellowings, not a bull's but Uncle Peter shouting and slamming around the house. Luckily this happened when the light was already broad across the uplands and the unmilked cows beginning to low plaintively in the shed, because (as often happens when the first snow falls) everyone slept longer than usual. Margaret dozed on, conscious at moments of the rummaging and thumping, until in the middle of a meaningless dream her shoulder was grasped and shaken hard. She opened her

eyes and saw Aunt Anne, still in her nightrobe, face taut
with worry, bending over the bed.

"Marge, Marge," she whispered.

Margaret sat up into the numbing air.

"What's the time?" she said.

"Marge, they've gone, Tim and Lucy, and they've taken
Pete's second pair of boots and a shoulder of mutton and
some bread. What shall I do?"

"Does he know what they've taken?" The habit of secrecy
kept Margaret's voice low.

"No. I noticed the boots. He's mostly cross because the
stove isn't lit and the porridge not on."

"I'll light it. Lucy must have heard Mr. Gordon talking to
you. I shouldn't tell him anything. Can't you just be sleepy,
Aunt Anne? If he's really angry he won't notice."

"He's milking the cows now. But what's happened to
them? In this weather, too?"

"Oh, I'm sure they're all right. Lucy knows what she's doing."

Margaret realized as she spoke that she'd got her emphasis a little too strong. Aunt Anne stared at her, opening and
shutting her mouth several times.

"What about Jo?" she hissed at last.

"Jo?" said Margaret, misjudging the surprise this time.
"Has he gone too?"

Aunt Anne's bony fingers dug into her shoulders and she
was shaken back and forward until her head banged the
wall and she cried out aloud.

"You know what I mean," whispered Aunt Anne.

"Yes," said Margaret, "but you can't stop Jo doing what he
wants to, can you?"

Aunt Anne sat on the bed and said, "No. No. Never."

"I'll do Lucy's work until you can find someone else. Can't
you tell Uncle Peter it'll be two mouths less to feed through
the winter? And you could tell him what Mr. Gordon said
too—then he'd know why they've gone—I'm sure he's worried about it. I was talking to him in the cowshed last night."

Aunt Anne began to rock to and fro on the bed, moaning
and saying, "Oh dear, oh dear." Margaret sat and waited for
her to stop, but she went on and on until Margaret was

frightened enough to slide out of bed and run along the passage to find Jonathan, who was yawning while he dressed.

"Come quick," she whispered. "Your mother's not well."

He walked to her room and stood for several seconds in the doorway, watching the rocking figure. Then he slipped his arm around her waist, pulled her wrist over his shoulder and walked her back toward her own bedroom.

"Get some breakfast for Father," he said as he went through the door. "Don't dress—go down in your gown."

So there was kindling to be fetched from the scullery and the fire to be lit in the still-warm stove and little logs to be fed into it through the reeking smoke (that chimney was always a pig in a north wind) and the pots and kettles to be arranged in the hottest patches. Uncle Peter stormed in before anything was ready and threw himself into his chair where he glowered and growled. Margaret tiptoed to the larder and found a corner of boiled bacon and one of yesterday's loaves; while she was looking around for something to appease an angry and hungry farmer she noticed the little bottles of cordial, so she unscrewed the top of one and poured it into a pewter mug, which she carried into the kitchen and put on the table at his elbow. He picked it up, sniffed it and took a sip. When she came back with the bread and bacon he was tilting the mug to swallow the last drop. He banged the pewter back onto the table.

"Ah, that's something like," he said. "You've the right ideas, Marge girl."

"I'm afraid it will be twenty minutes before I can give you anything properly hot, Uncle Peter."

"Never mind, lass, never mind. I'll make do."

He picked up the thin, gray-bladed knife and hacked off a crooked slice of bread and a crookeder hunk of bacon.

"Gone!" he shouted through a mouth full of yellow teeth and munched crumbs and lean and fat.

"Aunt Anne told me," said Margaret.

"But why, but why?" shouted her uncle. "After all we did for 'em, too!"

"I think she must have overheard what Mr. Gordon was

saying about Tim. Shall I fetch you another bottle of cordial?"

"Aye. No. Aye. No, better not. Bring me a mug of cider. What was Davey saying, then?"

"About Tim really being a witch. You were talking about it too, yesterday evening."

"Ah. He's a deep one, Davey. What do you think now, Marge, hey?"

"I don't know, I still don't see how a zany could be a witch. This porridge is warm enough to eat now—would you like some?"

"Leave it a minute more. I like it proper hot. You go and dress, lass, and I'll fend for myself. I must go and tell Davey Gordon what's up, and soon as may be."

Margaret spun out her dressing, and when she came down again the kitchen was empty. She opened the door into the yard and looked out; Uncle Peter's footmarks were the only blemish on the level snow, great splayed paces striding up toward the gate. If you knew what you were looking for you could just see two faint dimplings running side by side toward the shed—the lines made by the sledge runners when they'd come back, but covered with new-fallen snow; the marks of their outward journey had vanished. She turned at the sound of a light step behind her; Jonathan had sidled up to study the black-and-white landscape.

"Jo, I thought of something," she whispered. "Won't someone notice that the sledge is wet?"

"I left it under the hole in the roof, where there was piles of snow coming in. I put some bundles of pea-sticks over the place when we left, so the ground's fairly dry underneath too. It ought to look all right."

"How's Aunt Anne?"

"I don't know. Tell anyone who asks she's got a fever."

Then Mr. Gordon and his cronies came catcalling down the lane and trampled to and fro over the yard until even the marks of Uncle Peter's first crossing were scuffled out, let alone the lines left by the sledge. Mr. Gordon stood in the melee, head thrown back to sniff the bitter air.

"Clear!" he cried at last. "Sweet and clear! Peter, your

farm's clear of wickedness now, or my name's not Davey Gordon."

"The zany, was it?" cried one of the stonecutters.

"Sure as sure," cackled Mr. Gordon. "And that sister of his, too, like enough."

"She always had a sly look," said another of the men. "Where'd they come from, anyone know?"

"Bristol," called Margaret from the porch.

"Aye, so you told me before," answered Mr. Gordon. "That's where they'll be heading then. Out and after them, boys."

But it was a quarter of an hour before the men even left the farm, because they kept telling each other how right they were, and repeating old arguments as if they were new ones. Amid this manly furor no one spared a second to ask after Aunt Anne; and when they departed Uncle Peter went with them.

He left a hard day's work behind for two children who'd been up most of the night—the cowshed to be mucked out, hay carried in, ponies to be tended, sheep to be seen to, hens to be fed and their eggs found, the two old sows to be fed too—besides all the most-used paths to be shoveled clear before the snow on them was trodden down to ice too hard to shift. Jonathan ran down to the stream and fetched the hired man to help with the heaviest work, so by the time Uncle Peter came back, bored with the useless hunt and angrily ashamed with himself for leaving the farm when there was so much to be done, most of the important jobs were finished. Aunt Anne stayed abed all day, and Margaret was staggering with tiredness when she carried the stewpot to the table for supper; but she opened another bottle of cordial for him (Aunt Anne rationed him to a bottle on Sundays) and he leaned back in his chair and belched and scowled at the roofbeams.

"Glad we didn't catch 'em, sort of," he said suddenly.

Margaret cleared away in a daze of exhaustion and went to bed. When she looked down from the top of the stairs he was still lolling there, his cheeks red in the firelight and mottled with anger and drink, and his shadow bouncing black across the far wall. He looked like a cruel old god waiting for a sacrifice.

Too tired to bother with lanterns or candles she felt her way into bed and dropped at once into that warm black ocean of sleep which waits for bodies strained to the edge of bearing, and slept too deep for dreams.

Next day Aunt Anne seemed worse. She lay under her coverlet with her knees tucked almost up to her chin, and all she said when anyone tiptoed in to offer her a mug of gruel or a boiled egg was "Leave me alone. Leave me alone." Uncle Peter, after two attempts to comfort her (quite good attempts—worried, voice gentle), lost his temper with the unreasonableness of other folk and stumped off around the farm, furiously banging the milk pails together and when milking was done starting on the unnecessary job of re-stacking the timber pile and refusing to be helped. Margaret took him out a flagon of cider in midmorning (having poured half a bottle of cordial in first) but was otherwise far too busy with housework and cooking to pay attention to him or anyone else. Luckily Aunt Anne had done the baking two days ago, so there was bread enough for two days more, but even so there were hours of work to be done. When you have no machines, a household can only be kept sensible if certain jobs are done on certain days of the week, others on certain days of the month, others every day, and others fitted in according to season. Margaret usually hated housework; but now that Aunt Anne was moaning and rocking upstairs she was in charge, so she polished and scrubbed and swept with busy pleasure, humming old hymn tunes for hours on end.

It was only when she was laying the table for lunch that she realized that Jonathan was missing; she ran out to the paddock, and found that Caesar was missing too. Scrub trotted up for a gossip, but she could only spare him a few seconds before she ran back to clear the third place away, to pour the other half-bottle of cordial into Uncle Peter's tankard so that he wouldn't notice when she sploshed the cider in on top, and to think of a good lie. Luckily the stew smelled rich enough to tempt an angry, hungry man.

"Where's that Jo?" he said at once when he saw the two places.

She ladled out the best bits of meat she could find and added three dumplings (Aunt Anne would frown and purse her lips when she found how lavish Margaret had been with the precious suet).

"I sent him down to Cousin Mary," she said. "She's got a bad leg and I didn't know how she'd be making out this weather. I know Aunt Anne doesn't speak with her, but I thought she'd rather we did something than that we didn't."

Uncle Peter chewed at a big gobbet of meat until his mouth was empty enough for speech, if only just.

"We'd all be happier if we hadn't any relations," he growled. "None at all."

Margaret tried to sound shocked, because that was obviously what he wanted.

"What a horrid thing to say—why, you wouldn't have any of us!"

He laughed, pleasedly.

"Aye, maybe," he said, "but a man ought to be able to choose."

He scooped up another huge spoonful of stew, which gave Margaret time to think what she was going to say next.

"But then you wouldn't have anybody who *had* to stick by you. You'd only have friends and . . . and people like Mr. Gordon."

He munched slowly, thinking in his turn.

"Right you are," he said. "But mark you, I didn't choose him neither. He chose me. And what I say is . . ."

Between mouthfuls he told Margaret more about the village than he'd told her in years. Mr. Gordon was right, but he had too much power and influence for a man in his station, and that had maybe turned his head a trifle. It was squire's fault, and parson's. Squire was a ninny and parson was a drunkard. The whole village was sick. But you couldn't fight Davey Gordon and his gang, because nobody else would dare stand up for you. It was better to belong with them, and then at least you knew where you were. And, certainly, Davey had an uncanny nose for witchcraft of all kinds, and it was better to live in a sick village than

one riddled with witches. And mark you, Marge girl, witch
hunting was good sport—better than cockfighting.

When he'd finished his harangue Margaret fetched him
bread and cheese and went upstairs to see whether she
could do anything for Aunt Anne. She was asleep at last,
straightened out like a proper person. Margaret slipped out
and settled down to a long afternoon of housewifery. She
was feeding the eager hens in the early dusk when Jonathan
came back, riding Caesar, who looked bewildered by the
distance he'd suddenly been taken, as if he'd never realized
that the world was so large.

"How's Mum?" said Jonathan in a low voice.

"Better, I think; anyway she's asleep and lying properly. I
told your father you'd gone to see whether Cousin Mary was
all right."

"Good idea. Our lot are, anyway. Lucy's found a little row-
boat and tethered the tug right across the dock so that she
can't drift about—she's a clever girl, given the chance. And
she and Tim got Otto down into the cabin, where there's a
stove, so they won't freeze. I took them enough food for
three days, I hope."

"Did you try the footpath?"

"Yes, but there's a locked gate across it, so it was a good
thing we didn't try it. It would be faster than going through
Hempsted, if I can break the gate open. I didn't see your
dogs, but I heard them; if they smell Lucy and the others it's
going to be much more dangerous visiting the dock."

"But couldn't we tow them further along the canal, down
to the bit beyond Hempsted? No one lives there or goes
there."

"I can't start the engines, supposing they'll go, until Otto's
well enough to show me how, and once they're started
they'll bring people swarming round. When we do go, we'll
have to get down the canal and out to sea all in one rush."

"If you can break that gate, Scrub could tow them for a
few miles: that'd be enough."

"You and your Scrub! Could he really?"

"Oh, yes, I think so. You're so busy thinking about machines that you never remember what animals can do."

"Well, you think about them enough for both of us."

"Not so loud, Jo!"

"It's all right—it'd look funny if we spent all our time whispering to each other. Next time we can both get away I'll climb out the night before and hide that old horsecollar in the empty house at the top of Edge Lane. We mustn't be seen taking it."

But that wasn't for a full week. Aunt Anne's mind-sickness left her, but a strange fever followed it which made all her joints ache whenever she moved, so she lay drear-faced in bed or else tried to get up and do her duty as a farmer's wife with such obvious pain that Margaret couldn't possibly leave her to cope. Twice Uncle Peter had to carry her up to her bed. Then he asked around the village for somebody to take Lucy's place and found a cousin of Mr. Gordon's who'd been living over in Slad Valley. Her name was Rosie, and she was a bustling, ginger-haired, sharp-voiced woman of thirty, chubby as a pig and with sharp piggy eyes which watched you all the time. Margaret and Jonathan agreed it was like having an enemy spy actually in the house, but at least her presence gave them the chance to get away for a whole day. Jonathan had been to the boat again, alone, in the meanwhile, but they both knew that the food on *Heartsease* must be getting low now.

They picked up the hidden horsecollar and rode down to the canal, Caesar still absurdly astonished at the amount of exercise he was suddenly expected to take after years of slouching about unwanted in the paddock. It had snowed several times since their midnight journey, so the world was starched white except for the scribbled black lines of walls and hedges and the larger blobs where the copses stood; the colors of the famished hedgerow birds showed as sharp as they do in a painting. It had frozen most nights, too, and the surface of the snow was as crisp as cake icing but gave with a cracking noise when the hooves broke through to the softer stuff beneath. (This wasn't the cloying snow which would stick and cake inside the horseshoes, so there was no need to lard the ponies' feet.) The lane was hardly used this weather, but an old man waved at them from where he was chopping up the doors and staircase of an empty and isolated cottage to carry home for firewood.

"Seasonable weather we'll have for Christmas, then," he called.

"Yes," they shouted together.

"I'd forgotten about Christmas," muttered Margaret as they took the next slope. "It's going to make things much harder."

"Easier, I'd say," said Jonathan cheerfully. "With all those folk coming and going, no one will notice whether we're there or not."

"They'll notice if there's nothing to eat, so unless your mother gets better I'll have to be there."

"Won't Rosie . . ."

"If I leave her to do all the work she'll start asking people where on earth I can have got to—innocent, but meaning. You know."

"Um. Yes. We can't risk that, seeing whose cousin she is, too. And another thing, when we've shifted *Heartsease* we'd better go and call on Cousin Mary. Messages get sent at Christmas, and if we keep using her as an excuse and never go there, someone might hear tell of it."

"Besides," said Margaret, "she seemed terribly lonely when I did see her."

In front of the inn at Edge stood a group of men with short boar-spears in their hands, and rangy dogs rubbing against their legs. They waved, like the old man down the lane, but their minds were busy with the coming hunt and the ponies padded by as unnoticed as a small cloud. The runner-lines of a few sledges showed on the big road, but when they dipped into the lane the snow was untrodden— the Vale had little cause to visit the hills, nor the hills the Vale. As they twisted between the tall, ragged hedges Margaret glimpsed vistas of the flat reaches below, dim with snow, all white patches like a barely started watercolor. It looked very different from her earlier visits.

But when they were really down off the hills it felt just the same. As soon as the lane leveled out they came across a bent old woman gathering sticks out of the hedgerow. She glanced piercingly at them as they passed, but gave them no greeting. There was a black cat sitting on her shoulder. She looked like a proper witch.

She was the only soul they saw for the rest of the journey (not many, even of the queer Vale folk, cared to live so close to the city). When they crossed the swing bridge Jonathan reined Caesar to a willing halt and gazed up and down the mottled surface where the snow had fallen and frozen on the listless water. It looked a wicked surface, cold enough to kill and too weak to bear.

"I'm stupid," he said. "I should have known it would be like this. We can't tow her out till it thaws—for weeks, months, even."

"Wasn't it frozen when you came down on Tuesday?"

"There were bits of ice on it, but it was mostly water. I think the river must have risen high enough to flood over the top gates—that would have broken up the first lot of ice."

"What shall we do, then?"

"Go and see them, tell them to look out for the dogs, see how Otto is, give them the food. Then go and visit Cousin Mary."

The path by the canal was flat and easy, but long before they came to the dock area it was barred by a tall fence of corrugated iron. Jonathan led the way up the embankment, through a gap in a hedge and into the tangled garden of one of the deserted houses between Hempsted and Gloucester. Beyond the level crossing he pushed at a gate on the right of the road, picked his way between neat stacks of concrete drainage pipes and back to the canal. They were just below the docks.

"I found this way last time," he said. "There she is."

He pointed along the widening basin. The tug lay in its private ice floe right in the center of the dock, with a hawser dipping under the ice at prow and stern and a dinghy nestling against her quarter.

"It'll be easier from the other quay," said Jonathan. "We'll find a cord and throw it out so that they can pull the food sack across the ice—that hawser's shorter. Over this bridge is best."

"I can't see anyone on her," said Margaret.

"Too cold. They'll be keeping snug down below."

They moved in complete silence up the quayside and

around an arm of frozen water which stretched south from the main dock until they reached the place where the hawser was tied—a chilly and narrow stretch of quay under a bleak cliff of warehouse. Margaret peered nervously into the cavernous blackness between its open doors, and then squinted upward to where, eighty feet above her, the hoisting hook still dangled from the black girder that jutted out above the topmost door.

"Ahoy!" called Jonathan.

He was answered by a clamor of baying from the other side of the dock. There was a swirl of movement along the far quay, a shapeless brown and orange and black and dun weltering which spilled over the edge and became the dog pack hurling across the ice toward them.

"In here!" shouted Jonathan, using the impetus of Caesar's bucking to run him under the arch into the warehouse. Scrub followed, dragging Margaret.

"Door!" he shouted. She let go of the bridle and wrenched at her leaf of the big doors. It stuck, gave, rasped, and swung around into the arch. She could see the foremost dogs already on this side of the tug, coming in long bounds, heads thrown back and sideways, jaws gaping. Then Jonathan's door slammed against hers and they were in total dark.

"Sorry," he said, "mine was bolted."

He fiddled with the bottom of the doors while Margaret tensed her back against them and the baying and yapping rose in a spume of noise outside. The dark turned to grayness as her eyes learned to use the light from two grimed windows set high in the furthest wall. She could see the ponies now, standing quite still as though the dark were real night—just the way parrots go quiet when a cloth is thrown over their cage.

"I think that'll hold it," said Jonathan. "Hang on, there's a hook here too. That's better. Let's go up and see if we can see anything from above. If there isn't another way out we're in a mess."

The steps to the floor above were more of a broad ladder than a staircase. They found another long room, piled high with sacks of grain which had rotted and spilled their contents across the small railway that ran along the middle of the space from the doors overlooking the dock. The air smelled of mustiness and fermentation, sweet and bad.

"Let's go higher," said Jonathan. "They'll get excited again if we open these doors, but they mayn't notice if we go right to the top."

Each floor had the same layout, with the double doors at the end and the railway down the middle between the stacked goods. Different kinds of goods had been stored at different levels; on the second floor the trolley that ran on the rails had been left half unloaded, with two crates of canned pineapples still on it and a ledger loose on the floor. The very top floor was used for the most miscellaneous items—there was even a bronze statue of a soldier in one corner, swathed in the ropes that had been used to handle the crates on the hoist; beside him lay several truck axles. The roof had gone in a couple of places and patches of snow lay on the floor, but this meant it was much lighter; and when Jonathan pulled the double doors open it felt like sunrise. The girder arm of the hoist stuck out rigid above them, the big hook dangling halfway along. It was a gulping drop to the quay below. Out on the ice the dog pack were sniffing round *Heartsease* in an absentminded but menacing way. Jonathan leaned against his side of the doorway, quite unaffected by the chilling drop, and teased the back of his skull.

"We need a bomb," he said.

"Oh, surely they wouldn't store them here," said Margaret. "The army would have . . ."

He grinned across at her and she stopped talking.

"What's on that trolley?" he asked.

This one hadn't been unloaded at all. It was covered with small wooden boxes, no larger than shoeboxes, whose labels, still faintly legible, were addressed to the *Gloucester Echo.*

Margaret tried to pick one up but found she couldn't move it.

"Printing metal," said Jonathan. "Must be almost as heavy as lead. The boxes are small, so that a man can lift them. Now that's what I call a real bit of luck! Let's see if we can push it. Come on, harder! One, two, three, *heave!* Fine.

Leave it there and we'll try the hoist. It'll be electric, but there might be a hand control to run the hook out. Tell me if anything moves."

He tugged levers without result, then began to turn a large wheel.

"That's it," said Margaret excitedly, but still without any idea of what he was up to.

"Good. Now those bits of iron at the end of the rails must be to stop the trolley flying out over that quay if there's an accident, but there might be a way of moving them."

"Mine's got a sort of hook this side."

"So's mine, hang on, it's stuck. Can you see anything to bang it with? Yes, that'll do. Ouch! Don't worry, I only grazed my knuckles. Done yours? Fine. Now, just let me work this out."

"But, Jo, even if you get them right under here, on the quay, you'll only hit one or two, and . . ."

Jonathan stopped sucking his ravaged knuckle to grin at her.

"I've got a better idea. If it works," he said.

He looked outside, up at the hoist, back at the trolley, down at the drop. Then he wound the hook in, so that he could reach it. Then he made Margaret help him shove the trolley right to the giddy verge. Then he fetched the ropes which festooned the bronze soldier and spent several minutes contriving a lopsided sling from the hook to the trolley. Last of all he wound the hook out almost to the end of the girder and readjusted the ropes. Margaret suddenly saw what would happen if the trolley were pushed the last few inches over the edge—pushed with a rush: it would swing down and out, in a wide curve, trolley and boxes all moving together; but because the far end of the trolley was on longer ropes than the near end, the boxes would start to slide out forward, and when the swing of the ropes had reached its limit the boxes would all shoot on and be scattered right out across the ice, almost as far as *Heartsease;* and if the dogs could be lured onto the ice at the right moment . . . she knew what his next words were going to be before he said them.

"You'll have to be bait, I'm afraid."

"Bait?"

"Yes, as soon as I've found a lever. I want them on the ice halfway between here and *Heartsease*—it's the big ones that are the killers. Go down to the bottom, edge one door open, make quite sure you know how to shut it, slip through and shout. Look, they're bored with the tug and they're going back to where they were before, so you'll know just how long it will take them to get across. Stick it out as long as you can, Marge, but get back inside when the first dog is halfway between the boat and the quay—I don't want to drop a ton of lead on *you*. If I shout, you'll know it's not safe to open the door. All right?"

"All right," whispered Margaret, sick with terror. The stairs seemed longer going down, the rooms darker, the rustling of rats more obvious—perhaps they'd been scared into brief silence by the clamor of the dogs. Scrub and Caesar were restive: most ponies hate rats. She patted and talked to them both, until she realized she was only doing so to put off opening the door. She walked down between the rails and studied the bolt and the hook—the hook would be quite enough by itself. She was lifting it when she suddenly wondered whether she could hear him down all those stairs, supposing he was shouting to warn her of prowling hounds . . . come on, girl, of course you would—Jonathan wouldn't have suggested it if it wasn't going to work. She opened the door eight inches and slipped through the gap into the bitter daylight.

The dogs were over by a warehouse on the far side of the ice, squabbling over something edible. She could hear distant snarlings.

"Ahoy!" she called. Her voice was weak and thin.

"Ahoy!" came Jonathan's cheerful yell far above her head.

She saw two or three dogs raise their muzzles and look across the ice. She pranced about on the quay, waving both arms to make sure she was seen, because most dogs have poor vision and the wind was blowing from them to her, so that no scent would reach them.

At once it all became like the nightmares you have again and again: the same baying rose; the same swirl of color spilled down on the ice; the same dogs leaped yelping in front, their heads held the same way; the same panic lurched up inside her. She was yards from the door, after her prancing, and rushed madly for it, but when she reached it she saw that the dogs had barely come as far as the tug, so she still had to stand in the open, visible, edible, luring them on. Bait.

But it was only seconds before the first dog reached the rumple in the ice she'd chosen as a mark, and she could slip back in and hook the door shut. As she closed out the last of sky she thought she glimpsed black blobs hurling down.

Then there came a thud, a long, tearing crack, a lot of smaller bangings; the yelping changed its note, faltered and vanished; then there were only a few whimpers, mixed with a sucking and splashing. She unhooked the door, edged it open and poked her head out.

The whole surface of the ice had changed—it had been nothing like as thick as she'd thought and was really only snow frozen together, without the bonding strength of ice. Now the under water had flooded out across a great stretch of it and the part between her and *Heartsease* was smashed into separate floes, overlapping in places and leaving a long passage of open water. The smaller dogs had not come far enough to be caught and were rushing away to the far quay, but most of the larger ones were struggling in the deadly water. As she watched, one which had been marooned on a floating island of ice shifted its position; the ice tilted and slid it sideways into the water; it tried to scrabble back but could find no hold; then it swam across to the fixed ice and tried there, but still there was nothing on the slippery surface for its front legs to grip while it hauled its sodden hindquarters out; it tried and tried. Margaret looked away, and saw several others making the same hopeless effort around the edges of the open water. In the middle two still shapes floated—dogs which had actually been hit by the falling boxes. She shut the door and went trembling up the stairs.

Jonathan had shut his door and was sitting on a bale with his head between his hands. He looked white, even in the dimness.

"It worked," she said, "but I couldn't go on looking."

"Nor could I," he answered. "It's not their fault they're killers."

Margaret was surprised. She was so used, after five years of knowing him well, to his instant reaction to the needs of any happening that she hardly thought about it. Jo would say what to do, and he'd be right. Now, for the second time —the first had been when they'd crouched at the top of the stairs and listened to Mr. Gordon hypnotizing Aunt Anne— he'd buckled under the sudden load of his feelings. He felt the death of the dogs more than she did—she was only shocked, but he felt something deeper, more wounding, in his having done what he had to do. She put her hand under his arm and coaxed him to his feet.

"The ponies are getting worried," she said.

He followed her listlessly down the dusty flights; the ponies were stamping fretfully in the shadows, but as much from boredom and strangeness as from fear—or perhaps the stress the children felt was making them kick the cobbles in that fretful way. Jonathan walked up to Caesar and slapped his well-padded shoulder.

"Shut up, you fat idiot," he said. "We could stick it out for months here. Corn for you and pineapples for me and a million rats to talk to."

Caesar enjoyed being spoken to like that. Margaret fondled Scrub's nose and gently teased his ears until he was calm. Then she opened the door. The water was almost still now, though two dogs still paddled feebly at the far edge. A few more shapes floated in the middle of the water—the others must have got out somehow, or sunk when they drowned. As she looked, a hatch on *Heartsease* opened and a cautious head poked out—Lucy's. Margaret stepped into the open and waved; an arm waved back. Jonathan came and stood beside her, with his usual perky, cat-faced look.

"If they used their pole to break the ice around her," he said, "they could cast off the far hawser and we could haul her over."

"Scrub and Caesar could, anyway," said Margaret.

But it took five minutes of signaling and hallooing before Lucy grasped the idea and persuaded Tim to do the work. Meanwhile Margaret devised a makeshift connection be-

tween the near hawser and Scrub's horsecollar, and an even
more makeshift harness for Caesar to do his share of hauling in. Caesar didn't mind, but the ramshackle and once-
only nature of the whole contraption displeased Scrub's
conservative soul, and she had to bully him before he suddenly bent to his task like a pit-pony and began to haul the
inert but frictionless mass across the dock. Margaret led the
ponies back into the warehouse, so that they could pull
straight.

"Whoa!" shouted Jonathan from the quayside, and she
hauled back on the bridles. The hawser deepened its curve
until it lay like a basking snake along the floor, but it was
many seconds before she heard the dull boom of the tug
nudging up against the stonework. Three minutes later they
had shut the ponies back in the warehouse and were standing on the deck, where Tim was cuddling a draggled yellow
blob with a snarling black snout.

"What's he got?" said Margaret.

"Puppy," said Lucy. "He fished un off a bit of ice as the
boat ran past. Come and see Otto. He's better—in his mind,
that is. He can't move his legs still, and his side hurts him,
but he's better in his mind."

She led them below.

# Chapter 6

# WILL SHE GO?

It was glorious to be out of the fingering wind.

The cabin, an odd-shaped chamber with a tilting floor and walls which both curved and sloped, was beautifully warm and stuffy—warm from the round stove which crackled against the inner wall, stuffy from being lived in by three people. The witch lay in a corner, his feet down the slope of the floor, and watched them scramble down the ladder; the reflection of daylight from the open hatch made his eyes gleam bright as a robin's. He looked thin, tired, ill—but not dying, not any longer.

"Welcome to the resistance movement," he said in his strange voice, slow and spoken half through his nose. "What you got there, Tim? Another patient?"

Tim cooed happily and put his bundle on the floor, a wet, yellow, floppy pup, just big enough to have followed its mother with the pack but not big enough to fend for itself, nor to tilt off its patch of ice and drown. It snarled at them all and slashed at Tim's hand; he didn't snatch it away but let the puppy chew at it with sharp little teeth until Lucy handed him a mutton bone. The puppy took it ungraciously into the darkest corner and settled down to a private growling match.

Otto laughed.

"What shall we call him?" he said. "If it is a him."

"Davey," said Margaret without thinking. The other two children looked at her, surprised.

"Means something to you?" said Otto. "Okay, fine. What happened outside? We heard the noises but we couldn't figure them out. At least you won your battle."

Jonathan told him what they had done in dry sentences, as though it had happened to someone else and was not very interesting anyway. Otto listened without a word and then lay silent, twitching his eyes from face to face.

"Yeah," he said at last. "I reckoned I'd just been mighty lucky till now. I didn't know we had a thinker pulling for us."

"We can't do it if we're not lucky," said Jonathan without emphasis.

"Yes," burst in Margaret, "but we couldn't have got anywhere without Jo. He's made all the luck *work.*"

"The question is can we make the engines work," said Jonathan.

"What's she got?" said Otto.

"I think it must be diesel," said Jonathan. "It's very old; there's a brass plate on the engine saying nineteen twenty-eight. I can't see anywhere for a furnace, or for storing coal; and there are feed-pipes which look right for oil and wrong for water, and a big oil tank behind here."

He slapped the partition behind the stove. Otto whistled.

"Nineteen twenty-eight!" he said. "A genuine vintage tub, then. Isn't there anything newer?"

"Yes," said Jonathan, "the other tug, the one that's not sunk I mean, looks much newer and much more complicated. But it's in a mess, as though they were using it all the time just before the Changes came. But this one's very tidy, with everything stowed away and covered up and tied down. I thought perhaps it was so old that they didn't use it at all, but just kept it here, laid up. So they might have left it properly cared for, so that *they'd* be able to start it if they hadn't tried for a long time."

"Yeah," said Otto, "that they might. And another thing—a primitive engine is a simple engine—unsophisticated, not much to go wrong, provided she isn't all seized up. I'll get Tim to lug me along for a look-see as soon as my rib's mended, three more weeks maybe. And where'll you sail us then, captain?"

"We're in Gloucester Docks," said Jonathan. "There's a canal which goes down to the Bristol Channel. Margaret's explored it. It's about fifteen miles long, she thinks, and not many people live near it. The bridges over it open quite easily, though she didn't try them all. There's only one lock, out beyond the other docks at the far end. We thought we'd use the ponies to tow *Heartsease* right down there, and if anyone stopped us we could say it was a wicked machine and we wanted to get it away from our part of the canal— that would be a good argument in England now. And when we got there we could see if we could find enough fuel (or we could look for some here) and see if we can make the lock work. If we can we'll try to start the engines and get out down the Bristol Channel, and if we can't we'll think of something else."

"Sharpness," said Otto. "That's the name of the port at the far end; I remember it from my briefing. And another thing I remember—that the Bristol Channel's just about the trickiest water in Europe. Tide goes belting in and out, six knots each way, and drops thirty foot in two hours; then the river's nothing but mud flats and a bit of stream winding through the middle. We'll need charts."

"I'm hungry," said Margaret.

"Right," said Otto. "Food first, action after. What's on the menu?"

"We've nigh on eaten all you brought last time, Master Jonathan," said Lucy.

"We've brought enough for another three days, I hope," said Margaret.

"Anyway," said Jonathan, "the warehouse is absolutely full of cans."

"Given you can find a can opener," said Otto.

The shape of that forgotten tool was suddenly sharp in Margaret's mind, like an image out of a lost dream.

"I'll look for an ironmonger's," said Jonathan, "after I've burgled the offices for charts."

While they ate the firm cheese and crisp-crusted bread (one thing about Rosie, she baked better than anyone else in the village) they talked a little and thought a lot. Margaret was dismayed to find that they were less than halfway through their job; the most dangerous part was still to come. And she alone knew how huge and immovable-seeming were the steel gates down at Sharpness. She distracted herself from her worries by watching Tim coax the puppy into trusting him, so gentle, so patient that it was difficult to remember that he hadn't all his wits. The puppy was quite wild, but with generations of man-trust bred into it; savagery and hunger and fear fought with these older instincts, sometimes winning, sometimes losing. At last there came a moment when it took a fragment of bacon from Tim's hand without snatching and running away, then stayed where it was to let him rub the back of its skull with his rough, dirty fingers.

She looked around the cabin and saw that the others had been watching just as intently as she had, as though the fall of kingdoms depended on Tim's winning.

"He's not so hungry now," explained Jonathan with his dry laugh.

"Tim, you're marvelous," said Margaret.

"Why do you want to name him after Mr. Gordon, then, Miss Margaret?" said Lucy, soft and suspicious as of old.

"I don't know," said Margaret. "Mr. Gordon's a bit like that, I suppose, savage and doing what he does because something in him makes him. But I thought it might be lucky too, I don't know how."

"Who's Mr. Gordon?" said Otto.

It was not comfortable to explain, because if Mr. Gordon had not lived in the village Otto might never have been stoned. Even so, they found themselves trying to make as good a case as they could for the terrible old man, partly for the honor of the village but partly for reasons they couldn't put a name to.

Otto's good hand kept fingering the puckered tissues which were left after the healing of his smashed cheek.

"To think of you kids living with all this and staying like you have," he said when they'd finished.

"It's Aunt Anne, more than anything," explained Margaret.

"And that's true," whispered Lucy.

Jonathan didn't speak, but got up and climbed the ladder into the square of daylight. Margaret went with him and found that the tug had now drifted a few feet away from the quay. For the first time she really looked at *Heartsease* by daylight—a dirty old boat, black where it wasn't rusty, about seventy feet long; the bulwarks curved out from the uptilted prow about knee-high, and became shallower as they reached the rounded stern; the cabin was at the fore end, its roof barely a foot above deck level; then a narrow strip of deck beneath which lay the fuel tank; then the wheelhouse, which was really just a windowed shed much too tall and wide for the proportions of the boat. Behind that stood the big funnel, with its silly little hat brim running around it just below the top—she could still see the lines of color which showed which shipping firm the tug had belonged to. The funnel rose from the top of a low, flat roof, along whose side ran tiny rectangular windows, which could only allow the skimpiest ration of light through to whatever was below. The engine room. Under there must lie the iron monster which Jonathan was going to try to wake; it was the monster's weight which set the tug so much down by the stern, making it (even at rest) seem to tilt with an inward energy as though it were crouched to tackle huge seas. And last of all came an open area of deck rounded off by the curve of the bulwarks at the stern. This was what Margaret had been looking for—a place where she could tether Scrub when the time came.

Jonathan had opened the engine room hatch and was kneeling beside it, craning down into the gap, his trousers taut over his rump, his whole body as tense as a terrier at a rat hole. Margaret nudged his ribs with her shoe and he stood up frowning.

"Too difficult for me," he said. "At least, I'm sure I could understand it if Otto would teach me. If you'll show Lucy where the cans are I'll look for charts and a can opener."

"Don't you think Tim had better go with you, just in case?"

Jonathan agreed, and scuttled down into the engine room. He came back with a massive wrench, almost the shape of a caveman's club. Margaret explained to Lucy, who frowned and stood biting her thumb in the cabin. It was difficult for her: danger for Jonathan meant danger for Tim; but they would never get away if Jonathan went into danger alone and was caught by the dogs; and Tim couldn't decide for himself, so . . .

She sighed, shook herself and tried to explain to Tim that he was to go with Jonathan to stop him from being hurt. At last he grasped the idea that something was dangerous, and took the big wrench. Jonathan led him off. Every few yards he brandished the wrench and snarled right and left.

"Do you think he'd actually hit a dog if he had to?" said Margaret.

"I dunno," whispered Lucy, "but he'd surely fright 'em."

She gazed after the hulking back with just the same smile as a mother's who watches her pudgy toddler playing some private game. Margaret had never liked her so much.

The ponies had become fretful in their strange dark stall, all rustling with rats, but it seemed safe enough to lead them out and tether them on the quay. On the first floor of the warehouse Margaret found a sack which seemed not to have gone musty, so she tilted a double helping of corn into the fold of her skirt, carried it down and spread it in two piles on the snow. The ponies sniffed it, then gobbled greedily at it.

By the time the girls had carried their third load of cans aboard, Jonathan and Tim were back, both too laden with looted goods to fight off a single hungry terrier. Luckily they hadn't even met that. They had charts and tide tables, books for Otto, a can opener and knives and forks. Jonathan dumped his load on the deck and opened a blue metal case.

"Look, Marge," he said. "Aren't they *beautiful?*"

There was a wild light in his eyes, as though he had drunk some drug, when all he had found was an expensive tool chest full of shiny wrenches and firm pliers.

When all their treasures were stowed away they said good-bye to Otto, jumped ashore and pushed the tug out along the channel through the ice with a scaffold plank Margaret had found. No dogs barked as they rode away. It was too late to visit Cousin Mary; in fact it was drawing toward dusk when the ponies plodded down the last slope toward the farm, Scrub sulky because he hadn't been far enough and Caesar sulky because he'd been anywhere at all.

That night Margaret had the second of her nightmares about the bull at Splatt Bridge. Two nights later she had the same dream again; again the bull was pelting toward her; again Scrub vanished from beneath her; again she was waist-high in clinging grass, unable to turn or run or cry for help; again she woke with a slamming heart and lay sweating in the dark, telling herself it was only a dream. And the same a few nights later; and twice next week; and so on, for six weeks, while the frost locked hill and vale in its iron grasp.

No more snow fell, but even the sun at noon had no strength to melt what already lay. Where the earth was bare it boomed when you struck it with a stick, as though the whole round world were your drum. Christmas came with carols and trooping into the tomb-cold church to hear a long service in Latin (the parson was sober this year) and cooking big slabs of meat and bread in case the revelers felt hungry while they were shouting in the farmyard (you couldn't call it singing); all the men's faces were cider-purple in the feast-day firelight, but surly and ashamed next morning.

Aunt Anne slowly recovered, and began to eat a little and smile a little, especially when Jonathan was in the room. Mr. Gordon visited them several times, but seemed more like a bent old gossip than a dangerous slayer of witches.

Every third day the children took it in turns to ride down to the docks. They had no need to think of an excuse now, because Cousin Mary's leg was worse and she had taken to her bed. She and Aunt Anne forgave each other the silver teapot, and began to exchange long weepy letters on scraps of hoarded paper, chatting over the adventures of their own girlhood, and the children carried them to and fro. Uncle

Peter worked hard and said little. He slept in the kitchen, preferring it to Aunt Anne's sickroom.

*Heartsease* froze hard into the ice again, twelve feet from the quay. Jonathan found a ladder and raided the ironmonger's for nails, so that when Margaret next rode down she found a bridge between shore and ship which a human could clamber across but a dog couldn't. The pack could have crossed the ice again, of course, but never came—they were scared of the docks now, and no wonder.

But Jonathan had hit trouble in the business of clearing the towpath down to Hempsted Bridge. Not one gate, but several, blocked it, where different industrial estates had sealed off their own territories. He toiled away steadily with looted crowbars and hacksaws and bolt cutters. He also found two or three inlets of water on that side: they would have to get enough way on *Heartsease* to let her drift past while they led Scrub around the edge.

In the middle of January, Margaret found that Otto had been moved into the engine room. Reluctantly she climbed down iron rungs into a chilly chamber whose whole center was occupied by a great gray mass of iron, bulging into ponderous cylinders, flowering with taps and dials. Otto's bed was in the narrow gangway which ran all around it. There was a much smaller engine outside the gangway on either side.

"Did you ever see anything like it?" he said. "It's so primitive it ought to be made of flint. A Dutch diesel, my pop would have called it—they used to have tractors like it when he was a kid. See those things on top of the cylinders that look like blowlamps? You light 'em up and let 'em blow onto the cylinder heads; then you get the auxiliary going—that's this motor here; we won't need the other one, it's only electric—and pump up the air bottles, over yonder. Then, when the cylinder heads are good and hot, you turn on the fuel, give her a blast of compressed air from the bottles and she's going. Got it?"

"No," said Margaret. "It's not the sort of thing I understand. But *will* it go?"

"Tim's turned her over for me, and the parts all move. So

far so good, that's the best you can say. But I can't see why she shouldn't."

"Have you told Jo?"

"Uh-huh," said Otto. "He's fallen in love with her, I reckon."

"You won't let him touch it, will you?" said Margaret urgently. "Not until we're ready to go?"

"Why so?"

"Otherwise he'll get himself all covered with rust and oil and begin to smell of machines. And even if he doesn't actually *smell*, Mr. Gordon will nose him out."

"This Mr. Gordon," said Otto, "I'm beginning to think he's a bit of a baddie. If he was a cowboy he'd wear a black hat."

"It isn't like that," said Margaret. "Nobody's like that. It's all caused by things which happened long ago, long ago, and probably no one noticed when they happened. I don't even know if he was always a cripple—I must ask Uncle Peter."

Otto stared at her for a long time. Then he said, "Forget it —I was only joking."

"I'm sorry," said Margaret. "I didn't understand. We aren't used to jokes in our world."

"Okay," said Otto, "I'll keep your Jonathan away, best I can, but his fingers are itching."

"I'll talk to him. Is there a lot to do to the engine?"

"Injectors to be cleaned is the main thing," said Otto. "That's them on top. Lucy can do it, if she can show Tim how to loosen 'em off."

Lucy gave a funny little bubble of laughter over in her corner.

"When I go to heaven," she said, "there won't be no cleaning. I spent four years cleaning the farmhouse, and then I'm cleaning Otto, and now I'm going to clean a hulking great lump of iron."

"Sweetie," said Otto, "if we get home I'll see to it that the United States government buys you a dishwasher, three clothes washers and eighteen floor polishers."

"I should like that," said Lucy.

That night Margaret gave Jonathan a long, whispered sermon about staying away from machines. He made a comic disappointed face, but nodded. Then, after his next visit, he crept into the kitchen reeking of a heady, oily smell. Luckily Uncle Peter was out, tending a sick heifer. Margaret took Jonathan's clothes and poked them one by one into the back of the fire, which roared strangely as it bit into them; and she made Jonathan take a proper, all-over bath in front of the hearth. They had just tilted the water out down the pantry drain when there was a rattle at the bolted door—Rosie, back from calling on her cousin. She sniffed sharply around the kitchen the moment she was in.

"Funny kind of whiff in here," she said.

"I fell in a bog," said Jonathan.

"Fool of a boy," said Rosie. "Give me your clothes and I'll put 'em to soak."

"I've burned them," said Margaret. "They smelled awful— I think there must have been something wicked in the bog."

"Nice to be rich folk," said Rosie sharply. "Some might say wasteful."

"I'll ask Mr. Gordon, shall I?" said Margaret. "He'd know if I was right."

"Maybe," said Rosie, and went sniffing upstairs.

Jonathan winked at Margaret from his swathing towels, but she was shivering with the nearness of the escape. Later, when they went out to water the ponies, he explained that he had checked the fuel on *Heartsease* and there was plenty of diesel oil but not enough kerosene for the blowlamps on top of the cylinders; he'd found some drums of the stuff in a shed, but the one he tried to roll outside had been so rusted through that it split and spilled all over him. Margaret tried to scold him, but already he was talking excitedly about something called the bilge, which he'd shown Tim how to empty; the point was that the tug had hardly leaked at all.

Next time Margaret visited the docks Lucy was sitting with a piece of dirty machinery in her lap, swabbing at it with a clear, smelly liquid, the same that Jonathan had reeked of—kerosene. Margaret ran up the ladder again, fearful that the stink of the stuff would get into her hair. Tim was on deck, carefully cleaning his way around with a brush; the puppy, Davey, crouched watchfully beside him and as soon as he had gathered a little mound of rustflakes and dirt would leap on it with a happy wuff and scatter it around the deck. Luckily Tim enjoyed the game too, and seemed prepared to go on all day, sweeping and then seeing his work undone. But between games (perhaps while Davey was snoozing) the tug had become cleaner; the windows of the wheelhouse had been wiped, too, and the bigger flakes of peeling paint removed. But to set against this tidiness there was a nasty little pyramid of used cans on the ice under the bows—Lucy's style.

Margaret knew that she herself would have carried them out of sight, but she couldn't any longer despise Lucy for not doing things her way. And if she wasn't going to nag there was nothing for her to do, so she called her good-byes down the hatch and was answered by two preoccupied mumbles, Lucy busy with her cleaning and Otto with his charts and tide tables. Scrub had never learned to approve of the docks and walked off briskly the moment she was mounted.

Cousin Mary was much worse, too poorly even to write; she raised her fat hulk onto an elbow to give Margaret a few word-of-mouth messages to Aunt Anne, but almost at once sank back sweating with pain. Even having someone in the room obviously tired her. Margaret left quickly.

They were trotting up the lane toward the main road when Scrub suddenly faltered into a limping walk. Margaret jumped down and saw that he was shifting his off foreleg in obvious distress; when she lifted the hoof she found a ball of snow packed like iron inside it, which it took her several minutes to pry out. The other three hooves were nearly as bad. She straightened when she had cleared them and looked at the landscape with new eyes: the ash by the lane was dripping its own private rainfall onto the pocked snow beneath; the wind smelled of the warm sea and not of the icy hills; there was a tinkling in the ditch beneath the crust of snow. The whole Vale was thawing, thawing fast.

She had to clear Scrub's hooves twice more before they reached the first house in Edge, where a tiny woman lent her enough lard to smear into them to stop the gluey snow from sticking.

Jonathan was so fidgety with excitement that evening that

Rosie kept looking at him with the sour glance of someone who is being kept out of a secret. Margaret knew what he was thinking: He had only two more gates across the towpath to demolish. In a few days the canal, too, would be clear, and they could tow the tug down, by stages, to Sharpness and work out how the lock gates functioned and watch the pattern of the tides. He chattered about it next morning when they were picking up the eggs, their whispers safe from inquisitive ears amid the scuttling and clucking of disturbed hens.

"Jo," she said in a pause, "I don't want to come with you."

He looked up with a puckered stare from groping under the nesting box where Millicent always hid her egg.

"Why not?"

"I'm frightened. Not of the journey, or what people will do if they catch us. I'm frightened of that too, of course, but it's different. I'll help you get away, but then I want to come back here."

He stood up and sighed.

"You can't," he said. "Mr. Gordon—all of them—will know you were in it. Think what they'll do then. You'll have made fools of them."

She stared at the straw until it grew misty; then she shook her head to clear the half-started tears. Jonathan bent to search for Millicent's hidden treasure again.

"We'll find room for Scrub," he said without looking at her.

It seemed a long week before it was her turn to ride down again. The farmyard became mushy, the fields squelched, the ditches gushed and the millstream at the bottom roared with melting snow. A slight frost most nights slowed the thaw up, but when at last she headed Scrub down into the Vale the only snow lay in wavering strips along the northern side of walls and hedges. She dismounted at the bridge and prodded the ice with a stick; there was an inch of water above it, and it gave way when she pushed—it would be gone next day. On *Heartsease* the engine was fitted together again and Otto was reading *Oliver Twist*. Lucy was cooking on the cabin stove, hemmed in by the piles of tools and rope and tackle and oddments which Jonathan had been looting from deserted ironmongers' and ships' chandlers. Tim was exercising Davey on the quayside. There was nothing for her to do again, except to warn them to be ready for the slow, three-day tow to Sharpness. Already they all seemed to have settled into such a routine of danger that she was hardly worried by the thought of that stretch of the adventure: it all ought to be quite straightforward, she thought. They could simply pick their time.

But when she rode into Hempsted there was a funeral cart at Cousin Mary's door. Their excuse for visiting the Vale was gone.

# Chapter 7

# ENGINES

Jonathan thought for almost a minute, biting the back of his knuckle while his breath steamed in the early moonlight. Then he picked up his side of the big bucket and helped her edge it through the paddock gate and tilt the water into the trough.

"I'll ride down tomorrow night," he said, "and warn them to get ready. Then we can both go down two nights after that and start the towing in the dark. We'll be halfway to Sharpness before they even miss us, and they'll never guess which way we've gone."

"We must say good-bye to Aunt Anne somehow," said Margaret.

"I'll write her a letter. I'll do it tomorrow so that I don't have to do it at the last minute, and I'll hide it in my room. Cheer up, Marge, she'll feel better when we've gone because she'll stop worrying about us. That's why she's been so ill, knowing what'd happen to us if we're found."

"But she doesn't know what we're doing," said Margaret.

"She knows we're doing something, though."

Margaret remembered the haggard face, and the bony hands that had banged her to and fro in bed.

"Yes," she said.

He was in his room all next afternoon, toiling away (Margaret knew) at his half-taught, baby-big handwriting. He would tell Aunt Anne everything, too, because she had a right to know the truth, a right to know the real reasons why he had to go. Margaret went to bed feeling guilty in the awareness that he was keeping himself awake so that when the house was still he could climb out and ride the tiring journey down to their companions; but she was quickly asleep. Perhaps she stirred and frowned when the board outside on the landing creaked as someone trod on it in the darkness, or perhaps the stirring and frowning were caused by the first waves of terror as she began on the old, horrible dream about the bull.

But this time the dream never finished. Instead she was wide awake, staring at darkness, heart slamming, because something out of the real world had woken her—a shouting and stamping on the stairs, three hammering paces on the landing, and the door of her room opening like a thunderclap. Uncle Peter towered there, a lantern in one hand and in the other several sheets of paper, all different sizes.

"What's this? What's this?" he bellowed, and shoved the papers under her nose. She put out a hand to take them, though she knew quite well what they were, but he snatched them away. His face was so tense with rage that she could have counted the different muscles of his cheeks. Rosie hovered in the doorway behind him.

"What's what?" quavered Margaret—no matter how scared she sounded, because she would have been scared even if she'd known nothing.

"A letter!" he shouted. "A letter to your aunt! Jo wrote it. Says he rescued that witch and he's going to get him away from Gloucester Docks in a filthy wicked boat! What *d'you* know about it, my girl?"

"Where did you find it?" asked Margaret in a wobbly voice.

"Rosie brought it to me," he growled. Rosie's acid tones took over.

"I was leaning on my sill," she said, "looking out at the night, when I saw Master Jonathan ride away into the dark of the lane. So I puzzled what he might be about, and went along to his room to see if there was nothing there to tell, and sure enough I found this letter, so I took it to the master. No more than my duty, was it?"

"No," said Margaret. "I'm sure you did right. Have you told Aunt Anne, Uncle Peter?"

"None of your business!" he shouted, so she knew he hadn't. "He talks about *we*—we did this, we're planning that. *You're* in it!"

"Oh, no, Uncle Peter! You can't think that. I don't know anything about machines—I hate them and I wouldn't understand them anyway. Don't you think he might mean Lucy and Tim?"

Uncle Peter peered for a moment at the paper, too dazed with anger to read or think. Then he shoved his face close against Margaret's, so that she could smell his cabbagy breath, and stared into her eyes.

"Maybe," he growled deep in his throat, "maybe not—we'll know the morning. He says he's not planning to be off these two days, so likely he'll be back by dawn. Till then I'll just lock you in while I go and rout Davey Gordon out. Rosie can watch out of the parlor window, so there'll be no nonsense like you tying your sheets together and climbing down, see!"

"Of course not!" said Margaret.

He took his face away and stood brooding for a moment at the lantern.

"Dear Lord in Heaven," he said softly, "have I not been tried enough?"

When he'd gone, followed by Rosie, she sat in the dark pierced through and through with pure despair. First she thought, if I stay where I am it'll look as though I had nothing to do with it. Second, and much stronger, came the thought, I must warn them—if I dress I might just be able to get down from the window and run to Scrub before Rosie catches me. I'll have to ride him bareback, because there'll be no time to harness him, and I doubt if he'll like that, but it's the only chance.

She was putting a big jersey on and still trying to think of a way to distract Rosie from the parlor window when the door scraped faintly—the bolt was being drawn back. Margaret stiffened at the creak of the hinges; now she was going to be caught fully dressed, with no possible lie to account for it.

"Marge, Marge," whispered Aunt Anne's voice, "get dressed as quick as you can."

"I am dressed."

"Oh, thank heavens. He was too angry to think of locking your pony up. You've just time to saddle up and ride to warn Jo. I'll keep Rosie busy while you get through the kitchen."

"No," said Margaret, "I'll climb down from Jo's window— she can't see that side of the house. Then you can bolt the door after me and go back to bed and seem too sick to move, and they won't know what's happened."

"Marge, please, Marge," said Aunt Anne, "if the Changes ever end, bring him home."

"He'll come anyway," said Margaret. "I'm sure."

"And Marge, remember Pete's a *good* man, really. A very good man."

"I know. I like him too."

As she tiptoed down the passage she heard a noise like sobbing, but so faint that the grate of the closing bolt drowned it.

Scrub was waiting for her at the paddock gate, as if there was nothing he wanted more than a midnight gallop. As she tightened the girth of the heavy sidesaddle she heard a new noise in the night—men's excited voices. That meant the lane was blocked, so she swung herself into the saddle and set Scrub's head to the low place in the far wall, which she'd often eyed as a possible jump if it hadn't meant going over into Farmer Boothroyd's land. But tonight she didn't care a straw for old and foolish feuds.

Scrub must have thought about the jump too, for he took it with a clean swoop, like a rook in the wind. Then came a good furlong down across soft and silent turf to the far gate;

then the muddy footpath along the bottom of Squire's Park; a steep track up, and they were out in Edge Lane.

Potholed tarmac, unmended through five destroying winters, is a poor surface for a horse to hurry over in the dark, especially when it tilts down like a slate roof between tall hedges. In places Margaret could risk a trot, for they both knew the road well by now, but mostly there was nothing for it but a walk. Luckily Scrub had sensed the excitement and urgency of the journey, so he didn't loiter; but the dip to the stream was agonizingly slow and the climb beyond slower still. Then they could canter along the old main road —though they nearly fell from overconfidence in the pitchy blackness beneath the trees; the descent to the Vale was slow again, before they could hit a really fast clip along the bottom.

Margaret did sums. Caesar was a slower pony, and Jonathan wouldn't be hurrying as much as she was. But he'd left at least an hour before she had—probably two hours. Suppose he spent half an hour at the docks, making arrangements (he'd have thought it all out in his head on the way down, and would know exactly what he wanted)—she'd gain at least half an hour on him on the journey, almost a whole hour; so they'd meet on the big road at the bottom, or the bridge, or the towpath if he'd dallied. She began to strain her ears for distant hooves. The far cry of a dog made her shiver with sudden terror, but it might have been miles away.

The iron bridge rang beneath Scrub's shoes, but that was the only sound in the wide night. She must have missed him; he'd found some clever way home, across fields. Desperately she hurried Scrub along the matted grass of the towpath, leaning low over his neck and peering forward for the place where they turned up past the deserted house into the road.

"Marge!" called a voice out of the shadows behind her. She reined back; hooves scuffled, and a small shape led a larger shape out into the unshadowed path behind her.

"I thought it must be you," said Jonathan. "What's happened?"

"Rosie found your letter and took it to Uncle Peter."

"But I hid . . . Oh, never mind. It all depends what they do. We'd best go back to the tug and talk to the others."

They led the ponies through the ruined garden.

"If they come down here and find us," mused Jonathan, "we'll be done. We could run away, but we'd have to leave Otto, and Tim will be hard to hide. We could turn the horses loose and all hide in the city, but then we'd be worse off than before. But if we can start the engine, and if the canal is deep all the way down, we can get clear away, provided they don't try to cut us off. In a chase we'll go faster than they do, and keep going, and that should give us about two hours at Sharpness. That would be enough if the tide's right, and Otto's worked a tide table out. We'll have to see."

"Couldn't we start to tow her down while you're working on the engines?" said Margaret. "That would save time."

"Not worth it. We've got to run the auxiliary for at least an hour before we can start the main engine, and if we try to do that while we're towing through the countryside people will come swarming out and catch us helpless. Once we go, we must go fast, because of the noise. But you'll still be useful, you two."

She could hear from his voice that he was grinning in the dark.

"You'll have to ride ahead and open the bridges," he said.

"Yes, I think I can do that; nobody lives near them, except for the two at that village down at the far end."

"It's called Purton on the map. We might be able to stop and tow her past there. You're going to have to ride fast, Marge—she does nearly ten miles an hour, flat out, Otto thinks."

"That's too fast. We could do it for a bit, but we'd never keep it up."

"I'll talk to Otto," said Jonathan.

The tug lay still and lightless, a dull black blob on the shiny black water, but Davey yapped once, sharply, as they came along the quay. They heard a quick scuffle as Jonathan crossed the ladder—Tim, presumably holding the muzzle of a struggling pup.

"It's all right," said Jonathan's cheerful voice, pitched just right for everyone to hear, "it's me again."

The scuffling started again, then stopped with the ludi-crous gargle of a dog who has been all set to bark and finds there is no need. The hatch from the cabin, where Lucy slept amid Jonathan's loot, rose.

"Forgotten summat, Master Jonathan?" said her soft purr. "Why, you've a body with you, Miss Margaret is it? There's trouble, then?"

"I think it'll be all right, Lucy, provided we start tonight. Father found the letter I wrote to Mother."

Lucy came swiftly out of the hatch and looked into his face.

"And I'll lay he took it straight up to Mus' Gordon," she said.

"Yes, he did," said Margaret.

"I must take Tim away, then," said Lucy.

"You can if you want to," said Jonathan, "but I'm going to try and start the engines and run down to Sharpness. It's sixteen miles, so we should do it in three hours. If we get the engines going just before dawn I'll be able to see to steer, and Marge can ride ahead and scout and open the bridges. You'll be no worse off if you have to run from Sharpness than from Gloucester."

"I've been looking at them maps," said Lucy. "If they've a morsel of sense they'll head to one of the bridges halfway down and catch us there."

"Yes, I've thought of that," said Jonathan, "but it's not their style. I said in my letter we weren't going for two days, so they'll wait for us to come home tonight, and when we don't they'll come blinding down here in the morning. If we get a start we'll be far away by the time they reach here. You think it out while I talk to Otto; if you still want to leave us, you should go at once, but we won't need to start the auxil-iary for another two hours."

"I don't like it, neither way," whispered Lucy, and settled chin in hand on the bulwarks.

"You go and lie in her bed, Marge," said Jonathan. "I shan't need you until dawn."

"What about the ponies?"

"Tie them up on the quay. I'll keep an eye on them."

"Scrub's all taut inside—he knows something's up. He needs a roll."

"Oh, goodness!" said Jonathan angrily. "He'll have to roll on cobbles, then."

Margaret scrambled across the bridge, thinking so that's why Caesar is such a broody and difficult character—Jo's never understood him. All horses get tense, after any sort of expedition, and need to work it off, to unwind. She tethered them side by side to a rusty ring set in the quay, fetched Tim's bailing pan and a bucket, and dredged up nasty oily water from the dock for them to drink. She fondled Scrub's neck for a while to calm him, tried to be nice to Caesar (who sneered sulkily back) and crossed the ladder again. The blankets were warm and Lucy-smelling, but the boards beneath them were so hard that they seemed to gnaw at her hip—small chance of going to sleep; but in a minute she was in the middle of a busy dream, senseless with shifting scenes and people who changed into other people, all hurrying for an urgent reason which was never explained to her.

She was woken by clamor for the second time that night. But now it was not Uncle Peter roaring up the stairs, but a noise which England hadn't heard for five years, fuel exploding inside cylinders to bang the pistons up and send the crankshaft whanging around—the auxiliary engine pumping air into the big storage bottles, to provide the pressure which would start the main diesel.

On deck, light glimmered through the glass roof over the engine, a new light whose nature she didn't remember. She knelt at the hatch and peered in: on top of each of the tall cylinders a roaring flame spread across the metal; the auxiliary clattered away; Jonathan was walking down the narrow gangway by the engine peering at the blowlamps—in their light she could see a smear of oil down both his cheeks, like war paint. He must have felt the cold air when she raised the hatch, for he glanced up and gestured to show that he was coming out in a moment. She still felt the repugnance against engines which had been half her thinking life, so she moved away and sat on the bulwarks, looking at the clifflike warehouses which at this chill hour loomed so black that even the night sky seemed pale. It was pale, too.

The stars were fewer and smaller. Soon they would fade, and the tug would rumble out through that strange interworld between dark and day.

Jonathan, reeking of engines, came and plumped himself down beside her. She could feel his nerves humming with the happiness of action.

"All set," he said. "Tim and Lucy are staying. They've brought a load of cans out of the warehouse, and a couple of sacks of corn for the ponies. Scrub won't mind canal water, will he? It's less oily outside the docks. And I've found four drums which we can fill for the sea journey—it oughtn't to be more than a day to Ireland."

"What do you want me to do?" said Margaret.

"Two things, one easy and one difficult. The easy one is help start the engines. The difficult one is scout ahead and get the bridges open. That *could* be tricky. You see—"

"*Must* I help with the engines?" said Margaret.

There was just enough light flickering through the engine room roof to show how he looked at her, sideways and amused, but kind.

"Not if you don't want to," he said. "But we won't be able to manage if you don't do the bridges. I've just done the first one—it was different from the others—hydraulic—but I managed."

"I'll do the bridges."

"I've got two good maps of the whole canal—they were pinned up in offices—so we can each have one. Otto and I are going to aim for about six knots—nearly seven miles an hour—because you won't be able to keep ahead if we try to do more. That means we'll have something to spare if we're chased, provided we don't pile up a wave in front of us down the canal. You'll have to average a fast trot."

"The towpath's quite flat, except for one bit," said Margaret. "We should be able to do that."

"It's not as easy as it sounds, because you'll be stopping at the bridges. And you'll have to go carefully around the bends, especially the ones just before the bridges, in case you gallop into trouble. I found a bolt of red flannel which I've cut some squares off for you to take. If there's something wrong you can go back a bit and tie a square to a bush by the bank, so that we've time to stop. If it's something serious, Caesar will have to tow us through."

"He'll get terribly sore. He hasn't worn a collar for years."

"Poor old Caesar," said Jonathan, as though it didn't matter. "He'll have to put up with it. I think that story will work, provided they haven't spotted the smoke."

"Smoke?"

"You'll see. I want to start in quarter of an hour. You could go on now and get well ahead, if you like."

"I'd better wait and help you get Caesar aboard. He won't fancy it."

"How do you know?"

"Like you know about engines."

"Well, let's try now."

Margaret was right. They climbed ashore, took the ladder away and slowly pulled *Heartsease* toward the quay until she lay flush against the stonework, her deck about two feet below the level where they were standing. Jonathan untied Caesar's reins and led him toward the boat, but one pace from the edge of the quay the pony jibbed and hoicked backward, so that Jonathan almost fell over. Then Margaret tried, more gently, with much coaxing and many words; she got him right to the brim before he shied away.

"I hate horses," said Jonathan.

"Let's see if Scrub will do it," said Margaret. She crossed to her own pony, untied him, pulled his ears, slapped his shoulders and led him toward the boat. He, too, stopped at the very verge. Then, with a resigned waggle of his head and a you-know-best snort, he stepped down onto the ironwork deck. Caesar lumbered down at once, determined not to be left alone in this stone desert. Margaret tied his reins to an iron ring in the deck, poured out a generous feed of corn for him and led Scrub ashore. Before she could mount there came a thin cry from the engine room.

"They're ready!" cried Jonathan. "Come and see!"

He scuttled down the ladder. Margaret knelt by the hatch and peered down to where the weird lamps flared with a steady roaring, while the auxiliary battered away at the night. Lucy was standing down at the far end, by the two further cylinders, her hands on a pair of cast-iron turncocks just above shoulder level. Margaret could see two nearer ones—*she* ought to have been standing there. Otto lay in the corner directly below her, and Jonathan made signs to him through the racket, meaning that he would do Margaret's job as well as his own. He pulled briefly at a lever beside the nearest cylinder, and a spout of oily black smoke issued from the four cylinders, just below the turncocks. He glanced around at Otto, who raised the thumb of his left hand. Jonathan pulled hard down on the lever and left it down. There was a deep, groaning thud, followed at once by another, and another, and the whole tug began to vibrate as though two giants were stumping up and down on its deck. Lucy was already twisting her turncocks when Jonathan pranced around beside her and started twisting his. The beat of the heavy pistons steadied; the roaring flames at their heads died away. Margaret straightened up from the clamorous pit and saw a slow cloud of greasy blackness boiling up from the funnel. When she looked back, Jonathan was already halfway up the iron ladder; she made way for him.

"Like a dream!" he shouted.

"What now?" said Margaret. She wanted to get off the boat as soon as she could.

"Lucy will stay down there, to set the engine to the speed I signal for. I'll steer from the wheelhouse. You move off and open the first bridge. We'll follow in five minutes, and you ought to be nearly at the second one by then."

Margaret stood quite still. She knew there was something in the plan that didn't fit. She was just turning away when it came to her.

"Some of the bridges open from the wrong side!" she said urgently. "I'll have to wait till you're through and shut them before I can ride on."

Jonathan shut his eyes, as though he was trying to draw the mechanism on the back of his eyelids.

"I'm a fool," he said at last. "They seemed so simple that I didn't really think about them. We'll have to go slower and let you catch up."

"Let's see how we get on," said Margaret, and swung herself up into the saddle. She was cold, and there was a scour-

ing northwest wind beginning to slide across the Vale, the
sort of wind that clears the sky to an icy paleness, and keeps
you glancing into the eye of the wind for the first signs of
the storm that is sure to follow. But in the shelter of the
docks the water was still the color of darkest laurel leaves,
and smooth as a jewel.

Behind her the beat of the engines deepened. It was surprising how quiet they were, she thought, once you were a
few yards away. But when she looked around she saw, black
against the paling sky, the wicked stain of the diesel smoke.
If it's going to be like that all the way, she thought, we'll
rouse the whole Vale. But even as she watched in the bitter
breeze the smoke signal changed; the black plume thinned
and drifted away, and in its place the funnel began to emit
tidy black puffs, like the smoke over a railway engine in a
child's drawing; the wind caught the puffs and rubbed them
out before they had risen ten feet—not so bad, after all.

This last time she decided to risk going right through
Hempsted village, instead of dismounting and leading
Scrub down through the difficult track to the canal. They'd
always gone by the towpath and the empty house before, in
case any of the Hempsted villagers should become inquisitive about their comings and goings. But now it wouldn't
matter anymore. Hempsted slept as she cantered through.
This was one of the bridges that opened from the easy side;
she lifted the two pieces of iron that locked the bridge shut
and cranked the whole structure open; it moved like magic,
with neither grate nor clank.

If she had been good at obeying orders she would have
mounted and ridden on, but she felt she owed something to
the villagers of Hempsted, though she couldn't say what. At
least they had left the children to work out their plot in
peace—and that man *had* tried to warn her about the dogs.
So she couldn't leave them cut off, bridgeless (no one would
care to shut a wicked bridge like this, even if they could
remember how). Besides, she wanted to watch *Heartsease*
come through.

Jonathan slowed down the engines and shouted something from the wheelhouse as the tug surged past, but she
waved to show she knew what she was doing, and swung

the bridge slowly (how slowly!) back to its proper place. She heard the beat of the engines quickening and saw the black cloud boil up again. Just as she was bending to put the first locking-bar back she heard a shout. Without looking to see who it was, she slung herself into the saddle, shook the reins, and let Scrub whisk her onto the towpath. Now, over her shoulder, she saw a little old man in a nightshirt standing at the other end of the bridge shaking a cudgel. She waved cheerfully back.

*Heartsease* was already around the next bend when Margaret caught up, the funnel still puffing its ridiculous smoke rings against the pearly light of dawn, the throaty boom coming steadily from the huge cylinders. She was surprised to find, as she cantered level with the boat, that even she felt an odd pride and thrill at the sense of total strength which the shape of the boat gave because of the way it sat in the water. She slowed to a trot to watch it.

At once Jonathan moved his hand on the brass lever that jutted up beside the wheel; the boom of the engines altered; *Heartsease*, no longer shoved by the propellers, began to lose speed as Jonathan edged her in toward the bank. He opened the door of the wheelhouse.

"It'll be all right," he called, "provided you can keep that sort of speed up. You must think of a story, just in case you're caught on the wrong side with a bridge open. What about . . ."

"They wouldn't believe it," Margaret interrupted. "We'll just have to swim. That old stableboy who came when the earl came told me horses can swim with a grown man on them. But Jo, try to keep your engine going the same speed all the time. It makes a horrid black cloud when you speed up. People could see it for miles, but you can't in there."

"Thanks!" said Jonathan. He shut his door, signaled down to Lucy in the engine room, and, as the water churned behind the tug's stern and the black smoke rose again, steered out for the center of the canal. Scrub was happy to go. The wind was even colder now, out from the sheltering buildings.

Scrub was in good form, happy with the tingling early morning air and the excitement of having something to do.

Margaret was sure he knew how much it mattered, that he sensed her own thrill and urgency. The towpath was a good surface, hard and flat underneath but overlaid with rank fallen grasses which softened the fall of his feet. She had to rein him in firmly as they took the bend at the end of the long straight, and he was fidgeting with the bit all the three hundred yards down to the next bend. Just around it was another bridge. This one opened from the wrong side.

Already it was almost a routine, she thought as she hitched the reins to the rail, hoicked up the locking-piece and began to crank. But as the bridge swung over the water there was a shrill burst of barking in the lane behind her.

Margaret panicked. In a flash she had untied the reins, flung herself up to the saddle and hauled Scrub around to set him up at the awkward jump from the end of the bridge to the bank. It wasn't impossibly far, but it was all angles. He took it as though he'd been practicing for weeks, and climbed up to the towpath. From there Margaret looked back.

The smallest dog she had ever seen, very scrawny and dirty, was yelping in the entrance to the far lane.

Jonathan had slowed *Heartsease* down, but even so the tug was almost at the bridge, and there was no way for Margaret to cross and finish her job. She was turning Scrub toward the bitter water, nerving herself for the shock of cold, when she looked up the canal and saw her cousin gesticulating in the wheelhouse—he had another plan, and he didn't want them to swim.

His hand moved to the big brass signal lever and pulled it right over. The tug surged on for a second, and then there was a boiling of yellow water beneath the stern as the propeller went into reverse. *Heartsease* suddenly sat differently, slowed, wavered and was barely moving, drifting through the water, nudging with a mild thud against the concrete pier on Margaret's side of the gap. The bridges were still high at this end of the canal, because the surrounding land was high: it was only the mast and the funnel which wouldn't slide under. Delicately, with short bursts of power from the propeller, Jonathan sidled round the projecting arm, just scraping the corner of the wheelhouse as they went past. Once through, he opened the wheelhouse door to lean back and watch the oily smoke fade as *Heartsease* settled down to her six-knot puff-puff-puff.

"Sorry!" shouted Margaret. "I was too frightened to think."

"Not surprised," he shouted back. "But it looked funny from here—you two great animals routed by that little rat of a dog. Couldn't you lean down and turn the handles from the saddle?"

"No. They're too low. How far is it to the next bridge? Scrub doesn't understand about maps—the flapping makes him nervous."

"Half a mile. Then a mile and a half to the one after. Get ahead and come up to that one carefully, just trotting along. There used to be an inn there, and more folk'll be about by now."

The next bridge opened from the right side and no one barked or shouted at her. Then came the stretch of bad towpath, all muddy hummocks, so she took to the fields and cantered along on the wrong side of the hedge, wondering why the canal wasn't all in that kind of condition. The answer came to her at once, as she pictured the boiling khaki wake behind *Heartsease*. No ships had been using the canal for five years, so the water had barely moved; it had been when large engines had churned the surface about that the banks had needed constant looking after.

As she came up toward Sellers Bridge and the inn beside it, she settled Scrub to his easiest trot, and made sure that there was a square of red cloth loose at the top of her saddlebag.

She remembered the pub from her first exploration—a large white square building with broken windows. It hadn't looked as if anyone lived there, but she slowed to a casual trot as a gentle curve brought the bridge into view. The whole narrow world—the world between the enclosing banks of the canal—seemed empty of people, but who could say what enemies mightn't be about beyond them? As she wound at the handle she felt the blank windows of the ruined inn watching her, she felt the vast silence of the Vale listening like a spy to the slow clack of the cogs beneath her. This bridge was slightly different from the others: even though it opened from the "good" end, it turned on a pivot so that when it was open she was left with an awkward leap down to the bank. She decided it was safer to close it, but by the time she had watched *Heartsease* pass and had cranked the bridge shut she was shivery and sweating.

The next bridge was already open, and now the land fell away on either side of her so that she could feel the teeth of the wind out of Wales—and the banks would no longer hide the tug. Now they would be parading their wicked engine before all the watching Vale, twenty miles wide. At the bridge after that all went well, though it opened from the wrong side, but as Margaret was cantering on she heard a shrill cry and looked back to see a woman brandishing a saucepan while an arthritic old man hobbled away down the lane—for help, probably, for somebody young and strong to pursue them. Margaret bent over Scrub's neck and let him stretch to a full gallop; she was sure they could outrun any pursuit, provided they weren't halted in their flight. Hungry, she felt into her saddlebag as soon as they were past the tug, and found a hunk of Rosie's bread to gnaw.

It was two miles to the next bridge, a flimsy affair for foot traffic, where the canal crossed the narrow little barge canal from Stroud, all reeded and silted. Then a short stretch to Sandfield Bridge, which opened from the "good" side; then nearly a mile more to the bridge between Frampton and Saul. That one lay amid brooding woods which screened the next expanse of country, and it was already open. Frampton, she remembered, lay only a furlong from the canal, and beyond the woods was a long straightaway through windswept and shelterless country; so, as she was now well ahead of the tug, she took Scrub down the embankment, dismounted and led him along by the overgrown gardens of Saul Lodge. The canal here ran ten feet higher than the land. She was completely under cover as she walked below the stretching arms of the pine trees to a point, thirty yards on, where the curve was finished and she could climb up again until only her head showed as she spied out the long straightaway.

For five endless seconds she peered around a clump of withered nettle stems.

Then she had wrenched the startled pony around and was running back along the awkward slope. Up onto the path the moment it might be safe; into the saddle; galloping back and reaching at the same moment for the square of red cloth. *Heartsease* was only fifty yards the other side of the open bridge; desperately she waved her danger signal.

The water creamed under the stern as the propeller clawed at it to slow the tug down, but already they were through the bridge and Margaret could see that the momentum would take the tug around the curve before she could be stopped. Jo twirled the wheel and the bow swung toward the towpath; two seconds later it slid into the bank with a horrid thud. She jumped from her pony and ran along the path, but before she came to the place the still-churning engine had lugged the boat out into midstream again. Jonathan moved the lever to the stop position and opened the wheelhouse door.

"I hope that was worth it," he called.

"Oh, Jo, we're done for! Come and see! Can you turn the engine off without making smoke?"

He fiddled with the lever and the wheel, so that a quick spasm of power sucked *Heartsease* backward to lie against the bank. Margaret caught the rope he threw and tied it to a thornbush; he scuttled down the engine room hatch, and almost at once the puff-puff-puff from the funnel died away. Lucy came up behind him, her face all mottled with oil and dirt, but stayed on the deck while he leaped ashore. Caesar fidgeted with his tether in the stern.

Margaret led Jonathan along under the embankment. The children peered again around the hissing nettle stems, down the mile-long line of water which rippled grayly in the sharp wind, to where Splatt Bridge sat across the dismal surface like a black barricade.

There were people on the bridge, about a dozen of them, tiny with distance but clearly visible in the wide light of the estuary. Above them rose a spindly framework with a hunched blob in the middle.

"What on earth have they got there?" said Jonathan.

"Mr. Gordon's litter."

# Chapter 8

# KNIFE AND ROPE

There was no mistaking it. The freshening northwester had cleared every trace of haze from the fawn-and-silver landscape.

"Bother," said Jonathan. "It's strange how you never expect other people to be as clever as you are yourself."

He spoke in an ordinary voice, but looking at him Margaret could see the hope and excitement fading in his eyes as the colors fade from a drying seashell.

"Oh, Jo," she cried. "What are we going to *do*?"

"If we can't think of anything else we'll turn round, go back and hide again. Where's that bull you told me about?"

"Bull?" whispered Margaret.

"Yes. You said you were chased by a tethered bull at Splatt Bridge."

"We can't see him from here, if he's still where he was then. We might if we go further along the wood."

"Wait a moment. Let's watch them a little longer. It all depends whether they've seen us."

Margaret's heart was beginning to bounce with a new dread, the terror of her remembered nightmares. The palms of her hands were icy patches. To stop herself from thinking about the bull she screwed up her eyes and peered along the narrowing streak of water until the bridge seemed to dance and flicker. But between the flickerings, the tiny people appeared lounging and unexcited. There was a small flurry, and the litter tilted, but it was only a change of bearers.

"All right," said Jonathan. "Let's find your bull."

The children crept along the edge of the leafless wood, away from the canal; it was difficult not to walk on tiptoe.

"There he is," said Margaret.

Even at this distance the bull looked dangerous, tilted forward by the weight of his huge shoulders and bony head. The cruel horns were invisible, but Margaret knew their exact curve.

"No cows with him," said Jonathan. "He'll be in a real temper."

"What are you going to do?" whispered Margaret.

"I don't want to turn round and go back if we can help it," said Jonathan. "Some people must have seen us pass, even if they couldn't get out in time to try and stop us, so they'll probably be hunting down the canal after us. And even if we do get through, they'll probably stir up enough people to hunt us down in Gloucester. But if I can cut the bull's tether and bait him toward the bridge, he'll clear the men off for long enough for me to open the locking-pieces, and then you could simply barge the bridge open. They haven't brought horses. They won't catch us after that."

"You'll have to borrow Scrub. Caesar would be hopeless at that sort of thing."

"So would I. I'll do it on foot."

Margaret felt cold all over, a cold not from the bitter wind but spreading out from inside her. She knew Jonathan hadn't a chance of beating the bull on foot, any more than she had a chance of managing *Heartsease*. The plan was the wrong way around.

"I'd rather do the bull," she said. "I can ride Scrub. We'd both be better at our jobs that way. How do I cut the tether?"

Jonathan tilted his head sideways and looked at her until she turned away.

"It's the only hope," she said.

"Yes. It's better odds. And if it goes wrong at least you've a chance to get away. We'll try it like that. I found a carving knife in the ironmonger's in Gloucester—I liked it because it was so sharp—and if you can slash at the rope when the bull has pulled it taut you should be able to cut it in one go. *Heartsease* will make a tremendous cloud of smoke when she starts again, and they'll all be watching the canal after that. Then it will be six or seven minutes before I reach the bridge if I come down flat out. You'll have to time it from that, because you don't want to clear the bridge too early, or they'll simply dodge the bull and come back."

"What about Lucy and Tim?"

"I'll need Lucy to control the engine."

"Couldn't we cut a pole for Otto to do that with? Then Lucy and Tim and Caesar could come down after me, and get away if things go wrong. I'm going to ride down behind that long bank over there—it's called the Tumps on the map —so that I can't be seen from the bridge. If it all works, the men will be on the wrong side after the bridge is open, so we could wait for Lucy and Tim beyond it. If it doesn't, they might be able to escape."

"Um," said Jonathan. "I'll go and talk to them. And Otto. But I'll need Lucy to help me start the engines, so she won't be able to leave until you're almost in position—they'll be a long way behind you."

"Never mind," said Margaret. "At least it means Tim won't try to stop me teasing the bull."

Jonathan laughed.

"He doesn't look as if he needed much teasing," he said. "You move off while I show Lucy where to go. I'll give you twenty minutes before I start up."

"The knife," said Margaret.

"Yes, of course."

They went back to the boat. Lucy was sitting on the bulwark with her head in her hands; Tim was tickling Davey's stomach on the foredeck. Jonathan scampered aboard while Margaret looked over Scrub's harness and tightened the girth a notch. He came back with a knife which was almost like a scimitar, with a knobby bone handle made from the antler of a deer; she tried it with her thumb and found that it had the almost feathery touch of properly sharpened steel. Too scared to speak, she nodded to her cousin, raised her hand to Lucy and led Scrub away under the trees.

After a hundred yards they worked through a broken fence into an overgrown lane, with another small wood on their left; beyond that she turned south, still screened by trees, parallel with the canal but four hundred yards nearer the great river. At the far corner of the wood she found she could see neither Splatt Bridge nor the bull, so, hoping that meant that none of her enemies could see her either, she mounted and cantered on over the plashy turf. Scrub was still moving easily, his hooves squirting water sideways at every pace as he picked the firmest going between the dark green clumps of quill grass that grew where the ground was at its most spongy. Two furlongs, and their path was barred by a wide drainage ditch, steep-banked, the water in it flowing sluggishly toward the Severn. Scrub stretched his pace, gathered himself for the leap and swept across. Now they were riding along the far side of the Tumps.

This was a long, winding embankment, old and grassy, built (presumably) to stop the Severn from flooding in across Frampton long before the canal was dug. The map showed that it dipped sharply in toward Splatt Bridge. They reached the place far sooner than she wanted, but she dismounted at once and whispered to Scrub to stay where he was and taste the local grass. Then she wriggled to the top of the bank.

The bridge was three hundred yards away, straight ahead but half hidden by the patchy saplings of a neglected hedge. Much nearer, more to her right, stood the enemy of her dreams. The bull was already disturbed in his furious wits by the crowd on the bridge, and had strained to the limit of his tether in the hope of wreaking his anger and frustration on them. The best thing would be to snake through the grass and cut his tether while he fumed at Mr. Gordon and his cronies. Surely he wouldn't notice if she came from straight behind. There was plenty of time.

But she couldn't do it. To be caught there, helpless, too slow to escape the charging monster . . . She lay and sweated and swore at herself, but her limbs wouldn't take her over the bank.

Suddenly a savage cackling and hooting rose from the bridge. Through the bare branches of the hedge she could see arms pointing upstream. She looked that way herself. Clear above the distant wood rose a foul cloud of murk, that could have come only from some wicked engine.

She ran back to Scrub, mounted and trotted him along the bank until she thought they were opposite where the bull was tethered; then she nudged her heel into his ribs and he swept up over the bank, and down the far side. She'd been hoping to catch the bull while he was straining toward the shouting voices; but he must have heard the drub of hooves, for his head was already turned toward her and even as Scrub was changing feet to take the downward slope the horns lowered and the whole mass of beef and bone was flowing toward her as fast as cloud-shadow in a north wind. She could see from the circle of trampled grass how far his tether reached; she was safe outside it, but she could never cut the rope unless she took Scrub inside it.

Scrub saw the coming enemy and half shied away, but she forced his head around and touched his ribs again to tell him that she knew what she was up to. When the bull was so close that she could see the big eyes raging and the froth of fury around the nostrils, she jerked sideways at the precise moment in Scrub's stride which would whisk him to the right, and as the bull belted past she leaned forward to slash at the tautening rope.

The first slash missed completely, and the second made no more than a white nick in the gray hemp; then the enemy had turned.

The bull was dreadfully quick on his feet, considering how much he weighed; he seemed to flick his mass around and be flowing toward her before she had really balanced herself back into the saddle. But Scrub was still moving toward the center of the trampled circle, and even before she asked him he accelerated into a gallop. She knew he didn't like this game at all.

But he turned when she told him, out on the unchurned grass, and they tried again. It was a question of swaying out around the charge of the bull, allowing for the extra width of the sweep of his awful horns, and then at once swaying in to come closer to the rope than they had before. And this time she would have to lean backward, away from the pommel and stirrups of the sidesaddle. But Scrub's pace was all wrong, and she knew this before they reached the circle, so she took him wide out of range with several yards to spare. They halted on the far side of the circle and prepared for another pass. In the stillness between the two bouts of action she heard the men's voices again, deeper and more menacing than before. She glanced up the canal and saw the black funnel about three hundred yards away. It would have to be this time.

By now Scrub seemed to know what was wanted of him. As the eight hooves rushed the two animals together he swayed sideways at the last moment in a violent jerk, and then in again. Margaret couldn't tell whether she'd controlled him into this perfect movement, or whether he'd done it on his own, but there was the rope, taut as a bowstring, beside her knees. She stabbed the knife under it and hacked upward. The rope broke and the bull was free.

She flashed a glance over her shoulder; the bull had already turned and was coming at her again. Something about the way he held his head told her that he too knew that the rules of the game had changed. Now all that mattered was which of the two animals was faster. And where was the best gap in the ruined hedge.

There was no time to think. She saw a wide hole in the bushes a little to her left, just behind the bridge, so she nudged Scrub toward it. The men were making such a clamor now that she couldn't hear the hoofbeats of the bull. As she came through the gap she saw that her moment was exactly ripe: the men were on the bridge still, all their attention toward the tug which was booming down toward them with a solid wave under its bows; two of them had arrows ready, tense on the pulled strings; the rest had spears and

billhooks. Above them all Mr. Gordon crouched in his swaying litter, his face purple, his fist raised to the bleak sky.

Margaret gave a shrieking yell, and two heads turned.

A mouth dropped open, an arm clutched at the elbow of
one of the bowmen. More heads turned, and the color of the
faces changed. Then, like reeds moving in a gust of wind,
the whole group of bodies altered their stance—no longer
straining toward the tug, but jostling in panic flight away
from the bull. As Margaret reached the white railing that
funneled in to the bridge, a half-gap opened in the crowd.
She leaned over Scrub's neck, yelled again, and drove him
through it. His shoulder slammed into the back of one of
the litter bearers and she saw the crazy structure begin to
topple, and heard, above all the clamor, a wild, croaking
scream. Then she was over the bridge and wrenching him
around to wait beside the canal while the rout of men fled
down the lane and the bull thundered behind them.

She rushed Scrub back onto the bridge and leaped down
by the crank. The wreck of the litter hung half over the
railings and something was flopping in the water below her,
but she hadn't time to look. She snapped the locks up and
began to turn the handle. The bull was snorting in the middle of the lane while the men struggled through hedges. One
man lay still in the middle of the road, and the legs of another wriggled in a thorny gap. She cranked on, and suddenly found that the handle would turn no more. The
bridge was open, and pat on time *Heartsease* came churning
through.

"Look out!" yelled Jonathan from the wheelhouse, pointing up the road.

She looked over her shoulder. The bull had turned. Beyond it two men with spears hesitated by gaps in the hedges.
The bull snorted, shook its head, lowered its horns and was
surging back toward her; and the men behind it were coming in her direction too.

"I'll wait for you," shouted Jonathan. Margaret swung
onto Scrub's back and skipped him from the end of the
bridge onto the little path that ran up beyond the deserted
cottage where the bridgekeeper had lived. Forty yards further up, *Heartsease* was edging in to the bank, and by the

time they reached it, was almost still; without orders Scrub picked his way over the bulwark and stood quivering where Caesar had been. Margaret slipped down and caressed the taut neck while the engine renewed its heavy boom and the smoke rose, puff-puff-puff, from the ridiculous funnel.

When Scrub had stopped quivering she walked along to the wheelhouse.

"Father was there," said Jonathan.

"I didn't see him."

"I think he got away all right."

"There was one man lying in the lane, but his trousers were the wrong color. And somebody fell into the water, I think."

"That was Mr. Gordon—I saw him topple. I wish Father hadn't come."

"Perhaps he was going to try and do what he could for us if we were caught."

"I hope so."

"How long must we wait for Tim and Lucy?"

"I'll pull in here. Marge, you were quite right—I couldn't have managed that, not possibly. Now I want to go and tell Otto what happened. Just watch the bridge, in case they get across while I'm below."

Splatt Bridge was half a mile astern now, looking almost as small as it had when they had first peered over the bank at the other end of the straight. Margaret tied the hawser to a sapling on the bank and then led Scrub ashore; the pony moved off a few yards and began to browse among the withered grasses, looking for blades with sap in them; then he found a small pool and drank. The bleak wind, scouring the fens and hissing through leafless thickets, seemed to be made of something harder than ordinary air, and colder too. Margaret crouched in the shelter of the wheelhouse and watched the men on the bridge.

They were bending at the rails, and at first Margaret thought they were trying to fathom the workings of the crank; but they moved, and she saw they were busy with something in the water.

A hoof clopped on stone; peeking around the wheelhouse

she saw Lucy leading Caesar out of the meadow on their
left, with Tim walking beside her.

"Did you kill him?" said Lucy, her voice almost a whisper.

"Who?"

"Mr. Gordon. I saw him fall in."

"Ah, please God no!" cried Margaret. Lucy smiled at her—
the same smile as she sometimes watched Tim with.

"Aye," she said. "Best dead, but not when one of us has to
be killing him. Shall we be sailing on now?"

"As soon as possible, I think," said Margaret.

But nothing would make Caesar go aboard the tug again,
not though Scrub stepped daintily on and off a dozen times.
After Jonathan had tugged and bullied, after Margaret had
flattered and coaxed, they decided to leave him.

"Perhaps he'll follow us," said Jonathan.

"Perhaps," said Margaret. "Anyway the winter's over, and
he'll be all right. Nothing the weather can do can hurt a
pony—that's what the old stableboy told me."

"Only four more bridges," said Jonathan with a slight
change of voice which made Margaret realize that he'd only
been pretending to worry about Caesar to keep *her* happy—
left to himself he'd have abandoned his pony long before.

"One of them's in Purton," said Margaret, "and there's
people living there."

"Two on the map," said Jonathan.

"I only remember one."

"Well, you'd best get right ahead and scout. It's four miles
yet, and round a bend. If we have to, we'll stop the engine
and let Scrub tow us through."

"Do you think they'd allow us to open the bridges if we
told them our story?"

"Let's hope."

*Heartsease*, as if in triumph over the battle of Splatt
Bridge, spouted her largest and nastiest plume of smoke
when she restarted. Scrub cantered easily down the towpath, quite rested from his battle with the bull. The first gate
moved like the others, but the second, in the middle of a
huge emptiness with only the white spire of Slimbridge
Church to notch the horizon, was stuck. In the end Jonathan had to ram it open, backing *Heartsease* off and charg-

ing a dozen times with fenders over the bow before something in the structure gave way with a sharp crack. Then Tim and she together just managed to wind the opening section around so that the tug could go through. It seemed too much work to shut it again, so Jonathan ferried them across to the towpath.

"I didn't enjoy that at all," he said. "Purton's about two miles on now. You get well ahead and see what's best, and I'll wait half a mile out until you come back—if I've got the contours right there's a little hill which will screen us."

So there was a long, easy canter, dead level, with Scrub's hooves knocking out the rhythm of rapid travel. The estuary gleamed wide on her right, at about half-tide—so if it was ebbing they'd have a dangerously long nine hours to wait before high tide, and if it was flooding they'd have a bare three. Three seemed nothing like enough to be sure of finding out how the lock worked, but quite long enough for angry men to come swarming after them.

Scrub suddenly became bored with hurrying when they were almost at the last bend and slowed to a shambling walk, so Margaret dismounted and led him along the towpath. She'd have liked to leave him to rest and browse while she went on alone to explore, but she hadn't quite the courage to go among dangerous strangers without her means of escape—Scrub could gallop faster than the angriest man in England could run. The first bridge was open, which was why she hadn't remembered it, but the second was shut. Worse still, a fishing rod was lashed to the further railings, its float motionless on the gray water, and that meant that someone must be watching the bridge. But at least the locking-bar on her end was open. She led Scrub across, peering over hedges on either side of the street.

He was in the garden of the first house on the right, a fat lump of a man lying almost on his back in a cane chair, wrapped in blankets and coats against the bitter wind. A straw hat covered most of his face, so that Margaret couldn't tell whether he was watching the float through a gap in his fence, or listening for the bell at the end of the rod, or sleeping.

"Good morning," she called—softly, so as not to break his precious sleep, if he was asleep.

The hat was brushed back by a mottled hand, and an angry blue eye peered at her from above a purple cheekbone, but he said nothing.

"You're a long way from your rod," said Margaret cheerfully.

"Three seconds," the man grunted, and shoved his hat forward.

Margaret felt sick. He was much too big and much too close—it took forty seconds to open a bridge, even if it moved easily. She walked back over the bridge but stopped close by the handle.

"Lame?" she said, as if she was talking to a baby. "Oh, you are a big softy—let me have a look. Why, it's only a tiny pebble. There, that's better, isn't it?"

Scrub was not a good actor; anyone actually watching could have seen how puzzled he was to have a perfectly sound hoof lifted up, peered into, poked at and put down again. While she was kneeling Margaret flipped the locking piece of the bridge over, and as she rose she gave the handle a single turn, trusting the fidgeting hooves to drown the noise, to see whether it would move at all. It did, and at the far end she could see the crack in the film of dried mud which showed where the join had begun to part. Then she mounted and rode slowly up the canal and told Jonathan what she had seen and done.

"Three seconds is useless," he said. "We'll have to lure him away. Are there a lot of other people in the village?"

"I didn't see any, but I think there must be—all the gardens are dug and weeded."

"Probably they're having dinner. If you rode back in a frenzy and said there was something wicked coming down the canal but you could only see it properly from the other bridge, he'd run up there and you'd have time to get that bridge open. If you time it right, you could point to the smoke."

"I'll try," said Margaret, though she didn't feel from the look of the fat fisher's eye that he would be an easy man to lie to. She cantered back reining Scrub in every few paces and then letting him go again so that he would seem properly fretful when they reached the village. She rehearsed cries—was "Help!" a better beginning or "Please . . ."?

No need. The rod was there, but the fat man was gone from his garden.

She jumped down and started to wind frenziedly at the handle. The end of the bridge had moved a yard when there was a shout behind her and something flicked past her ear, banged on the railing and dropped into the water; she looked around—he was behind the fence, his hand raised to throw another stone. She gave a meaningless shout and, still cranking, pointed with her free hand to the space between rooftops where the familiar black puffs rose before they were scattered by the wind. He wheeled around, stared, ran to the far hedge, stared again, and bellowed. Windows in the village opened with bangs or squeaks.

"Oi, you girl, you lay off!" he shouted. "We'll catch un here!"

Nearly far enough. Margaret cranked on. Pain blazed into her left shoulder. She gave the handle five more turns, dodged sideways and heard the splash of a stone, turned thrice more and ran to where Scrub waited out on the arm of the swinging bridge. Her shoulder was still fiery with pain when she twisted up into the saddle and urged him forward. A stone grazed his quarters and rapped her heel. Startled, he gathered himself and sprang straight out over the waiting water. There was a roaring splash, freezing water blinding her eyes, burning her nostrils, panic. But she'd remembered to lean right forward, and kept her seat as Scrub's body tilted into its swimming posture. The roaring died, though the deadly cold remained, and they were swimming slantways toward the far bank with Scrub's head and her own head and shoulders rising above the water but the rest of them covered from the old man's stones. Then she heard shouts behind, and a tinkle of breaking glass. They'd stopped throwing at *her*.

She looked back up the canal and saw half a dozen men bending and flinging as *Heartsease* surged around the curve, but they were too lost in the rage and drama of action to think of crowding onto the open bridge, from which they could have boarded as the tug went past. She was still watching the fight when something tickled her neck—a blade of grass. Scrub had reached the bank, but it was too steep for him to climb. She scrambled soddenly up, and with her weight off him he managed it. But she knew she would die of cold in ten minutes unless she could find something dry to wear.

Jonathan must have known it too, for he was already slowing the tug as he came abreast of her.

"Dry clothes in the cabin!" he shouted through a smashed window, his face streaming with blood.

"Are you all right?" she called back, in the accents of a fussing mum.

"Only bits of glass. Doesn't hurt. Get aboard."

The stove was still going in the cabin, and the close air warm as a drying cupboard. Margaret stripped and rummaged through a big cardboard box full of clothing. Jonathan must have raided a department store for Lucy. She dried herself on a blanket and then put on a vest, two pairs of jeans and two thick jerseys—it didn't seem the time for the tempting little frocks. Then she started to hang out her own sodden clothes to dry over the stove, but there wasn't room, so she took them all off the line again and rolled them into a tight bundle tied with her belt. She took the blanket up to rub down Scrub.

They were already far down the last arm of the canal, where it ran tight against the river with only a thirty-yard-wide embankment to separate its listless waters from the rushing tides of the Severn. Only when the pony was nearly dry did she remember about Jonathan's face.

His left eye was glued shut with drying blood, and his lip swollen to a blue bubble, but he hummed to himself as he stood at the large wheel, twitching it occasionally to keep the tug dead in the center of the canal. The main cut in his forehead had stopped flowing, and he said nothing while Margaret sponged and dabbed. She found he wasn't as injured as he'd looked, and the moment she stopped worrying about him she felt the pain nagging again at her own shoulder. He must have noticed the sudden tightening of her movements.

"Did he hit you?" he said. "He looked too close to miss."

At once she was ashamed.

"Only one stone," she said. "It just hurts when I think about it."

"You've got us through twice now," he said. "I was an idiot second time; and an idiot to let Caesar go, too. He could have towed us through."

"I don't think they'd have allowed us to open the bridge anyway."

"I didn't think about towing till too late—you get in a mood when you're just going to blind through, and you don't *want* to stop to think. They're right about machines, somehow—Mr. Gordon and his lot, I mean. Machines eat your mind up until you think they're the answer to every-thing. I noticed it that morning when you stopped Mr. Gordon hypnotizing Mother; all I could think of was some sort of *contrivance*, and there wasn't one."

"Lucy says I killed Mr. Gordon," said Margaret.

"No you didn't!" said Jonathan hotly. "I saw his litter keel over and tip him in, and I didn't see him climb out. But if he's dead, he killed himself. Something like this was going to happen, for sure. He'd have pushed somebody too far— somebody like Father with a mind of his own—and they'd have gone for him with a billhook."

"Yes," said Margaret. "But it was me."

She stared through the shattered windows at the wide, drear landscape. It was so different from the hills because, though you could see just as much of the scurrying and steely sky, you couldn't see more than a few furlongs of earth. The land lay so flat that distances lost meaning—even the mile-wide Severn on their right looked only a grim band of water between the muddy band of bank in the fore-ground and the reddish band of cliffs beyond. And the hills of home, the true hills, the Cotswolds, might just as well have been clouds on the left horizon, so unreachable seemed the distance to them.

"Lord, that's a big tower!" said Jonathan. He pointed ahead to where the warehouse at Sharpness soared out of the flatness, less than a mile away.

"High tide just under three hours," he added. "Otto

worked it out from old tide tables—it's time we got him on
deck. Could you ask Lucy to persuade Tim? And there's a
dustpan and brush in the cabin, if you felt like getting rid of
this broken glass."

Scrub was standing in the oval of space behind the engine
room roof, watching with mild boredom as the bank slid
past. Margaret knelt at the engine room hatch; the torrid
air, blasting through the small opening, smelled of wicked
things: burned fuel, reeking oil and metal fierce with friction. Each cylinder stamped out its separate thud above the
clanging and hissing. Otto lay in his corner, watching Lucy
and the signal dial. She stood by the control lever and
watched it too, frowning. Tim slept in the middle of the
racket, crouched in a gangway like a drowsing ape, with
Davey asleep in his arms. Margaret hated the idea of going
down, so she yelled and yelled again. Lucy glanced up. The
oily face smiled, and said something, and an oily hand gestured at the dial. Margaret nodded, beckoned and pointed
forward. Lucy shrugged and left her post.

"Sorry," said Margaret as her head poked out of the hatch.
"Jo wants Tim to bring Otto on deck."

Lucy nodded and stared across the choppy estuary.

"Shouldn't fancy living in these parts," she said. "I'll wake
Tim."

Margaret found the dustpan and brush and swept out the
wheelhouse. When she threw the last splinters overboard
she saw that they'd finished with hedges and fields and were
moving between sidings and timber yards; and *Heartsease*
was going much more slowly too.

"Are the bridges the same as the others?" called Jonathan.
"One's got a railway on it. You'll have to land and open
them."

"There's one high one, but I don't remember the other,"
said Margaret.

"Funny. . . . Anyway, there's the high one—we can get
under that. And there's the other, and it's open. Lord, that *is*
a big tower!"

The huge, windowless column of concrete on the south
side of the dock came nearer and nearer. The canal widened
as it curved. Around the corner lay the big ship which had

so astonished Margaret; *Heartsease* seemed like a dinghy beside it. Then, right across the water, ran a low, dark line with a frill of railing above it in one place. The line was the quay at the bottom of the docks, and the frill was the guard-rails for the narrow footpath on top of the lock gates. It was here the canal ended—and their escape, too, if they couldn't find how to open the lock gates.

# Chapter 9

# WILD WATER

Otto lay out on deck beside Scrub, as pale as plaster with his illness and long hiding from daylight. Tim knelt by him, bubbling worriedly—and Margaret thought that the paleness might also be pain, the pain of being heaved with ribs half mended up a vertical iron ladder. But he smiled wickedly at her as she walked aft.

"Hi, Heroine of the Resistance," he said. "I sure wish I'd taken a movie of you playing your bull, just to show the folks back home. You look like a girl back home, too, in that rig. Nice."

Margaret felt herself flush, and glanced down at her primrose-yellow jersey and scarlet jeans. They made her feel like someone else.

"Pity your own folk can't see you," said Otto.

"Uncle Peter would whip me if he did," said Margaret. "And strangers would throw things at me. Women mustn't wear trousers—it's wicked."

"And what do you—" Otto began. "Hey! How do we know the Horse of the Resistance won't step on me?"

"He's much too clever," laughed Margaret. "Did it hurt a lot being carried up?"

"So-so," he said, "but Tim . . . hold tight! He's misjudged it!"

The tug swung suddenly, and then the whole length of it jarred as it thudded into the quay. Margaret was flung to the deck, almost putting her arm through the glass of the engine room roof. As she went down she saw Scrub prancing sideways toward Otto in a desperate attempt to keep upright; but when she rose he'd stopped, with his forelegs actually astride the sick man. Delicately he moved himself away.

"I told you he was clever," said Margaret with a shudder.

"Sorry!" called Jonathan from the wheelhouse. "I made a mess of that. Is Lucy all right?"

"Fair enough," answered Lucy, poking her head through the hatch. "I burned my arm on that engine of yours, but not enough to notice."

"Margaret can put some cream on it," said Jonathan. "In the first-aid bag in the cabin, Marge. But first, Lucy, can you get Tim to carry Otto ashore to look at the sluices?"

Tim thought it was an unwise move. Margaret was astonished by how much you could tell from the tone of his bubbling and the way he moved his head; now he was arguing that his patient had been under quite enough of a strain coming up from the engine room, and must rest before he attempted anything else. He began to back away as Lucy talked softly to him.

"Ah, come on, Tim, my old pal," said Otto suddenly. "I can stand it if you can."

Tim stopped backing away and knelt beside him, making little worried noises.

"Ah, come on," said Otto gently. "Jo's been stoned, Marge has fought a mad bull, Lucy's kept that engine going all morning—why can't I earn my medal too?"

Tim slithered an arm beneath his shoulders and another beneath his thighs and picked him up tenderly. He must have been very light with illness, as light as a dry bone. Margaret took Lucy below to dress her burn, which was a nasty patch of dead whiteness surrounded by angry red on the inside of her left forearm. There were aspirins, too, in the bag—Jonathan must have raided half the shops in Gloucester. Lucy grimaced as she chewed them up.

"D'you think I'm doing right, Miss Margaret?" said Lucy.

"How?"

"Taking Tim to America. Otto doesn't think they can make him *clever*, not like you nor me, but they might find drugs for him which'd make him two parts well; and Otto's uncle has a farm where we can live, he says. But what frights me is they might take Tim away and shut him up with a lot of other zanies—they wouldn't do that, would they?"

"Not if Otto says they won't. He owes you a lot—both of you."

"Aye," sighed Lucy. "But will they listen to him?"

"I wish I weren't going," said Margaret. "I wish none of this had ever happened. It's awful knowing nothing can ever be smooth and easy again."

Lucy grinned—not her usual secret smile but a real grin.

"I reckon we got no choice," she said. "Neither you nor me. Master Jonathan blows us along like feathers in the breeze. Let's look what he's at now."

Jonathan was down a deep hole in the quayside; the hole had a lid, which they'd opened, and Otto was propped on the rusting lip of iron which surrounded it.

"It's hydraulic," called Otto, "so there must be some kind of cylinder with a piston in it and a shaft. Then the shaft might thrust down on an arm and the other end of that might haul the sluice up. They'd be sure to have fixed it so you could haul it up by hand, in case the hydraulics failed. See anything?"

"I've got the main cylinder," said Jonathan as matter-of-factly as if he were talking about laying the supper table. "But the rest of it's not . . . oh, I see. How far would the sluice travel, do you think?"

"Four, five feet, I guess. Could be only two or three, if it's broad enough."

"That's it, then. There's two rings which'd take a hook, one to shut and one to open. I can't begin to shift it, though."

"Don't try," called Otto urgently. "Fetch out that block and tackle you looted from the garage. We'll put a beam across."

Jonathan popped out of the hole and began scampering to the tug. All he'd done since yesterday evening didn't seem to have slowed him down at all.

"Come and help, Marge," he called as he disappeared down the cabin hatch.

By the time she got there he was handing up a thing which didn't look any use at all, made of two hooks and two pulley wheels and a great tangle of rusty chain. Margaret struggled with the heavy and awkward mess of metal back to where Otto lay, while Jonathan rabbited down into the engine room.

"Is there more of it?" she asked Otto.

"No, that's all. It ought to do the trick—got a twenty-to-one ratio, just about."

"Then we've still got to find something strong to lift it—Scrub could pull, I suppose."

"No need," he said, grinning. "See where the chains run over that top wheel? That pulley's double, and one side of it's a mite smaller than the other, so when the pulley goes round the loop in the middle, that bit there which the other pulley hangs from gets slowly bigger or smaller. But you've got to pull the chain outside the pulley a good yard to make the loop a couple of inches smaller, so you're pulling about twenty times as hard. You can lift twenty times your own weight. Got it?"

"No," said Margaret.

"You'll see," said Otto. "What's the gas for, Jo?"

Jonathan was bending beneath the weight of two big cans, just the same shape and size as the one he'd used to scatter petrol over the stones the night the whole fearful adventure began.

"Gas?" he said, putting them down. "It's petrol. Marge, will you and Lucy take a can each up to where the timber piles are thickest; there'll be men hunting us down from Purton soon. I saw a boat on the canal up there, so I think they'll cross and come down the towpath. Pull a lot of planks out across the path, spray the petrol about, stand back and throw a lit rag on to it. Take rags and matches.

Then go and do the same thing on the road the other side of the sheds—there's more timber beyond it, and if you can get it really blazing they'll never get through. I may have to harness Scrub to the capstan to open the gates—d'you think he'll do it for me if you aren't back?"

"Oh, yes," said Margaret. "How much have you got to do?"

"Shut the bottom sluice, open the top one, open the top gate when the water's level—it's only got about four foot to come up because the tide's high in the basin—put *Heartsease* in the lock, shut the top gate, shut the top sluice, open the bottom one, let the water go down again, open the bottom gate and we're out. Hurry up, though—I can't move *Heartsease* without Lucy in the engine room."

The girls trudged up beside the dock, straining sideways under the twenty-pound weight of the petrol cans. The wind bit at the backs of their necks and fingered icily through their clothes in spite of the exercise.

"Fine breeze for a bonfire," whispered Lucy.

Margaret did most of the timber hauling, but she didn't mind because Lucy seemed happy to handle the petrol. It was hard work, but quick once she'd found a stack of planks light enough for her to run out across the quay in a single movement. At the back of the shed the road and railway ran side by side, making a forty-foot gap before the further sheds. The girls toiled away, one on each side of the road, hauling out planks to make a barrier of fire, until Margaret saw that they were going about the job in an un-Jonathan-like way.

"That's enough," she said. "We'll never be able to pull out so much that there's fire right across the road. But if the sheds really catch it'll be too hot to get through."

"Right," said Lucy. "Shall I start this end, then? Wind's going round a bit, I fancy. Ugh! Wicked stuff, this petrol. You stand back, Miss Margaret, while I see what I can do with it."

She soaked several rags, scattered half of one can all over Margaret's pile and the wood beside it in the stack, then the other half over her own. In the shelter of the stacks the harsh wind eddied, blowing the weird reek about them.

Lucy tied a stone into a soaked rag so clumsily that Margaret was sure it would fall out. She lit it and threw.

Half a second's hesitation, and with a bellowing sigh the spread petrol exploded. In ten seconds the pile was blazing like a hayrick, huge sparks spiraling upward in the draft. One of these must have fallen into the second pile, for it exploded while Lucy was still tying another stone into a rag. Margaret picked up the other can and ran between the stacked planks to the quayside. Already they could hear the coarse roar of fire eating into the piled hills of old pine, dry with five summers, sheltered by the shed roofs from five winters. By the dock Lucy splashed the petrol about as though she were watering a greenhouse. The wind, still shifting around toward the northeast, smothered them with an eddy of smoke from the first fire, and in the gap that followed it Margaret thought she saw through her choking tears a movement far up the canal—a troop of men marching down the towpath; but the same booming whoosh of fire blotted out land and water.

The flames at the far end of the shed were already higher than the roof. Smoke piled skyward like a storm cloud. Timber stacks which they hadn't even touched were alight in a dozen places. Heat poured toward them on the wind, like a flatiron held close to the cheek. They ran back to the lock. The gates at the top were open.

"I thought I saw men coming down the towpath," gasped Margaret.

"Me too," said Lucy. "Nigh on a score of them."

"They won't get through that lot," said Jonathan, nodding toward the inferno of the timber yard. "Lucy, will you go and be engineer while we get her into the lock? Marge, as soon as she's in will you make Scrub haul on that capstan bar to close the gate? Otto and Tim might as well wait here."

As the tug nosed through the narrow gap left by the single gate being opened, Margaret studied her next job. The capstan was really a large iron cogwheel in a hole in the ground, protected by an iron lid which Jonathan had opened; below it lay inexplicable machinery; from the cog a stout wooden bar about seven feet long stuck out sideways, shaped so that it rose just clear of the rim of the hole. Scrub was harnessed on awkwardly short traces to the end of this pole: if he pulled hard enough, the cog would turn.

Margaret patted his neck and said, "Come on, boy." He hated horsecollars but was sensible enough to know that he had to endure them sometimes, so he leaned into the collar, hesitated when he found that the weight behind him was more than he was used to, then flung himself forward. With tiny, labored steps he moved over the cobbles; the moment the gate began to move, its slow momentum made the strain less; Margaret led him round and round, talking to him, telling him how strong and clever he was, but looking all the time over her shoulder to make sure they were pulling at right angles to the capstan bar.

At last Otto gave a shout, and she eased the pony off and untied the rope from the capstan. Jonathan was already down the sluice hole, hauling at a clacking chain which ran over the double pulley. Margaret leaned over and saw the lower hook gradually inching upward, but she still didn't understand how it worked.

"Strong hoss," said Otto, as she led Scrub toward the lower capstan.

"I don't know if he can do two more," said Margaret. "It's a horrid strain, and he always gets bored with that sort of thing rather quickly."

"Only one more, I hope," said Otto. "The gates out into the river, on the other side of the basin, they float open as the tide comes in. They're open now, see?"

And they were, too. That made the escape seem easier. Jonathan scurried past with his chains and pulleys, and Tim followed with the squat balk of timber from which the pulleys were to hang. Davey came last of all, grabbing frivolously at Tim's heels. The flames gnawed into the timber with a noise like surf among reefs, and a rattling crackle told them that another stack had caught. In the shifting wind long orange tongues of fire flowed clean across the dock, reflected dully by the dull water. Jonathan worked his magic with the block and tackle and the lower sluice. *Heartsease* disappeared down into the lock, until only the top half of the funnel, the windows of the wheelhouse and a

few feet of stubby mast were showing. Then she stopped—
the lock water was level with the basin.

But this time Scrub couldn't move the capstan, for all
Margaret's praise and coaxing. Lucy came up from the engine room to watch; then Jonathan said "Rest him a moment" and ran across the quay to a low office building, on
whose side were arranged three shaped pieces of wood,
each on its separate pair of hooks. He came back with them
and fitted their square ends into the holes in the top of the
capstan: they were the other capstan bars, by which the
locks had been worked before the Changes if ever the power
failed. He led Tim up to one bar, and showed him how to
push. He and Lucy strained their backs against the other
two, and Margaret led Scrub forward, watching the group
around the capstan over her shoulder. Nothing moved.

"Come on, Tim," gasped Jonathan. "Push, Tim. Push hard.
Like this."

Tim gazed at him, slack-jawed, bubbling. Then he leaned
his broad shoulders against the bar and heaved, and they all
fell to the ground together as the capstan turned. Jonathan
was on his feet in a moment, but Lucy lay where she was,
rubbing her head and looking sulkily across to where Otto
lay laughing on the quayside.

"It's all right for some," she hissed, but Otto only laughed
the more, while Scrub and Margaret circled slowly around,
easing the gate open.

On the other side of the dock a petrol dump exploded like
a bomb. Then the wind shifted right around to the true
northeast and they were all coughing and weeping in the
reeking smoke, dodging desperately toward what looked
like clear patches but were only thinner areas of smoke
where you still couldn't breathe, and then another onset of
fume and darkness rushed down and overwhelmed them.
In the middle of it all Scrub, still harnessed to the capstan,
panicked. He pranced about the quay trying to rush away
from the choking enemy and always being halted with a
tearing jerk at the end of the short rope. He was too crazed
to notice where his hooves were landing.

"Get down and crawl!" yelled Otto from the ground. "It's
okay down here! Crawl to the boat!"

Margaret dropped. He was right. Under the rushing clouds there was a narrow seam of air which could still be breathed, if she chose her moment. In it she could see Jonathan already crawling toward the lock, and Lucy crouching low and trying to drag Tim down. The zany bent at last, then dropped on all fours and immediately scampered with a rapid baboon-like run toward Otto. Otto spoke to him, but Margaret couldn't hear what he said.

She never saw how Tim carried him to the boat, either, for suddenly an eddy of air pushed all the smoke aside so that she could see Scrub, mad with terror of burning, wallowing at the end of his rope. At once she was on her feet. For several seconds Scrub didn't know her and she could do nothing but hold his bridle and dodge the flailing hooves. Then, as she crooned meaninglessly to him, like Tim talking to a sick beast, he found a tiny island of trust in his mind, steadied and stood still. Before the smoke overwhelmed them again she managed to back him to a point where she could loose him from the traces, her fingers moving so fast among the straps and buckles that she didn't have to tell them what to do. As the horrible smoke swept over them she took hold of the bridle and forced Scrub's head down toward the cobbles; bending double she scuttered toward the lock. He saw the patch of calm and smokeless air below him and skipped delicately down to the deck, where he stood snorting and shivering.

"Ship's crew mustered!" cried Otto. "Horse and all! We're away!"

The big engine boomed. The water churned in the lock and the quay slid backward. Then they were out in the wide acre of the tidal basin, with the smoke streaming past a foot or two above their heads. Only the far gates now, and they'd escaped.

But the gates were shut. For the first time Margaret saw Otto look worried.

"Tide must have started to ebb and sucked 'em in," he said. "They were open quarter of an hour back, weren't they, Marge?"

"Couldn't we pull them open?" called Jonathan from the wheelhouse. "If we got a hawser up there quickly."

"Worth a go," said Otto.

"I'll take it up," said Margaret. "It'll take longer if you do it, Jo. Lucy, make Tim look after Scrub, or he'll think I'm leaving him."

It was an awkward six-foot scramble, up a rusty projection which supported a screw-topped bar; the heavy hawser tugged at her belt. She had to lie flat on her face on the catwalk at the top of the gate to fasten the hawser to a stanchion below her—the rails on either side of the catwalk didn't look strong enough. Panting, she backed off the top of the gate onto the quay, trying to work out how much the tide had fallen since the gates had closed—barely a couple of inches, she thought. She watched anxiously as the slack of the hawser rose dripping from the basin, became a shallow curve, became a stiff line. Jonathan put his signal lever over and the water under the stern erupted into boiling foam. The bows came up. The rope groaned. The gate moved an inch, three inches, and Margaret could see the creased lines at the gap where the water hunched and poured through. Then everything altered as the gate swung past the pressure line. *Heartsease* backed off with a jerk like a rearing pony and the gate swung fully open with the basin water tearing through. The hawser snapped like wool, but with a deep twang, as the tug reached the end of its tether; but Margaret had already grasped the spare length of hawser which she'd left beyond the place she'd tied it (Jonathan's suggestion, of course) and before the gate could swing shut she'd taken three turns around a bollard on the shore.

The fierce haul of the engine dragged the tug out toward the middle of the basin before Jonathan could halt it and make for the gap again. He headed slowly in, anxious not to spoil his victory at the last minute by charging into the wall or the other gate. The smoke was thinner here, but still rushing past in choking and tear-producing swirls. As Margaret crouched under it, waiting, she heard a hoarse cry. She hopped around, still crouching, and saw a big man galloping toward her through the murk with an ax swung up over his shoulder. He was thirty yards off, but he'd seen her —it was her he was coming for. She scrambled through the two sets of railings on top of the gate, hung for an instant to a stanchion as she leaned out and tensed herself, then leaped for the nearing bows of *Heartsease*. The world reeled and hurtled, and the bulwarks slammed into her knees and she was turning head over heels on the rough iron of the deck. Her ear must have hit something, for it was singing as she started to heave herself up. The ax clanged onto the iron two feet in front of her face, bounced and rocketed overboard. The man was trying to follow it, but *Heartsease* was through the gap before he could disentangle himself from the double railings. He stood and shook his fist, gigantic amid the smoke. Margaret, her head still ringing, walked aft.

"I saw him coming before you did," said Jonathan through the broken window. "Tell you later—Otto says I must shave this breakwater close as I can."

They were racing along beside a strange structure of huge beams, all green with seaweed, which stretched out into the estuary. There was another on the far side of the harbor entrance, curving away upriver, and between the two breakwaters the river surface was level and easy; but out beyond them Margaret could see the full Severn tide foaming seaward. She thought Jonathan had misjudged his course, that they were going to ram one of the enormous beams right on the corner, but it whisked by barely a yard from the bulwarks. She wanted to lean out and touch it—the last morsel of England, maybe, that she would ever feel—but it was too far for safety.

Then the whole boat heeled sideways for an instant as the racing waters gripped it, before Jonathan turned the bow downstream and they were moving toward Ireland with the combined speed of a six-knot tide and a ten-knot engine. Margaret looked aft to where the streaming pother of smoke was marked at the actual places where the wood was burning by the orange glow of house-high flames. Just as she was thinking how fast they were moving away from that hideous arena she saw Scrub skitter sideways as the boat lurched in the tide race. He almost went overboard. She ran back to him, staggering along the gangway, took his bridle and tried to gentle and calm him while he found his sea legs. Soon he was standing much more steadily, his legs splayed out and braced, so she tied his reins to a shackle just aft of the engine room roof and poured out a little hill of corn for him to nose at.

That made her realize how hungry she was. She walked forward to where Otto lay on the raised bit of deck in front of the wheelhouse; he had his chart spread out beside him, and Tim had propped him on a rolled tarpaulin so that he could watch the far shore and try to pick out the landmarks which would steer them down the twisting and treacherous channel.

"When's dinner?" she said.

"Just about as soon as you've got it ready, Marge. You're cook, because Lucy can't leave the engine and Jo and I must get this hulk ten miles downriver before the tide goes out. This is some cranky bit of water, and I don't like the feel of the wind, neither."

Margaret looked at the sky. Now that they were out from under the pother of smoke she could see that it had indeed changed. All morning it had seemed like a neutral gray roof over the bleak flats—it had been the wind that hurt, but the sky had seemed harmless. Now, to the northeast, it had darkened like a bruise. The wind must have risen, too, for it seemed no less and they were moving with it at fifteen knots. The waves, even in these narrow waters, seemed to be growing bigger. She looked anxiously aft to where Scrub was feeding in snatches as the deck bucketed beneath him.

"Easy!" shouted Otto. "There's Berkeley—three points right, Jo, to round Black Rock. If you can spot the line of the current, steer a mite outside it on the way out, then inside it on the way in."

"I can see two buoys still there," called Jonathan.

"Lift me up, Marge," said Otto. "Manage? Fine. Outside both of 'em, Jo, then sharp back inshore. Marge, food!"

She opened cans in the cabin and spooned chilly messes of stew into the plastic mugs which Jonathan had stolen— but the spoons were elegant, stainless steel with black handles, marked MADE IN SWEDEN. The crew took their helpings without a word, and began at once to eat with one hand while they did their work with the other—except Tim, who fed himself and Davey with alternate spoonfuls. It would have been a horrid meal if they hadn't all been hungry enough to eat anything. She found a bucket for Scrub and half filled it with the nasty water of the canal from one of the big oil drums; she had to hold it up under his nose while he drank, because the boat was fidgeting too much in the churning tide for it to stand safe on the deck. When she'd finished she looked around again and saw that Jonathan had steered them right out to the far shore of the estuary, and they were now heading back toward England under the gigantic tracery of the Severn Bridge. The blackness from the north was covering half the sky and there were feathers of snow in the wind. Tim had come on deck and was trying to coax Otto below, but Otto just grinned at him and shook his head, so Tim clambered down into the cabin and returned with a great bundle of blankets which he spread around his patient; Otto allowed himself to be babied, but all the time he was watching the shore and glancing down at his flapping chart.

As Margaret was collecting the empty mugs the first real wave came washing along the scuppers, knee-deep and foaming. She had just time to fling herself up to the stretch of higher deck between the wheelhouse and the engine room roof as it ran sucking past; she lay panting on the tilted iron. As she rose Jonathan opened the wheelhouse door with a hand behind his back.

"Shut the engine room hatch as you go past," he shouted, still peering forward. "And for the Lord's sake hang on tight. I can't turn to pick you up in this."

He shut the door before she could tell him how furious she was at his having swept them all into this stupid adventure, so she clawed aft, holding on to anything holdable. The engine room was the same oil-smelling, clamorous hole, but now she couldn't really hear how noisy it was because the wind and the waves were making such a hissing and smashing that anywhere out of their power seemed quiet. She shouted down to Lucy that she was closing the hatch. Lucy must have heard her voice but not the actual words, because she looked up inquiringly. Margaret made signals; the tired face nodded; Margaret shut her in.

Scrub must have fallen once—there was a slight bleeding from his knee—but he was on his feet now, legs spread wider than ever. The waves rinsed down the scuppers and out of the ports on either side, sometimes washing right over his hooves as he braced himself on the reeling deck. No human can know what a horse really thinks. They have a memory, certainly, for a hunter will often find his way home unerringly across country which he hasn't seen for a year or more; but their idea of before and after must be different from ours, weaker, less useful; *now* is what matters. And *now*, for Scrub, was a rusty, clanging platform which reeled from side to side, and beyond it dangerous frothing water, such as never ran in any river a horse could drink from; no turf, no trees, no stables, only a senseless whirling universe which he couldn't escape from because he was tied to a shackle in the middle of the deck. He was on the edge of madness when Margaret stroked his desperate neck and spoke to him.

She stood there for almost an hour, watching the storming estuary and the muddle of charging clouds, and trying to guess which way the deck would next cant, so that she could help him prepare for the new posture. Snow whirled and stung. Sometimes she could barely see fifty yards from the boat, but then there would come a space between squalls, and land loomed in sight on their left, less than half a mile away, wheeling backward. The waves were not ordered; they came at *Heartsease* in all shapes and from all directions, with none of the ranked inevitability of midocean—the only inevitable thing was that they became steadily larger. And the sky became blacker. It would soon be night.

But there was still a long stretch of this rough ocean to cover, and poor Scrub was still burdened with all his harness, including the heavy horsecollar and the ponderous sidesaddle—no point in either of them any longer. She loosed the reins from the shackle and, talking to steady him all the time, lifted the collar over his head and laid it down on the deck.

A roar like cannon split their closed world, and a single bolt of lightning turned boat and sea and sky into a blinding whiteness which printed itself on her retinas through closed eyelids. Scrub shied toward the bulwarks, and at the same moment the tug (Jonathan must have been startled enough to let the wheel go) swung sideways onto the waves. One big hill of water heaved across the deck and smothered her, bashing her into knobs and surfaces of iron until it pinned her to the bulwark and poured away. She lay and gasped for an instant, then wrenched herself onto hands and knees to see what had become of Scrub.

He was overboard.

She cried aloud as she saw his neck and shoulders spear up above a wave, slip into a trough and rise again. He was trying to follow the boat, to follow her.

"Stop! Stop!" she yelled, but already the shape of the water under the stern was different as Jonathan backed perilously up into the following seas. But there was no hope of hauling the pony aboard, not even with Tim to help, no way for him to reach the deck with his forelegs and heave himself into safety. Her mind was made up, certain, before she could think. She ran to the forehatch, opened it and scrambled down. Her own clothes—the only ones it would be safe to wear—were still in the sodden bundle she had made after the swim in the canal. She picked them up and climbed out.

Otto had made a tent round his charts with his blankets, but he poked his head out like a tortoise.

"What gives?" he said.

"Scrub's fallen in," said Margaret.

"Horse overboard, hey? Let him go, Marge—he'll swim ashore. He'll be all right, honey."

"I'm going too," said Margaret.

"You can't!" That was Jonathan, shouting through the broken glass of the wheelhouse. Margaret would have stopped to put her tongue out at him if she hadn't been afraid that he might decide to order full speed ahead and steam away, leaving Scrub to toil on, toil on and drown. She raced along the wallowing deck to where the pony's head bobbed level with the bulwarks, stepped up, balanced for an instant on the narrow barrier and then slid herself down across the brown shoulders into the bitter sea, the bundle of clothes hung from her right hand across the saddle.

"Home, boy," she said, and he immediately turned away from the unclimbable hull. Margaret gripped the saddle as hard as she could, twisted in the water and raised her left arm to wave; she thought she saw an answering wave through the misted glass of the wheelhouse before she allowed herself to slide down into the sea, clasped the pommel of the saddle with her left hand and trailed her legs out behind to offer the least resistance to the water while at the same time it carried as much of her weight as possible.

Scrub swam steadily, his feet kicking below the impulse of the waves, his head arched high like a sea serpent's. Margaret could do nothing but trust him; she was in a blind world where she could sometimes see a few feet of the wrinkled upslope of a disappearing wave, sometimes snatch a full breath, but mostly was hard put to it to keep her eyes open and the burning salty water out of her nose and throat. The only constant thing was the sturdy beat of the legs moving against her ribs, the slippery leather of the saddle and the roughness of the living hide. Once, looking back from the top of a wave, she caught a glimpse of *Heartsease,* end on to her: she thought Jonathan had decided to come and pick her up, though she knew he wouldn't attempt anything so impossible—it wasn't his style. But next time she saw them the tug was bow on to the weather and tide, still almost level with her. Tim was holding Otto up so that he could watch the shore—Jonathan must have circled perilously upstream so as to be certain that she had come safe to land. At that moment Scrub's swimming motion hesitated, stopped, and he rose six inches out of the water. The waves were lower here, and Scrub had been moving with them, but now they began to stream past. He must be standing on firm land.

She heaved herself onto his back, to lessen the resistance to the hurrying torrent; the shore seemed very close, and the tug, when she looked back, far away. She raised her hand and waved. Otto and Tim waved back. She felt a sudden choking pang that she had not said even this remote kind of good-bye to Lucy.

As Scrub battled shoreward *Heartsease* began to wheel side on to the tide again. There was something about the smell of the storm that made her believe it was ending, though the clouds seemed no less dark—but perhaps that was the real night. Up in the wind the water in her clothes chilled and chilled; a cold like death felt its way toward her bones.

Scrub had to swim across two narrow channels before at last they were really riding out of the waves to the true shore, with water streaming from her thighs and calves and her whole body shuddering like a twanged wire. On the pebbly beach, under low cliffs, she wrung the water out of the clothes in her bundle, stripped and changed. She hid the jeans and jerseys in a cranny between two boulders, then piled pebbles into the gap until no shred of cloth could be seen. Her ears were singing and her head lolling from side to side when she led Scrub up a steep little path to the coarse sea turf above the reach of any tide. The hill sloped up and up, but she knew from the way he hung his head that he too was near the last morsel of his strength, so she led him dizzily on. Halfway up the seemingly endless slope she had to stop and be sick. Perhaps it was just the salt water she had swallowed; or perhaps she was really ill.

There was a path. It must go somewhere, so she followed it right-handed, looking a bare yard in front of her feet but still stumbling every few paces. Around the shoulder of the hill the path dipped and they came out of the full blast of the wind, so she stopped and looked about her.

It was almost night, true night. They had climbed far above the deadly waters which stretched away on her right into dimness. There lay Wales, invisible in storm and dusk; ahead, though, a fault split the level clouds and a thin streak of gold evening sky showed through it, the last light of day gleaming off the water. Into this gold gleam on the sea crawled a black fleck, dirty as cinders; above it, just visible, rose its indomitable signal, puff-puff-puff. She waved again, though no one could possibly see her, then stumbled on along the path.

# Chapter 10

# AND HOME . . .

The path started to climb again, curving through the dusk, then dipped; it was hard to sce now that night was turning all colors to different shades of dark gray. She kept falling, and Scrub waited while she picked herself up. She tried to mount him once, but was too weak to pull her own weight up to the sodden saddle. She kept her eyes on the ground, only aware of the few feet of bristly turf around the dimming path. She could no longer feel anything, even the cold, but she knew that if they didn't come to warmth and shelter soon she would die.

A gate blocked the path. Cattle snorted and fidgeted in the darkness down the slope. The voice of a hen tickled the night. She looked up at these homelike sounds and saw, not twenty yards away, the orange square of a lit window. The gate led into a farmyard. She fumbled at the chain with unfeeling fingers.

A tied dog lunged yelping at her the moment she had it open, but she edged around the limit of its reach, trying to think of a story. A door opened and a man's voice shouted, "Quiet, you! Who's there?" The dog slipped back to its kennel, duty done, and Margaret reeled toward the black figure outlined against firelight and lantern light.

"We fell in the river," she gasped, clinging to Scrub's neck to hold herself from falling.

"Martin!" he shouted. "Horse to see to!"

A boy, younger than she, ran out and took Scrub confidently by the reins. The man grunted and caught her by the elbow as she melted toward the paving. Then she was lifted and carried into warmth and light, and the lovely smells she knew so well—curing bacon and fresh bread and a stew on the hob and woodsmoke and old leather and cider.

"Cold as a side of beef," said the man's voice, "and dripping wet."

"She'll have pneumony on her, likely," said the soft voice of a woman.

"What'd we best do?" said the man. "She's nobbut a girl."

"Put her in my chair," said the woman, "and fetch me two blankets and some towels. You can go and help Martin while I strip her off and dry her. I shan't be ten minutes."

"Aye," said the man. "Horse'll need a good rubbing down, given it's as drenched as she is."

Margaret heard a door close, and flickered her eyelids up to catch a picture of flecked green eyes in a large red face with a straggle of gray hair around it. She tried to say thank you, but her lips wouldn't move.

"There, there," said the woman, "we'll soon have you to rights, my dear. Warm and dry and sleeping like the angels."

Then there was darkness.

Voices swam in the dark, and pictures which shifted into each other before they could really mean anything. Uncle Peter snorted in his chair by the fire, and the bull snorted toward her over the mashed turf, and Mr. Gordon raised his blackthorn stick and cried, "The Devil has taken his own!" Then they were all on the sledge, including Aunt Anne, racing along the hissing snow in glorious freedom, but the snow had melted and Tim was trying to haul the sledge through a plowed field, only now it was a capstan and the rope broke like a strand of wool and Uncle Peter, swinging

his ax, galloped at her out of the smoke and she leaped for
the tug but it wasn't there and she was falling, falling, falling.

There were many dreams like that, sometimes with the
dogs hurtling after her, sometimes with seas of petrol reeking over her, sometimes Mr. Gordon rocking and clucking
till she forgot the lifesaving lie and blurted out the truth.
But at last she woke to a strange ceiling with a black beam
straight above her head, motes dancing in the sunlight,
limed walls. A large woman in a gray dress sat by her bed,
knitting placidly but looking very serious. Her eyes were the
color of plovers' eggs, and flecked with the same brown
spots. She spoke as soon as Margaret opened her eyes.

"Don't tell me anything. I don't want to know. You talked
enough—more than enough—in your fever."

"Oh," whispered Margaret.

"Four days you've been lying here," said the woman, "and
talking I don't know what wickedness."

"No," said Margaret. "It wasn't like that, it really wasn't.
Please, I'd like to tell you. You look as though you'd understand."

The needles clicked to the end of the row and the woman
put them down.

"Tell me one thing first," she said, "before I decide to listen. Do you believe, right in the honest heart of you, that
you've done God's will?"

"I've not thought of it that way," said Margaret. "But yes, I
suppose so. Once we'd begun we couldn't have done anything else. It would have been wrong to stop."

"If you believe that," said the woman, "really and truly,
I'll hear you out. Don't you tire yourself, mind."

So Margaret told her story while the needles rattled and
the fat fingers fluttered and the motes drifted and shafts of
sunlight edged across the room. All the words she needed
came to her just when she wanted them. She never changed
her voice, but let the story roll out in a steady whisper, even
and simple, like water sliding into a millrace. All the time
she watched the woman's face, which never changed by the
smallest wrinkle or the least movement of the mouth corners, up or down. When the story was ended she shut her

eyes and tried to sink back into the darkness which had been her home for four days.

"Aye," said the woman, "it's wicked water, the Severn. No, I don't see what else you could have done, my dear. Thank you for telling me. My men are out sowing—that's my husband and my son—and we won't tell them what you and I know. They wouldn't understand the rights and wrongs of it like we do, being women. My name's Sarah Dore, and you're welcome to stay here as long as you like."

"Oh, you are kind," said Margaret. "But really I must go and tell Aunt Anne what's happened to Jonathan."

"Maybe you must," said Mrs. Dore, "but not till you're well inside yourself. Two days you were that nigh death I fairly gave you up."

"How's Scrub?" said Margaret.

"Right as rain. My Martin's got a way with horses, so he's pulling a cart up in Long Collins."

Margaret smiled.

"He won't like *that*," she said and fell asleep again, a silky, dreamless, healing sleep that lasted until she woke to the hungry smell of frying bacon. She got out of bed, found a dressing gown on the chair where Mrs. Dore had sat and, holding weakly to walls and banisters, traced the smell down to the kitchen, where the Dores greeted her as though she'd belonged in that family ever since she could crawl. She stayed with them eighteen days, and at last rode off after trying to say thank you in a hundred different ways, none of which seemed nearly enough. Indeed, the day before she left Martin brought up from the beach a gull with a broken wing, which he set before bandaging the bird into a fruit basket so that it could not harm itself with its struggles. Margaret looked into its desperate wild eye and tried to tell it that it was safe here.

The gale had blown the winter away, and weald and wold were singing with early spring. Really singing—innumerable birds practicing their full melody among the still-bare branches of every hedge. As she crossed the smooth upland behind the Dores' farm she saw a dazzling blink of black and white, gone before she could see the true shape of it, but she was sure it was wheatears. And then there were curlews, playing in the steady southwest wind. The color of the woods had changed—beeches russet with the swelling of their tight little leaf buds, birch tops purple as a plum. And the larches were a real red with their tasseled flowers, and the sticky buds of chestnuts glistened when the sun came out from behind the lolloping fat clouds which rode up off the Atlantic.

But, more than anything, every breath she took was full of the odor of new growth, a smell as strong as hyacinths. In winter there are no smells, or very few and sour—woodsmoke and reeking dung heaps and the sharp odors man makes with his toil. But there comes a morning when the wind is right and the sun has real pith in it, and then all the sappy smells of growth are sucked out of the earth, like mists from a marsh, and the winds spread them abroad, streaming on the breeze with a thrilling honey-sweetness which even high summer—the summer of bees nosing into lime blossom—cannot equal.

It was through such a world as this that Margaret rode home, with Scrub dancing and happy beneath her and all her blood and all her mind well again. (To be fair, Scrub was probably mostly happy not to be pulling the Dores' cart.) She had to fetch a wide circle around Bristol, which seemed an even bigger city than Gloucester, and ask her way north many times; but all the people she spoke to were full of the kindliness of the season and answered her like friends. That night she slept in an isolated barn beside a beech hanger, north of Chipping Sodbury. The air turned cold but she snuggled deeper into the tickling hay and made herself a nest of warmth where she dozed until the dawn birds began their clatter of small talk again.

It was another dew-fresh day, chilly but soft, with scarfs of mist floating in the valleys. The sun, an hour after it was up, became strong enough to strike caressingly through her coat, and the wind was less than yesterday's and herding fewer clouds. She had started so early that she was hungry enough for another meal by midmorning. As she settled to eat it in the nook of a south-facing dry-stone wall she saw, almost at her feet on the strip of last year's plowland, a tuft of wildflowers: yellow and white, marked out with strong brown-purple lines which made each flower a quaint cat face. Wild pansies, heartsease. They must have been the very first of all the year.

She reached out to pick them so that she could carry home with her a token of that grimy but heroic tug, then drew her hand back and left them growing. All the time she munched the good farmbread and the orange cheese, she kept looking at them, so frail and delicate, but fluttering undamaged above the stony tilth.

It was dinnertime in the village when she came to Low Wood. She had worked her way around by well-known paths so as to be able to come to the farm without passing another house. Now she tied Scrub to a wild cherry, just big enough for the hired man not to have felled it, in the hollow of a little quarry where he couldn't be seen from the road. She tried to tackle her problem Jonathan-style, so she used a knot which Scrub would be able to loose with a jerk or two —just in case she was trapped by vengeful villagers. The safest thing would be to creep up and hide until she could talk to Aunt Anne alone.

Primroses fringed the quarry, and celandine sparkled in the wood. She walked up the eight-acre, keeping well in under the hedge; then stole through the orchard. There seemed to be no sound of life in the whole village, though most of the chimneys showed a faint plume of smoke; no men called, no bridles clinked. She tiptoed along the flagged path at the edge of the yard and peeped carefully through the kitchen window.

They had finished their meal but were still sitting at the table—not in their own chairs at either end but side by side on the bench where the children used to sit. Aunt Anne's hand lay out across the white deal, and Uncle Peter's huge fist covered it. Their faces were shaped with hard lines, like those a stonecarver's chisel makes when he is roughing out a figure for a tombstone. They both looked as though they had lost everything they had ever loved.

Margaret changed her mind about hiding; she stepped across to the door, lifted the latch and went in. They looked up at her with a single jerk of both heads and sat staring.

"May I come back, please?" she said.

"Where's Jo?" said Uncle Peter. His voice was a coughing whisper.

"Safe in Ireland, I think. There was a storm, and Scrub and I were washed overboard, but we climbed a hill and I saw the boat going on into what looked like calmer water; and it was still going properly, too. He'll come back, Aunt Anne, I'm sure he will—as soon as the Changes are over, and that can't be long now."

"Please God," said Aunt Anne faintly. Margaret now saw that the whole of Uncle Peter's other side was hidden by a yellow sling.

"What have you done to your arm?" she said.

He gave an odd little chuckle.

"What've *you* done, you mean, lass. Your friend the bull broke it after he'd knocked Davey Gordon into the water and drowned him. But it's mending up nicely enough. I went down with them to see what I could do for you, supposing you got caught in your craziness. Leastways I think I did."

"That's what I told Jo," said Margaret. "Where's Rosie?"

"Sent her packing," said Uncle Peter triumphantly. "What call had she to go nosing among my son's belongings in the middle of the night, eh?"

"Did he tell you why we did it?" said Margaret.

"He tried," said Aunt Anne with a tiny smile, the first that Margaret could remember for months. "But he's a poor hand at explaining himself, at least on paper. You must tell us over supper."

"You know," interrupted Uncle Peter, "I needn't have troubled myself to traipse down there getting my arm broken. I might as well have stayed at home milking for all the help you needed of me, you and Jo."

He sounded really pleased with the idea—proud of them, almost.

"Thank you for coming home," said Aunt Anne. "We need you, Pete and I."

"Shall I be able to stay?" said Margaret. "I could dye my hair and pretend to be the new servant girl, I thought."

"No need, no need," said Uncle Peter.

"The village is different now, isn't it, Pete?" said Aunt Anne.

"It is that," he answered. "All different since Davey died. Not that you can lay it against him, honest—he just brought out of us what was in us. Oh, he piped the tune all right, but we'd no call to dance to it if we hadn't the lust in us. But never mind that: winter's gone now, and the season of idleness. Spring's on us, and that means hard work and easy hearts. What could a man ask more, hard work and an easy heart?"

"I saw some heartsease in a field above Dursley," said Margaret.

"That's very early," said Aunt Anne. "It's always been my favorite flower, with its funny face. Like Jo, I used to think."

"Oh," said Margaret, surprised at the reason—surprised too that she hadn't thought of the likeness. "I nearly picked them to bring you, but it seemed best to leave them growing."

"I'm glad you did," said Aunt Anne.

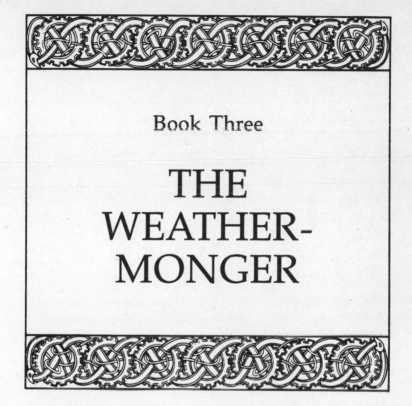

Book Three

# THE WEATHER-MONGER

# The Feel of Ending

There were no more storms. The little tug puffed its sturdy
way westward and met up next morning with an Irish
trawler. The trawler's radio carried the unlikely message to
the mainland, and within a couple of hours a U.S. naval
patrol boat came creaming out to meet them. Otto's bosses,
out of the mere habit of secrecy, hushed up the failure of his
mission. Otto took Lucy and Tim to his uncle's farm in Ne-
braska, where they both settled down happily. Lucy in particular liked civilization, with all its glossy, effort-free benefits.
But Jonathan insisted on staying in Ireland, as near home as
possible. He went to school, worked hard at science, and
waited for the end. As he'd told Otto, he knew it was coming
soon.

It's odd how sometimes we can sense things drawing to a
close—a piece of unfamiliar music, a child's tantrum, a period in our own lives. Up and down Britain people had felt
the same, sensing it dimly and in fear. A housewife making
tallow candles might look up from the slow and smelly job
and sigh, suddenly remembering how once in that very same
room she'd been able to summon good, bright lights at the
touch of a switch. And then she would shudder, no longer
from horror of the thing itself, but from fear that she had
thought of it. If anybody should find out! She dared not even
tell her husband, though he perhaps would come in that evening from his backbreaking labor at the saw pit with his own
mind full of the secret memory of how quickly and accu-
rately the big circular saws used to slice the tree trunks into
planking.

People like these were warned by the fate of anyone who

tried to anticipate the end—that obstinate old ship's engineer in Weymouth, for instance, who converted an old mill on the river to weave coarse cloth. All Dorset knew what the weavers did to him.

Again, a stranger coming to Felpham, where the Sikhs had settled, might notice how rich the fields were, how fat the cattle, how healthy the village children. If he'd picked up a rumor in a nearby village he might hint at witchcraft, and get a surly answer from the villagers. But the villagers themselves were careful not to be about when Kewal brought his wagon of artificial fertilizers back from a raid on some big abandoned warehouse, or to ask what Cousin Punam actually put into the potions which she gave them for a sick child.

And the Power that had caused the Changes still was strong. It came in pulses. There were days when even Mr. Maxie would have presided at the trial and execution of his closest ally if he'd been shown hard evidence of witchcraft. There were places, too, especially in old forests, where it seemed always strong. And strong or weak it was there; on certain days the weathermongers might sense that they would need to put forth more of their mysterious gift to summon the wind or draw the molecules of water vapor into a rain cloud; but they could still do it.

But the end was coming. Unconsciously the island waited for it. But what kind of an end? A peaceful accounting of gains and losses? Or time of worse ruin even than the beginning, as the Power that had been woken by the man in the tunnel threshed to and fro in its last delirious convulsions?

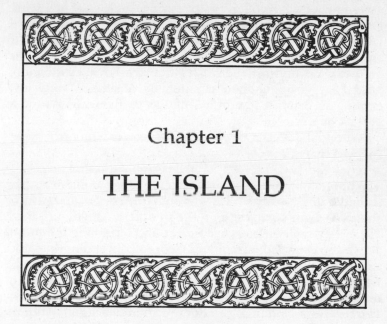

# Chapter 1

# THE ISLAND

He woke up suddenly, as if from a deep sleep full of unre-coverable dreams. He was very uncomfortable. The light was too bright, even through closed eyes, and there was something sharp and hard jutting into one of his shoulder blades. His head hurt too.

He moved his right arm in search of something familiar, a sheet or a wall, and found a quite different feeling—hun-dreds of rough, scratchy lumps on a warm but slimy sur-face, like iron pimples. Familiar, though—barnacles on a sea rock. He was lying on a rock. He opened his eyes and sat up.

His skull yelped with pain as he did so, and his hand moved instinctively to touch the smooth round thing that should have been hanging around his neck, and wasn't.

A voice beside him said, "They took it away. They hit you on the head and took it away, so that you wouldn't be able to use it."

She was a girl, about twelve, a kid with pigtails, very

dirty, her face swollen with crying, but wearing what looked like an expensive dress of green brocade with gold trimmings that would have come right down to her ankles if she'd stood up. She was sitting beside him, her knees under her chin. Beyond her the sea lay flat as a Formica tabletop, hard blue, joggling in one patch by a sunken rock just enough to catch a few glints of the vertical noon sun. A perfect day.

"Who took it?" said Geoffrey, not even remembering what "it" was.

"They did."

Without looking around she jerked her chin over her shoulder and he turned. He was on a tiny rock island, which shouldn't have been there, in the middle of Weymouth Bay. The pretty dollhouses ranged right and left along the Front above the crowded beach, and George III's great gilt statue stood pompous at the far end. The pier was gone though, with only a few tarred and tilted timbers to show where it had been, and the crowd wasn't a holiday crowd either. They were all standing, shoulder to shoulder, looking out to sea, and all fully dressed. There wasn't a bathing suit anywhere. As he turned they roared, a long jeering moo. They were looking at him.

"What on earth are they up to?" he said.

"They're waiting for us to drown. When the tide comes in."

"Well, don't let's wait for them. It's still quite shallow. Come on."

"They won't let you ashore, but they want you to try. That's what they like. I've seen it."

"Oh, rubbish! Come on."

Without waiting to see whether the girl would follow, Geoffrey hitched up his robes and stepped into the sea. A pleased hum throbbed through the crowd, like the purr of a huge cat. The water was beautifully warm; it must have been a first-rate summer; he couldn't remember. He sploshed toward the shore, hampered by his silly dressing gown of a robe, worried about spoiling its precious gold fabric with salt water, but comforted by the real, everyday feel of watery sand under his feet. As he waded the front row of the crowd opposite where he stood looped forward into the fringe of the sea. They were all men, rather small men, but carrying what looked like spears. The whole of Weymouth Bay seemed to have shrunk a bit.

Once they had worked out where he was aiming for, the spearmen bunched there in a close line and lowered their spears. They weren't only small—they were oddly dressed, with a history-book look about them. Most of them had ordinary jackets, very patched, but some were wearing crisscross leggings and others a sort of sacking kilt, and they all had beards. When he was a couple of feet from the spearpoints, which looked dead sharp, he stopped. The crowd was still as an empty beach.

"What the hell do you think you're doing?" he said to the man directly in front of him. "Come off it."

It felt odd to be talking to a grown-up like that, but they were really behaving a bit daft, and anyway he was quite as big as they were. His voice came out round and firm, without that stupid squeak.

The man (he was bald, with a coppery beard, his face tanned dark as a gypsy's, with a mesh of tiny crimson veins running under the tan on his bulgy nose) said nothing, but the line of spearmen moved another pace into the water, and the man's spear touched Geoffrey's robe, pierced it, pricked his skin. Quite right, the points *were* sharp, so it hardly hurt at all. Geoffrey stood his ground.

With a happy grin the man prodded the steel a quick half inch further in and twisted. That hurt like mad. Geoffrey forgot his robe and the water and tried to jump back, but tripped and sat down in the clammy wetness. The crowd bayed and cheered. Geoffrey scrambled up from his defenseless sprawling, but the man made no further attack. He just stood, watching and grinning. Geoffrey looked down at the gold robe, where the blood was beginning to make its own pattern among the threads; he felt the tears of pain and defeat in his eyes, and (so that the crowd on the beach shouldn't see them) turned and waded back to the tiny rock island that shouldn't have been there.

As he was climbing onto it, he saw that it was really a platform made of broken slabs of concrete roughly heaped

together—a platform for drowning people from. The girl
had been crying again, but had stopped.

"I told you so," she said. She sounded not smug but sym-
pathetic and miserable. Geoffrey stared at her, wondering
who she was and what the people on the beach could be up
to, trying to drown a couple of kids. He felt again at his
chest, where the round, smooth whatever-it-was should
have been, dangling from its gold chain.

"They took it away," she said. "I told you. Can't you remember *anything*?"

"Not much."

"Don't you even know who *I* am?"

"I'm afraid not."

She started to snivel again.

"I'm Sally," she said between gulpings, "your sister Sally."

Oh, Lord! Geoffrey sat down on the concrete and stared
out to sea. The water had only a couple of inches to come
and it would cover their island. And somewhere he'd lost
five years. No wonder the bay was smaller and people were
smaller. But why had they all gone mad? He'd have to do
something for Sally now, anyway, even if she was a different Sally and not the cocky six-year-old clown he knew.

"Why do they want to drown us?"

"For witches. They came to ask you about making
weather and found you putting a bit of machinery from the
boat into the oven. Then they banged you on the head and
took your talisman away, and then they rummaged around
the house and found my pictures, so they rang the church
bells and brought us down here to drown."

"Making weather?"

"Yes. You did it with your talisman. You're the weathermonger in Weymouth. Every town has one. *I* think that's
really why they want to drown you, because you're one of
the richest men in Weymouth and they want your money.
They paid you pounds and pounds for a good harvest."

"But *Quern*'s still there?"

"Oh, yes, that's where the bit of engine came from which
told them you were a witch. You sneak down and fiddle with
her almost every week. I've seen you out of my bedroom
window, though what use she is without sails *I* don't know."

"What would happen if we tried to swim round to her?"

"They'd run along and get into boats and prod you in the water. We saw a man try it last Whitsun. I laughed and laughed. Oh dear."

She started off on her gulping again. Geoffrey stared glumly at the rising water. Only half an inch to go now.

"Look," he said, "I think our best bet's to wait until the tide's right in and try and float round with our noses just out of the water and perhaps they'll think we've drowned."

"But I can't swim. I'm not a witch. I've never touched an engine since the Changes came. I only drew pictures."

Blast. Geoffrey thought he might possibly be able to swim around to the harbor undetected. It's surprising how little you can see from the shore of something that's barely moving and barely projecting from the water. But he couldn't do it if he had to lifesave Sally all the way.

"Fat chance of our getting it this weather," he said, "but what we want is a good old sea fog."

*A breathing out of the water. No wind that you could feel, and nothing you could see, if you looked at any particular patch of sea. But all along the coast, from Bournemouth to Exeter, the water breathing up and being condensed into a million million million droplets in the cold layers of air above the oily surface. Cold out of the lower deeps. An unnumberable army of drops, which even the almighty sun could not feel through, breeding more layers of cold in which more armies of drops could be breathed out. And now the wind you could not feel, pushing the fog from the south, piling it up in heavy swathes against the seaward hills, thick, gray, cold. Thicker. Grayer. Colder. Thicker. Grayer. Thicker. . . .*

Sally was shaking him by the shoulder. He was sitting in six inches of water and could see about a yard through the grayness. There were shoutings from the shore, a noise of contradictory orders being given in many voices.

"I think they're getting boats and coming to throw us in," said Sally. "You could swim now. It didn't matter their taking it away after all. D'you think you can take me with you?"

Geoffrey stood up and took off his sopping robe. He folded the expensive cloth carefully and tied it in a roll with the belt, with a loop which he put around his neck so that the roll lay on his chest, where the whatever-it-was should have been. He stepped down into the deep water, on the far side of the island. It came up to his neck.

"I don't know if we'll be able to find our way in this," he whispered, "but it's better than being drowned a-purpose, like a kitten. You lie on your back and I'll hold you under your arms and pull you round. Take off your dress, though, and do it like my robe. Fine. Good girl. Off we go. Try to breathe so you've got as much air as possible in your lungs all the time. It helps you float. And pinch my leg if you hear anything that sounds like a boat."

There was no trouble finding the way in the fog. It was *his* fog, after all—he'd made it and knew, if he cared to think about it, how its tentacles reached up into the chalk valleys behind the town and its heart drifted in slow swirls above the obliterated beach. But he thought about it as little as he could, for fear of getting lost in it, mind-lost, again. He lay on his back and gave slow, rhythmic frog kicks out to sea. He hoped it wouldn't be too smelly when they went through the patch by the outflow from the town sewer, where the best mackerel always were. Sally lay very still, like a girl already drowned.

He was beginning to worry about her, to think of risking a few words, when he felt her hand moving over his shin. She pinched him hard and he stopped kicking, slowing to a barely moving paddle. She was right. There was a squeaking of wood on wood in the grayness, between them and the beach, and it was coming nearer. A voice said, "What's that, over there?" Pause. More squeaking. Another voice said, "Lump o' timber. This is right useless. Let's be goin' in. Who'd have thought the young wickeder would have had another talisman?" Another voice said, "We'll be lucky if Dorset sees a morsel of dry hay this summer. Never cross a weathermonger, I always say. *And* he was a good un, for a young un." "He was an evil witch," said a more educated voice, fiercely. "Thou shalt not suffer a witch to live." The voices wrangled away into silence.

Geoffrey kicked on. He seemed to have been doing it for hours, and his legs were flabby after their rest. He began to count kicks, in order to keep going. Seven, eight, nine, eighty, one, two, three, four . . . the water was greasy with electricity under the grayness. They disturbed a gull, which rose effortlessly from the surface and vanished. There didn't seem to be any smell where the sewer came out—perhaps they weren't using it anymore . . . eight, nine, six hundred, one, two . . . nine, a thousand, one, two . . . around the corner and into the straight. Not all that far now. There was the heeling black side of the old Jersey ferry. Lord, she was rusty. Ouch!

He'd banged his head against something—a dinghy. The varnished planks seemed like a welcome home to a world he knew, after all that wet and grayness.

"Hang on here," he whispered, showing Sally where to clutch the gunwale. "Don't try to climb in."

He worked his way around to the stern, gave a final kick and heaved himself over, barking his belly a little. His legs felt empty and boneless, like one of those toy animals with zippers that women keep nighties in. Or used to, anyway. Heaven knows what they did now. He had a struggle getting Sally in—she was near the end of her strength—but managed it with a lot more noisy splashing than he cared for. There weren't any oars in the dinghy, of course, but at least he could paddle with the footboard. He moved to the bows and hauled on the painter until a blue stern solidified in the fog. *Schehallion IV* it said—Major Arkville's boat. Well, *he* wouldn't mind lending his dinghy.

"Where's *Quern?*" he whispered.

"Further down on the other quay, but it's no use going there. You want a boat with *sails*, Jeff. This one would do. You could always make a wind."

"I'd rather have an engine."

"But you haven't got the *stuff*. They burned it all, every drop they could find. I saw it. There was a great big whoof noise, and fire everywhere. The poor old mayor got roasted, because he stood too near."

Geoffrey felt obstinate. She was probably right, providing he *could* make a wind (but in that case who'd steer, supposing he "went under" like when he made the fog, if he *had* made it? And anyway, if he could sail so could they—faster, probably, and the wind would blow the fog away). But he wanted to see *Quern* again, if only for Uncle Jacob's sake. He didn't want to ask Sally about Uncle Jacob, because he knew something must have happened to him. There'd have been no question of drowning kids if Uncle Jacob had been about. He paddled clumsily away from the blue stern.

*Quern* was tucked right in under the quay, with a line of sailing boats lashed outside her. He tied the dinghy to the outermost and crept across the decks. The ones nearer the quay were in a very lubberly condition, but *Quern* herself seemed okay. Somebody (himself, Sally said) had been looking after her. Let's hope he'd been looking after the engine too. He lifted the hatch.

The engine was speckless, but the tank was quite empty. Geoffrey ducked into the cabin and crawled through the hatch in the forward bulkhead to where Uncle Jacob kept the spare cans. ("As far from the engine as possible, laddie. Fire at sea is a terrible thing. I've seen it.") There were three big jerricans, all full, which had evidently been missed at the time of the mayor-roasting. He lugged one back and rummaged for dry clothes in the port locker. Two oily jerseys, two pairs of jeans—terrific.

Sally was peering down into the engine hatch, shivering.

"It's like one of my pictures," she said.

"You'd better get into these."

"But they'll beat me if they find me wearing trousers. It isn't *womanly*."

"If they find you they'll . . . ach, never mind. But I can't remember whether it's womanly or not, and no one else will see you. Off you go, and I'll try and get this thing running."

She crept into the cabin, and Geoffrey bent to the engine. He filled the tank, turned the petrol switch, closed the choke, flooded the carburetor and swung the handle. It wasn't as stiff as he expected, which meant that he must have been turning it over from time to time. He swung again. Nothing. And again. And again. Nothing. He looked at the filter glass under the carburetor and found it was full of water—of course. There'd have been quite a bit of condensation in the tank. He unscrewed the glass and let the petrol flow for a little into the bilge. As he was preparing to swing again he realized that the magneto cover was loose, and lifted it off. No magneto. No hope then. Wait a sec, though; there might be a spare. Uncle Jacob was a maniac for spares, always taking up good locker space with things he'd be unlucky to need once in a lifetime. His cronies had said that he sailed about with a complete spare ship on board.

There was a magneto in the big locker in the cabin, sealed in a polyethylene bag. Sally gasped when she saw it.

"Jeff, that's what you were putting in the oven when they came and banged you on the head. Really they'd only come to ask for a night shower. Did you know?"

"In the oven?"

Oh, yes, of course. If he'd been looking after the boat he'd have taken the magneto up from time to time to dry it out. Bad luck to be caught with it. He adjusted the spare, clipped the cover into place, and swung the engine again. It coughed, died, coughed again and caught—though it didn't sound too happy. He opened the choke a little, adjusted the engine to idle, climbed the iron rungs to the quay and cast off every rope he could see. There was a babble of shouts from the direction of the town. A window slammed up above his head and a woman, screeching, began to throw candlesticks at him. He jumped down into the cockpit, put the throttle hard down and the gear to forward, and swung the wheel to port. The whole raft of boats started to move. There was open water between them and the quay. A noise of boots running on cobbles came through the fog. The locked boats wheeled out into the harbor, slowly, slowly. There was a four-foot, a five-foot gap now, with the black harbor water plopping muddily against weedy timbers. A man, a bearded man in a knitted cap, jumped with a grunt onto the deck, but only just made it. As he stood teetering with his knees against the rail, Sally charged yelling out of the cabin and butted her head into his stomach. He went over backward, arms windmilling, with a luscious splash. Now they were in the middle of the harbor, safe until boats could be got out.

Geoffrey, one hand still on the wheel, throttled down, put the gear to neutral and felt in the fire-fighting locker for the hatchet. Still there. He ran along the deck, hacking through the painters that lashed them to the other boats. The last ropes parted with a slap and twang. Back in the cockpit he revved up and put the gear to forward. Free after five years' idleness, *Quern* danced away down the harbor (a rather sick dancer).

"Well done, Sal."

She laughed, and he recognized at last the six-year-old he'd known.

# Chapter 2

# THE CHANNEL

Twenty minutes later they came out of the fog: a soft south wind was putting a tiny lop onto the water, making it flash, million-faceted, under the sun. It heaved sleepily too, stirred by the slow remains of Atlantic rollers. England, behind them, was still lost in grayness.

Geoffrey went into the cabin and found his gold robe. The saltwater stains were leaving it mottled and blobbed, but it was still too damp to show how bad the final result would be. He took it out to spread on the cabin roof. Coming out, he noticed how much sicker the engine was sounding than when he'd started, and realized at the same time how much the spear-prick in his chest was beginning to hurt. The first-aid box was in its proper locker. ("Never stint yourself for splints and bandages, laddie. I've seen men die for want of a proper dressing.")

"What happened to Uncle Jacob, Sal?"

"The weavers killed him. They came from all over Dorset and threw stones at him, and the neighbors watched out of their windows. It was because of something he was trying to do in the big shed by the stream. Shall I help you with that?"

She wasn't much help, not knowing how adhesive tape worked, but he managed quite a neat patch, with some analgesic cream (rather thick and crumbly with age) on the actual cut. Then he decided he ought to do something about the engine, or try to. He'd watched Uncle Jacob tinkering often enough, and done simple jobs himself, but he knew that it would have to be something pretty easy and obvious if he was going to tackle it alone. At least the tools would be there. ("No use trying to do a complicated job with a knife and fork, laddie. I've seen ships lost at sea for the lack of the right wrench.") He put the engine into neutral and stopped it. When he opened the hatch a blast of scorching air weltered up at him and there was a guggle of boiling water in the cooling system.

Oil? He'd been so cock-a-hoop about finding the petrol that he'd forgotten to check the oil. Just like him to get this far and then land himself, by sheer stupidity, with a hopelessly buckled crankshaft. But the dipstick, too hot to hold without a cloth, showed reasonably clean oil up to the "Full" mark, though it smoked bluely and gave off a bitter smell of burning.

Cooling system, then? Yes. There was far more water in the bilge than there should have been, and both hoses were dripping and hissing. He took off his jersey and bent down to try the intake hose. Damn! His arm seemed to come back of its own accord, like a recoiling snake, five inches of skin scorched white by the quivering metal. He rubbed some cream in and tried again more carefully. Both hoses were perished, useless.

"Is there anything for me to do, Jeff?"

"I don't think so. Wait a sec while I look at the spare hose."

There was a decent length of it in the locker, but this too was mostly cracked and powdery. He needed about eight good inches for the intake: the outlet could take care of itself, really, provided they didn't mind a bit of bailing. One stretch in the middle of the spare felt not too bad, and while he was reaching down to measure it against the rotten piece his eye was caught by the filter bowl under the carburetor. It was dark with little crumbly bits of brown stuff, like coffee grounds—rust off the inside of the jerricans. Much more of that and the jet would be choked. He went into the cabin and found two plastic buckets and a plastic sieve.

"Look, Sal, if you pour the petrol out of this can into those buckets through this strainer, all but a little bit, you can give the last drops a good swill around and empty it over the side. Then you can pour it back into the can through this funnel—and we'll have some clean petrol. And keep an eye on the coast. This sun will clear the fog up in a jiffy and they'll spot us."

"You could make another one."

"I dunno. I've a feeling that's all there is, by way of fog, for the moment. It takes an awful lot of cold. You can't make bricks without straw. I daresay I could make a calm."

"They've got rowing boats, quite big ones. They go terribly fast. Do you really mean that you can't remember how you make weather?"

"I can't remember anything, Sal. It must be something to do with being hit on the head. You'll have to explain to me what's been going on."

"The Changes, you mean? I don't know much. We weren't supposed to talk about them."

"Well, tell me what you know later. It's more important to get that petrol clean now. And keep a good lookout."

He went back to the perished hose. The good bit of spare would just about do. The trouble was that to get a screwdriver into the bulldog clip at the inner end involved working with his hands slap up against the scorching cylinder block. He got a towel out of the cabin, soaked it in the sea and hung it, hissing, down the side of the engine. The screw was very stiff, and before he got it to move the towel was dry and turning toast-brown in places. He soaked it again, and this time moved the screw a quarter-turn before he had to damp the cloth again. Three more goes and it was loose. The other end ought to be easy.

"Jeff, there are boats putting out."

She was right; he could see half a dozen water beetles, just outside the mole, scratches on the surface of the blue-glass sea.

"Okay, Sal, I'll see what I can do. When you've finished that you might see if you can do something about the outlet hose—this thing here. I haven't got enough spare to change it, but if you cut a piece out of one of the sou'westers in the cabin—there ought to be scissors in the galley drawer—you could bind that round and round with insulating tape—here —as tight as you can. Several layers, and then it shouldn't do more than drip. I don't know how long I'll be."

He hadn't put his jersey back on, so the robe lay next to his skin. The gold threads were full of the warmth of the sun. All around the Channel basked, like a sleeping animal, and on its skin the beetles moved toward them, murderous. They were larger now. He sat on the roof of the cabin with his chin on his knees, judging his time.

Now.

*A squall, from the southwest. Airs gathered over the Atlantic, moving steadily eastward under the massaging of the high stratospheric gales, in their turn moved by the turning world, dangling behind it like streamers. The march of airs flawed and splintered on meeting the land mass of Europe, some sucked back in whirlpools, some shoved on in random eddies, funneled by invisible pressures. One here, now, crumpling the water, a fist of wind, tight, hard, cold, smashing northeast, hurling a puny fleet of beetles about in a pother of waters and broken oars and cries that carried for miles, then on, inland across the unyielding oaks of the New Forest, to shiver into eddies and die out among the Downs.*

When he came to, Sally was making a neat finish to the outlet hose. She had bandaged it over and over, like the broken leg of a doll. She smelled of petrol and looked sad.

"I hope there wasn't anyone we know," she said. "You broke two of the boats, and the other four picked a lot of people out of the water and they all went home."

"Fine."

"Look, Jeff, I found this in the cupboard where you got the tape from. I didn't know you had another one."

"That's an ammeter. You use it for measuring electric currents. What do you mean, another one?"

"Oh, *but* . . . oh, Jeff, it was your talisman—the thing they took away when they hit you on the head. They thought you couldn't make weather without it. You wore the other one on a gold chain round your neck, and you *hit* me once when I touched it. You're much nicer, now, since they tried to drown you, you know."

"I'm sorry, Sal."

Funny, he thought. Perhaps if you have powers that seem magical you are a bit frightened of them, and so you have to pretend to yourself that the magic isn't in you but in something that belongs to you, a talisman. He still felt like that— superstitious, so to speak—about the gold robe. It would be interesting to try and make weather, something easy like a frosty night, without even that. Not now, though. He took the robe off and lay on the deck planks to detach the outer end of the hose and fit the new piece. The cylinder block was cool enough to touch now.

"Tell me about the Changes, Sal."

"I really don't know very much. They happened when I was a little girl. Everyone suddenly started hating machines and engines. No, not everyone. A lot of people went away, over the sea. They just started feeling miserable in England, I think. There are whole towns, quite empty, or that's what they say. And after that anyone who used a machine, or even anyone who just seemed to like machines, they called a witch. And I think everyone started to become more and more old-fashioned, too. Really, that's all I know. I'm terribly hungry; aren't you?"

"Yes, I am. Famished. Go and see if there's any gas in the butane cylinders. I saw some cans in the larder. You could rustle up some grub while I finish this lot off."

"I'm afraid you'll have to show me how."

The butane hissed happily, but most of the matches in the larder were duds. Geoffrey worked almost through a whole box before he got a light, and then he panicked and dropped the match. The second box was better, and he got the cooker going. There was fresh water in the tank, quite sweet, which was another sign of how carefully he'd been servicing

THE CHANGES: A TRILOGY

*Quern* in his forgotten-dream world. He had to show Sally how to put a saucepan on and how to open a can. Then he went back to his engine. It took him about half an hour to fit the hose and clear the carburetor jet, and when he turned the crank it moved quite easily. He must have stopped the engine just in time, before the heat could do any real damage. It started at once when he switched the petrol on and swung it again; it sounded fine now. He turned *Quern*'s head south. France seemed the best bet. He thought about all the people who had left England—there must have been thousands, millions of them, unable to live in a world without machines. How'd they get out? How many had died? Where had they gone?

He locked the wheel, after five minutes' pointless guessing, and went in to see what sort of a mess Sally had made of supper. It was beef stew and butter beans, and it was delicious. They ate it out in the cockpit, with the engine churning smoothly and the first stars showing.

"Is France the right place to go, Sal? We could turn around and land somewhere else on the English coast, where they don't know us."

"We couldn't land in this. They'd kill us at once. France is where all the others went, Uncle Jacob said. When he found out about me drawing pictures he wanted us all to go there, but you wouldn't. You liked being one of the richest men in Weymouth too much."

"I'm sorry."

"Anyway, we're going to France now."

"Okay. I'll go and see what charts we've got. I wonder if we've got enough fuel to go all the way to Morlaix."

There was a message in the middle of the big Channel chart, written in Uncle Jacob's backward-sloping hand on a folded piece of tissue paper. It said:

Good luck, laddie. I should have taken you and Sal south long ago, before you got hooked on this weather thing. Now I don't think I shall last long. I'm going to try and wean these fools of burghers from their cottage industries by building them a water-driven power loom. Can't be much harm in that, but you never know. This antimachine thing seems a bit erratic in its effects—it's pretty well worn off me now, but it seems just as strong as ever with most of the honest citizens of Weymouth. I can't be the only one. It's not sense. But everyone's too afraid even to drop a hint to his neighbor (me too). We'll just have to see what happens.

One thing I'd like to do is go nosing about up on the Welsh borders, Radnor way. There's talk about that being where the whole thing is coming from.

You'll find a spot of cash in Cap'n Morgan's hidey-hole.

Geoffrey went and looked in the secret drawer under his old bunk. If you felt under the mattress there was a little hook which you pulled, and that undid the catch and you could push the panel in. Uncle Jacob had made it for him to keep his spare Crunchie Bars in, but now all it held was a soft leather purse containing thirty gold sovereigns. In a fit of rage he thought of the men he'd spilled into the roaring sea with his squall, and hoped that some of the people who had stoned Uncle Jacob had been among them. Then he thought about that last trip to Brittany, in the summer holidays when he was ten, and decided to go to Morlaix if they possibly could. He did some sums and realized it would be a close thing: but he needn't make up his mind until they were on their last can of petrol.

"Time you turned in, Sal. One of us ought to be awake all the time, just in case. I'll give you four hours' sleep, and then you can come and be captain while I have a snooze."

When the time came to wake her he couldn't, she was so deep under. And he was tired all through, so that unconsidered nooks of his body screamed at him for sleep. He cut the engine, turned off the petrol and rolled into his bunk, wondering whether a night's dreaming would bring back his memory of the lost five years.

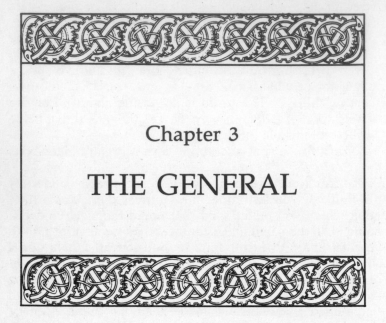

# Chapter 3

# THE GENERAL

A noise like the end of the world woke him. The room was bucketing about. His first thought was Earthquake! Then the noise came again as the two cans from last night's supper rattled across the floor, and he remembered he was on *Quern*. She was rocking wildly. He ran out on deck and saw a big oil tanker belting eastward, trailing the ridged wake that was tossing them about. Sally came out too, still almost asleep, staggering and bumping into things. She blinked at the tanker and put her thumb in her mouth. It was just after eight, supposing he'd set the clock right the night before. He started the engine and went to look for some breakfast. Supper out of cans can be fine, but not breakfast. They ate ham and spaghetti.

They saw a few more ships on the way over, and about midmorning the first of the big jets whined above them. Sally put her thumb in her mouth again and said nothing. Geoffrey realized that the previous afternoon they hadn't seen a single proper ship or airplane in all their twenty-mile circle of visibility.

It was about four, and raining, when they chugged up the listless waters of Morlaix estuary and made fast to the quay, with a cupful of petrol left in the tank. An absurd train, a diesel, hooted as it crossed the prodigious viaduct that spans the valley where old Morlaix lies. Sally cried out when she saw it.

"Oh, that's another of my pictures!"

There were proper cars slamming along the roads on either side of the mooring basin. She stared at them, and her thumb crept to her mouth yet again.

"Don't they go fast?" she said. "Why don't they hit each other? They look awfully dangerous. And they smell."

Yes, they *did* smell. Geoffrey hadn't remembered that. Or perhaps five years in a land without exhaust fumes had sharpened his senses. There was a very French-looking boy fishing wetly in the corner of the basin. Geoffrey dredged in his mind for scraps of language.

"Nous sommes Anglais," he said, shy with the certainty that he wouldn't be able to manage much more.

"Oh, are you?" said the boy. "So'm I. You mean you've only just come over? I say, you *are* late." He gave a short laugh, as if at a joke he didn't expect anyone else to see. "I'll take you along to the office, though it's probably shut—practically no one comes over any more. Monsieur Pallieu will be tickled pink to have a bit of work to do."

The "office" was upstairs in a harsh but handsome building close to the quay. It said DEPARTEMENT DES IMMIGRES on the door. There were voices inside.

"You're in luck," said the boy. "He's probably brought some crony back from lunch to help him swill Pernod."

He tapped on the door and lounged in without waiting for an answer, as though it were his own house. From behind they saw a ludicrous change come over his demeanor, as he clutched off his dripping beret and jerked his insolent slouch into respectful attention. He spoke politely.

"I've brought two new *immigrés* to see you, Monsieur Pallieu. They're kids."

"Diable!" said one voice.

"Thank you, Ralph," said another. "Let them come in."

The room was extremely hot, and smelled of dust, paper, gasfire, wet umbrellas and people. There were two men in it, a small gray gentleman who didn't look like anyone in particular and introduced himself as M. Pallieu; and a larger man in an untidy tweed jacket who looked distinctly like somebody—he had a square, tanned face, close-cut black hair above it, and a bristling little moustache in the middle of it. M. Pallieu said he was General Turville, Inspecteur du Département. The two were sitting behind a desk which was covered with neat piles of paper, all containing rows of figures.

The General muttered in French to M. Pallieu, and went over to stare out of the window at the rain. M. Pallieu fetched two chairs for the children.

"Please sit down," he said. "The General has kindly consented to wait while I take your particulars. We were, in fact, discussing the possibility of closing this office down, so you have arrived in the nick. Now"—he reached for a form —"names, please."

"Geoffrey and Sally Tinker."

"Your ages?"

Geoffrey looked at Sally.

"I'm eleven and he's sixteen," she said.

"Do you not know your own age, young man?" said M. Pallieu.

"They hit me on the head yesterday," said Geoffrey, "and something seems to have gone wrong with my memory."

"Ah." M. Pallieu didn't seem at all surprised, but went on asking questions in his beautiful English and filling in the form. He had nearly finished when he said "Do you possess any money?"

"I've got thirty gold sovereigns, and I suppose we could sell the boat if we had to."

"You came in your own boat? It is not stolen?"

"No. It belonged to my Uncle Jacob, but he's dead, and Sally is sure he left it to me."

"Ce bâteau-là?" the General barked from the window, so odd and abrupt a sound that at first Geoffrey thought he was only clearing his throat.

"Yes, that's her. She's called *Quern.*"

The General jerked his head at M. Pallieu, who went across the room and looked out of the window. He sounded a little less kindly when he turned back and spoke again.

"Let us have this clear. You claim to have come from Weymouth in that white motorboat we can all see down there?"

"Yes," said Geoffrey. "Why?"

"He doesn't think we could have done it in a *motor*boat," said Sally.

"Exactly," said M. Pallieu. "Furthermore, it is well known that the government of France is extremely interested to meet *immigrés* upon whom the English scene does not appear to produce its customary symptoms, and there have been a number of impostors who have made this claim. They expected to be given money."

"Did they come in motorboats?" asked Geoffrey.

"Of course. That appeared to substantiate their claim."

"Oh dear," said Sally.

"On the other hand," said M. Pallieu, "they were not children. Nor did many of them have as much as thirty gold sovereigns. With the General's permission, we had better hear your story and then we can perhaps judge."

"They were trying to drown us for being witches," said Sally, "but Jeff made a fog and swam me round to the harbor and found some of the stuff you put in the engine to make it go and I pushed a man overboard and we got out of the harbor and then the engine stopped and the fog went away and the men came after us in boats and Jeff made a wind and abolished them and mended the engine and I helped him and then I made supper on a sort of oven that went whish with blue fire which came out of a bottle and here we are."

"Let us take it more slowly," said M. Pallieu.

He asked questions for what seemed hours. Sally had to do most of the answering. The General leaned over the desk and barked occasionally. They kept coming back to the starting of the engine in the harbor and the mending of it out at sea. At one point the General himself tramped down to *Quern* and nosed around. He came back with some odd things, including a mildewy burgee and a packet of very moldy biscuits. At last they had a low-voiced talk in French. Then M. Pallieu turned to the children.

"Well," he said, "we think that either you are telling the truth or that some adult has arranged an extraordinarily thorough piece of deception and used you as a bait. Even so, how would he obtain five-year-old English gingersnaps? So, really, we do not think you are impostors, but we wish there was some way of proving your story. There are many things about it that are most important—this business about making weather, for instance. That would explain much."

"Would it help if Jeff stopped the rain?" said Sally.

The two men looked at him, and he realized he would have to try. He reached up under his jersey, under his left arm, and pulled out the rolled robe. He unrolled it and hung it over the back of a chair while he took his jersey off. Then he put the robe on. Odd how familiar the silly garment felt, as a knight's armor must, or a surgeon's mask, something they'd worn as a piece of professional equipment every time they did their job. He opened the casement and leaned his hand on the sill, staring at the sky. He did not feel sure he could do it; the power in him seemed weak, like a radio signal coming from very far away. He felt for the clouds with his mind.

*From above they were silver, and the sun trampled on them, ramming his gold heels uselessly into their clotting softness. But there were frail places in the fabric. Push now, sun, here, at this weakness, ram through with a gold column, warming the under air, hammering it hard, as a smith hammers silver. Turn now, air, in a slow spiral, widening, a spring of summer, warmth drawing in more air as the thermal rises to push the clouds apart, letting in more sun to warm the under air. Now the fields steam, and in the clouds there is a turning lake of blue, a turning sea, spinning the rain away. More sun . . .*

"He always goes like that," said Sally. "We never knew when to wake him."

In the streets the humps of the cobbles were already dry, and the lines of water between them shone in the early evening light. The cafe proprietor on the far side of the basin was pulling down a blue and red striped awning with CINZANO written on it.

The General was using the telephone, forcing his fierce personality along the wires to bully disbelieving clerks at the far end. At last he seemed to get the man he wanted, changed his tone and listened for a full two minutes. Then he barked "Merci bien" and put the receiver down. He turned and stared at the children.

"Vous ne parlez pas français?" he said.

"Un peu," said Geoffrey, "mais . . ." The language ran into the sand.

"And I too the English," said the General. "How they did teach us badly! Monsieur Pallieu will speak, and I will essay to comprehend."

"The General," said M. Pallieu, "has been speaking to the meteorological office at Paris. We wished to know whether this break in the clouds was just coincidence. After all, you might have felt a change coming, and risked it. But, apparently, he is satisfied that you, Mr. Tinker, did the trick yourself. Now, you must understand that the only phenomenon we have actually been able to observe over England during the last five years has been the weather. Most Western powers—France, America, Russia, Germany—have sent agents in to your island, but very few have returned. Some, we think, were killed, and some simply decided to stay: 'went native,' you might say. Those who did return brought no useful information, except that the island was now fragmented into a series of rural communities, united by a common hostility to machines of any sort, and by a tendency to try to return to the modes of living and thought that characterized the Dark Ages. The agents themselves say that they felt similar urges, and were tempted to stay too.

"Of course, at first we tried to send airplanes over, but the pilots, without exception, lost confidence in their ability to fly their machines before they were across the coast. Some managed to turn back but most crashed. Then we tried with pilotless planes; these penetrated further, but were met before long with freak weather conditions of such ferocity that they were broken into fragments.

"Despite these warnings, a number of English exiles formed a small army, backed financially by unscrupulous interests, and attempted an invasion. They said that the whole thing was a Communist plot, and that the people of England would rally to the banner of freedom. Of the three thousand who left, seven returned in two stolen boats. They told a story of mystery and horror, of ammunition that exploded without cause, of strange monsters in the woods, of fierce battles between troops who were all parts of the same unit, of a hundred men charging spontaneously over a cliff, and so on. Since then we have left England alone.

"Except for the spy satellites, though even these are to some extent affected by the British phenomenon. They send us very poor pictures, with no detail, but at least we can see the weather pattern. This is very strange. For centuries, the English climate has been an international joke, but now you have perfect weather—endless fine summers, with rain precisely when the crops need it; deep snow every Christmas, followed by iron frosts which break up into early, balmy springs; and then the pattern is repeated. But the pattern itself is freckled with sudden patches of freak weather. There was, for instance, a small thunder area which stayed centered over Norwich for three whole weeks last autumn, while the rest of the country enjoyed ideal harvest weather. There are some extraordinary cloud formations on the Welsh border, and up in Northumberland. But anywhere may break out into a fog, or a storm, or a patch of sun, against all meteorological probability, in just the way you brought the sun to us now.

"So you are doubly interesting to us, Mr. Tinker. First, because you explain the English weather pattern. And secondly, because you appear to be genuinely immune to the machine phobia which affects anyone who sets foot in England. You seem to be the first convincing case in the twenty million people who have left England."

"Twenty million!" said Geoffrey. "How did they all get out?"

"The hour brings forth the man," said M. Pallieu, "especially if there is money involved. All one summer the steamers lay off the coast, on the invisible border where the effect begins to manifest itself, and the sailing boats plied out to them. Most had given all they possessed to leave. They came by the hundred thousand. I had twelve men working under me in Morlaix alone, and in Calais they had three whole office buildings devoted to coping with the torrent of refugees. That is what you English were, refugees. When I was your age, Mr. Tinker, I saw the refugees fleeing west before Hitler's armies, carrying bedding, babies and parrots, wheeling their suitcases in barrows and prams, a weeping, defeated people. That is how they came to us, five years ago.

"And nobody knows how many have died. There can, one imagines, be no real medicine. Plague must have ravaged the cities. We know from the satellites that London and Glasgow burned for weeks. And still we do not know what has caused this thing."

"Why does it matter so much to you?" asked Geoffrey. It was the General who answered.

"If this can arrive to England," he said, "it can arrive to France. And to Russia. And to America. Your country has a disease, boy. First we isolate, then we investigate. It is not for England we work, but for Europe, for the world, for France."

"Well," said Geoffrey, "I'll tell you everything I can, but it isn't much because I've lost my memory. And so will Sal, but I honestly don't think she knows much about what happens outside Weymouth. Really what I'd like to do is go back, if you'll help me, and try and find out—not for France or the world or anything, but just to know." (And for Uncle Jacob: and he wasn't going to tell them about Radnor, if he could help it.)

"Can I come too?" said Sally.

"No," said Geoffrey and M. Pallieu together.

"Yes, she must go," said the General.

"I don't think I like it here," said Sally. "I think those things are horrible."

She pointed out of the window at a Renault squealing ecstatically around a right-angled bend at sixty mph and accelerating away across the bridge, watched by a benign gendarme.

"You would soon be accustomed to them," said M. Pallieu.

"You'd better stay, Sal," said Geoffrey. "Honestly, England sounds much more dangerous. Nobody is going to drown you here, just for drawing pictures."

The General grunted and looked at Sally.

"You are right, mamselle, you must go," he said. "Your brother has no memory of what arrives in England today. He must have a guide, and you are the only possible. Michel, it is necessary." He spoke firmly in French to M. Pallieu, and Geoffrey, used now to the sound of the language, grasped that he was saying that the children had not much to tell, but might possibly find out more than previous agents. Then he turned to Geoffrey.

"Young man, with your powers you have weapons that are stronger, in the conditions, than the antitank gun. If we send you to England, what will you do? You cannot explore a whole island, two hundred thousand square miles."

"I think I'd go and explore the freak weather centers," said Geoffrey. "That one on the Welsh borders sounds interesting."

"Why?" The General pounced on him, overbore him, wore him down with stares and grunts. In the end it seemed simplest to tell them about Uncle Jacob's message, and the gossip about the Radnor border.

"Understood," said the General. "We must direct you to that point. You will find the location and the cause of the disturbance. And when you are returned, you can make us some more French weather. For the five years past we have endured your horrible English weather. The rain must go somewhere, is it not, Michel?"

He laughed, a harsh yapping noise, as if he were not used to the exercise.

"Yes, General," said M. Pallieu sadly.

# Chapter 4

# BACK

A fortnight later, in a warm dusk, they were lounging up the Solent under the wings of a mild wind from the southwest, passengers only, on a beautiful thirty-foot ketch skippered by Mr. Raison, a solemn fat furniture designer who'd been one of the first to leave England. The General had chosen him, hauled him all the way up from Nice, because he had once kept a yacht on Beaulieu River, with his own smart teak bungalow by the shore. He had spent every weekend of his English life sailing devotedly on those waters, until he could smell his way home in a pitch-black gale.

The crew was English too. They were brothers called Basil and Arthur. Six years before they had lived near Bournemouth, fishermen in the off season, but making most of their livelihood out of trips for tourists in the delicious summer months. Now they owned a small garage in Brest, which the General had threatened to close down unless they joined the adventure—but Geoffrey, knowing them now, re-

alized they would have come of their own accord if they had
been asked in the right way.

The ketch belonged to an angry millionaire, who hadn't
been willing to lend it until he received a personal telephone call from the President of France. (His wife had put
on her tiara to listen to the call on an extension.) It was the
best boat anyone knew of which did not have an engine.
The point was that they still knew absurdly little about the
reaction of England to machines. Would the people sense
the presence of a strange engine, even if it wasn't running?
Would the weather gather its forces to drive them back?
Sally thought not, but it wasn't worth the risk.

They were going to have to rely on an engine in the end.
This was the upshot of the second lot of arguments in
Morlaix. (The first had been about whether Sally should
come at all, Geoffrey and M. Pallieu versus Sally and the
General. Sally's side had won hands down, partly because
Sally really was the only one who knew what she was talking about, and partly because the General had enough will-
power to beat down three Geoffreys and twenty M. Pal-
lieus.) The problem had been how the children should move
the hundred and fifty miles across England to the Welsh
borders. Should they walk, and risk constant discovery in a
countryside where every village (Sally said) regarded all
strangers as enemies? Obviously not, if they could help it.

At first they'd assumed that any mechanical means were
out of the question, and the General had scoured the country for strong but docile ponies. But the riding lessons had
been a disaster: Sally was teachable, but Geoffrey was not.
Five minutes astride the most manageable animal in northern France left him sore, sulky and irresponsible. They per-
severed for five days, at the end of which it was clear that he
would never make a long journey in that fashion, though he
could now actually stay in the saddle for perhaps half an
hour at a time. But he obviously didn't belong there. The
most dimwitted peasant in England would be bound to
stare and ask questions.

It was M. Pallieu who came up with the mad, practical
idea. He pointed out that the engine of *Quern* had worked,
at least. This implied that the English effect was dormant in

the case of engines which had been in England all along, without running. England had got used to their presence. Would not the best thing be to find a car which had been abandoned in England and was still in working condition?

"Impossible," barked the General.

But no, argued M. Pallieu. It happened that his friend M. Salvadori, with whom he played belotte in the evenings, was a fanatic for early motorcars. Fanatics are fanatics; whatever their subject, stamps, football, trains—they know all there is to know about it. And M. Salvadori had talked constantly of this fabulous lost treasure store, not two hundred kilometers away over the water, at Beaulieu Abbey: the Montagu Motor Museum.

When the Changes came, Lord Montagu had been among the exiles; but before he left he had "cocooned" every car in his beloved museum, spraying them with plastic foam to preserve them from corrosion. (Navies do the same with ships they don't need.) Could they not take a car from the museum? They could choose a route that avoided towns and villages. They would come so fast that nobody would be ready to bar their way and they would outrun any pursuit. They might meet casual obstacles, but some of the great old cars were built almost like tanks, enormously simple and robust. They could be further strengthened. . . . M. Salvadori suggested the famous 1909 Rolls-Royce Silver Ghost.

The General had sat quite still for nearly two minutes. Then he had spent two hours telephoning. Next morning a marvelous old chariot trundled into Morlaix, with a very military-looking gentleman sitting bolt upright and absurdly high behind its steering wheel, and all the urchins cheering. So Geoffrey had his first driving lessons on that queen of all cars, the Silver Ghost, taught by a man to whom driving was a formal art and not (as it is to most of us) a perfunctory achievement.

It had not been easy. In 1909 the man who drove had to be at least as clever as his car. Nowadays they built for idiots, and most cars, even the cheap ones, have to be a good deal cleverer than some of their owners. So Geoffrey, sweaty with shame, groaned and blushed as he crashed those noble gears with the huge, long-reaching lever, or stalled the impeccable, patient engine. But he improved quite quickly. Indeed, before the messenger sent by the General to Lord Montagu in Corfu returned, the military-looking gentleman went so far as to tell him that he had a certain knack with motors. The messenger had brought back sketch plans of the abbey and the museum, and, best of all, keys.

So now here they were, heading up the estuary through the silken dusk, with fifty gallons of petrol in the cabin, a wheelbarrow on deck, together with two big canisters of decocooning fluid, spare tires, two batteries, a bag of tools, cartons of sustaining food, bedding, and so on. Beside them lay the "ram," a device like a cowcatcher to be bolted on to the front of the Rolls—Basil and Arthur had welded it together in their garage, because Sally had said they might need it. But an even more curious item, perhaps, was Sally's pouch of horse bait, in case the Rolls was a flop and they had to trudge into the New Forest and steal ponies after all. The General had dug up a professional horse thief, a gypsy. He had been very old and smelly, and had smiled yellowly all the time, but he'd pulled out of pocket after pocket little orange cubes that smelt like celestial hay. He had whined horribly at the General for more money, but when he realized that he'd been given as much as he was going to get he had changed his personality completely, becoming easy and solemn, and had said that Sally was born to great good fortune.

They could see the banks of the estuary now, on both sides, a darker grayness between the steel-gray water and the blue-gray sky. The rich men's yachts were all gone. There was a noise of hammering and a flaring of lights from Buckler's Hard, as if the old shipyard were once again building oaken seagoers, in a hurry after two hundred years of idleness. The banks came closer. There were houses visible by the shapes of their roofs against the skyline, but few showed any lights in a land where once again men went to bed at dusk and rose at dawn. A dog howled and Geoffrey cringed a little in the darkness, sure that the animal spoke for the whole countryside, that somehow it had sensed them and their cargo, alien and modern; sure that they would land to meet a crowd of aroused villagers, bristling with staves and spears (like the soldier men at Weymouth) who would chump them all into shapeless bloody fragments, like the jaws of some huge, mindless hound. But no dog answered; there was no calling of voices from dark house to dark house, no sudden scurrying of lanterns; the ketch whispered on through the darkness between the black, still woods on either side of the water.

After an endless time the two brothers held a low-voiced talk with Mr. Raison, crept forward and brought the mainsail down with a faint clunking. They drifted along, barely moving, under the jib. Staring forward, Geoffrey saw the reach of water down which they were sailing darken in the distance, as if it were passing through the blackness under trees. Mr. Raison gave a low whistle and put the wheel over. The jib came down, flapping twice like a shot pheasant. The anchor hissed overboard (its chains had been replaced with nylon rope at Morlaix). They were there. The ketch lay in the center of the pool below the abbey. The blacker patch of water had been land.

Sally pulled the trailing dinghy in by its painter and Geoffrey eased himself in, then stood, wobbling slightly, to receive stores, stowing canisters and bedding all around him until there were only three inches of freeboard left, and barely room for Basil to lower himself in and row them ashore. He really was an expert. He pulled with short, tidy strokes and caught the oars out of the water with a cupping twist of the wrists that made neither swirl nor splash. The only sound was that of a few drops from the oar tips.

They unloaded their cargo over a patch of bank slimy with the paddling of ducks, and Basil went back for more. Geoffrey sat on a drier patch higher up the bank and stared at the star-reflecting water. The ketch itself was invisible against trees.

Thank heavens, anyway, he hadn't needed to make a wind for them. The breeze, which had been perfect, was now dying away to stillness, and soon there'd be an offshore wind to take the ketch out. But they'd a good four hours' work to do before then, and four hours seemed nothing when you thought that before next nightfall Sally and he would, like

as not, be dead. Funny to think of all those distinguished
officers scampering across Europe, bullying underlings over
the telephone, just in order to land a couple of kids in
Hampshire to steal a motorcar, when the odds were that all
three, the Rolls and Sally and himself, would finish up
among the rusting rubbish at the bottom of a duck pond.

He began to worry again about Sally, though she'd been
happy and excited on the way over. She'd hated France with
its whizzing cars and jostling citizens. The only aspects of
civilization she'd really enjoyed had been Coca-Cola and ice
cream, and she'd got on best with the smelly old gypsy man.
After he'd left she had filled every spare nook of her clothes
with the orange horse bait, which she kept pulling out to
sniff during their endless planning sessions.

Suppose that by some crazy fluke they brought it off and
England became again the England he remembered, would
Sally ever be happy? And then there was the General. At first
Geoffrey had worshipped him, a magnificent manifestation
of absolute will, whose orders you obeyed simply because
he was giving them; but then he'd found himself puzzled by
the great man's actual motives: the readiness to slaughter a
couple of kids on the off chance of pulling off a farfetched
coup—did he really know what he was up to? Or was he like
a mindless machine, pounding away toward some un-
thought-out purpose.

You couldn't blame him so much, thought Geoffrey, for
not being very interested in how the children got back to
France, supposing they ever did. Any plan so remote had to
be vague, and the best they could hope for was to hide the
Rolls near their target, nose around, drive home by a different road, buy or steal a boat and sail south once more. M.
Pallieu had suggested that they might carry a homing pigeon, trained by another crony of his, but then they were
disappointed to find that the crony's pigeons could only find
their way home from the south—that being how pigeons are
trained: you take them a little way from their loft and let
them fly home; then you take them further in the same direction; and further; and further. So the General vetoed the
idea. Children, he seemed to think, make much more flexi-
ble and reliable messengers. And just as expendable.

They were taking the devil of a time about reloading the dinghy. Perhaps Sally was having second thoughts—be a good thing if she did, really. It was damned unfair blackmailing a kid to come on a business like this, and that went for himself, too. Why did it have to be *them*? Had the General honestly made an effort to find anyone else who was immune to the Effect, or had he just seized on their chance arrival as an opportunity to exercise his own self-justifying will? Serve the great man right if the Rolls turned out to have been burned by angry peasants. In that case he was certainly not going to go loping off into the dark to steal ponies—and they'd hang you now for that, Sally said—Blast! The dry patch he was sitting on wasn't as dry as he'd thought, and the cold came through the seat of his trousers like a guilty conscience. He stood up and stared at the stars, then walked up onto the road.

When the dinghy came back he was exploring the potholes in the unrepaired tarmac and wondering whether they'd brought enough spare tires. Sally came up the bank to him.

"Sorry we've been so long," she whispered. "We couldn't get the ram and the wheelbarrow and us in all together. They're going back for it now."

Geoffrey slithered down to the water and found the wheelbarrow, which he hauled up to the road. By the time he'd brought the rest of the stores up the dinghy was back, with all three men in it.

"Thought I'd take her back, seeing as you were making the extra journey," whispered Mr. Raison. "Don't want some busybody coming along and spotting her. Remember I can't get out if we have to leave after four a.m. I'll skip off if you two aren't back by then, Bas, and you'll have to lay low all day. Try and get down to that broken staging just below Buckler's Hard. I'll look for you there about eleven, and if you aren't there I'll try and come up here, but it won't be easy single-handed. Same the night after. Then I won't try anymore, and you'll have to steal a boat. Okay?"

"Aye, aye, sir," said the brothers together. As Mr. Raison sculled away into the shadows they picked up the ungainly ram and carried it up to the wheelbarrow. Geoffrey helped

stack whatever stores they could around it, and the rest—
mostly petrol—they hid in deep shadow under the old abbey
wall.

The main gate was locked, and though the key fitted the
lock it wouldn't turn it. Arthur produced an oil can from a
pocket and they tried again. Geoffrey was just feeling in the
barrow for the big bolt-cutters when the corroded wards
remembered their function. Arthur oiled the hinges, and after one ugly screech the gates swung silently open. Geoffrey
shut them behind him.

The lock to the front door of the museum would not move
at all, but the smaller door around on the far side gave easily enough, and they were in. The cars lay ghostly to left and
right, lumpy blobs under their plastic foam and dust sheets.
The floor was gray with dust, and Geoffrey was surprised
that he could see it, until he realized that the moon must
now be up—he hadn't noticed in the tense crouching over
the locks. He looked behind him, and saw in the dust four
sets of footprints, like those black shoe-shapes which comic
artists draw to show the reeling passage of a drunk along a
pavement. Between them ran the telltale track of the barrow's rubber tire—a risk, but worth it for the sake of silence. Arthur lit a pencil torch, and in its stronger glow
Geoffrey saw hummocks of white stuff, like fungus, scattered between the cars. Basil walked across and pushed one
with his foot.

"Plastic foam, that is," he whispered. "Right old mess they
made."

"Forgotten how to use the equipment then?" said Arthur.
"Just let's hope that don't start happening with us, eh?"

Silence lay around them like a dream. As they turned the
corner to where the Rolls should be, Geoffrey felt that the
thud of his excited blood was the loudest noise in the night.

"That's her," said Basil. "Drape a bit of bedding on a line
atween those other two, Jeff, and we won't hardly show no
light."

Arthur was already scratching with a fingernail at the
white foam on the hood. He tore a strip of the stuff away
and shone his torch on the hole. They all saw the overlapping red RR.

"Aye, that's her," said Arthur, and chuckled in the darkness. Geoffrey ran a cord between projections from the two
white lumps on their right and draped sleeping bags into the
gap. Arthur lit a small lantern torch and began tearing systematically at the cocooning plastic. Geoffrey untied the
dust sheets that covered the rear two-thirds of the machine
and found that the dash and the controls had also been cocooned. He helped Sally into the driver's seat and set her
pecking sleepily away, then went off with the barrow to
fetch the rest of the stores. By the time he'd finished his
third trip, Basil and Arthur had torn off all the cocooning
that would come easily, and were working under the hood,
swabbing down the plastic with solvent. It shriveled as the
sponges touched it to a few small yellow blobs, which they
wiped away with cloths. Sally was fast asleep on the front
seat, sucking her thumb in a mess of white plastic. She
grunted like a porker as Geoffrey heaved her into the back,
but stayed there. He covered her with a blanket, swept out
the litter of cocoon and started to swab away at the dash.
She'd done pretty well, really. He finished the dash, cleared
the steering wheel, gear-lever and brake, and climbed down
to see how the brothers were doing. They'd almost finished.

"I'll nip down and get the last jerrican," he said. "Then I'll
give you a hand with the wheels and the ram."

"Okay, Jeff. I reckon she'd start now—if she'll start at all."

Outside the moon was well up, leaving only the big stars
sharp in a black sky. And something else was different. He
stood still, and realized that the night was no longer noiseless. There was a muttering in the air. As he walked down to
the gate he recognized it as the sound of low, excited voices.
There was dim, flickering light beyond the bars—a lantern!
He crept through the clotted mat of grasses that had fallen
during five summers of neglect into the drive, and peeped
around the stone gatepost. There were three or four men on
the grass bank where they'd landed on the other side of the
road. The one with the lantern knelt and pointed. Another
ran off to the sleeping houses. They must have spotted the
tread marks of the barrow's tire. As quickly as he could
move in silence, Geoffrey loped back to the museum. The

brothers had hauled the ram into position in front of the bonnet and were standing scratching their heads.

"There's no time for that! They've spotted the barrow tracks, or something. One of them ran off to the village!"

"Ah," said Basil, slowly, as though someone had told him crops were moderate this year.

"What'd we better do?" said Arthur, as though he already knew the answer but was just asking for politeness.

"Do you really think she'd start?"

"Aye. We've put some petrol in her, and primed her, and pumped her. Mebbe we could be getting off to some tidy spot in the Forest now, and put the old ram on there."

"What about the tires?"

"Reckon we must go chancing that, Jeff. They don't look too bad to me. I'll be pumping the tires while Basil cranks and you can see if she'll go. Oil's okay."

Geoffrey and Basil unfastened the absurd great straps which held the top forward, eased the framework back and folded the canvas in. Sally said "I'm all right" as he lugged her back into the front seat to make room for the stores, but she stayed asleep. Then he settled himself behind the wheel, whispering to himself, "Be calm. Be calm." Arthur was standing by the left front wheel, methodically pawing away at the footpump, when Geoffrey moved the advance/retard lever up and switched on. Basil swung the starting handle, but nothing happened. The same the second time, but at the third swing the engine kicked, hiccuped and then all six cylinders woke to a booming purr. He revved a couple of times, and Arthur grinned at him through the easy note of power. This, thought Geoffrey, was far the most beautiful toy that man had ever made for himself. The idea was spoiled as a snag struck him. He gazed up the narrow and twisting path between the shrouded cars to the intractably locked main doors.

"How are we going to get out?" he shouted, though there was no need to shout. At low revs the engine made no more noise than a breeze in fir trees, but panic raised his voice.

"Ah," said Basil. He walked around and kicked the wall behind the car.

"This is no' but weatherboarding here," he said. "I got a

saw somewhere, and I'll be through that upright in a brace of shakes."

Arthur didn't even look up from his pumping. His long, pale face was flushed with the steady pumping, and there was a pearl or two of sweat on his moustache.

"All I ask is have a care the roof don't come down atop of us," he said.

Basil scratched his jaw and looked up at the crossbeam.

"Don't reckon she should," he said. "Not till we're out, leastways."

He took his saw from his toolbag and sawed with long, unhurried strokes at the upright timber. When he was through at the bottom he stood on two jerricans and started again about seven feet from the ground. Arthur packed the pump into the back and went around the car, kicking the tires thoughtfully. Basil jumped down from his pedestal and heaved the cans into the back. He looked over the door at the sleeping Sally, climbed up, picked her up gently and stowed her on the floor in front of the passenger seat. Then he lifted the sleeping bags off the cord and tucked them around and over her, until she was cushioned like an egg in an eggbox. He knelt on the seat and reached over into the back, feeling in his toolbag, and brought out two hefty wrenches. He handed one to Arthur and settled into the passenger seat.

"What's the wrench for?" asked Geoffrey.

"Bang folk with—if it comes to that. You see us out, Art. Follow us sharpish. I dunno how long that bit o' timber will stand. Reverse her out, Jeff, nice and steady. You got three ton o'metal there, pushing for you. Right?"

"Right," said Geoffrey, and moved the long lever through the gate into reverse. He let the hand brake off, revved gently and put the clutch in. There were about five feet to go, and Arthur, standing a little to one side, shone the torch onto the back wall. They were rolling backward. With a foot to go Geoffrey put the accelerator down a full two inches, so that they would hit the wall slowly but with full power. He felt a dull jar, and at the same time the huge engine bunched its muscles and shoved. Timbers groaned and cracked. Splintered ends of wood screeched against the metal. The air was cold around his neck and shoulders, and he was no longer breathing dust and exhaust fumes. They were out.

He stopped, and Arthur walked out of the black cavern they had left, still holding the torch. The hut leaned a little sideways, but decided to stay up.

"Very nice," said Basil. "Reckon the drive's up thataway. You can push straight through that bit of old hedge. No, Art, don't you stay on the running board. They might clutch you off. I left a spot for you to squat on them cans, so you can look after that side, in case anyone tries to board us."

"What about the gates?" said Geoffrey.

"They'll give outwards, easy enough. I noticed that when we come in."

"Okay," said Geoffrey.

He put the gears into first and drove forward across the tangle of old lawn at the hedge. The ground was true and firm under the four-foot grasses, and the hedge gave easily. Then up to the drive, which seemed no wider than a bridle path now that they had the full width of the Rolls to occupy it. He turned toward the gates, outlined against several jigging lanterns, and changed (badly) into second. The villagers must surely have heard the crash.

But suddenly, behind the left-hand wall, stood up a great smoky flame, blazing into the night to a belling of whooping voices.

"Oy-oy," said Arthur, "they've found a spot of petrol. D'you leave a can there, Jeff?"

Before he could answer, the tone of the voices changed; someone had heard the crash of gears, and now had seen the Rolls. The gates banged open and the drive was blocked by a barricade of people, black against the glare.

"Keep going," said Arthur, "fast as you can, remembering you got to get round the corner outside. Don't you pay no heed to *them*. They'll claw us limb from limb if you stop."

Geoffrey stayed in second, not risking a stall during another gear change, and put his foot down. The people leaped toward him, black and screaming. Arthur leaned forward and squeezed the bulb horn, which pooped its noble note. Basil stood up and bellowed, "Out of the road there! Jump for it!" He couldn't help hitting someone now, but he kept accelerating, remembering the spearman on Weymouth beach. The villagers, it turned out, were fewer than they looked and well inside the gates with room to scatter to safety. The car missed them all, somehow, and a volley of stones clunked into the bodywork as Geoffrey took her through the gate. He braked hard in the entrance, swung left, and revved again. There was a barrier of burning petrol across the road; a man in priest's robes and holding a cross leaped for the running board and clung there, screaming Latin, until Basil rapped him fiercely on the knuckles and he dropped off, howling, at the edge of the flame.

They were in it. Through it. In blackness. Geoffrey, blinded after the light, eased to a crawl for fear of going off the road. Arthur passed the torch forward and Basil adjusted its beam to shine twenty feet in front of them. It wasn't much, but it was enough. They were away.

A couple of miles on they stopped and listened for pursuit. Geoffrey kept the engine idling while the brothers fixed the main acetylene lamps. Then they drove on through the darkness, looking for a glade to hide in for the rest of the night. The road was awful.

# Chapter 5

# NORTH

There was a breakfasty smell when Geoffrey woke, cramped on the backseat. Arthur had built a small wood fire and was frying bacon.

"I wasn't certain as how I could get the stove going," he said uneasily. "We'd better be starting on the old ram afore we can't tell one end of a wrench from t'other."

Sally was mooning around in the long grasses of the clearing, not looking at the Rolls. When they sat down on groundsheets for breakfast she made sure she had her back to it.

"Are you really going to be all right, Bas?" said Geoffrey.

"I reckon so. We got some oldish things on, and we *are* sailors. We can say we're going looking for work at Buckler's Hard. On'y thing is, do we *look* right? They don't all wear beards, do they, Sal?"

"No. It's just that they don't like shaving. It hurts. But the fussy ones go to the barber's to be shaved once a week."

The brothers sat around when they'd finished eating, as if

they didn't want to start work. Geoffrey noticed Basil glancing sulkily at the car, and looking away again. In the end he
had to say "Come on," and go and try to drag the ram
around by himself. It was heavy and awkward, a pointed
prow of cross-braced girders which kept poking sharp corners in under the mat of fallen grass and sticking. After he'd
lugged it a few feet, Arthur came and helped. Between them
they carried it around to the front of the Rolls, where Arthur tried to line it up back to front.

"Are you feeling all right, Arthur?" said Geoffrey.

"I dunno. I'm fine in myself, I suppose, but I don't feel
certain of anything no more. Here, catch ahold of this, Bas,
and help me hold it up for Jeff to buckle on. He can't do it
hisself, not possibly."

Basil came across, muttering, and helped his brother lift
the contraption and hold it in place while Geoffrey clamped
it onto the dumb-irons in front of the car and then lay under
the machine to fasten the long arms that ran back from it to
the chassis. It took much longer than it should have, because the brothers were so awkward, Arthur giggling a little
at his clumsiness, Basil sullen and ashamed. When he'd finished he went around to the front and looked at the result.
Arthur came and stood beside him, hands on hips.

"Do you think it will really do the trick, Arthur?"

"Should do. Leastways we worked it out pretty careful in
France. But I wouldn't be knowing now. Not beautiful, is
she?"

Geoffrey wasn't sure whether he was referring to the ram
alone, or (now that the effect of England was clearly beginning to work on him), to the car itself. The ram was certainly ugly, crude in its red-lead paint, brutal, jutting out
three feet in front of the proud radiator like a deadly cowcatcher. They'd feel pretty silly if they turned out not to
need it at all, Geoffrey thought, as he primed the cylinders
and pumped pressure into the tank.

"D'you feel like helping me with the tires?" he said.

"Not really, to speak honest, Jeff. You can manage 'em by
yourself, surely."

"I expect so. I'll have to take her out on to the road so that the jack doesn't sink, and perhaps you and Basil could keep a lookout for me. . . . What is it, Sal?"

She came running from the end of the glade.

"There's something enormous in the woods, Jeff. I can hear it crashing about. Do you think it's a dragon?"

Geoffrey laughed. "Most likely a pony," he said. But neither Arthur nor Basil looked amused.

"Best get everyone into the car," said Arthur. "Think you can start her by yourself, Jeff?"

They could all hear the crashing now. It sounded like a tank blundering about in the undergrowth. Then the noise changed, as the thing began to charge straight toward them, ignoring thicket and brake. Geoffrey swung the engine and ran around to the driver's seat. They all waited, looking sideways toward the noise, where the midmorning sunlight stood in shafts of warmth against the darkness under the oaks. A bush convulsed and opened, and in a patch of light stood a prodigious boar, tusked, hairy, slavering, not twenty yards away. It shook itself and swung its low-held head from side to side, inspecting the glade. Its tiny red eyes seemed to blaze as it spotted the car, and it grunted as though that was what it had come for. At once it was careering toward them, a wild, fierce missile of hard muscle and harder bone. Geoffrey let the clutch in with a bang. The wheels spun on the grass, then gripped, and they were moving, accelerating, out over the layer of leaves the brothers had spread to camouflage their tracks, into second, third, doing fifty over the potholes, away.

Three hundred yards down the tarmac he eased up and craned over his shoulder. The boar was sitting on its haunches in the middle of the arch under the trees, watching them go. It still looked enormous eighty yards back.

"They don't come that big," said Basil in a low voice. " 'Tisn't natural."

"I don't know," said Geoffrey. "You get farm pigs as big as that, with proper breeding. I wouldn't be surprised if a lot of farm pigs have escaped and gone wild since the Changes. How close did it get?"

"Six foot or so," said Arthur. "Dunno that it would have

done any real harm, unless it had nicked a tire. Hope there's not many of them about, eh, Bas?"

"Looked like it was coming for the car, not for us," said Basil.

They both sounded sick and bewildered, quite different from the calm and assured couple who had helped him steal the Rolls. Geoffrey realized that he had them on his hands now, and that he ought to make it as easy as possible for them to get back to the river by nightfall.

"Let's have a squint at that map," he said. "Look here. I think the best thing would be if I took you on up to Lyndhurst and then turned south. I've got to go there—there doesn't seem to be any real way around it. Then I can run you down almost to Brockenhurst and you can take the B3055 back to Beaulieu—it looks about six miles, and you don't want to come back along the road we left by. You needn't go into the village at all, actually, which is a good thing because it's probably still humming. I can go off this side road here, almost to Lyndhurst, and then right up this one here, which'll bring me back onto the road I was going to take anyway, up through the Wallops. Cheer up, Bas. I daresay you'll feel better once you're away from the Rolls."

"Hope so."

Lyndhurst was a ghost town, almost. There were no money-bringing tourists now, and the Forest, wilder than before, did not provide enough income to support a community. They boomed down deserted streets, left and left again. An old man leaning on a staff watching sheep graze a stretch of close-nibbled common turned at the sound of the motor, shook his fist at them and shouted something undistinguishable. But a curse, for certain.

When he judged he was just out of earshot of Brockenhurst, Geoffrey stopped. The brothers climbed out and stood dully in the road.

"Now listen," Geoffrey said. "You go down here for about half a mile and turn left. Got that? It's just where the stream crosses the road. You'd better take your bag, Basil, but leave out anything modern. Here; I'll sort it out for you. Saw, hammer, chisels, cold chisel, these square nails should be okay, hand drill, bits, brace, no, not the hacksaw, I should think—that'll have to do. Here are four gold pieces, in case you have to lie up for a bit, and need to buy food."

"They'll have to think of a story for them," said Sally. "They're a lot of money, and people always ask."

"All right. Now listen. You've been working in a shipyard at Bristol as carpenter and mate, and the master died and you didn't like the new master. So you thought you'd try your luck down this way. Got that?"

Basil glanced sideways at Arthur, doubtfully, but Arthur nodded. Geoffrey realized that he'd been speaking loud and slow, as if to a stupid kid. He went on at the same pace.

"Don't go into Beaulieu if you can help it. Wait for two nights at the disused piles below the Hard. If you don't meet Mr. Raison, steal a boat and sail south. Take food with you, and don't try to do it in a rowing boat. It's too far. It's a hundred miles. Got it? Okay, off you go. Good-bye, and thank you very much for all you've done. I'll wait till you're clear, off our road, so that people aren't watching for anything special when you pass. Good luck."

Basil spoke, slowly and thickly.

"I wonder if we done right, after all."

He was looking with loathing at the Rolls.

Geoffrey caught Arthur's eye and jerked his head sideways.

"Come along now, Bas," said Arthur. "We best be stepping along. 'Bye, Jeff and Sally, and good luck to you, I suppose."

The brothers turned together and walked off down the road, their shapes black in the stretches of sunlight and almost invisible in the shadows of the trees. At first they trudged listlessly, like tired men (which indeed they must have been), but after a while their backs straightened, their heads moved as if they had begun to talk to each other, and their pace became springier. At the curve of the road, beyond which they would no longer be seen, they stopped in the sunlight, turned and waved—a real good-bye this time, friendly and encouraging even at this distance. Then they were out of sight.

"I hope they'll be all right," said Geoffrey. "I was dead worried when they went all fuzzy like that, but they seemed to perk up once they were a bit away from the car. We'd

never have got here without them. Does this thing worry
*you,* Sal?"

"Some of the time. But I don't think it really bothers me
*inside* me, if you see what I mean. Not like Arthur and Basil.
It was something in their minds coming out which made
them go all funny. But with me it's really only that I'm not
used to engines. I'm used to thinking they're wicked. Parson
preached against machines every Sunday, almost. He said
they were the abomination of deserts and the great beast in
the Bible. He watched the men stoning Uncle Jacob."

"But you aren't suddenly going to drop a match into our
petrol tank?"

"I don't expect so. I don't feel any different from France. I
hated those little French beetles whining about, but I think
some machines are lovely, like the train on the bridge. And
this one too, I suppose."

She ran a dirty hand over the old red leather.

"Then you must be immune, too, or you'd have started
going like the brothers. Do you think it runs in families?
There was Uncle Jacob, and you, and me. Do you really
think we're the only ones?"

"I don't know. I don't *feel* like an only one."

"Nor do I. I think I must have been immune before I got
hit on the head, or I'd never have been able to look after
*Quern.* I suppose Uncle Jacob told me—"

"Jeff, I think there's another animal coming. I can feel it."

"Okay, Sal."

He let the big engine take the car slowly away, trying not
to disturb the murderous forest which had sent the boar,
but it was too late. A gray stallion, wild, swerved into the
road ahead of them, snorted as it saw the car and reared
with whirling hooves to meet them. Geoffrey increased his
speed, nudged the wheel over so that the ram pointed directly at the beast and pooped the horn. The stallion
squealed back. At the last moment, when they were doing
nearly forty, he jerked the wheel to the left and back again,
so that the huge car skittered sideways and on. The horse,
clumsy on its hind legs, couldn't turn in time to block them,
but a hoof, unshod, banged on metal somewhere at the back
of the car.

They drove quietly around the outskirts of Brockenhurst until they came on a group of children playing a complicated sort of hopscotch in the middle of the road. Some ran screaming into the houses, but others picked up clods and stones out of the gutter and showered them at the Rolls, which clanged like a tinsmith's shop as Geoffrey nosed through. The windshield starred on Sally's side, where a flint caught it. A man came and stood in a doorway with a steaming mug in his hand. He shouted and flung it at the car, but missed completely in his rage and the mug shattered against the wall of a cottage on the far side, leaving great splodges like blood on the white stucco.

Geoffrey laughed as he accelerated away. "Tomato soup," he said.

Sally was crying. "It's everybody hating us, even the children. It's horrid."

"They hate the car, really. They'd have been sure to hit one of us if they'd really been aiming at us. Cheer up, Sal. We're not going through any more towns. We've chosen a whole lot of little lanes that ought to miss them completely, and you'll have to do the map-reading. I'll teach you as soon as we come to a safe bit of straight where we can't get surprised."

They found a good place almost at once, by a stream under some willows. Geoffrey stopped the car and switched off the engine.

"It's quite easy," he said, "especially as we're going north so everything's the right way around. These yellow and green and red lines are the roads. That's all that matters for the moment, but you'll learn the other signs as we go along. That's Brockenhurst, which we've just been through, and we're here. We want to get up to this road with the pencil mark beside it, which is the one we're supposed to be on, so we go up here, see, to the A35. That's about three miles. Then we turn right, and quite soon come to a bridge—this blue line is the river. Then a bit over a mile further on, when we're almost in Lyndhurst, we turn left through Emery Down and we're on our proper road. Try and tell me what's going to happen next about a mile before we get to it. Right? Off we go."

What happened next was a tree across the road. It had evidently been there a couple of years, but nobody had tried to move it. Instead, passersby had beaten a rutted track around the roots, which Geoffrey had to follow. The Rolls lurched and heaved at a walking pace, with the ruts, hardened by months of summer, wrenching the steering wheel about. Geoffrey remembered what the military-looking gentleman had told him about Silver Ghosts being used in the First World War to carry dispatches through the shell-raddled terrain behind the trenches. He realized, too, that he still had the five-year-old tires on. The ram was a nuisance in the tight curve of the track, poking ahead and catching in brambles and weeds, but the big engine wrenched it through. It might come in useful soon: the A35 was the old main road between Southampton and Bournemouth, and there was that bridge. He swung back thankfully onto the remains of the old tarmac.

A couple of miles later he eased cautiously out onto the main road. Its surface was no better than that of the side lanes—worse, if anything, as it seemed to have seen more traffic—but it was wide enough for him to pick some sort of path between the potholes. They swirled past a cart, leaving the driver to shout the usual curse through their long wake of dust. Now that they were coming out of the Forest, there would be more people about, of course. The road dipped toward the stream, and there was the bridge.

And there, on the bridge, was the tollgate. Sally had mentioned tollgates to M. Pallieu, who had informed the General. The ram had been built on his instructions. It was his sort of weapon.

The gate looked hideously solid, with a four-inch beam top and bottom, set into a huge post at either side. Geoffrey changed down to third and second, double-declutching anxiously. The tollkeeper, a fat woman in a white apron, came to the door of her cottage, stared up the road and screeched over her shoulder. Geoffrey changed down (beautifully—the military-looking gentleman would have been delighted) into first, glanced at the gate—now only twenty feet away—decided he was still going too fast and eased off, to a trot, to a walk. With the gate a yard off he accelerated. The whole car

338 THE CHANGES: A TRILOGY

jarred through all its bones as the ram slammed into the
bottom beam—they weren't going to make it. With a deep
twang the hinges gave, the structure lifted and leaped sideways, and the car surged forward. A big man with an orange beard pushed out from behind the woman, swinging a
sledgehammer, but before he got within smiting distance a
yellow thing looped out of the car behind Geoffrey's head
and caught him in the face. Unbalanced by the swing of his
mallet he fell backward, bringing the fat woman down too.
Geoffrey drove on.

"What on earth was that that hit him?" he asked.

"I threw your smelly stove at him," said Sally. "I never
liked it anyway. I hope the gates aren't all as exciting as
that."

"With luck we won't meet many. We'll hardly be on main
roads at all. But rivers are almost the only thing we can't
find a way around, so we've got to go over bridges. I didn't
expect the gates to be quite so strong."

"We turn left quite soon," said Sally. "When are we going
to have lunch?"

"Let's go on a bit. I don't really want to stop till I need a
rest from driving. There ought to be some biscuits somewhere. If we get a puncture we'll just have to stop."

# Chapter 6

# ROUGH PASSAGE

They found an open upland of chalk an hour later, between Winchester and Salisbury, roughly, where an old chalkpit opened off the road. Geoffrey drove in between the high banks and discovered that the place had been used, in civilized days, as a graveyard for abandoned cars. There were a dozen rusting sedans amid the nettles and elders.

The floor of the pit was hard enough to hold a jack. Sally climbed up with the food to the untended grassland above the pit and kept a lookout while he changed the tires. (These came already attached to their steel rims, which were then bolted to the wooden wheels—it couldn't have been easier.) That left him with two good spares and the four old ones. He climbed up and joined Sally.

The Rolls was invisible from a few yards, but they could see for miles. The countryside to the south, which had once been mile-square fields, had reverted to a mosaic of tiny, unrelated patches, some worked, some abandoned. About half a mile away to the south he could see a piece of green

with a row of dots spread across it at the line where the
green changed texture. He ate a slab of bread and Camem-
bert and saw that the dots had moved—they were a team of
men mowing a hayfield with scythes. Behind them came
another pattern of dots, again altering the texture of the
green: more men (or probably women) tossing the hay out
of its scythe-laid rows so that every stem and blade was
exposed to the reliable sun. A few fields away they'd got
beyond that stage and were loading the pale, dried hay onto
a wooden wagon. Elsewhere the cereal crops were still
tender green, oat and wheat and barley each showing its
different shade in long narrow strips. The sun was very hot,
and there were lots of butterflies, all the species regenerated
since men stopped spraying. Geoffrey felt tired as tired.

"I think I'd better try and have a nap, Sal, or I might drive
off the road. Wake me up the moment you see anything
funny. You'd better put everything back in the car, so that if
we really are caught napping we can say we had nothing to
do with it. We just found it, and were waiting for someone
to come along and tell us what to do next. I'll stick to my
robe, just in case. Remember, I'm your idiot brother, deaf
and dumb but quite harmless, and you're in charge of me,
trying to get us north to stay with our married sister in, um,
Staffordshire. You take the grub down, and I'll see if I can
find a place without too many ants."

"When do you want to wake up, supposing nothing happens?"

"Give me a couple of hours, about."

He rolled up his jersey with the robe inside it for a pillow,
and wriggled round for a place where his hip felt comfortable. The grass ticked with insect life. The sun was very
bright. A seed-head tickled his cheek. Hell, he wasn't going
to be able to sleep here. . . .

"Wake up, Jeff. Wake up."

He sat up, the side of his face nubbly with the knitwork of
the jersey. The sun had moved, and the mowers were near
the end of their field. The wagon was gone, and the air was
still and heavy with grass pollen.

"I'm sorry, Jeff. You've slept for about three hours, but
they've pulled that hay cart on to this road, and I think

they'll be bringing it up the hill. They're going awfully slowly. There. You can see them coming out by that copse."

A green-gold hump heaved into sight out of the trees. There was a man in blue overalls lying on his back on top of it, with his hand behind his head. The wagon was about the size of a toy, and it would be ages before the horses brought it creaking up the hill.

"Anything happen while I was asleep?"

"Nothing, except that a rabbit came and nibbled one of the wheels, but I threw stones at it and it ran away."

Geoffrey lunged down the slope to look at his tires. On the left front there were a series of strong gouges, running in pairs—not nibbling, but a determined attack. The cart was still a good twenty minutes off, he decided—not worth risking a tire like that over these roads. He got the jack out, fumbled it into position, pulled himself together and changed the wheel deliberately. Eight minutes, not bad. There was time to fill up with petrol. Its stench rose shimmering into the untainted air. Four gallons gone.

As they backed out onto the road there were shouts from down the hill. Three men with hayforks, very red in the face, were running slowly up toward them. They must have spotted the tire treads in a patch of chalk dust on the untended tarmac. Lucky he'd been given as much as three hours' sleep—the countryside must be fantastically empty for nobody to have come up the road in all that time. The Rolls whined to the top in second and hummed down the far side, leaving the haymakers shouting. One of them had been wearing a smock, of the kind you used to see in particularly soppy nursery rhyme books.

On the next long stretch of road he stopped and sorted out the most obviously French blanket. This he folded in two, with the tent pole in the fold; he ran about six feet of cord from each end of the fender at the back of the car to the two projecting ends of pole; then he made a couple of holes through the blanket and tied the pole in.

"What's that for?" said Sally.

"Sweep out our tracks, with luck."

"It won't last very long, I'd have thought. Haven't you got anything tougher, like a piece of canvas or something?"

"No."

"What about cutting some branches out of the hedge. You could tie them in two bunches, and it wouldn't matter if they wore a bit, because there'd always be more twigs coming down."

"I suppose that'd work, too, but let's see how we get on with this first."

They drove on, Sally kneeling in her seat and looking backward. The blanket lasted about three miles. Sally hummed perkily as she helped him cut two large besoms of brushwood and tie them where the blanket had been. Off they went again, Sally still watching backward.

"It's making a terrible lot of dust, Jeff—much more than before."

Hell. He ought to have thought of that, with the roads so white with powder from the chalk hills. They were sending up a signal for miles in every direction. Better to leave tracks behind than warn people you were coming. He stopped, climbed down again and cut the bundles free.

Just outside Over Wallop they came around a corner to find a high-piled hay cart clean across the road, maneuvering to back into a farmyard. Geoffrey braked hard. There was no hope of turning in the narrow lane before the farm workers were on them—he'd have to reverse out and find a way around. But before he came to a complete stop the cart horses panicked, rearing and squealing as they struggled to escape through the quickset hedge opposite the farm gate. The cart came with them, up to its shafts, leaving a possible gap behind it. He wrenched the gear into first and banged through, misjudging it slightly so that the near fenders grated against the farm wall. Amid the grinding and shouting he was aware of a portentous figure poised in midair above him, arms raised, spear brandished, like St. Michael treading down the dragon. He ducked as the man on top of the hay flung his missile, but the hayfork clanged into the hood and stuck there, flailing from side to side as he drove on into the village. He couldn't afford to stop and pull it out until he was well clear of the houses, by which time it had wrenched two hideous wounds in the polished aluminum.

Thank heavens Lord Montagu wasn't there to see how his toy was being treated.

The railway bridge over the road at Grately was down, and they had to grind up the embankment, jolt over the deserted rails and lurch down the far side, the ram twanging the rusty fence wire as if it had been thread.

Three quarters of an hour later they were driving toward Inkpen Beacon, just south of Hungerford. The westering sun lay broad across the land, and under the bronze, horizontal light the hollows and combes were already filling with dusk. Above the purr of the engine and the hiss of the passing air they heard a hallooing on the hill above them; the gold horizon was fringed with horsemen, who were careering along the ridge of down to cut across their path where the road climbed to the saddle. Geoffrey grinned to himself. There was still a couple of hundred yards of flat to allow him to take a run at the incline, so there was no need to change down. He pressed firmly on the accelerator and the sighing purr rose to a solid boom; the feel of the wheel hardened in his hands and the rose-tangled hedges blurred with backward speed. The military-looking gentleman had told him that a single-seater Silver Ghost, stripped for racing, had done a hundred miles an hour at Brooklands; this one was supposed to do seventy in its whining sprint gear, but he wasn't using that on a hill—third should do it. The needle stood just over fifty as the hood tilted to take the meat of the twisting slope. Sally laughed beside him.

The horsemen were hidden now, behind the false crest of the down, and the engine, losing the impetus of its first rush, changed its note to a creamy gargle and swung them up the hill at a workaday forty. The hedges gave way to open turf as the Rolls swept toward the top and there were the horsemen again, coming along the ridge track at a whooping gallop, a dozen of them, barely fifty yards away. They hadn't a hope, except for the little man who led them on the big roan with a hawk on his wrist and his green cloak swirling behind him. He was barely six yards off when the Rolls, bucketing in a bad patch of potholes, hurtled over the saddle and whisked away down into the sudden cutting on

the northern slope. Sally twisted in her seat to watch the
hunters.

"That was fun," she said.

"Yes. What did they do?"

"They talked and waved their arms and then one of them
started to gallop off that way. Wait a sec while I look at the
map. I think he was going to Hungerford."

"Bother. That front chap looked like someone important,
and he'll get them to send messengers out to warn the countryside. That means it won't be safe to stop for at least another twenty miles, and I'd been hoping to camp for the
night before long. I'd better fill up with petrol now, to be on
the safe side. D'you think there'll be another tollgate at—
where is it?"

"Kintbury."

There was. They left it in spillikins, crossed the A4 and
boomed up the hill to Wickham, where they swung left on
to the old Roman road to Cirencester, Ermine Street. It was
busier than any road they'd been on. Haymakers were coming home now, through the dusty brown shadows of evening; old crones led single cows back to the milking sheds;
courting couples walked entwined through the shadier pas-
sages beneath arched beeches; the odd rider spurred toward
some engagement. Twice Geoffrey had to swing on to the
verge and jolt round a towering wagon with its team of fear-
crazed horses (small horses—five years is nothing like long
enough to revive the strain of the huge, strong, patient
Shires, which hauled for our ancestors for generations before the tractor came). The second time, Sally was hit on the
arm by the blunt side of a flung sickle, just at the moment
when Geoffrey felt his left front wheel slithering into a hidden ditch beneath the grass. Raging, he wrenched at the live
wheel and stamped on the accelerator. It happened to be the
right thing to do, and the car roared free, nudging the corner of the wagon so that the whole cargo, already unsettled
by the antics of the horses, tilted sideways and settled on the
man who had thrown the sickle.

"It's not bad," said Sally, "honestly. It's just a sort of thin
bruise. Crimminy though, this thing's sharp on the other
side."

At Baydon there was some sort of merrymaking or religious procession or something in the main street (which is all Baydon consists of). Anyway, it involved a lot of hand-drawn carts with a ring of candles round the rim of each, very pretty in the dusk-tinged night. The villagers were all in fancy dress, looking like dolls on a souvenir stall, but jumped squawking for safety as Geoffrey, still stupid with rage at a society where grown men felt it was proper to throw deadly tools at his kid sister, clove into the procession. The ram splintered the handcarts. Candles cartwheeled into the shadows. Women shrilled and men bellowed. On the other side of the village they were in blackness, real night, with a lot of stars showing.

"Time to find somewhere to sleep, Sal. See if you can spot a place which looks empty on the map. I don't mind turning off this road if we have to."

"Anywhere for the next six or seven miles, I think." (Sally had Arthur's pencil torch out.) "After that we come to a sort of plain which seems absolutely crammed with villages, and then we've got to turn off and start wiggling, which I'd rather not do in the dark."

They found a spot, a couple of miles on, where the road dipped over the shoulder of a hill and eased to the right to take the gentler slope. But a still earlier age had preferred to cut the corner, and it was possible to drive down the old track—as old, perhaps, as the Romans—into a natural pull-off. They were only fifteen yards from the road, but hidden by a thorn thicket. Geoffrey left the engine running and scouted off into the dark to make sure he could get out at the far end, if need be. Then, while Sally rummaged for a cold supper and the engine clicked as it cooled, he unrolled a ball of twine and rigged a kind of trip wire all around the car. They sat, backs to the warm radiator, in the balmy dark and ate garlic sausage, processed cheese, bread and tomatoes, and drank the last of the Coca-Cola.

"You aren't frightened of *this* car, Sal?"

"No. Not any longer. Really it's more like an animal—a super charger for rescuing princesses with. We've been frightfully lucky so far, haven't we, Jeff?"

"I suppose so. That was a nasty bit when we found the

wagon across the road, and I suppose the other man could have hit you with the sharp side of his sickle." (He'd found it on the floor of the car, and it really had been sharp, honed like a carving knife.) "And other places too, honestly. I was scaredest at that first toll bridge, because it was something we'd planned for and didn't seem to be working. But we've *got* to be lucky, Sal, so there's no point in thinking about it."

"You're all like that. Boys and men, I mean. If there's no point in thinking about something, you don't. Are we going to sleep on the grass or in the car?"

"In the car. We aren't really far enough from Baydon for comfort. I'll prime the cylinders and put a bit of pressure in the tank, just in case we have to be off in a hurry. I wonder whether it's worth making a hill fog. It wouldn't be difficult tonight."

"Funny how you know about that when you can't remember anything else."

"I don't have to *remember* it. I just know."

"Anyway, don't let's have a fog. It would be a pity to spoil the stars."

It would too. It was a night when it was easy to believe in astrology. He tucked Sally into the backseat, filled the tank with petrol, put a quart of oil into the engine, looked into the radiator and realized they ought to stop for water at the first stream they came to, primed the cylinders, pumped the tank, tied the loose end of his trip string around his thumb and attempted to find a comfortable position across the front seats. He tried several positions, but really he was too long for the width of the car—it was as if a grown man was lying down in a child's cot. In the end he lay on his back, knees up, and started to count the ecstatic stars.

He was woken by Sally pinching his ear. It was still dark.

"Don't do that. Go back to sleep at once. Did you have a bad dream?"

"Shh. Listen."

League upon league the fields and woods lay around them, silent in an enchantment of dark. No, not quite silent. Somewhere to the south there was a faint but continuous noise, a rising and falling hoot, or howl, very eerie.

"What's that?"

"Hounds. Hunting. I've heard them before."

His mind flickered for an instant to the dog that had bayed on the banks of Beaulieu estuary, but whose cry had gone unanswered.

"What on earth are they hunting at this time of night?"

"Us."

Yes, possibly. The village of Baydon might have come swarming after them, like a hive of pestered bees. More likely the man with hawk had sent a messenger to Hungerford and got a thorough pursuit organized. If he was important enough he could have commandeered fresh horses, fresh hounds even, all the way up. It wasn't all that distance.

"How far away are they? What time is it?"

Sally looked at the stars for a moment.

"Between three and four. I don't think they're as far off as they sound."

She was right. The hound cry modulated to a recognizable baying, only just up the road, a noise whose hysterical yelping note told that the dogs had scented their presence and not just their trail. The best bet was to start on the magneto: he switched on and flicked the advance and retard lever up and down. Too fast. He took it more slowly and the engine hummed alive. As he moved off there was a sudden biting pain in his right thumb. The damn string. He declutched and tugged. No go. He leaned over and tried to bite the taut cord free, but achieved nothing more than saliva-covered string, as strong as ever. Suddenly the cord gave and something bonked into the bodywork beside his head—Sally had slashed the cord through with the sickle. The hounds sounded as if they were almost on them as Geoffrey eased the car over the loose rubble of the old road, jerked up onto the newer tarmac and accelerated downhill. The white dust of the road (limestone here) made the way easy to see under a large moon. They whined down the incline and curved into a long straight, overhung with beeches on the left and with a bare, brute hill shouldering out the stars on the other side. The surface was almost unpocked, and Geoffrey did fifty for six miles on end.

"Jeff! Jeff! You must slow down. I can't read the map in the dark at this speed. We've got to turn off somewhere

along here and there's a stream just before. It may be another gate. No, it wasn't—that must have been it. Now we
turn right in half a mile and then left almost at once, and
then—oh, I see, you've only done that to get round Stratton
St. Margaret. It's awfully wiggly. Couldn't we go straight
through at this time of night?"

They did, the exhaust calling throatily off the brick walls
down the long street. Half the roofs showed starlight
through them.

"Right here! Right!"

He only just got the car around onto the A361.

"I thought you said straight through."

"Well, it's straighter than going round, anyway. I'm sorry.
We turn left in about three miles. I think I'll be able to see
soon without the torch. Bother. We could have gone straight
through and branched off later. It would have saved us a lot
of wiggling."

"Never mind. If that's the main road to Cirencester there's
probably quite a bit of stuff on it in the early hours—folk
going to market and so on. I hope it gets lighter soon."

It did. The gray bars in the east infected the whole sky.
The stars sickened. For about five minutes, while his eyes
were adjusting to their proper function, he drove through a
kind of mist which was really inside his own mind, because
he couldn't decide how far down the road he could really
see. Then it was morning, smelling of green grass sappy
with dew. They breakfasted early, before the dew could
clear and the haymakers would be about with their forks
and scythes. Geoffrey filled the radiator from a cattle
trough, still a bit shaken by the distance the hunt had managed to cover (assuming that it came from Hungerford—
and he was sure it did—he was obsessed by the small man
on the big horse with a hawk on his wrist) in seven hours or
so. He got out the map and did sums. They'd done about
twenty miles between Inkpen Beacon and stopping for the
night, and roughly the same again this morning. At that rate
the hunt, if it kept going, would be about twelve miles behind now. Allow an hour for breakfast, and it would be six
miles—say four for safety. That should be okay.

But they must have spotted the general direction the Rolls

was going by now, and they might send messengers posting
up the main road to Cirencester and Cheltenham. If they
took it seriously enough (and, considering Weymouth Bay
and the fuss since the Rolls had been stolen and everything,
there was no reason why they shouldn't), they might then
send more messengers along the main roads radiating from
those towns, ordering a watch to be kept. Obviously all the
bridges west of Gloucester would be closely guarded. The
first danger point would be crossing the Fosse Way, a few
miles on; then the A40 and A436. Besides, once people were
about to mark their passage, there'd be messages and rumors streaming into the towns from the farmland, and the
hunt would know which way its quarry had passed. Better
not allow an hour for breakfast, really. They might be able
to have a bit of a rest when they were up beyond
Winchcombe and had turned sharply left.

Perhaps it was just luck, or perhaps it was because they'd
kept going and left the chase miles behind, but they had
almost no trouble all morning except for shaken fists and
thrown stones. They motored in flawless summer between
the walled fields of the Cotswolds, dipping into steep valleys
where loud streams drove booming waterwheels, or where
gold-gray wool towns throve in the sudden prosperity which
the defeat of the machine had brought back from the North.
Then up, hairpinning through hangers of beeches, where
herds of pigs grunted after roots, watched by small boys in
smocks. Or along molded uplands where huge flocks of
sheep nibbled at fields still rich from the forced harvests of
six years back.

The only real excitement came from such a flock, which
they met not far from Sudeley Castle in a bare lane with
well-kept walls rising five feet on either side. The road
foamed with fleeces for hundreds of yards, and beyond they
could see a group of blue-clad drovers beginning to gesticu-
late at the sight of the car. There was time to hesitate. Geoffrey thought for a moment of plowing on through a carnage
of mutton, but realized he'd bog down almost at once.

"How far have I got to go round if we go back, Sal?"

"Miles."

"Oh well, let's see what happens."

He pulled over as far to the left as he could, and then swung right. This wasn't going to be like a gate. He slowed below a walking speed before the ram touched the wall. The whole car groaned, jarred and stopped, wheels spinning. He backed and charged the same spot, and this time saw the top of the wall waver. Third time it gave, and the Rolls heaved itself through the gap, one wheel at a time because of the angle, like a cow getting over a fence. The grass on the other side was almost as smooth as a football field, and they fetched a wide circuit around the flock. A flotilla of sheepdogs hurled across the green and escorted them, yelping, to a flimsy gate which the ram smashed through without trouble. Soon after he had settled to the road again he realized that the car did not feel itself.

"Lean out and look at the wheels, Sal."

"There's something wrong with this one on my side at the back. It's all squidgy."

He could see nothing through the wake of dust, but when he stopped and listened there seemed to be no sound of pursuit. He climbed down, leaving the engine running, and looked at the right rear wheel. The tire was flat, with a big flap of rubber hanging away from the battered rim. When he was halfway through changing it there was a snarling scurry in the road and a black sheepdog sprang toward him, teeth bared. He lashed at it with the wrench, and it backed off and came again. He lashed again, and again it retreated. As it darted in for the third time a stone caught it square on the side of the jaw and it flounced, whining, out of range.

"I think I can keep it off for a bit, Jeff."

"Great. My, you're a good shot, Sal. Where did you learn that?"

"Scaring rooks."

When he had two nuts on she spoke again.

"There's someone coming down the road, and I think I saw a man running behind the wall over there. Something blue went past the gate at the other side of the field."

He hurriedly screwed on a third nut, hoping that that would be enough to hold for a few miles, and lowered the clumsy jack. As he drove off half a dozen men appeared from behind walls to left and right, like players at the end of a game of hide-and-seek. Heaven knows what kind of an ambush they'd been planning, given five minutes more. He stopped and put the remaining nuts on just before they turned left on the A438. They banged through another toll-gate, over the Avon and climbed the embankment onto the M5 motorway near a place called Ripple. The great highway was a wound of barren cement through the green, lush pastures. It was deserted. Where they joined it was a strange area, a black, charred circle covering both lanes. Two miles later they came to another.

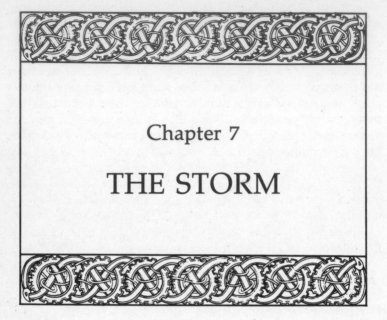

# Chapter 7

# THE STORM

"Funny," said Geoffrey. "It looks as if someone had been lighting a series of enormous bonfires down here. D'you think they've been trying to burn the motorway?"

"It isn't quite like bonfires—it's too clean. There's always bits and bobs of ends of stick left around a bonfire, and the ash doesn't blow away either, not all of it. It makes itself into a sticky gray lump. It *is* funny. I suppose they *could* have come and swept it up."

There was something else funny too. Geoffrey felt it in a nook of his mind as being wrong, out of key with the solid sunshine of the day. There was a flaw in the weather ahead of them, a knot in the smooth grain of the sky. Nothing to see, unless it lay hidden beyond the hills of the Welsh border. It worried him, so much so that he kept glancing at the horizon and almost drove headlong into a vast pit in the road where a bridge had once carried the motorway but was now a scrawl of rusted and blackened iron. He let the weight of the car take them down the embankment and stopped in the lower road to look at the wreckage.

"It must have been a bomb did that, Sal."

"They don't have bombs. It's been burned, hasn't it?"

Very odd. The destruction didn't look as if it had been done by people at all. He felt thoroughly uneasy as he drove up the far embankment. The flaw in the weather was insistent now, either stronger or closer—he thought he could see a change in the hue of the air just north of one of the hills on the western horizon. Another three miles and he was sure. Soon the shape of the hammerheaded cloud that brings thunder was unmistakable. Odd to see one of them, all alone, but nice to know what it was that had been worrying him. He drove on, relieved.

But soon his relief was replaced by a greater unease. Thunderclouds didn't move like that—they planed slowly across the countryside in straight lines, diffusing energy, grumbling, like an advance of arthritic colonels. This one was compact, purposeful, sweeping eastward down a single corridor of wind between the still regions of summer air. He increased his speed to get out of its path, the Rolls exulting up to seventy. At this speed they'd be clear of the cloud's track in no time.

Or would they? He slacked off and gazed at the hills again. The corridor must be curved, for the cloud was still advancing toward them, moving at the pace of a gale. A few miles more and there was no doubt about it—the thing was aimed at the Rolls, following as a homing missile follows its target. He stopped the car.

"Out you get, Sal, and up the bank. Two can play at that game."

He followed her slowly through the clinging weeds, gathering his strength, resting his mind. The motorway ran here through a deep cutting, from whose top he could see for some distance. He unrolled his jersey, took out the robe and put it on. Then he sat beside Sally and stared at the charging cloud, blue-black beneath and white with reflected sunshine through its two miles of height. The thing to do was nudge it aside. Wind from the southwest.

\* \* \*

*The island drowses with heat. The hills are baked. The mown hayfields drink sun. The woods breathe warmth. And over them all lies air, air twice heated, first as the jostling sunbeams plunge down, again as the purring earth gives back the warmth it cannot drink. Isle-wide the air swells with sunlight, lightening as it swells, rising as it lightens, sucking in more air beneath it, cold from the kiss of the Atlantic. Now it comes, broad-fronted over the Marches, comes now,*

> *here,*
>> *now,*
>>> *here,*
>>>> *now in this darkness, in this up-and-down roaring of black, rubbing itself together, three miles high, generating giant forces, poised, ready, smiting down with a million million volts on to the thing it was aimed at. . . .*

Mastered, overwhelmed, Geoffrey crumpled into a gold shambles. Sally alone, thumbs uselessly in her ears, watched the storm heave its bolts of bellowing light down on the Rolls. The air stank with ozone. The clay of the bank vibrated like a bass string. She rolled onto her belly, buried her face in the grasses and screamed.

The noise was gone, except inside her skull. Dully she sat up and looked down the embankment at the motorway. The Rolls, charred and twisted, lay in the center of a circle of blackened cement like the others she had seen. Tires and upholstery smoked, the stench of burned rubber, leather and horsehair reeking up the bank on the remains of Geoffrey's wind. The wind had carried the cloud away, appeased. Her brother lay beside her on his back, with bruise-blue lips and cheeks the color of whitewash. She thought he was dead until she slid her hand under the robe and felt the movement of his breathing.

When a person faints you keep him warm and give him sweet tea. She must get his jersey on, but not over the robe in case someone came by. It was like trying to dress a huge lead doll, and took ages. But it was three hours more before he woke.

\*   \*   \*

Geoffrey came to to the sound of voices. There seemed to be several people about. He kept his eyes shut for the moment.

"You'm sure he baint dead, missie?"

"Yes," said Sally. "You can see. His face is the proper color now."

"Ah, he's a brave one to call a storm like that. I never seed our own weatherman do the like, not living so near the Necromancer as we be. It's surely taxed un."

"It always does," said a voice like a parson's. "You say he's a bit simple, young lady?"

"No, I didn't. He's quite as clever as me or you, only he can't talk and sometimes he looks a bit moony."

"Did you see no one in the wicked machine then?" asked one of the rustic voices. "We did get word as how there was two demons a-driving of it, spitting sparks and all."

"They been hunting un," said another peasant, "all along up from Hungerford way. Lord Willoughby seed un out hawking and give the word. And they damn near caught un last night, I do hear."

"Only she go so mortal fast."

"Hello," said the parsony voice. "I think he's stirring."

Geoffrey sat up, groaned and looked about him. There were more people around than he'd expected, mostly tanned haymakers, but also an oldish man in a long blue cloak with an amber pendant around his neck. Down on the concrete the superb car reproached him with smoldering, stinking wreckage. He smiled at it, what he hoped was a pleased, idiot smile.

"Yes, Jeff," cooed Sal. "You did that. You *are* a clever boy." He stood up and shifted from foot to foot as the people stared at him. "Please," said Sally, "could you all go away? I don't want him to have one of his fits. It's all right, Jeff. It's all right. Everybody likes you. You're a good boy."

Geoffrey sat down and hid his face in his hands.

One of the rustic voices said, "S'pose we better be getting back along of the hayfield then. Sure you be all right, missie? We owe you summat, sort of."

"No thank you, honestly. We don't want anything."

"You get along, chaps; I'll set them on their road and see

that they're properly treated." This was the parsony voice. Then there was a diminishing noise of legs swishing through grass, and silence.

"You made a mistake there, young lady. If he'd really made the thunderstorm you'd have asked for money, but of course he didn't have anything to do with it. He might have made that funny little bit of wind from the southwest, but the storm came from the Necromancer, or I'm a Dutchman."

"I wish you'd go away," said Sally. "We're quite all right, really."

"Come, come, young lady. I have only to go and tell those peasants in the hayfield that I can see what looks like a spot of engine oil on our dumb friend's trousers, and then where would you be? Can he talk, as a matter of interest?"

"Yes," said Geoffrey.

"That's more like it," said the man in the blue robe, sitting beside them and gazing down the embankment.

"What was it?" he asked. "Something pretty primitive, by the look of it."

"A 1909 Silver Ghost," said Geoffrey, nearly crying.

"Dear, dear," said the man. "What a pity. There can't be many of those left. And where were you making for?"

Geoffrey peered at the horizon, working out in his mind the curve of the thundercloud's path in relation to the hills. He pointed.

"Curious," said the man. "So am I. A pity we have no map. I was coming up from the south when I first sensed the storm, and you were coming from the northeast. We could do some crude triangulation with a map, but the point is academic. It would have saved us a deal of trouble."

"I *have* got a map," said Sally, "but I don't know how far it goes. I was still holding it when we got out of the car, but I hid it under my frock when we heard people coming."

"Oh, how perfectly splendid," said the man. "You stay up on the bank and keep watch, young lady, while my colleague and I do our calculations down here out of sight."

As he moved down, Geoffrey saw a gold glint beneath the blue robe.

"Are you a weatherman, too?" he asked.

"At your service, dear colleague."

"Are you the local chap? Did *you* make the storm?"

"Alas, I am, like yourselves, a wanderer. And alas too, it is beyond even my powers to make such a storm as that—though I should certainly have claimed the credit for it had I arrived on the scene in time, and profited more from it than you did. You are something of a traitor to the guild, dear colleague, refusing fees; but we will mention it no more."

"I thought weathermongers stayed in one place and made weather there. What are you doing wandering about?"

"I might ask the same of you, dear colleague, and even more cogently. Your circumstances are dangerously peculiar. Why did you leave your own source of income, wherever it was?"

"Weymouth. I can't remember much about it, actually, because they hit me on the head, but when I woke up they were trying to drown me and Sal for being witches."

"Ah. They were trying to hang me in Norwich."

"For being a witch too?"

"No, no. For being a businessman. It had long seemed to me that the obese burghers of East Anglia did not adequately appreciate my services, so I announced that I proposed to raise my fees. Of course they refused to play, so to bring them to their senses I made a thunderstorm over Norwich and kept it there for three weeks at the height of the harvest. Unfortunately I had misjudged their temper, and when I heard the citizens come whooping down my street it was not, as I hoped for a moment, to yield to my reasonable demands but to stretch my neck. I left."

"And why do you want to go to Wales?"

"Doubtless for the same reason as yourself. But no, you are too young. You go to find out, do you not?"

"Yes, I suppose so."

"And so, in a way, do I. In my journeyings after leaving Norwich—and let me advise you, young man, that folk do not welcome two weathermongers in a district, and still less does the operator already in possession—in my journeyings I began to hear talk of the Necromancer, subdued talk round inn fires when men had a quart or two of ale in them.

Ignorant country gossip, of course, and full of absurdities, but pointing always, and especially as one drew westward, to a source of power in the Welsh hills."

"Yes, that's what we heard," said Geoffrey.

"No doubt. Now, if I am to return to my easy life—oh, so much more agreeable than my old trade of schoolmastering —I need power, power to oust a local weathermonger in some fat district, power more than lies in a mere chivvying of clouds. Some such thing is hidden just over that horizon, and I mean to find it if I can. There is gold in them thar hills, pardner. Let us study the providential map."

It was a one-inch survey, still crackling new, which they spread on the bank, banging it to make it lie level on the grasses.

"Hmm, less providential than I thought. You must have been coming almost directly toward the source, and my poor legs do not carry me fast enough to make much difference. I fear we shall have a very narrow base for our triangle."

"Well," said Geoffrey, "we were up here when I first felt it, and about here when I really saw it. It brewed up a little south of west, beyond the north slope of a biggish hill, this one I think. My line runs like this."

"Ah, more useful than I had feared. I had not realized that the motorway curved north as it does, and I had forgotten how fast a motor vehicle can travel. Now, if I lay my line along here, where does that carry us to? Off the map. No, not quite. This is a painfully crude method of measuring, which would not have satisfied me when I had the pleasure of instructing the young in mathematics, but if we were to head for Ewyas Harold we would certainly be going in the right direction, though our destination must be a step or two beyond that."

"It looks an awfully long way, without the car. You don't seem to mind about the car."

"I went through a period," said the weatherman, "of revulsion from machines, but it has passed. Still, it is not safe to say so, though I suspect that there are more of us about than care to admit it. Certainly, the Black Mountains are a tidy step."

"The thing is I don't know whether Sal is up to it. Couldn't we buy horses?"

"No doubt, given the wherewithal. I myself, I regret to admit, am in somewhat reduced circumstances, but if you have the equivalent of nine gold pieces on you I daresay we could purchase nags of a sort. It would not be money wasted. A horse that can be bought can always be sold again."

"I've got some money."

"Then let us be moving. We will eschew Ross-on-Wye. Townspeople ask tiresome questions of strangers. Which do you think is the better way round?"

"Look, we could head up here through Brampton Abbots, then jiggle down to the railway line and over to Sellack. Then, if we take this footpath we can cut through along the riverbank here and get on to this road which runs all the way to Ewyas Harold."

"That will do passably well," said the weatherman. *"Marchons mes enfants.* Good heavens, what a pleasure it is to be able to speak in a civilized manner after all these years. But we must be cautious. I think, dear colleague, that you had best revert to the dumb idiocy which you portrayed so convincingly to the yokels a while back. You might well be my servant. A leech—I usually travel in the guise of a leech, and do less harm than most of the profession—might well have picked up some poor creature brought to him for cure. I think, however, that we will not afflict the young lady with loss of speech—the strain would be too great for her. She shall be my ward, and as such should call me Dominus. Do you know Latin, young lady?"

"Yes," said Sally. "I'm hungry, and where are we going to sleep?"

"You shall eat at the first likely farm, while I haggle for a horse. We are unlikely to pick up more than one at any one place, because horses are still scarce, now that the tractors are no more. Big farm horses command huge sums, but there is a plethora of ponies left behind by the pony clubs. We shall contrive something before dusk, I doubt not. Perhaps it would be more verisimilitudinous if Geoffrey were to disburse what coin I am likely to need while we are still hidden. It would not do for me to have to ask my servant for gold."

Geoffrey brought out his purse and gave the weatherman ten gold pieces. He still felt dazed, and was glad after that hideous careering and decision-taking to put himself into the hands of this self-assured adult. He felt hungry too. They had breakfasted at dawn and missed lunch, and the world was now heaving over toward evening. At least they ought to be sure of a fine night, with two weathermen on the staff, if it came to sleeping out.

They crossed the motorway, not looking at the ruined Rolls. Up on the other side, a field away, lay a small road along which they walked slowly, sending up puffs of summer dust at every step. Sally seemed very tired, her face drawn and sullen, mouth drooping, skin gray beneath the dirt and tan. In a mile they found a cottage beside the road where the weatherman, leaning on his staff, sent Geoffrey to knock on the door. A mild old dame, stained beyond the wrists with blackcurrant juice, came out into the sunlight and answered the weatherman's imperious questions. Yes, she knew for sure that Mr. Grindall up at Overton had a roan foal for sale. He'd taken it to Ross Market only last week but hadn't been offered a price. And mebbe he had another. And at Park Farm they might have horses to spare. Folk were afeard, living so close to the Necromancer, and there wasn't always men to work the horses. They'd all gone east, to easier climes, including her own two sons, and times were terrible hard. . . .

The voice trailed away into a whining snivel. Unmoved, the weatherman stared at her, as if she were telling him lies, until she hauled up her long black skirts and scuttled back into the cottage.

"We must move on a few paces," he said in a low voice, "so that we may look at the map unseen and hope that Overton is on it."

"It's up that track there," whispered Geoffrey, back to the cottage. "I remember from the map. And Park Farm's a bit beyond it."

"What! Total recall! I have always regarded it as an obscene myth. Still, I must take advantage of your faculties just as you must take advantage of mine—social contract, in effect. Rousseau *would* have been pleased."

At Overton Farm the weatherman's demeanor was completely different. He became soft and smooth, rubbing his hands together and cooing at the girl who opened the door, and then at the sturdy farmhouse wife who pushed her aside. He was a leech from Gloucester, he said, hasting north at the command of my Lord Salting, to attend the birth of an heir. Now they were late, having stayed by the way to succor a village oppressed with a running sickness. They were tired and hungry. Could they rest awhile and buy milk and bread? And if by chance there were any illness in the house, he would be glad to do what he could in recompense for hospitality.

The farmwife led them indoors to a room where the pattern of embossed wallpaper still showed through whitewash. The fireplace had undergone an upheaval in order to install a great open range, unlit at this time of year, with hooks for curing hams in the chimney and a bread oven jutting across the hearth beside it. The furniture was hard oak, crudely made. Sally and the weatherman sat on a long bench and Geoffrey stood against the wall, pulling faces at random to sustain his reputation for idiocy, while the farmwife and her maid clattered in the scullery beyond.

His dizziness was gone, and he was beginning to have doubts about the weatherman. There was something too slick about him, and he really had been horrid to the poor old woman at the cottage. But he did know his way about. He was being very useful now, and rather cunning not mentioning horses at all.

The farmwife came back with a leg of cold mutton, and the maid brought ale, milk, butter and rough brown bread. They ate for a while in silence, but soon the farmwife started asking where they'd come from and why they hadn't gone through Ross. She didn't sound suspicious, just curious, and the weatherman satisfied her by saying that Geoffrey tended to have fits in towns. They all sighed and glanced at him, and to keep them happy he pulled another face. Then the weatherman asked about crossing the Wye, and was told to take the path down to the old railway

bridge, keeping an eye open for thunderstorms in case the
Necromancer chose to throw a bolt at it. It was only at this
point that he mentioned horses, in the most casual way, as
though he wasn't really interested and honestly preferred
walking. It was just that they were so late for this important
birth, and his lordship was not a man to displease. The
farmwife's face turned hard and greedy and she called to
the maid to go and fetch the master from the cowshed.

He was a small, dark, beaten-looking man, and even
when he was there his wife did most of the talking, speaking
of the superexcellent quality of the farm's horses, and how
exceedingly lucky the travelers were that there should be, at
this moment, not one but two to spare, which were a bargain at seven sovereigns. The weatherman nodded and
smiled until the two horses were led into the yard. One was
a lean, tall roan and the other a restless piebald. The weatherman grunted and strolled over to them, feeling their legs
and sides, forcing their mouths open, slapping their shoulders. At last he stood up, shook his head and offered the
farmwife three sovereigns for the pair, or four with harness
thrown in. At once there was a cackle of dismay, as if a fox
had got into a henhouse, and they settled down to hard bar-
gaining, with the weatherman holding the upper ground, as
he could claim both that they didn't want horses and also
that two horses were no good to them in any case—they
really wanted three.

The haggling grumbled back and forth, like a slow-mo-
tion game of tennis, until the farmer broke into a pause.

"If you be wanting three horses," he said, "we got a pony
as might do for the young lady. He's a liddle 'un, but he's a
good 'un."

He shambled off around the corner of a barn and returned with the most extraordinary animal, a hairy, square
thing with four short legs under it, dark brown, the texture
of a doormat, with a black mane and a sulky eye. It snarled
at the people, and when the weatherman was feeling its
hocks it chose its moment and bit him hard in the fleshy
part of the thigh. He jumped back, his face black with rage.

"Ah," said the farmer, "you want to watch un. He's strong,
but he's willful. Tell you what, you take the other two for

five-an-a-narf sov, an' I'll give un to you, saddle an' all. Ach, shut up, Madge. He eats more than he's worth every month, an' *we've* no use for un."

The weatherman rubbed his thigh, pulled his temper together and looked at Sally.

"What do you think, my dear," he said. "Can you manage him? He gave me a vicious nip."

"What's his name?" said Sally.

"Maddox," said the farmer, "I dunno why."

Sally felt in a pocket of her blouse and brought out a small orange cube. Geoffrey recognized it at once by the smell: it was a piece of the gypsy's horse bait. She broke it in half and walked stolidly toward the pony, holding a fragment in the flat of her palm. The other two horses edged in toward the sweet, treacly smell.

"Keep them away," said Sally. "This is for Maddox. Come on then, boy. Come on. That's a nice Maddox. Come on. There. Now, if you're a good pony and do what I tell you, you shall have the other half for your supper. You *are* a good pony. I know you are."

She scratched as hard as she could through the doormat hair between his ears, and he nuzzled in to her side, nearly knocking her over, looking for the rest of the horse bait.

"Well," said the farmer, "I never seed anything like it. I'll just nip off an' fetch his harness afore he changes his mind. Five-an-a-narf sov it is then, mister?"

"I suppose so," said the weatherman, and counted the money out into the farmwife's hand. She bit every coin.

The horses jibbed at the railway bridge, disturbed by the machine-forged metal, until Sally led Maddox up onto the causeway and the other two followed. It really was evening now, a world of soft, warm gold, with the hedge-trees black on their sunless side and casting field-wide shadows. They plugged on (Geoffrey very unhappy on the piebald) through Sellack, along the path by the riverbank onto the road again near Kynaston, and up the slow westward hill. It was almost dark, with Sally yawning and swaying in her saddle, before the weatherman agreed to stop for the night.

The place he chose wasn't bad, a disused huddle of farm

buildings backing onto a field which was a wild tangle of weeds and self-sown wheat. There was a big Dutch barn of corrugated sheeting, half its roof blown off in some freak wind, but filled with rusting tractors, combines, balers, hoists and such. It didn't look as though they'd been afflicted by any special visitations from over the horizon, no such holocaust as had destroyed the Rolls. Given time and petrol, Geoffrey felt that he could have got some of them to go. But the moment a cylinder stirred, the wrath of the Necromancer would be down on them.

They ate and slept in another barn, floored with musty straw. The weatherman had bought bread and a bagful of mutton at the farm, and they sat with their backs against decaying bales and munched and talked. Sally, curiously, did most of the talking—about life in Weymouth, and the respect Geoffrey was held in, and the inadequacy of other Dorset weathermen compared to him. When the weatherman spoke he did so in smooth, rolling clauses, full of long words such as schoolmasters use when they are teasing a favored pupil, but he told them very little about himself. His talk was like cotton candy, that huge sweet bauble that fills the eye but leaves little in your belly when you've eaten it. At last he gave them both a nip of liquor from a flask "to help them sleep," and they wormed themselves into the powdery straw, disturbed by tickling fragments at first, then cozy with generated warmth, then miles deep in the chasms of sleep.

When they woke in the morning the weatherman was gone, and so was the roan, and so was Geoffrey's purse.

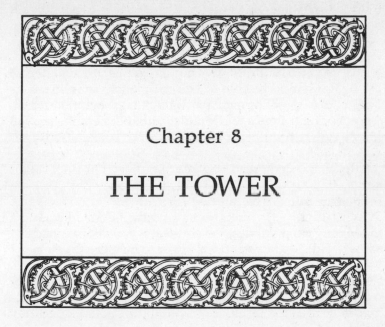

# Chapter 8

# THE TOWER

He had left the piebald horse and Maddox. Also a square of red cloth containing some bread and mutton and a letter.

Dear Colleague,

I know you will understand when I tell you that I have changed my mind. I am not really (as you so evidently are) the stuff of which high adventures are made. So, learning that there was a decent billet for a weathermonger of my abilities at Weymouth, I realized that it ill became me to deprive you of a share in the honor and glory (if any). You have but twenty miles to go, while I have half a country. I was sure (and therefore decided that it was kindest not to wake you) that you would, in the circumstances, have pressed upon me a loan which it would have been embarrassing to refuse. If the burghers of Weymouth are as free with their money as your sister implies, I shall be in a position to repay you next time you pass that way, when no doubt we shall have much to talk about.

Meanwhile I remain
your devoted admirer
CYRIL CAMPERDOWN (not, of course, my real name)
P.S. You should be able to sell the piebald for two sovereigns (ask three) provided you don't let the purchaser inspect his left hind foot. Maddox might be edible, stewed very slowly for several hours.

Sally said, "He never liked poor Maddox, not since he bit him."

Geoffrey said, "What are we going to do?"

"What he says, I think, except for eating Maddox. If it's really only twenty miles, we could sell your horse and take turns to ride Maddox, and we ought to be there for supper."

"And what then?"

"Oh, Jeff, I don't think that's a very sensible question. Absolutely anything might happen, so there's no point in thinking about it, like you said last night. I think we've done jolly well to get as far as we have done, honestly."

"I expect you're right."

He felt muddled by the weatherman's treachery—sorry that somebody he'd liked and who'd been helpful should turn out such a stinker; glad to be on their own again. They ate the bread and mutton and decided on a story—Sally couldn't cope with Geoffrey remaining officially dumb. It seemed easiest to stick to the weatherman's basic lie, simply adding that they'd been sent ahead but had missed their master on the road and had to sell the piebald to get home.

This worked surprisingly well. The first farm they tried didn't want another horse, but gave them each a mug of milk for nothing. The second was full of squalling dogs so they gave it a miss. But at the third the farmer seemed interested. Geoffrey held the piebald and Sally kept Maddox as close to the suspect foot as she could. The farmer went through the ritual of prodding and feeling, but when he came around to the off hind quarter and bent down Sally gave Maddox a little more rope and he lunged and bit the farmer's ear. The man swore. Geoffrey apologized and spoke crossly to Sally. The farmer's wife leaned out of an upstairs window and jeered at him. He didn't seem to fancy any more feeling and prodding, but took the horse for two and a half sovereigns.

It turned out that Maddox wouldn't let Geoffrey ride him, even with Sally leading. This suited Geoffrey very well, as it allowed Sally to ride and rest (it wasn't like real riding—no bumpity-bumpity—more like traveling on a coarse, swaying sofa) while he walked beside her. The pony's pace exactly matched his, and they ambled west in a mood extraordinarily different from yesterday's. Then they had felt invaders, alien, blasting their way between the growing greens of early harvest; now they were part of the scenery, moving at a pace natural to their surroundings. Haymakers straightened from scythes and waved to them, shouting incomprehensible good-days. For two miles, between Orcop and Bagwy Llydiart, they walked with a girl of about Geoffrey's age, a plump, bun-faced lass who talked to them in a single incessant stream of lilting language—about her relations and acquaintances, never pausing to explain who anybody was, but assuming that they both knew Cousin William and Mr. Price and Poor Old John as well as she did. The idea that anybody really lived outside the span of the immediate horizon—closer now as the foothills of Wales grew steeper —was clearly beyond her. Two or three times she referred casually to the presence of the Necromancer, twelve miles westward, as one might refer to the existence of a river at the bottom of the paddock—a natural hazard that must be reckoned with but which nothing in the ordinary round of life could affect or change. She left them before Bagwy Llydiart, in midsentence. Geoffrey and Sally got the subject and verb, and the girl who opened the farm door to her got the object.

In the village, which is really only an inn and a couple of houses, they bought bread and bacon and cider. Geoffrey had been rehearsing his story for the last half mile up the hill, but found it wasn't needed. The bar had five old men in it, all talking eagerly about the demon-driven engine which had been slain on the bad road by a storm from over the mountains. The accounts of the two demons were exciting but confusing, because two different stories seemed to have arrived in the village together. In one the car had been driven by monsters, horned, warty, blowing flames from their noses; in the other by a man and woman of surpassing but devilish beauty. Both stories agreed that no remains had been found in the car, which made the supernatural quality of the drivers obvious. Then the landlord joined in the talk, after doing complicated sums with Geoffrey's change—England seemed to have some very peculiar coins these days.

"I did hear," he said, "as how Lord Willoughby had hunted un all the way up from Hungerford, and precious near caught un two nights back. And they'm sending south for his lordship's hounds, as may still have the scent in 'em, after nosing round where the engine stopped in the dark. *I* don't reckon 'em for demons. What need would there be for the likes of demons to go stopping in the dark? You mark my words—they was nobbut wicked outlanders, who seed the storm a-coming and left their engine in time. S'posing his lordship brings the dogs up in coaches, they'll be on the bad road two hours since. Then there'll be fine hunting."

"Lot o' s'posins," said one of the old drinkers. "They'm demons for my money."

The argument circled back onto its old track, and Geoffrey left, sick with panic. Fifteen miles start, perhaps, and there'd been a good stretch yesterday evening when everyone was riding. That should confuse them. On the other hand the hunt must have guessed where they were making for by now, and once they'd been traced to Overton Farm there'd be descriptions available, of a sort.

Sally had become bored with waiting, and was trying to balance, standing, like a circus rider, on Maddox's back. It can't have been difficult on the broad plateau of his shoulders, but she looked nervous and sat down the moment she saw Geoffrey.

"What's the matter?" she whispered.

"Nothing. I hope."

"Oh, you must tell me. It isn't fair being left in the dark."

"Something they said in the pub. It looks as if we're still being hunted by those hounds."

"Oh bother. Just when everything seemed so easy and right. What are you going to do?"

"I don't know. Plug on, I suppose. They can hunt us wherever we go, you see."

"I suppose perhaps if we got close enough to the Necro man they might be too frightened to follow us."

"It's a chance—the best one probably."

"I wonder if they'll start hunting our weatherman too. That would surprise him."

Indeed it might, but no doubt he'd talk his way out of it. Geoffrey decided not to stop for lunch but to eat walking. Maddox decided otherwise, and won. They ate their bacon (smoked, not salted, and very fatty) and drank their sweet unbubbly cider a mile out of the village, where the hill sloped gently down in front of them. Maddox found a stretch of grass which appealed to him and champed stolidly. Geoffrey and Sally sat on the gate of an overgrown orchard and looked west. Now, for the first time, they could see how close the ramparts of the Black Mountains loomed, a dark, hard-edged frame to the green and loping landscape. Nothing on the near side of the escarpment looked at all peculiar. The haymakers were at work, as they had been in Wiltshire; an old woman in a black dress, leading a single cow, came up the road toward them and gave them good-day. Perhaps fewer of the fields were worked here, and more had been let go, but that might be simply because the soil here was less rewarding than in the counties they had passed through yesterday. You couldn't tell.

Maddox took nearly an hour to finish his meal. Without event they covered the long drop into Pontrilas, where they crossed the Monnow and found a two-mile footpath up to Rowlstone. Here the country grew much steeper, so that Geoffrey realized how tired his legs were, and that there was a blister coming on his left heel. On the crest of Mynydd Merddin they rested and looked back.

"See anything, Sal?"

"No. They couldn't be coming yet, could they?"

"Not unless they were dead lucky. We ought to have three or four hours yet. What we really need is a stream going roughly the way we want to go, and then wade down it, but there doesn't look as if there's anything right on the map. This one at the bottom's too big, I think. On we go."

Clodock, in the valley, was an empty village with its church in ruins, but the bridge still stood. The mountains heeled above them. Geoffrey led Maddox up a footpath, very disused and overgrown, to Penyrhiwiau, where the track turned left and lanced straight toward the ramparts. Already it was steeper than anything they'd climbed, and the contour lines on the map showed there was worse to come. The hills were silent, a bare, untenanted upheaval of sour soil covered with spiky brown grass and heather. He'd been expecting to see mountain sheep and half-wild ponies, but not an animal seemed to move between horizon and horizon, not even a bird. He felt oppressed by their total loneliness, and thought Sally did too. Only Maddox plodded on unmoved.

His heart was banging like an iron machine and his lungs sucking in air and shoving it out in quick, harsh panting, like a dog's, when they took the path southwest for the final climb. This path slanted sideways up the hill, so that they could look out to the left over the colossal summer landscape. No road could have taken that hill direct: its slope was as steep as a gable, and was topped with a line of low cliffs, where the underlying bone of the hills showed through the weatherworn flesh. Their path slanted around the end of these and then (the map said) turned sharply back, down through terrain just as bleak to Llanthony. It looked as though there was a stream they could wade down starting almost on the far path. His legs were too accustomed, by now, to the rhythm of hurrying to move at a slower pace, but when they rounded the cliff at the top he knew that he had to rest.

Sally slid off Maddox and lay on the grass beside him, looking back over their route. The pony nosed disgustedly among the coarse grass for something worthy of his palate. Geoffrey swung the map around and tried to work out exactly where they'd been. Mynydd Merddin seemed no more than a gentle swelling out of the plain, until you realized for how far it hid the country behind it. Then that must be their path, coming down by the tip of that wood, and into

Clodock, which was easy to spot by its square church tower. Of course, he would not be able to see the footpath from here—it had been so overgrown that . . .

He *could* see it. Not the path itself, of course, but the horsemen on it. And, in a gap, the wavering pale line which was the backs of hounds.

He stared at them hopelessly.

"Come on, Jeff. We can't give up now, after getting so far. Do come on."

He shambled up the path, too tired to run, to the crest of the hill. Perhaps he'd be able to run a bit down the far side; then, if they could get to the stream, or at least if he could send Sal off down it, there might be hope. Eyes on the track, he weltered on.

"Oh!" cried Sally, and he looked up.

They were on the crest, and the Valley of Ewyas lay beneath them. It was quite crazy. Instead of the acid, barren hills that should have been there, he saw a forest of enormous trees beginning not fifty yards down the slope with no outlying scrub or thicket to screen the gray, centuries-old trunks. Beneath the leaves, beyond the trunks, lay shadows blacker than any wood he had ever seen. Above, reaching north and south and out of eyesight, the green cumulus obliterated the valley. Out of the middle of it, a single monstrous tower, rose the Necromancer's castle. It could be nothing else. Their path led into the wood and straight toward it.

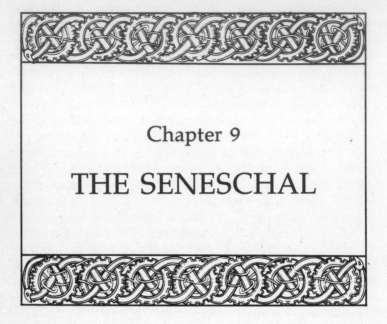

# Chapter 9

# THE SENESCHAL

A crooked tissue of wind brought the sound of hallooing from over the cliffs behind them.

"Come on," said Sally, "it's the best bet. Maddox, you're going to have to see if you can go a bit faster."

With the help of the downward slope the pony managed to produce out of his repertoire a long-forgotten trot. In a way he was like the Rolls, a rectangular, solid, unstoppable thing. Geoffrey, now in a daze of tiredness, let the path take him down in a freewheeling lope, which he knew would end in fainting limpness the moment the path flattened to a level. They plunged into the trees.

It was darker than he'd thought possible. This was a quite different sort of forest from the gone-to-pot New Forest which they'd breakfasted in yesterday. That had seemed, somehow, like a neglected grove at the bottom of a big garden—after all, its trees had been tended like a vegetable crop only six years before. But this one had not seen a forester's ax for generations of trees. The oaks were prodigious, their trunks fuzzy with moss, and the underwoods were a striving, rotting tangle, tall enough to overarch the path for most of the way—this was what made the shadows so dark. The silence was thick, ominous, complete; even the noise of Maddox's hooves was muffled by the moss on which they ran, a soft, deep, dark-green pile which would surely be worn away in no time if the road was used much —used at all. Why had the forest not swallowed it? It lay broad as a highway between the tree trunks, without even a bramble stretching across it.

"Jeff, what was that?"

"What?"

"That. Listen."

A noise of dogs howling. The hunt, of course. But it came from the wrong direction, forward and to their right, and was different from the baying they'd heard last night— deeper, more intense, wilder.

"Jeff, there aren't any *wolves* in England today, are there?"

"I hope not. But anything—"

There it was again. No, that *was* the hunt this time, behind them and distinctly shriller—they must be at the crest now. The new noise welled up again, closer, but still to their right, up the hill, and the hunt behind them bayed its answer. And here, at last, was the stream.

"Look, Sal, this is the only hope. Get off and lead Maddox down there, keeping in the water. I'll run down here a bit further and then come back. Keep going down the stream till I catch up with you."

"You *will* come back won't you? Promise."

"All right."

"Promise."

"I promise."

She led Maddox gingerly into the stream, which was steep and stony, and Geoffrey pounded on down the mossy ride. He thought at once that he ought to have brought Maddox too, and bolted him on downward while he climbed back to the scent-obliterating water, except that Maddox wasn't the sort to fit into elaborate schemes of deception. Hurrah, here was another stream, too small to be marked on the map; if he went back now the hunt might waste time exploring this one.

The climb seemed like a crawl, and the woods swayed round him. This was hopeless—he must have somehow branched onto another path without noticing—there wasn't a sign of his footprints on the moss. He looked back, and saw that he'd left no track there either, which would help the deception supposing he got back to the first stream on time. The two choruses of baying clashed out at each other again, and the hunt sounded fearfully close. At last he splashed down into the stream, his weak legs treacherous on the wobbly boulders, and waded downstream. He caught Sally up only a few bends down.

"You ought to have got further. You shouldn't have waited."

"I didn't, but Maddox felt thirsty. Come on now, boy. Not far. Oh!"

Her quack of surprise was almost inaudible in the yelping and baying that shook the wood. Somewhere on the path the two packs must have met. Above the clamor he could hear human voices shouting and cursing; they did not sound as if they were in control of the situation.

He followed Sally down to a lower road, which also seemed to lead toward the tower; without a word they turned off along it, padding in a haze of silence down the endless mossy avenue while the battle in the woods above them whimpered into stillness. He realized with surprise that the darkness was not only caused by the double roofing of leaves; it was drawing toward night outside, and the tower, whatever it might hold, was the only chance of escaping from the fanged things that ranged these woods. And at least they would have arrived, against all odds, at the target at which the General had aimed them three whole days ago in Morlaix. And he hadn't had a proper sleep since then. A voice somewhere, confused by the booming in his ears, started saying "Poor old Jeff. Poor old Jeff" over and over again. It was his own.

He was drowning in self-pity when they stepped out of the forest into the clearing around the tower. It was enormous, three times as high as the giant trees, wide as a tithe barn, a

piled circle of rough-hewn masonry sloping steadily in toward the top—the same shape as those crude stone towers
which the Celts built two thousand years ago in the
Shetland Islands, but paralyzingly larger. Around its base,
some distance away from it, ran a stone skirting wall about
as high as an ordinary house. Just outside this was a deep
dry ditch, and then the clearing they stood in. There was no
door or window in this side of the wall, so they turned left,
downhill, looking up at the monstrous pillar of stonework
in the center with a few stars coming out behind its level
summit. The black wood brooded on their left.

They rounded a sharper curve by the ditch, and saw the
line of wall interrupted. Eighty yards on was a bridge across
the dry moat, and two small turrets set into the wall. As they
trudged through the clinging grasses toward it no sound
came from the tower, no light showed. Perhaps it was
empty. They crossed the bridge and found the gate shut.
Geoffrey hammered at it with his fist, but made no more
noise than snow on a windowpane. He crossed the bridge
again to look for a stone to hammer with, but Sally pointed
above their heads.

At first he thought there was a single huge fruit hanging
from the tree above the path, then he realized it was too big
even for that, and decided it must be a hornet's nest. He
moved and the round thinned. When he was under it it
looked like a thick plate, something man-made.

"What is it, Sal?"

"I think it's a gong. You come along here on your charger
and bonk it with your lance and the lord of the castle comes
out to answer your challenge. If you stood on Maddox's
back you might be able to reach it. Come here, Maddox.
That's a good boy. Up you get, Jeff. Oh, Maddox, you are
*awful.* I'll see if I've got any horse bait left. Here. Stand still.
That's right. Now Jeff!"

He scrambled on to the broad back. The gong was just
above his head and he struck at it with the fat edge of his
fist. It made a tremendous noise, a sustained boom that died
away at last into curious whinings all the way up the diapa-
son. Nothing stirred in the tower. He struck the gong several times, judging its internal rhythm so that each blow

produced a louder boom. At last Maddox decided that enough was enough and shied away; Geoffrey slithered down and the three of them stood listening to the resonance of bronze diminish into whimperings.

In the new silence they realized they could hear another noise, one that they had heard several times that afternoon. The baying of wolves (or whatever they were) was echoing through the valley, seeming to come at times from all around the compass, but at other times from the hill they had themselves descended. It was getting nearer.

"Jeff! D'you think we ought to go on?"

"We'll give it another minute and then we'll climb a tree. Maddox will have to . . . Look!"

In the near-dark they could see a movement of light behind the postern tower. A few seconds later they heard a rattle of chains and the grate of rusty metal drawn through metal. In the big gate a small door started to open and they ran toward it. A face thrust through, with a long white beard waggling beneath it.

"Well," said the face, "what is it? Do you realize how late it is? I was just shutting up."

"Please," said Sally, "but we got lost in the wood and it seems to be full of wolves or something and could we come in for the night, please?"

"Ah," said the face, "benighted travelers. Yes, yes, I'm sure he would think that proper, as far as one can be sure of anything. Come in. Goodness me, what an extraordinary animal! Is it a dog or a horse? Oh, it's a pony, according to its lights. Well, well. Come in."

The small door swung wide open, so that they could see his whole body. He was a little, bent man, holding a flaming branch which had been soaked in some sort of tar or resin which made it flare in the dark. He wore sweeping velvet robes, trimmed with ermine around the edges; a soft velvet cap, patterned with pearls and gold thread, sloped down the side of his head. Sally led Maddox in, and as Geoffrey stepped over the threshold there was a snarling in the trees and a pack of dark shapes with gleaming eyes came swirling toward the door. The little man pushed it almost shut, poked his head out again and said "Shoo! Shoo! Be off with you! Shoo!"

He shut the door completely, pushed two large bolts across, swung a huge balanced beam into slots so that it barred the whole gateway and laced several chains into position over it.

"Nasty brutes," he said, "but they're all right if you speak to them firmly. This way. We'll put your animal into the stables and then we'll go and see if there's anything for dinner. I expect you'll be hungry. Do you know, you're really our first visitors. I think he doesn't fancy the idea of people prying around, reporters from the newspapers, you know, which is why he put the wolves there. But benighted travelers is quite different—I think he'll appreciate that—it's so romantic, and that's what he seems to like, as you can see."

He waved a vague arm at the colossal tower, and led them into a long shed which leaned against the outer wall. It was crudely partitioned into stalls.

"Tie him up anywhere," said the old man, "there ought to be oats in one of those bins, and you can draw water from the well."

"Poor old Maddox," said Sally, looking down the empty length of stables, where black shadows jumped about in the wavering flare of the torch, "I'm afraid you're going to feel lonely."

"Oh, you can't tell," said their host. "Really you can't. Having one pony here might put ideas into his head, and then we'd wake up to find the whole place full of horses, all needing watering and feeding. I don't think he has any idea of the work involved, keeping a place like this going, but then he doesn't have to."

The bins were all brimming with grain, and there was sweet fresh hay in a barn next door. Geoffrey worked the windlass of the well, and found that the water was only a few feet down. They left Maddox tucking in to a full manger, like a worn traveler who, against all the odds, has finished up at a five-star hotel. As they crossed the courtyard to the keep they realized it was now full night, the sky pied with huge stars and a chill night breeze creeping up the valley. The door to the keep was black oak, a foot thick, tall as a haystack. The old man levered it open with a pointed pole. Geoffrey noticed that it could be barred both inside and out.

Beyond the door lay a single circular chamber, with a fire in the middle. It was sixty feet from where they stood to the fire, and sixty feet on to the far wall. The fire was big as a Guy Fawkes Day bonfire, piled with trunks of trees, throwing orange light and spitting sparks across the rush-strewn paving stones. Around it slept a horde of rangy, woolly dogs, each almost as large as Maddox. The smoke filled the roof beams and made its way out through a hole in the center of the roof, which, Geoffrey realized, high though it seemed, could not have come more than a third of the way up the tower. He wondered what lay above. Around the outside wall of the chamber, ten feet above the floor, ran a wide wooden gallery supported on black oak pillars. It reached up to the roof, with two rows of unglazed windows looking out across the chamber. Beneath the gallery, against the wall, stood a line of flaring torches, like the one the old man carried, in iron brackets. Between them pot-shaped helmets gleamed. On either side of the fire, reaching toward them, ran two long black tables, piled high with great hummocks of food, meat and pastry and fruits, with plates and goblets scattered down their length and low benches ranged beneath the tables. They walked up toward the fire between an avenue of eatables.

"Oh, splendid!" exclaimed the old man. "Perhaps he heard the gong and decided it was time for a feast. Often he doesn't think about food for days and days, you know, and then it starts to go bad and I have to throw it out to the wolves—I used to have such a nice little bird table at my own house—and I don't know which way to turn really I don't. Now, let's see. If you sit there, and you there, I'll sit in the middle and carve. I suppose we ought to introduce ourselves. My name's Willoughby Furbelow and I'm seneschal of the castle."

"I'm Geoffrey Tinker and this is my sister, Sally. It's very kind of you to put us up."

"Not at all, not at all. That's what I'm here for, I suppose, though it isn't at all what I intended. Really this place ought to be full of wandering minstrels and chance-come guests and thanes riding in to pay homage and that sort of thing, only they don't seem to come. Perhaps it's the wolves that put them off, or else you're all too busy out there in the big world. I keep trying to tell him he ought to do something about the wolves, but he doesn't seem very interested and my Latin isn't very good—I keep having to look things up in the dictionary and I never thought I'd need a grammar when it all started, all those tenses and cases you know I find them very muddling and he does get terribly *bored*. In his lucid intervals, I mean. Now, this thing here is a boar's head. Actually there isn't a lot of meat on it, and it's a pig to carve (pardon the pun) and though some bits of it are very tasty others aren't, and besides it seems a pity to spoil it just for the three of us, it looks so splendid doesn't it? Would you mind if I suggested we had a go at this chicken? You mustn't mind it looking so yellow. Everything seems to get cooked in saffron, and it really does taste quite nice, though you weary of it after a few years. Which part do you fancy, Miss Trinket, or may I call you Sarah?"

"Everyone calls me Sally and may I have a wing and some breast, please? There don't seem to be any potatoes. And what's that green stuff?"

"Good King Henry. It's a weed really, but it's quite nice, like spinach. I'm afraid they didn't have any potatoes in his day, any more than they had the fish fingers you're used to, but there are probably some wurzels down below the salt, if you fancy them. You do realize you've got to eat all this in your fingers, like a picnic? I used to have such a nice set of fish knives and forks, with mother-of-pearl handles, which my late wife and I were given for a wedding present. I think I miss them as much as anything. But the bread is very nice when it's fresh and you can use it for mopping up gravy and things. There. Now, Geoffrey?"

"Please, may I have a leg? I didn't understand what you said about lucid intervals."

"That's what I call them, but I doubt if a psychiatrist would agree with me. I don't mind confessing I'm at a loss which way to turn. Perhaps I should never have started. The result has been very far from what I intended, I promise

you. But now . . . he's so *dangerous* . . . so uncontrolla-
ble. So strong, too, of course. I did try to administer seda-
tives at one point, several years ago now. I thought I might
contrive to return him to his previous condition, but he was
angry. Very angry indeed. I was terrified. Oh dear, don't let's
talk about it. You have no idea how powerful he is, really
you haven't. But he built this whole place in a single night,
and all the forest too, and the wolves. I often wonder if he
interferes with telly reception outside the valley. Just think
what he might do if he were really enraged—especially now
he's so much worse than he used to be. Why, he might destroy the whole world. It says so on his stone. Is that enough
or would you like a bit of breast too?"

"That's fine, thanks," said Geoffrey. Mr. Furbelow was one
of those men who cannot talk and do anything else at the
same time, so Geoffrey's helping had been mangled off
somehow between sentences, and then the high, eager, silly
voice rambled on. The old man helped himself to several
slices of breast and both oysters, and then began to worry
about drink.

"Dear me, I don't know what my late wife would say
about Sally drinking wine. She was a pillar of the Abergavenny temperance movement. I had a little chemist's
shop in Abergavenny, you know. That's what made the
whole thing possible. As a chemist, I cannot advise you to
drink the water, and though there is mead and ale below the
salt, I myself find them very affecting, more so than the
wine. I trust you will be moderate."

The chicken was delicious, though almost cold. Geoffrey
was still hungry when he had finished and helped himself
from a salver of small chops, which were easy to eat in his
fingers, unlike the Good King Henry, which had to be
scooped up on pieces of dark soft bread. His knife was desperately sharp steel, with a horn handle bound with silver.
His plate seemed to be gold, and so did the goblet from
which he drank the sweet cough-syrupy wine. All the while
Mr. Furbelow talked, at first making mysterious references
to the "he" who owned the tower and provided the feast,
and then, as he filled his own goblet several times more,
about the old days in Abergavenny, and a famous trip he

and his wife had made in the summer of 1969 to the Costa Brava. It took him a long time to finish his chicken. At last he pushed his plate back, reached for a clean one from the far side of the table and pointed with his knife at an enormous arrangement of pastry, shaped like a castle, with little pastry soldiers marching about on top of it.

"You *could* have some of that, if you liked, but you never know what you'll find inside it. If you fancy a sweet there might be some wild strawberries in that bowl just up there beyond the peacock, Sally dear. Ah, splendid. And fresh cream too. No sugar of course. Now you must tell me something about yourselves. I seem to have done all the talking."

This had been worrying Geoffrey. He didn't know what a seneschal would feel about a traveling leech's dependents. Would he come over snobbish, and send them down below the salt? Or would the chemist from Abergavenny be impressed by the magical title of Doctor?

"Honestly," he said, "there isn't much to say about us. We're orphans, and we were traveling north with our guardian, who is a leech, when he had to hurry on and help someone have a baby, a lord's wife, I think, and he told us where to meet him but we made a mistake and got lost, and when we heard the wolves in the forest we ran here."

"Dear me," said Mr. Furbelow, "I'm afraid your guardian will be worrying about you."

Sally, her mouth full of strawberries, said sulkily, "I don't like our guardian. I think he'd be glad if we were eaten by wolves."

"Oh, Sally, he's been awfully kind to us." (Geoffrey hoped he didn't sound as though he meant it.)

"You said yourself that he couldn't wait to get his hands on the estate. I bet you he doesn't even try to look for us."

"What's a leech?" said Mr. Furbelow.

"A doctor."

"Do you mean," said Mr. Furbelow, "that this"—he waved a vague hand at the tower and the hounds and the Dark Ages appurtenances—"goes on outside the valley?"

"Oh, yes," said Geoffrey. "All over England. Didn't you know?"

"I've often wondered," said Mr. Furbelow, "but of course I

couldn't go and see. And how did this doctor come to be your guardian?"

"He was a friend of Father's," said Geoffrey, "and when Dad died he left us in his care, so now we have to go galumphing round the country with him and he treats us like servants. I shouldn't have said that."

"But it's true," said Sally.

"You poor things," said Mr. Furbelow. "I don't know what to do for the best, honestly I don't. Perhaps you'd better stay here for a bit and keep me company. I'm sure *he* won't mind, and I'll be delighted to have someone to talk to after all these years."

"It's terribly kind of you sir," said Geoffrey. "I think it would suit us very well. I hope we can do something to help you, but I don't know what."

"Well," said Sally, "*I* can speak Latin!"

Oh, Lord, thought Geoffrey, that's spoiled everything, just when we were getting on so well. She's tired and had too much wine, and now she's said something he can find out isn't true in no time. Indeed, the old man was peering at Sally with a dotty fierceness, and Geoffrey began to look around for a weapon to clock him with if there was trouble.

"Dic mihi," said Mr. Furbelow stumblingly, "quid agitis in his montibus."

"Benigne," said Sally. "Magister Carolus, cuius pupilli sumus, medicus notabilis, properabat ad castellum Sudeleianum, qua (ut nuntius ei dixerat) uxor baronis iam iam parturiverit. Nobis imperavit magister—"

"How marvelous," said Mr. Furbelow. "I'm afraid I can't follow you at that speed. Did you say Sudeley Castle? I went there once on a coach trip with my late wife; she enjoyed that sort of outing. Oh dear, it *is* late. We must talk about this tomorrow. Now it's really time you were in bed. He might put the torches out suddenly. Perhaps you'd like to share the same room. This castle is a bit frightening for kiddies, I always think."

He said the last bit in a noisy whisper to Geoffrey, and then showed them down to the far wall where a staircase, which was really more like a ladder, led up to the gallery. There were several other ladders like it around the hall.

Upstairs they found a long, narrow room, with a large window looking out over the hall and a tiny square one cut into the thickness of the wall. Through this they could see the top of the outer wall, and beyond that a section of forest, black in the moonlight, and beyond that the blacker hills. There were no beds in the room, only oak chests, huge feather mattresses like floppy bolsters, and hundreds of fur skins.

"Where do you sleep?" asked Geoffrey.

"Oh," said Mr. Furbelow, "I've got a little cottage near the stables which I bought for my late wife. He didn't change that. I have my things there and I like to keep an eye on them. I do hope you'll be comfortable. Good night."

Before they slept (and in the end they found it was easiest to put the mattresses on the floor—they kept slipping off the chests) Geoffrey said, "How on earth did you pull that off?"

"Oh, I *can* speak Latin. Everybody can at our school. You have to speak it all the time, even at meals, and you get whipped if you make a mistake."

The furs were warm and clean. In that last daze that comes before sleep drowns you, Geoffrey wondered where the weatherman had got to.

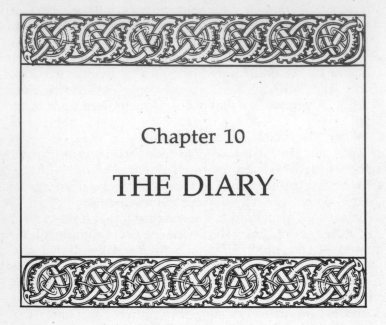

Chapter 10

# THE DIARY

Geoffrey couldn't tell what time he woke, but the shadows on the forest trees made it look as if the sun was quite high already. Sally was still fast asleep, muffled in a yellow fur and breathing with contented snorts. He looked out of the window into the hall and saw that the feast was still there, though the dogs had been at it in places, scattering dishes and pulling the whole boar's head onto the floor, where two of them wrenched at opposite ends of it. He felt stupid and sick, which might have been the wine, and very stiff, which must have been yesterday's climbing and running. His clothes were muddy and torn. In one of the chests he found some baggy leggings, with leather thongs to bind them into place, and in another a beautifully soft leather jerkin. There was a belt on the wall, too, carrying a short sword in a bronze scabbard, pierced and patterned with owls and fig leaves. He buckled it around the jerkin and went down into the hall to see if the dogs had left any of the food undefiled.

They were enormous things, very woolly and smelly, big-

boned, a yellowy-gray color. Wolfhounds, he decided. Two
of them lurched toward him, snarling, but backed away
when he drew his sword. He found that they'd only messed
up a tiny amount of the hillocks of food spread down the
tables, so he filled a silver tray with fruit and bread and cold
chops and looked around for something to drink. The
thought of wine or mead or ale made him sick, and after
Mr. Furbelow's warning about the water he decided it
would be safer to boil it, if only he could find a pot to put on
the fire. He was afraid the gold and silver vessels might
melt, and there didn't seem to be anything else.

In the end he found, hanging between two of the torches,
a steel helmet with a chain chinstrap and a pointy top. He
used his sword to hollow out a nest in the red embers of the
fire, settled the helmet into place and poured water in, spilling enough to cause clouds of steam to join the smoke and
waver up toward the hole in the roof. It boiled very fast. He
hooked it out by the chinstrap and realized that he couldn't
put it down because of the point and he had nothing to pour
it into, so he held the whole contraption with one hand
while he poured the water from one of the big jugs on to the
floor and then wine out of a smaller jug into the big one,
and at last he could pour his boiled water into the small jug.

When he went to put the blackened helmet back in its
place he found a new, shiny one already hanging there.
Chilly with fright he carried his tray up to the bedchamber
and woke Sally to tell her what had happened.

"He must have done it," she said matter-of-factly.

"Who? Mr. Furbelow?"

"Oh, Jeff, don't be tiresome. I mean the 'he' Mr. Furbelow
keeps talking about, the one who makes all the food and
could get rid of the wolves if he felt like it and might put a
lot of horses into the stable to keep poor Maddox company.
The Necro man."

"I expect you're right. I just don't want to think about it.
I've boiled the water, so it should be all right to drink, but
it's still pretty hot. There might be enough left to wash with.
You look a right urchin. I found my clothes in the chests,
and it mightn't be a bad idea if we looked for something for
you. I'm sure Mr. Furbelow would like that. He's got himself

some pretty elaborate fancy dress. Though I suppose Latin's our best bet. What do you think he means about lucid intervals?"

"I don't know. It ought to mean clear spaces, that's what the words mean in Latin. May I have the last chop—you've got three and I've only got two. Is he mad?"

"Mr. Furbelow? No, at least he's a bit loopy, but he's not just imagining things, or not everything. *Somebody* must have built this tower and put the forest there—they aren't on the map. And if you agree that far, it means that the somebody's still here. He brings the food and he built the tower and he put the helmet back just now. *He* might be mad. I think that's what 'lucid intervals' means—the times when mad people aren't mad for a bit. But I don't think Mr. Furbelow's mad."

"But I don't think he's *bad* either. I think he's made some sort of mistake and has gone on making it worse and doesn't know how to stop. But I think he might easily be rather touchy. We must be careful what we say to him."

"Yes. And don't push the Latin too hard. Just wait for a natural chance to come up again. Let's see if we can find some clothes for you."

Everything in the chests was really much too big for an eleven-year-old girl, but they found a long emerald tabard with bits of red silk appliquéd to it and intricate patterns of gold thread filling the gaps. On Sally it reached to the ground, almost, but when it was pulled in with a big gold belt it looked okay; there weren't any sleeves, so they left her brown arms bare. They found a silver comb in another small chest and did her hair into two pigtails tied with gold ribbon, and when Geoffrey had sponged the mud and sweat off her face she looked quite striking, as if she was about to play the queen in a charade. There was still no sign of Mr. Furbelow so they carried the tray down to the hall and started to explore the rest of the tower.

There were two stories of rooms in the gallery, all just like theirs, full of chests and furs. The ones in the lower story were all separate, but the higher ones ran into each other all the way around, with heavy curtains across the doorways, but with nobody in them at all. There was no sound in the whole tower except the crash of a log falling into the fire, followed by a squabble of disturbed hounds. It was very confusing, like a maze. Halfway around they found another ladder going up still further. It led them out onto the roof.

They stood in the open air, still only a third of the way up a dizzy funnel of inward-leaning stone. An open timber staircase climbed spirally up inside this tube of rough-hewn yellow boulders, and finished in a wooden balcony running all the way around inside the parapet. The roof they stood on was a flat cone, with the smoke hole at its point and drainage holes cut into the wall around its perimeter. As they climbed the endless timbers of the stairway Geoffrey noticed that you could still see on them the cutting strokes of a great coarse shaping tool. From the balcony they could see the whole valley, with the ridges of the hills mellow in the morning sunlight and the darker treetops smothering and unshaping everything in between. The children felt oppressed by those million million leaves. The bare upland beyond seemed suddenly a place of escape, if they ever did escape.

Geoffrey leaned over the parapet, his palms chilly with the knowledge of height, to study the courtyard. It was really nothing except the ground enclosed by the outer wall, against which leaned a higgledy-piggledy line of pitched roofs, tiled with stone and slate. They looked very scrappy from up here, like the potting sheds and timber stores and huts where mowers are kept which you can usually find behind privet hedges in the concealed nooks of a big garden. They seemed just to have grown there. In one place this ill-planned mess gave way to a neat modern building, set askew to the wall, finished in whitewashed stucco, with proper sash windows and steep slate steps leading up to a yellow front door. While they were staring at it the door opened and Mr. Furbelow came out carrying a tray. The old man stood for a moment, blinking in the keen sunlight like a roosting bird disturbed by a torch beam, and then tit-tupped down the steps with an easy little run that showed he'd done it a thousand times before.

"He's going to come a cropper one of these days," said Geoffrey.

"What's that he's carrying?" asked Sally.

She wasn't tall enough to see over the parapet, so she'd wriggled herself up onto the warm gold stone and was lying on it facedown, craning over the dizzy edge. Geoffrey grabbed angrily at her belt.

"Don't be a nit, Sal. There's nothing to hold on to."

"There's no reason to fall off either. What *has* he got?" It was a large black tray, with several dishes on it, and jugs, and a jar. Two cloths hung over Mr. Furbelow's arm, and there was something about his bearing that didn't seem to belong to this world of battlements and saffron-soaked chicken and wolfhounds scratching and snarling around a central fire. A faint haze of steam rose above the largest jug. Suddenly Geoffrey saw a picture, sucked out of forgotten times but very clear—lunch in a big hotel with Uncle Jacob, with tea trolleys whisked silently across thick carpets and huge bowls of fruit in baskets; men walked like that, carrying trays like that, with cloths over their arms like that.

"He looks like a waiter," he said.

"Do you think he's going to wait on the Necro man? He must see him sometimes, if he knows that he's bored, and he keeps trying to talk to him in Latin."

They watched Mr. Furbelow move across the cobbles to what Geoffrey had decided was a second well, with a heavy, roped windlass above it. Here the old man put the tray down and started to crank the handle. He turned it for ages, so that it seemed as if the well must be enormously deeper than that from which they'd watered Maddox.

"Oh, look, Jeff. The stone's moved. I can just see the edge of it from here. It's enormous."

Geoffrey moved along the parapet and saw what she meant. The side of a thick flagstone, a huge one, had been heaved out of the ground and a pitch-black opening showed beneath. The handle-winding hadn't been because the well was deep, but because the windlass had to be highly geared to allow Mr. Furbelow to shift a stone that weight. At last he stopped cranking, picked up the tray and felt his way into the hole. From the jerky way his body moved as he disappeared they could see he was going down steps.

"Quick, Sal, now's our chance to find something out."

They belted down the long spiral of steps, through the trap in the roof, down the ladders and into the hall where the hounds lounged. The big doors were barred from the outside; Geoffrey shoved and tugged, but they moved as little as a rooted yew.

The children climbed back to the parapet and waited in the generous sun. They were feeling hungry again before Mr. Furbelow came out.

While he was cranking the flagstone back into place Geoffrey said, "I've had a thought—we don't want him to think we've been spying on him. Let's try and find a window downstairs from which we can see him going back to his house but can't see the windlass. If I leave my handkerchief on the balcony we'll be able to keep our bearings when we get down."

It wasn't easy, even so, and they got it wrong first time. Then they found a suite of rooms with the tiny square windows tunneled through the masonry, from one of which they could see the white cottage. The ratchet of the windlass was still clacking monotonously.

"We can shout, I suppose," said Geoffrey, "but he'll never see us in here. We might try poking a cloth out on a stick."

"I could wriggle along and poke my head out. Lift me up."

"Don't get stuck. It isn't worth it."

She squirmed into the opening, working herself along with toes and elbows. When she stopped, Geoffrey could only just reach her feet. The folds of the tabard completely filled the square, blotting out the sunlight and the noise of the ratchet. He was mad to let her go in without taking it off —it would ruck up as she came back and make it twice as hard for her to get out if she stuck.

"Mr. Furbeloo-ow! Mr. Furbeloo-ow! Please can you come and let us out?"

Faintly Geoffrey heard an answering shout, and Sally began to wriggle back. He reached into the hole and pulled at the hem of the tabard so that it couldn't bundle itself up and cork her in. She slid to the floor grinning.

"He nearly dropped the tray. He's gone into the house but

he says he'll be coming in a minute. Have I messed myself up?"

"Not too bad. Your cheek's dirty. I'll go and get some water."

"Use lick. I don't mind."

They went down and waited by the big doors. At last there was a squeaking and rattling outside and when Geoffrey shoved the door groaned slowly open. Mr. Furbelow looked tired, but was gushingly apologetic.

"My dear young things, I am so sorry. I am in the habit of shutting the dogs in, you see, and to tell the truth I had completely forgotten your presence here. On the days when I have to visit him I find it hard to think of anything else. I do apologize. And goodness, it must be nearly lunchtime. I hope he left some food for your breakfast. Shall we eat at once?"

"Please, Mr. Furbelow," said Sally, "may I go and see if Maddox is all right? And could I let him out into the courtyard for a bit?"

"Of course, my dear, of course. How well that attire suits you, like a little Maid Marian. You two go and look after your pony, and then come and join me for a bite of food."

Maddox was in a bitter temper, snarling at Geoffrey and trying to work him into a corner where he could be properly bitten. Sally pretended not to notice, scratched him between the ears, found another cube of horse bait and led him out into the courtyard, where he yawned at the magic tower, sneered at the delicious sunlight and began to scratch his sagging belly with a hind hoof. Then he noticed some green grass growing between cobbles and cheered up. They left him systematically weeding the whole paved area and walked into the cavern of the tower.

Mr. Furbelow was talking baby talk with a funny Welsh lilt to one of the wolfhounds; the uncouth monster lay on its back, legs waggling in an ecstasy of adoration, while he rubbed its chest with his foot.

"Aren't you afraid of them?" said Geoffrey. "They frightened me stiff this morning when I came down to get some food."

"Oh dear me, no, I'm not afraid. I love dogs, though I

really wanted corgis but I couldn't make him understand. But in any case he wouldn't let me be hurt—he said so. If you tried to hit me on the head or your pony tried to kick me he'd prevent it."

"Would he stop you hurting yourself—by accident?"

"I don't know. I hadn't thought of that. But I don't think it's likely to happen. Shall we have a go at this side of beef? They seemed to prefer it rather high, I'm afraid, but sometimes you can eat it. Oh dear. I think we won't risk it. You take that end, Geoffrey, and I'll take this, and we'll drag it to the fire for the dogs. Don't try to do it all yourself, it's much too heavy. Oh dear, what it is to be young and strong. I must ask you to give me a hand with one or two things this afternoon, too trivial to bother him about. Now, let's see."

He walked down the long table sniffing suspiciously at the mighty slabs of meat, muttering and clucking and shaking his head, and eventually settled for a peacock with all its tailfeathers in place. The dark meat was chewy but pleasant, but the stuffing was disgusting. Most of the strawberries had gone moldy overnight, but there were some delicious apricots. Mr. Furbelow insisted that they must peel these, as they had probably been ripened on dungheaps.

"Did he make all this food out of nothing?" asked Geoffrey. "Or does it come from somewhere? I boiled some water in a helmet this morning and when I'd finished there was another helmet on the wall. Did he really make this tower all at once, just like that?"

"Oh dear, I don't know how he does it. The tower came in a night, and he took my cottage away but I made him get it back because it had my medicines in it. I think this is all a copy of something; bits of it look so used and all those clothes seem to belong to real people. I think it's the same with the food. Sometimes these big pastry things look as if they'd been made for a special occasion. I often think they're not even copies—they're the real things and he's just moved them about in time."

"Then why aren't there any people?" said Sally.

"Oh dear, it is difficult, isn't it? I've asked him that, before I lost him completely, and he said something about 'natura.' I think he meant it was wrong somehow to do to people what he's done to the tower and the food—it's against nature. I suppose that's why he doesn't stop the food going bad, too, but he is so difficult now, and he gets so impatient when I have to look things up in the dictionary, and it's all so different from everything I meant."

"Would you like me to come and help?" said Sally. "I could do the Latin if you'd tell me what to say."

The old chemist, who'd been practically sniveling with misery at the end of his last speech, opened his mouth to say no, but instead he made a funny sucking noise, and sat for several seconds with his mouth wide open, staring at her. He looked as if he were going to cry, but instead he shook his head and sighed.

"Too late, too late. If you'd come four years ago, perhaps. But you cannot get through to him now, and even if you could . . ."

The old despairing voice dwindled into mumblings.

"If you could?" said Geoffrey at last.

"I don't *know*," said Mr. Furbelow irritably. "How *can* I know? There's nothing to go on. I've interrupted a process I don't understand—*nobody* could understand it—especially as I was waking him in gradual stages and he wouldn't let me continue once he was partially awake—he's wavering between two worlds, you might say, and now if I try to interfere again it will only make him worse, and then I don't know what he mightn't do, I really don't."

"Does he understand what's happened, do you think?" said Geoffrey. (Really it was a very awkward conversation, trying to lead the old man on into telling them more, but not to seem too inquisitive. Like a guessing game, not knowing who "he" was or what he did.)

"Sometimes, I suppose," said Mr. Furbelow. He'd lost his irritation and his voice had returned to its normal dazed lilt. "But a lot of the time it's not as if he were in this world at all. When he has a lucid interval, though . . . No, I doubt even then. It must be very difficult for him down there."

"Then," said Sally, "he probably doesn't know what he's done to the rest of us—how many people he's made leave their homes and run away."

"How many people have been killed," said Geoffrey.

"Is he good or bad?" said Sally.

"Oh, he's *good*," said Mr. Furbelow, leaning forward

across the table with such earnestness that his beard trailed through the greasy juices on his plate. "There's no doubt about that, none at all. You can feel it even when he's at his most completely lost."

"Then couldn't I try to explain to him?" said Sally. "About what's happened, I mean, and how much harm he's doing?"

Mr. Furbelow sniffed several times and stared into his goblet.

"Oh dear," he said, "I suppose we ought to try. I do confess I don't want to. I find him a very frightening creature. But it may be the only chance, the last chance. Ah, well . . ."

He drank the last mouthfuls of wine and stood quickly up.

"We must go now," he said. "There is some chance of catching him at a good moment, when this world is real to him, when he's not quite lost in dreams. He didn't say anything to me this morning, but he ate what I gave him— perhaps the contact with a real person and the taste of real food on his tongue may make him more conscious of what is really happening. Come, let us get it over with. Geoffrey, you can turn that filthy crank for me, but I will go down alone with Sally. You must promise not to follow us and come nosing down. I know how inquisitive young folks are. I put you on your honor."

"I promise," said Geoffrey. They followed Mr. Furbelow out of the hall.

The windlass was harder work than he'd supposed. There was a lot of friction in the wooden cogs and axles, and he wound on and on, surprised at the willpower that enabled Mr. Furbelow to drive his doddering body to work the contraption. At last the stone, a great tilted flap of paving, jarred against a crossbeam, and Geoffrey could see coarse steps leading into darkness.

"They're rather steep," said Mr. Furbelow. "I'll show you the way."

Sally followed him down.

At first Geoffrey mooned about the area around the windlass, but soon Maddox clumped up, snarling, and drove him off. The pony seemed to know where Sally was, and even

394 THE CHANGES: A TRILOGY

tried putting a foot on the top step, but thought better of it and stood staring down into the burrow like a cat nosing at a mousehole or a lover gazing at the window of his beloved. Geoffrey left him to it.

The second time he passed the white cottage he decided to explore. He could see Maddox from the steps, still standing like a stuffed animal in a museum. Any movement from the pony would be a warning that someone was coming out. The yellow door was ajar. The hall was a clutter of dumped objects, with just room to walk between them. There was that funny smell of damp and dirt that you sometimes find in houses where nobody does any proper cleaning. Upstairs were two rooms, one a dusty storeroom and the other a pretty, pink room with two beds in it. Downstairs was a kitchen with a gas range, but it didn't look as if it had been used for ages; a back door led out to the angle between the outer wall of the tower and the house. Opposite the kitchen, across the hall, was the room Geoffrey wanted.

This was where Mr. Furbelow lived and kept his belongings. There were rows of chemist's bottles on shelves, and more chemistry-looking things in cardboard cartons piled along a wall. Most of the books on the shelves were about chemistry and medicine, and there were piles of *Pharmaceutical Journal*s. The only furniture in the room was a very ragged sofa with some rugs on it, which looked as though this was where Mr. Furbelow usually slept, and a big desk with an upright chair. There was a photograph on the desk, of a smiling plump dark-haired woman with her hair in a big bun. Beside her lay two dictionaries, one Latin–English and the other English–Latin. In the middle of the desk was an account book. The latest entry, made only yesterday, read:

Very restless. Would not talk to me at all, but kept muttering to himself. Shouted "Quamdiu" several times, and once (I think) "Regem servavi dum infantem." I begin to believe his speech is more slurred than it was. Hope this is no bad symptom, but can find nothing in my books. He suddenly was disturbed by something, and almost stood up. Instead he went into a trance, and I heard a tremendous noise of thunder outside. There was a small storm disappearing over the eastern hills when I came out. Nothing like this for months.

Geoffrey glanced out of the window. Maddox was still at his post. The rest of the book was full of short entries, every other day, sometimes just the two words "No change." There was always at least that. On the bookshelf Geoffrey found four similar account books, all full of entries, and next to them a proper diary with the dates printed on each page. Each book covered one year, so the diary must be five years old. Geoffrey leafed through it; the first half of the year was almost empty, except for notes of visit to K's grave, but on the 17th of May there was a longer one:

A most extraordinary thing, which I must record in full. Last spring dear K planted at Llanthony a flowering cherry. *Prunus longipes* it said on the label. She used often to say, after Doctor H told us the ill news, that she would never see it in flower, but at our last visit before she went into hospital—because of the shop we could only come up at weekends—it was in perfect flower, but deep yellow. This was October, and it was supposed to bear white flowers in late April. We laughed and cried and imagined the nursery had made a mistake. But when I came up here last month—I could not endure to come before—it was in flower again, big white dangling bunches like upside-down powder puffs. Perhaps I ought to have got in touch with some botanical body, but I felt it would be a desecration of dear K's tree. Instead, thinking there might be some peculiarity in the soil, I took samples back to town for analysis. I did the work myself, and either I am mad or it is full of gold!

There were no entries for a week, then a short one:

I have begun to dig at Llanthony. Difficult without disturbing the roots of K's tree. I am tunneling down and then sideways. I feel compelled to do this.

Next weekend he had dug still further and had taken more samples, which were also rich with gold. The entry after that was longer; Geoffrey read it, glancing out of the window between sentences.

Now I know! But I do not know what to do. I have been digging for the past two weekends, leaving little Gwynnedd to care for the shop on Saturdays. It was not for the gold—I felt I had to do it, just to know. It was hard work for a middle-aged man, but I kept on, and yesterday at noon I struck a smooth, sloping rock. It seemed that I must be at the end of my tunnel, and either give in or dig somewhere else. Then I saw a crack in the rock that seemed too straight to be a fault. I cleared a larger area and uncovered a shaped, rectangular stone. With great difficulty I levered this out. There was a hole behind it, into which I crawled and found myself in a low cavern, full of a dim green light. I thought it must be an ancient burial chamber, for on a slab in the center there was the body of a very big man, and very hairy. I thought he must be dead, and preserved by some freak which produced the green light too, but when I touched him his flesh was firm and far colder than the coldest ice. It burned like solid $CO_2$. But I knew for certain he was alive. Then I saw that there were letters on the side of the slab. They said MER-LINUS SUM. QUI ME TANGIT TURBAT MUNDUM. Latin, I think, but I cannot buy a dictionary until tomorrow. I left, and leaned the stone back into its place.

There was a three-day gap, and then another entry.

I have decided what to do. I cannot leave him and go. I feel sure that I was *meant* to find him, and that the tree and the gold were signs for me, and me alone. I know that he has enormous powers. I could feel that in the cavern, and that in my hands he could use those powers for good. In what way I do not yet know. Perhaps he might even stop these wicked wars in the world, or bring dear K back to me.

The problem is how to wake him, so that I can best

direct him to exert his powers where they can do most good. I have been reading about the process of reanimating patients whose metabolism has been slowed by refrigeration for the purpose of certain surgical operations.

There appears to be a new synthetic stimulant which can be injected into the veins in very precise doses, so that its effect on the patient can be very carefully watched, and I see that this drug is in the catalogues of one of the American companies who manufacture pharmaceutical products in England. I shall attempt to order a quantity of this. Alas, I shall have neither the equipment nor the knowledge which is available in a big hospital, but I feel that it is my duty to take the risk. If I fail, only he (and possibly I) will suffer. And I really do intend to try and use him for the good of mankind. Pray heaven that I turn out to be justified.

The Latin, I think, means: I am Merlin. He who touches me upsets the world.

I have already touched him. I cannot change that.

Phew, thought Geoffrey, things certainly hadn't turned out as Mr. Furbelow intended. Fancy expecting to make Merlin his slave! Other way around, now, from the look of it. He began to turn the pages, looking for an account of the wakening, when out of the corner of his eye he saw Maddox move. Geoffrey put the diary back in its place and slipped out through the back door. He ran down a long empty shed full of perches for hawks and climbed through the open window at the far end. From here he was out of sight, and could saunter back toward the windlass, noticing for the first time, as he did so, the flowering cherry that had started all the upheaval.

Mr. Furbelow was already winding the slab down into position, and Sally was talking to Maddox, her face as white as a limed wall.

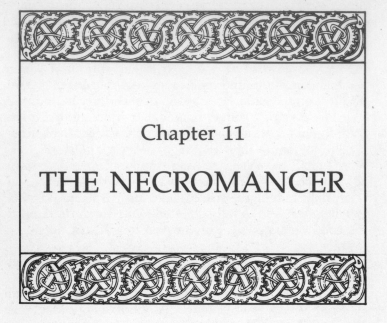

# Chapter 11

# THE NECROMANCER

Geoffrey sensed at once that it wouldn't do to ask how the interview had gone. He took over the crank in silence, and lowered the stone. Then Mr. Furbelow solicitously took Sally into his cottage and made her lie down on one of the upstairs beds, and he himself settled down for a nap on his sofa. Geoffrey was left to explore, but found nothing of interest, and spent most of the afternoon looking for birds from the tower over the outer gate. He didn't see anything uncommon, but he fancied he heard a wood warbler several times.

They supped early and went to bed when there was still gray light seeping through the outer window. As soon as he was lying down Sally, who had been very quiet all evening, spoke:

"Jeff, you've got to *do* something. He's killing him, really he is. It was all about making a sword this afternoon, but full of words I didn't know. It's awful. He doesn't know what's happening to him, and he's so marvelous, you can feel his mind all strong and beautiful, and Mr. Furbelow is just dithering around waiting for him to die. I tried and tried, but he wouldn't hear what I was saying. His Latin's a bit funny, the way he says it, but you soon get used to it. And goodness he's big. Do you remember—no, you won't—there was a dancing bear came to Weymouth once? *It* was beautiful and strong, and it had to do this horrible thing with everyone laughing and jeering and a chain round his neck. He's like that, only worse, much worse. It's horrible. Jeff, please!"

"Oh, Lord, Sal. I'll try and think of something. Did you know he was Merlin?"

"Yes. It said so on the stone where he was lying. How did you?"

He told her about the diary, but before he'd finished she was asleep. He lay on his back with his hand under his head and thought around in circles until he was asleep too. It all depended on Mr. Furbelow.

But next morning Mr. Furbelow had changed. He was still polite and kind, but when they tried to talk about Merlin he said that that was his concern; and at lunch he told them that he would prefer them to leave next day. They were upsetting things, he said. They needn't bother about the wolves, because they could give them the rest of the feast tonight and wolves sleep for twenty-four hours after a full meal. That was settled then, wasn't it? He'd be sorry to see them go, but really it was for the best.

In the afternoon, for an experiment, Sally managed to maneuver Maddox into a position where he could take a good kick at Mr. Furbelow as the old man snoozed in a ramshackle deck chair in front of the house. The pony shaped happily for the kick, but suddenly danced away as if it had been stung and would not go near the place again. So that was no good. Nor, presumably, would be hitting him on the head with something, even if Geoffrey had managed to bring himself to do it. Geoffrey trudged round and round the tower, frowning. Mr. Furbelow would hear the windlass clack if they tried to raise the stone when he was asleep. If only they could contrive a reason for Mr. Furbelow *sending* them down without him.

He came around the tower for the twentieth time, and saw Mr. Furbelow, awake now, do his funny skitter down the steps. If only he would fall on them he might break a leg. They really were hideously dangerous, and that was the only hope. He must be made to fall.

The three of them dined together very friendlily. Most of the meat was high by now, but they found a leg of sweet, thymy mutton. Then, in the dusk, Mr. Furbelow showed them some funny long wheelbarrows without any sides in one of the sheds, and they wheeled load after load of bad meat to the outer tower and threw it through the wicket gate. The wolves were already there by the time they brought the second load, snarling and tugging at the big joints. As they watched, more and more of the long shadowy bodies flitted out of the blackness under the trees. There were several mother wolves with cubs which waited, eyes green in the half-light, until their mother dragged a big hunk for them and they could begin a snarling match of their own.

When the last of the meat had been ferried away from the tables Mr. Furbelow barred the children into the tower. Two hours later Geoffrey stood at the parapet in his gold robe and thought of rain.

*All day the island had slumbered in the sun. It was warm, warm, and above it the warmed air rose, sucking in winds off the western ocean, disturbed winds heavy with wetness, only just holding their moisture over the smooth, tepid sea. And now meeting the land, already cool with night, cooler now, cooler still, and the hills reforming the clouds, jostling them together, piling them up, squeezing them till the released rain hisses into the hills' sere grasses. Now trees drip, leaves glisten in faint light, forgotten gullies tinkle. Rain, swathed, drumming . . .*

Sally, wrapped in drenched furs, led him down the long stairs to shelter. He squatted in a corner, deliberately uncomfortable, so that he woke every half hour. When it was still dark he put his soaking robe on over a dry jerkin and went up to the parapet again. The last rain had gone, and starlight glistened in every puddle and drip. It was very cold already. He thought of frost.

*Still air chilling the hills. Evaporation chilling the ground. The trees ceasing their breathing. An icy influence from the stars. Rivers of cold air flowing down, weaving between the trunks, coming here to make a deep pool of cold, crisping the grass. Cat ice now in crackles on the puddles, white-edged round hoof prints, ice glazing cobbles and stones in a shiny film. A deep, hard frost, making earth ring like iron. Deep, hard, deep . . .*

This time he was woken from the weather trance by the violent shivering of his own body. The robe was starched rigid with ice, and his legs so numb with cold and standing that he couldn't feel his feet. He had to clutch the guardrail all the way down to the roof, and even so he nearly fell twice on the ice-crusted steps. He warmed himself by the never-dying fire in the hall, watched by yawning hounds, and then went up to the gallery. As he snuggled into his furs he was struck by a nasty snag in his plans. The doors would still be barred, but if all went right Mr. Furbelow wouldn't be able to open them. Sulkily he crawled out of the warmth and rootled through several chambers for belts. Ten ought to be enough. He hacked the buckles off and tied the straps into a single length with a loop at the end. And then sleep.

It was bright day when he woke. Sally was shaking his shoulder.

"Okay, okay, I'm awake. Has Mr. Furbelow come out yet?"

"I didn't look. I've brought some fruit and bread up for breakfast."

"Hang on. I'll just go and see what's up."

He ran down the stairs, carrying his leather rope. The hounds were used to him by now. Up the third ladder, which led to the suite overlooking the cottage. He peered through the small, square opening. Mr. Furbelow had already come out, and was lying in an awkward mess at the bottom of the icy steps. He didn't move.

"Sal!" shouted Geoffrey, realizing in sweaty panic that

perhaps the kind old man was dead and he'd murdered him. "Sal!"

She came into the chamber, flushed from running up the ladder.

"Look, Sal, Mr. Furbelow's slipped and fallen on the steps. You've got to crawl out backward with this loop around your foot. Don't lose it. Then when you're over the edge you can stand in the loop and hold on to the straps and I'll let you down; then you can run around and open the door and we can go and see if he's all right."

"I'll take my dress off. Don't worry, Jeff, I'm sure he's all right. Anyway it was the only thing you could have done. You'll have to lift me up."

It was much more awkward getting her in backward, and the loop wouldn't stay on her foot. But then she was slithering down the tunnel, scrabbling at the edge, and then out of sight. The knots snagged on the far sill, so that he had to lower her in a series of jerks. When he was holding the last belt the whole contraption went slack and he heard her calling that she was down. He ran to the doors.

"Jeff, you'll have to wait. I can't reach the bar. I'm going to fetch Maddox."

Silence. A long wait. The hounds scratched and the fire, which he'd never seen fed, hissed sappily. Outside a pigeon cooed its boring June coo. Then the clop of hooves.

"Stop there, Maddox. Good old boy. No, stand still while I climb up. That's it. Golly, it's heavy. I don't think . . ."

A scratching noise and a clunk. Geoffrey heaved at the door and it swung open.

Mr. Furbelow was lying on one side, with his leg bent back under him. He was breathing snortily, with his mouth open. Geoffrey ran into the cottage, nearly slipping on the icy steps himself, and brought out the sofa cushions. They eased him onto these and straightened him out on his back. His left leg seemed to be broken somewhere above the knee. Geoffrey decided he'd better try and set it while the old man was still unconscious. Trying to remember everything that Uncle Jacob had shown him ("Decide slowly, laddie, and do it quickly and firmly. No room for the squeamishness in a sick bay.") he felt the bones into position. There was one place where they seemed right. Then he used his sword to lever the back off one of the kitchen chairs, bandaged the leg with torn strips of pillowcase from the bedroom, and lashed the uprights of the chairback down the leg with the knotted belts. It was very tiresome to do without unsettling the join, even with the leg propped on cushions, and when he'd finished it looked horribly clumsy, but felt as if it ought to hold the break firm for a bit. Sally went into the hall to fetch a jug of wine, but before she was back the old man blinked and groaned.

"Morphine," he muttered. "Top right-hand drawer of my desk. Hypodermic syringe, bottle of spirit there too. Don't touch anything else."

There was a box of morphine ampoules, three hypodermic syringes and what Geoffrey took to be the spirit bottle. Mr. Furbelow took the things onto his chest, dipped the point of the needle into the spirit and then prodded through the rubber at the end of the ampoule, withdrawing the plunger to suck the liquid out. Then he tilted it up, pressed the plunger until a drop showed at the point of the needle, and pushed the point into a vein on the inside of his left arm, squeezing the morphine slowly into his bloodstream. You could see the pain screaming from his eyes. Hell, thought Geoffrey, he's a brave old man and I've done a wicked thing. He decided to tell him the truth, but Mr. Furbelow seemed to have fainted again. They watched him for five minutes. Then he spoke, not opening his eyes.

"That's better. Have you contrived to do anything about my leg?"

"Yes, Mr. Furbelow. I hope I've done the right thing. I tried to set it, and it felt as if it was together properly, and then I put splints on it. I *am* sorry. It must hurt frightfully."

"What had we best do about *him*?"said Mr. Furbelow.

"If you'll tell me what to do, I'll try and do it properly. Sally can talk to him if necessary. If it's the best we can manage he'll have to put up with it."

"He will not like the change, I fear. He is the most conservative of creatures."

"Would you like us to try and carry you into your house? It won't be very easy, but I expect I could rig something up."

404  THE CHANGES: A TRILOGY

"Let us leave that, for the moment. Perhaps he will be so angry that he will destroy us all, or perhaps he will mend my leg. In either case the effort will have been pointless. Oh dear. Well, there's one comfort. I baked some oatcakes only yesterday. And I've put the water on to boil. He insists on water from the well, and I've always boiled it, but I haven't liked to tell him. He won't make his own food, though he doesn't mind bringing the oats out of nowhere, and I have to pound them up in a mortar and then cook them. And the bees hive in the stable roof, and I collect their honey every autumn. The honey's in the cupboard on the left of the passage, and the oatcakes are there too. The kettle's on the fire in my room."

He sighed and shut his eyes. Geoffrey started up the steps to look for this primitive meal, thinking how strangely different it was from the elaborate and moldering banquet which they'd thrown to the wolves the evening before.

"Wait," said Mr. Furbelow. "I'm only resting."

Geoffrey sat on the bottom step, where the sun had melted the ice and dried a patch of stone. The old chemist's face was gray as ash, the lines on it suddenly deeper, the nose pinched, but the wispy moustache wavered slightly below his nostrils as his breath went in and out. Geoffrey was wondering whether he'd gone to sleep when he spoke again.

"You must take a clean linen cloth and a clean towel," he said. "You will find them in the bottom drawer of the chest of drawers in my study. The kettle is a big one, so there will be plenty of water. First you pour about two pints into the silver jug on the mantelpiece; then you put that in the big earthenware jar in the back room to cool off, so that he can drink it. I've built a platform of stones in the bottom of the jar, so that you can put the jug in and leave it there, without unboiled water slopping in over the top. Then you can get the other things together—two oatcakes, the little silver bowl on the shelf full of honey, a linen cloth, a towel, and the bowl for the hot water in case he wants to be washed. Shall I repeat that?"

"I think I've got it," said Geoffrey.

"Then you can come back and I'll tell you what to do, while the drinking water is getting cold."

The oatcakes were not those thin saucer-shaped things you buy in tartan tins in Edinburgh: they were just lumps of cooked oatmeal, with no real shape at all. The honey was the palest yellow, very runny, and smelling of wilder flowers than the garden-and-orchard-scented honey which shops sell. And the cloths smelled of mountain streams and sunlight. Mr. Furbelow spoke more drowsily when Geoffrey came back.

"It all depends," he said. "Sometimes he just lies there and opens his mouth, like a bird in a nest, and you have to break bits off the oatcake, dip them in the honey and pop them in. Other times he sits up on his elbow and feeds himself. Sometimes he's asleep, and I just put the tray beside him on his stone. About once a week he likes to have his face and hands sponged and dried. But really, you'll find you know what he wants without his telling you. I should go as soon as the water's cool enough to drink. I shall try to sleep now."

The cranking seemed to take half an hour, but at last the stone gave the dull thud which meant it was high enough.

"I'll go first," said Sally. "It's not really as dark as it looks —he makes a sort of light at the bottom. You've got to feel each step with your foot because they're all different."

They felt their way down the coarse stone. The steps did not seem to be shaped work at all—more like flattened boulders from a riverbed, pitted with the endless rubbing of water and patterned with fossil bones. There were thirty-three of them. At the bottom a passage led away through rock toward a faint green light. It was eleven paces down the passage and into a long, low chamber whose rock walls sloped inward like the roof of an attic. The air in the chamber smelled sweet and wild and wrong, like rotting crab apples. Merlin was waiting for them.

He lay on his side, with his head resting on the crook of his arm, staring up the passage. Perhaps he had been aroused to expect them by the clack of the ratchet. He wore a long, dark robe. Colors were difficult in the strange light, but his beard seemed black and his face the color of rusted iron. His eyes were so deep in the huge head that they looked like the empty sockets of a skull until you moved across their beam and saw the green glow reflected from the lens, like the reflection of sky at the bottom of a well. The light seemed to come from nowhere. It was just there, impregnating the sick, sweet atmosphere.

He gave no sign, made no movement, as Sally crossed his line of vision, but his head followed Geoffrey into the room. Geoffrey found he was gripping the tray so hard that the tin rim hurt his palms. There was a widening of the stone slab where he could have put it down, but instead he turned away from Merlin (it was a struggle, like turning into a gale at a street corner) and put the tray on the rough rock behind him. When he turned back Merlin had moved, rearing up onto his elbow. He was a giant. The black hair streamed down in a wild mane behind him. His eyes were alive now, and the chamber was throbbing with a noiseless hum, like the hum of a big ship's engines which you cannot hear with your ears but which sings up from the deck through your feet, through your shoulder when you lean against a stanchion, and through your whole body as you lie in your bunk waiting for sleep. His lips moved.

"Ubi servus meus."

The voice was a gray scrape, like shingle retreating under the suck of a wave. Sally answered in a whisper.

"Magister Furbelow crurem fregit."

Merlin did not look at her. The green blaze of his eyes clanged into Geoffrey's skull, drowning his will in a welter of dithering vibrations. The lips moved again.

"Da mihi cibum meum."

As the huge wave of Merlin's authority washed over him, Geoffrey gasped, "Tell him what's happening."

"Magister . . ." began Sally.

"Tacite," said Merlin, and Geoffrey's tongue was locked in his mouth, as though he would never speak again. Mastered, helpless, he turned and picked up the tray and put it on the slab. The giant lay back and watched him out of the corner of his eyes. Geoffrey broke off a crumbling corner of one of the oatcakes and picked up the little silver pot of honey. The surface of the honey was curved, with the faint arc of its meniscus, and that of the shining curve of the silver below gathered the green light to a single focus, a spark of light in the gold liquid. The clean wildflower smell smote up through the sick air of the cave. Geoffrey stared at the gold spark. It was the sun, the outside world where the wheat was growing toward harvest. His mind clung to the light, hauled itself toward that tiny sun.

"Tell him Mr. Furbelow gave him poison," he croaked.

"Venenum . . ." whispered Sally out of the blackness beyond the sun.

"Mel?" said Merlin's voice.

"Venenum tibi dedit Magister Furbelow," said Sally.

"Quando?" The old voice was weary, disbelieving.

"Hic quintus annus," said Sally.

"Mr. Furbelow tried to wake him up with a synthetic stimulant," said Geoffrey. "But he got stuck halfway."

"What does 'synthetic' mean?"

"Made in a factory, out of coal or oil or something. Not grown. Not natural."

Sally started on a longer whisper. Geoffrey still didn't dare look at her—he still clung to the sun in the honey. When she reached the word *natura* Merlin gave an odd, coughing grunt, and Geoffrey saw, at the edge of his vision, a shape moving downward. At last he looked away from the little silver bowl, and saw that the shape had been Merlin's legs. Merlin had heaved his body up again and was now sitting on the slab, his legs dangling, his head bowed so as not to touch the roof. He must have been nearly eight feet tall, and now he was staring at Sally with a deep, steady gaze as though he was seeing her for the first time. She finished what she had to say.

"Dic mihi ab initio," he said.

"He wants me to tell him from the beginning," said Sally. "Where shall I start?"

"Start with Mr. Furbelow digging into his tomb. Tell him what he was trying to do. Say he's not a bad man, but muddled. Then tell him what England's like now—how cruel people are. Tell him about all the people who had to go away."

Twice while Sally spoke to him something seemed to shake Merlin like a branch shaken by a sudden gust. Both times Sally paused; the feeling that the chamber was throbbing wavered, increased, then steadied back. Both times

Geoffrey knew that Merlin had fought away the delirium which had engulfed him for the last five years. Sally's voice became pleading. She wasn't whispering now, but almost shouting. "Indignum est," she said several times, "indignum nominis tui." Her face became runneled with tears, as she tried to ram her message through five years of poisoned stupor—she was thinking of the dancing bear. In the end she was gasping between each syllable and her voice was cracked with pain. Merlin stared at her like an entomologist considering an insect, and at last sighed. Sally stopped shouting.

He turned to Geoffrey.

"Da," he said.

Geoffrey handed him an oatcake and the honey pot. He broke off a fragment, dipped it in the honey and began to eat. While he ate he talked. Sometimes Sally answered. The word *natura* came up again and again. Next time he wanted food he just held out his hand to Geoffrey for an oatcake while he went on talking to Sally. His palm was covered with fine black hairs.

His voice changed, as though he were not asking anymore, but telling. Sally just nodded. Then he handed the empty honey pot to Geoffrey, drank a few sips from the jug and settled back onto the implacable stone.

"Difficile erit," he said, "sed perdurabo, Deo volente. Abite vos. Gratias ago."

The green light dimmed. Geoffrey picked up the tray. They left.

As Geoffrey began to wind down the stone he said, "Tell me what all that was about."

"I didn't really understand everything," said Sally. "I told him what had happened, and then I said that what he was doing now was—there isn't a proper word for *indignum*—unworthy, dishonorable, something like that. Then he told me a lot about *natura,* which means nature—but it isn't anything to do with wild birds and hedges. It's all about what we really are, and what is proper for us. I remember he said machines were just toys for clever apes, and not proper for man—they prevent him from finding his own nature. But anyway the stuff Mr. Furbelow gave him was very bad for *his* nature, and now he's going to try and change it so that he can overcome it. He said it would be difficult. He said that all sorts of things might happen out here, because once you start interfering with the strong bits of nature the things around them get disturbed. It's like the whirlpools around an oar, he said. Then he said it would be difficult again, but that he would manage with God's will, and then he said thank you. You know, he didn't seem at all worried about what he'd done to the other people in England—it was just unlucky for some of them, but they didn't matter much."

"But he said thank you," said Geoffrey as the flagstone boomed back into position over the dark stair.

"Yes," said Sally.

# Chapter 12

# PORTENTS

It felt as if it should be later afternoon as they came up the steps, but it was still morning, the sun just sucking up the last of the melted ice from the night before. Not knowing whether it was the right thing to do, Geoffrey lowered the slab over the tunnel and carried the tray toward the cottage.

Mr. Furbelow had his eyes open. He too had been roused by the clack of the ratchet and was waiting for them.

"Did he miss me?" he said.

"Yes," said Geoffrey. "He noticed at once."

"Ah," said Mr. Furbelow. Silence. "And he took it from you all right?"

"I hope you won't be cross," said Sally, "but we found him in a lucid interval and we told him what was happening."

"You did what?"

"We persuaded him to try and go back into his sleep. I'm afraid he said it might be dangerous for us out here."

"Do you want us to try to carry you into your house?" said Geoffrey.

"No thank you. I am better here."

"Then we must try and build you some sort of shelter."

There were a lot of curious tools in one of the sheds, great adzes and odd-shaped choppers. There were blunt and clumsy saws, too, and another shed was a well-stocked timber store. Geoffrey prized out four cobbles at the corners of Mr. Furbelow's bed with his sword—they were pigs to move, each packed tight against its neighbors and jammed by century-hardened dirt. He loosened the exposed ground and walloped four pointed uprights into position, staying them with what he took to be bowstrings, which he tied to knives jammed between cobbles further out. He nailed a framework of lighter timbers onto the uprights, and fastened to this the most waterproof-looking of the furs Sally had brought out from the tower. The whole contraption took him about six hours to build, so, what with stopping for lunch (stale bread and cheese, apricots and souring wine) and ministering to Mr. Furbelow's needs (the old man was quiet and dignified now, but gave himself another shot of morphine toward evening) it was drawing on to dusk by the time he had finished. Venus glimmered in a pale wash of sky above the western hill line before the first symptom occurred.

All the hounds in the tower began howling together, a crazy, terrifying yammer, interrupted by choruses of hoarse barking. A moment's silence, and they spilled into the courtyard, howling again, dashing to and fro under the tower wall, biting fiercely at each other with frothing mouths until the yellow fur was streaked with dirty red blood. Geoffrey drew his sword and told Sally to run to the house if they came any nearer, but the madness stopped with a couple of coughs, like a fading engine, and the dogs crept away to lick their wounds and whimper under the eaves of the timber store.

The evening deepened and the air chilled. Geoffrey went to spread the lightest pelt over Mr. Furbelow and to let down the sheltering flaps at the side of his bed. One of the guy ropes had gone slack, and when he tried to tauten it he found that the crack into which he had driven its knife was now half an inch wide. The ground had moved.

"Sal, I think you'd better get Maddox out into the open. Anything might happen tonight. I'll look for more rugs and food, if there's any left."

He jammed the knife into another crack and went into the tower. One of the big doors was off its hinges. Inside all the flambeaux were smoking, and the fire, too, was sending up a heavy gray column which didn't seem to be finding its way out of the hole in the roof. The huge room was full of choking haze, and a voice was shrieking from the upper gallery: "Mordred. Mordred. Mordred." It went on and on. One of the long tables had been overturned, leaving a mess of fruit and bread and dishes spilled across the floor, but on the other he found a bowl of tiny apples and some untouched loaves. He carried them out to the cottage steps, where Sally sat wrapped in a white fur.

"Get as much wood as you can out of the timber store," he said. "We'd better have a fire. I'll find something to protect Mr. Furbelow's leg in case that contraption collapses. It sounds as though there's people in there now, Sal, but I can't see anyone."

"I don't think he'd hurt us on purpose," said Sally.

This time the smoke in the tower was worse. The voice had stopped but there was a clashing and tinkling on the far side of the hall, interspersed with hoarse gruntings. He couldn't see what was happening because of the smoke, but suddenly grasped that this must be the noise people make when they are fighting with shield and sword. He picked up a bench and began to carry it out, but before he reached the door there came a burst of wild yelling behind him and the running of feet. Something struck him on his left shoulder; he staggered and then something much solider caught him on the hip and threw him sideways across the bench he was carrying in a clumsy somersault. He crouched there as the feet thudded past, but saw nothing. When they had gone the voice began shrieking again: "Mordred. Mordred. Mordred." It was lower in tone now, but still the same woman's voice, hoarse and murderous. He picked up his bench and limped away, the pain where the thing had hit him nagging at his hip. Sally had gathered a useful pile of timber.

"We'll want smaller stuff to start it with," said Geoffrey,

THE WEATHERMONGER                413

"and straw out of the stables. Did you see anyone come out of the tower? Somebody knocked me over but it's so full of smoke that I couldn't see what was happening."

"I saw Maddox shying and neighing, and then he went off and made friends with the dogs, but I didn't see anything else. How are you going to light the fire, Jeff?"

"If you'll get straw and kindling, I'll get a burning log out of the hall."

"Do be careful."

"Okay. But I don't think being careful is going to make much difference."

The voice had stopped again and there was no noise of fighting. The smoke was thick as the thickest fog. Geoffrey crouched under it and scuttled across the paving until he could see the glow of the fire. Before he reached it he realized there was something in the way, and stopped. It looked like two new pillars, supporting a heavy, shadowy thing. At the same moment as he realized that the pillars had feet, the thing became the back of an armed man, motionless, squat, brooding into the fire. His armor was leather with strips of thick bronze sewn on to it. A tangle of yellowy-gray hair flowed over the shoulders from under the horned helmet.

Geoffrey crept away beneath the shelter of the smoke. When he reached the wall he found a tall stool, which he stood on to take one of the flambeaux out of its iron bracket. He decided not to go back into the tower again.

The flame of the straw flared into brightness and died down almost at once, but some of the kindling caught and with careful nursing they made a proper fire, leaning billets of timber into a wigwam around the crackling, orange heart. As soon as it was really going the hounds slouched over and arranged themselves in a sprawling circle, scratching, yawning, and licking the blood off their coats. Maddox followed and stood in the half-light on the edge of the circle, thinking obscure horse thoughts. Geoffrey placed the bench at right angles across Mr. Furbelow's sleeping form, and stayed it firm, to be a second line of defense if the shelter fell. He went into the cottage and brought out the rest of the blankets and the drawer of medicine, which he put into the shelter. Nothing noticeable happened for half an hour, while Sally and he sat on the steps and ate bread and apples.

Then came the storm. The stars which had been blazing down hard-edged as diamonds vanished from horizon to horizon. The sky groaned. Balefires pranced along the parapet and flickered down the edges of the tower. A few drops of rain fell, warm as blood, and then the valley cracked with lightning. Geoffrey could see that the dogs were howling again, but he couldn't hear them through the grinding bellows of thunder. There was no darkness. All down the valley the black cloud-roof stood on jigging legs of light, blue-white, visible through closed eyelids. The shed next to the stables caught fire and burned with orange flames and black, oily smoke. Maddox picked his way between the dogs and nuzzled under Sally's fur, shivering convulsively. The world drowned in noise.

When the storm finished he thought he was deaf. His head was full of a strange wailing, which he decided must be the effect of ruined eardrums. But then a log on the fire tilted sideways and he heard it fall—the wailing was outside, coming from the sky, swooping in great curves around the tower. As it crossed the now blazing stables he thought he saw a darker blackness in the night, bigger than a bird, but wasn't sure. The wailing rose to a tearing squeal and floated away westward.

Then, he afterward realized, the disturbances invaded his own mind. At the time it seemed like more portents crowding in around him. A new tower sprouted to the north, with people moving about at the top of it, carrying lanterns. A dark beast, toad-shaped, big as a barn, heaved itself out of the forest and scrabbled at the stonework. Uncle Jacob stalked across the cobbles, cracking his thumbs in a shower of sparks; he looked angry, did not speak, and walked on into the dark. The whole landscape started to drift, to float away after the wailing noise, faster and faster, with a whirling, bucking motion, sucked on a roaring current of time which toppled over the edge of reality. They were falling, falling . . .

The rest, for a while, was dreams, meaningless; shapeless, a dark chaos.

* * *

When he woke up it was still dark. The clouds had gone, the moon was well down in the sky, a few red patches of embers showed where the stables and the sheds beyond them had been, and the earth was heaving in sudden stiff jerks and spasms. Tiles were clattering off the sheds all around the courtyard, and from the forest came the groaning of toppled trees. The steps on which they were sitting had tilted sideways. Sally lay across him with her head in his lap.

"Wake up, Sal. Wake up and be ready to run. I think the tower might fall."

"Oh, Jeff, I'm frightened."

"So'm I. If it falls straight at us we're done for, but if it looks like going a bit to one side we must run the other way. Don't try to hide in any of the buildings—they might cave in too. I hope Mr. Furbelow will be all right."

You couldn't prepare for the spasms, because they weren't rhythmical, just shuddering jars from any direction, often with a deep booming noise under ground. Geoffrey looked around to see how the cottage was taking it, and saw in the moonlight a black ragged crack, inches wide, running up the stucco beside the door. They fell over twice as they moved away (it was like trying to stand in a bus without holding on and without looking where it's going). They had to be careful, too, where they put their feet, because of the way the gaps between the cobbles widened and snapped together. They found a patch of flagstones, which seemed safer, and sat back to back, looking up to where the dark wedge of the tower blanked out a huge slice of stars.

They waited for it to fall. It came down quite slowly.

First there were three grunting spasms, all together, and a section of the outer wall over to their right fell with a gravelly roar into the ditch, taking the timber store with it. Then they saw the ground in that direction humping itself up into a wave which came grinding across the courtyard, six feet high, throwing off a spume of cobbles in the moonlight. They stood up. Sally turned to run.

"Face it, Sal. Try and ride over it when it comes. Hold my hand. Run *up.*"

The shock wave reached the paved area, tilting the stones over like the leaves of a book being flipped through. Geoffrey ran forward, dragging Sally with him, climbing and scrambling. Sally fell and he leaned forward, heaving at her arm. The stone he was standing on tilted suddenly the other way, breaking his grip and shooting him up onto the crest of the wave and down the other side. A stone fell painfully across his leg, pinning him by the ankle, and then Sally came floundering on top of him.

"Are you all right, Jeff?"

"Yes. Oh, look!"

He pointed. The wave was past the tower now, but the tower was falling. First a big triangle of masonry slid out on the far side, broad at the top and narrow at the bottom, like wallpaper peeled downward off a wall. The boulders slid, coughing and roaring, down in a continuous avalanche that spilled away from the base right out to the windlass and flagstone over Merlin's chamber. Something deep underground must have given way, for the tower continued to tilt in that direction, slow as the minute hand of a clock it seemed, but spilling more small avalanches from the ruined lip. It tilted, still almost whole, until it looked as though it could not possibly stand at that angle. Then the flaw below the foundation gave way with a final shudder; the severe curve of the outline crumpled; it was falling in hundreds of colossal fragments; there was one last roar and the tremor of booming hammer blows jarring the ground beneath them; dust smoked up in a huge pillar, higher than the tower had been, a wavering ghost of the solid stone; silence.

The long hill of rubble, immovable thousands of tons, lay directly over the place where Merlin was buried.

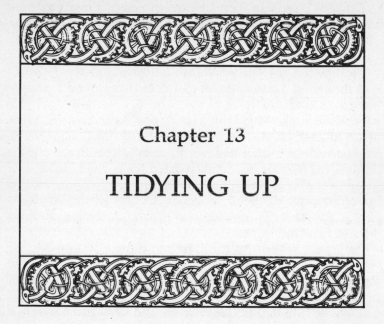

# Chapter 13

# TIDYING UP

That was the last upheaval. Soon there was a faint staining of dawn light over the eastern horizon. The courtyard was a wilderness of tumbled stones and half the outer wall was down. Two of the dogs were dead and a third was whining miserably, its leg trapped between cobbles. Maddox stood with his back to the worst of the wreckage, as if to make clear that anything that had happened wasn't his fault. At first Geoffrey, after he'd levered the flagstone away, had thought that his own ankle was broken, but he found he could just stand on it and hobbled over to see what had become of Mr. Furbelow. The shelter had collapsed, but the bench had fallen sideways across a protruding mound of cobbles and was still protecting the damaged leg. When Geoffrey cleared the furs and timber away he found the old man staring placidly upward.

"Would you like some more morphine, sir?"

"No, thank you. Aspirin will be adequate now. There is

some on the second shelf behind my desk. What has happened?"

"The tower fell down."

"Ah."

There was a long pause before he spoke again.

"I thought it was beautiful. Strange that we are the only three who ever saw it."

Geoffrey fetched the aspirin and took some himself. Then he tried to free the hound with the trapped leg, but it slashed with its teeth whenever he came close. In the end he threw a fur over its head and twisted the corners, making a sort of tough sack which Sally held tight while he unwedged the stones. They'd been loosened by the earthquake and gave easily. The dog limped away. The children lay down in piles of furs and slept.

They were woken by sunlight and hunger. Geoffrey's leg was very sore, so he took more aspirin and sat while Sally fetched bread and apples; there wasn't much left when they'd finished breakfast.

It was only then that Geoffrey noticed what had happened to the rockpile made by the ruins of the tower. It had contracted into a single solid ridge of unhewn rock, like the cliffs on the higher ground; small stonecrops and grasses already grew from its crannies. Merlin must still be alive, then, deep underground, and had drawn the whole ruin of his tower over him to keep him safe from any future Furbelows. Geoffrey tried to picture him, asleep in the greenish light, cold as solid carbon dioxide, waiting, waiting. . . . He spoke his thought aloud.

"What do you think he's waiting for?"

It was Mr. Furbelow who answered.

"I've thought about that a lot. I think he's waiting until there are more people like him. I think he became bored with people in his own time, galloping about and thumping each other, so he just put himself to sleep, until there were people he could talk to as equals."

"But there *can't* be anyone else like him," said Sally.

"Not yet, my dear, but one day, perhaps. You know, even after all this I still cannot believe in magic. Abracadabra and so on. I think he is a mutant."

"A what?"

"A mutant. I read about mutants in *Reader's Digest*, which my late wife regularly subscribed to. It said that we all have, laid up inside us, a pattern of molecules which dictates what we are like—brown hair, blue eyes, that sort of thing, the features we inherit from our parents. And the patterns of molecules govern other things, it said, such as having two arms and two legs because we belong to the species *homo sapiens*. A monkey is a monkey, with a tail, because of the pattern it inherits, and a fly is a fly, with faceted eyes, for the same reason. But apparently the pattern can be upset, by cosmic rays and atom bombs and such, and then you get a new kind of creature, with things about it which it didn't inherit from its parents and its species, and that's called a mutant."

"He was very big," said Sally, "and a funny rusty color."

"Yes, and he had hair on his palms," said Geoffrey.

"It appears," said Mr. Furbelow, "that most mutations are of that order, not mattering much one way or the other. Or else they are positively bad, such as not having a proper stomach, which means that the mutation dies out. But every now and then you get one which is really an improvement on the existing species, and then you get the process called evolution. I think I've got that right."

"It makes sense," said Geoffrey. "But we've got to think about how we're going to get out of here. He won't make any more food for us now. And we must decide what we're going to tell people when we do get out."

"But where did he get all that strength from?" said Sally. "Did he just have a bigger mind?"

"Perhaps," said Mr. Furbelow. "But that would not be necessary. Did you know there was a great big bit of your mind you don't use at all? Nobody knows what it's for. I read that somewhere else, in another *Reader's Digest* I expect. I've wondered about all this a lot, you know, and I think perhaps that Man's next bit of evolution might be to learn to use that part of his brain, and that would give him powers he doesn't have now. And I cannot see why this jump should not occur from time to time in just one case but fail to start a new evolutionary chain. There have been other marvelous men besides Merlin, you know, if you read the stories. Perhaps some of them put themselves to sleep in the same way, and are waiting. Quite often they did not die—they just disappeared."

"I suppose," said Geoffrey, "it was the delirium which made him change England back to the Dark Ages. He was muddled, and wanted everything to be just as he was used to it. So he made everyone think machines were wicked, and forget how to work them."

"Do you think there were people who could change the weather in his day?" asked Sally. "Like you can, Jeff. He must have given you the power for some reason. Or perhaps there were just people who *said* they could, and he forgot. He must have been very muddled between what was dream and what was real."

"Did you make the ice on the steps?" asked Mr. Furbelow.

Geoffrey felt like a thief caught stealing, but nodded. Mr. Furbelow was silent.

"You were justified," he said at last, "taking one thing with another. I thought about myself a lot in the night, when it seemed as if I were shortly to meet my Creator, and I discovered I had been blind and selfish. I tried to use him, you know—like a genie in a bottle. But he was too strong for me, and I let him lie there in his cave, lost and sick, lost and sick. It was a sinful thing to do."

"Do you think England will start being ordinary again now?" said Sally.

"Yes," said Geoffrey. "And we really must decide what we are going to tell people—the General, for instance. He'll start digging if we tell him Merlin's down there."

"General?" asked Mr. Furbelow.

They explained, Geoffrey feeling more like a thief than ever. Mr. Furbelow looked to and fro between them with sharp, glistening eyes.

"Goodness me," he said when they'd finished, "I never heard of anything more gallant in all my born days. Fancy their sending two children on a journey like that! And your carrying it off so! Do you mean that all the tale of the leech, your guardian, was an invention? It quite took me in, I must confess. Well, that *has* given me something to think about! Where were we?"

"Trying to decide what to tell the General," said Sally. "If we ever see him again. We must go before the wolves get hungry."

"Does everyone agree that we cannot tell the truth?" asked Mr. Furbelow.

"Yes," said the children together.

"Then we must have a story," said Mr. Furbelow. "You had best work one out, Geoffrey, as you seem to have the knack."

"Simple and mysterious," said Sally. "Then we needn't pretend to understand it either."

"Have you got any horse bait left, Sal?" said Geoffrey. "We've got to make a sort of litter for Mr. Furbelow, and Maddox will have to carry it."

"I've got four bits. Two to get him up this side, and two down the other. Then we can go and get help."

They worked out the story while Geoffrey labored and contrived: there had been no tower; the outer wall had been built by a big man with a beard, who had simply appeared one day, had sat down in front of Mr. Furbelow's house and begun to meditate. He had never spoken a word, but the walls and the forest had grown around him, and the dogs had appeared. He had produced food out of thin air, and Mr. Furbelow had felt constrained to wait on him. When the children came he had become enraged, wrecked the place and left, stalking off down the valley. That was all they knew.

"What about our clothes?" said Sally.

"We'll have to hide them," said Geoffrey. "And Mr. Furbelow's medicines."

By some miracle the true well had not caved in. Sally threw down it anything that spoiled the story, and then piled hundreds of cobblestones on top. They found some old clothes in chests of drawers in the cottage, mothy but wearable. The litter was a horrible problem, as most of the usable materials had been destroyed by fire or earthquake, and Geoffrey's ankle seemed to be hurting more and more.

He was still hobbling around looking for lashings when the first jet came over, in the early afternoon.

It was very high, trailing a feathery line of vapor, and curved down out of sight beyond the hills. Ten minutes later it came back again, squealing down the valley at a few hundred feet. Sally waved a piece of the sheet which Geoffrey had been tearing into strips for the litter.

"He'll never see that," he said. The pain in his leg made him snarly. "We ought to try and make a smoke signal or something. Damp straw would do it."

"What can we light it with?" asked Sally.

"Oh hell. There might be some hot embers in the stables if you went and blew on them. You'd need something to scoop them up with, and—"

"He's coming back."

The jet came up the valley, even lower, flaps down, engine full of the breathy roar of a machine not going its natural pace. Sally waved her sheet again. The wings tilted, and they could see the pilot's head, but so small that they couldn't be sure whether he was looking at them or not. The wings tilted the other way, then toward them again, then away.

"He's seen us," said Geoffrey. "He's waggling his wings."

The engine note rose to its proper whine, the nose tilted up and up until the plane was in a roaring vertical climb. It twisted its path again and whistled southward. In less than a minute it was a dot over the southern horizon, trailing its streak of vapor.

"He was looking for *us*," said Sally.

"Yes," said Geoffrey. "We'd better stay. The litter wasn't going to work anyway."

"I hope they come soon," said Sally. "I'm hungry."

"I have just remembered," said Mr. Furbelow, "there might be some cans in the cupboard in the kitchen. I haven't thought about them for five years. It was not the sort of thing he would have cared for."

There was some stewing steak and the trick with the embers worked, so they supped by a crackling fire in the open, like boy scouts, and slept under the stars.

Five helicopters came next morning, clattering along below a gray sky. A group of very tough-looking men jumped out of each machine and ran to the outer wall, where they trained their automatic weapons on the silent forest. Sally ran to warn them not to shoot the wolfhounds, who, restless with hunger, had gone hunting. One of the men aimed a gun at her as she talked, and she came back. Officers snapped orders, pointed out arcs of fire and doubled onto the next group. Three men stood in the middle of the courtyard in soldierly, commanding attitudes. They watched the activity for a while and then strolled over toward the cottage. The one in the middle was the General.

Geoffrey stood up, forgetting about his ankle. Ambushed by the pain he sprawled sideways, and stayed sitting as the three approached.

"Aha!" barked the General. "You do not obey the orders, young man. I say to you to make a *reconnaissance* (he pronounced the word the French way) and you defeat the enemy, you alone. That is no path to promotion. But this is the enemy, then?"

He pointed at Mr. Furbelow. He seemed very pleased.

"No," said Geoffrey. "This is Mr. Furbelow. He broke his leg in the storm, and I tried to set it, but I think he ought to go to hospital as soon as possible."

"But the enemy?" snapped the General. He didn't seem interested in Mr. Furbelow's leg.

"You mean the Necromancer," said Sally. "We only just saw him. He got angry when we came and he went away. Mr. Furbelow can tell you far more about him than we can."

The General turned again to the old man on the ground, and stared at him in silence.

"How did you find out so quickly?" said Geoffrey.

One of the other men answered, an Englishman.

"Half a dozen radio hams suddenly came on the air. They hadn't a clue what was up, but the fact that they could work their sets at all encouraged us to send reconnaissance planes over. One of them spotted this place—we knew where you were heading for, of course—and here we are."

"Your Necromancer," said the General, "what is he?"

"Honestly we don't know. He just sat and thought, Mr. Furbelow says. He's been living with him for five years, but he's really much too tired to tell you anything now. Why don't you send him off to hospital, let him have a good rest, and then I'm sure he'll tell you all he knows?"

The Englishman spoke to the General in French, and the General grunted. The third man yelled an order, and two soldiers doubled over from one of the gun positions. They ran to the helicopters and ran back with a stretcher, onto which they quickly and tenderly eased Mr. Furbelow. They must have practiced the job a hundred times in their training.

"Where will you take him to?" said Sally.

"Paris," said the Englishman. "I expect you will be coming too, young lady."

"No thank you," said Sally. "I want to take Maddox to Weymouth as soon as Geoffrey's foot is better. If you could find us another horse, we could ride down. And we'll need some money. The weatherman stole all ours."

The General grunted and sucked his lower lip over the little moustache.

"We had expected Mr. Tinker to come to Paris to make a report," said the Englishman.

"Can you *make* me?" said Geoffrey. "I'll come if I have to, but I'd much rather not. We don't know anything, Sally and I. He went when we came. I'll write to Lord Montagu and explain about the Rolls. It was struck by lightning."

"You have already one horse?" barked the General.

Geoffrey pointed. Maddox was coming disconsolately around the courtyard looking for tender fragments of green weed and finding nothing. Some he'd eaten already, and the rest the earthquake had obliterated. He was in a bitter temper, but stumped over toward the steps to see if Sally had any horse bait left. The General was in the way. Maddox plodded toward him, snarling, then stopped. For a moment these two manifestations of absolute willpower gazed at each other; then the General laughed his yapping laugh and stepped aside.

"I am no more astonished that you have succeeded. With a weapon of that caliber."

The staff officers smiled obediently.

"Thomas," said the General, "envoyez des hommes chercher un bon cheval. Au delà de ces collines j'ai vu des petites fermes. We will talk to Mr. Furbelow in Paris. Good-bye, M'sieu."

As the stretcher-bearers stooped to the poles Mr. Furbe-low turned to the children.

"I trust I shall see you again, my dears," he said. "I have much to thank you for."

"You are not alone," barked the General. "I too, England too, all have much to thank them for."

"The General will send you to Weymouth to stay with us," said Sally, "when your leg's better."

"I should appreciate that," said Mr. Furbelow.

He was lifted into a helicopter, which heaved itself row-dily off the ground, tilted its tail up and headed south. Five soldiers left to look for a second horse, but before they'd been gone ten minutes there was a noise of baying, followed by shots.

"Oh, Lord," said Geoffrey, "I forgot about the wolves. I hope your men are all right."

The Englishman grinned. "Excellent practice," he said.

"This Mr. Furbelow," snapped the General, "he will tell me the truth."

"Yes," said Geoffrey, "as much as he knows."

The General looked at him, sucking his moustache, for ages.

"Could somebody please look at my ankle?" said Geoffrey.

The third man shouted again, and one of the stretch-ermen ran over. He had very strong, efficient hands, like tools designed to do a particular job, and he dressed Geof-frey's leg with ointments and a tight bandage. He spoke friendlily to Geoffrey in French, which the Englishman translated. Apparently there was only a mild strain, but the pain was caused by bruising. The General strutted off to listen to a radio in one of the helicopters. Watching him, Geoffrey realized why he had been so helpful about sending them back to Weymouth: it wouldn't do to have *two* heroes returning to France.

The soldiers began to lounge at their posts, but still kept a sharp watch on the forest, a ring of modern weapons di-rected outward against an enemy who all the time lay in their midst, deep under the ridged rock, sleeping away the centuries.

They rode south three days later. The General had left six men to guard them, and together they went up the higher track. Half the oaks had fallen in the earthquake, and the ride was blocked every few yards. They saw no wolves. On the shoulder of the hill they said good-bye to their escort and went on alone.

The countryside was in a strange state. At almost every cottage gate there would be a woman standing to ask for news. On the first day, as they passed a group of farm buildings, they heard a wild burst of cheering and a rusty tractor chugged out into the open followed by a gang of excited men. Later they passed a car which had been pushed out into the road. Tools lay all around it and a man was sitting on the bank with his head between oily hands. The sky was busy with airplanes. They bought lunch at a store which was full of people who hadn't really come to buy anything, but only to swap stories and rumors. One woman told how she'd found herself suddenly wide awake in the middle of the night and had stretched out, for the first time in five years, to switch on the bedside light. Other people nodded. They'd done the same. Another woman came in brandishing a can opener, and was immediately besieged with requests to borrow it. There was an old man who blamed the whole thing on the atom bomb, and got into an angry argument with another old man who thought it had all been done by Communists.

While they were eating their lunch it began to rain. They sheltered under a chestnut tree, but the rain didn't stop and drips began to seep between the broad leaves.

"Oh, Jeff, please stop it!"

Geoffrey felt under his jerkin for the gold robe, but didn't put it on. He realized, with a shock of regret, that now that the Necromancer lay asleep again other things had settled back into place, and his own powers were gone. Nothing that he could do would alter the steady march of weeping clouds, or call down perfect summers, or summon snow for Christmas. Not ever again.

And the English air would soon be reeking with petrol fumes.